I Lost My Heart to The Belles

Pete Davies is the author of
All Played Out and *Storm Country*,
and two novels, *The Last Election* and
Dollarville. He lives in Yorkshire with
his wife and two children, having moved
there to write about the Belles.

D1471996

Also by Pete Davies

non-fiction
Storm Country★
All Played Out★

fiction
Dollarville
The Last Election

★*available in Mandarin*

Pete Davies

I LOST
MY
HEART
TO THE
BELLES

Mandarin

Thanks are due to the following for providing photographs:
Pictures 1, 2, 3, 4, 5, 6, 12, 13 and 15 © Julian Barker; pictures 7, 8, 11
and 16 © Lisa Woollett; pictures 9 and 10 © Jane Baker; picture 14
© Philip Brown; picture 17 © The Independent/Adam Scott.

Published in the United Kingdom in 1997 by
Mandarin

3 5 7 9 10 8 6 4 2

Copyright © Pete Davies 1996

The right of Pete Davies to be identified as the author
of this work has been asserted by him in accordance
with the Copyright, Designs and Patents Act, 1988

First published in the United Kingdom in 1996 by William Heinemann

Arrow Books Limited
Random House UK Ltd
20 Vauxhall Bridge Road, London SW1V 2SA

Random House Australia (Pty) Limited
20 Alfred Street, Milsons Point, Sydney, New South Wales 2061, Australia

Random House New Zealand Limited
18 Poland Road, Glenfield
Auckland 10, New Zealand

Random House South Africa (Pty) Limited
Endulini, 5a Jubilee Road, Parktown 2193, South Africa

Random House UK Limited Reg. No. 954009

A CIP catalogue record for this book is available from the British Library

Papers used by Random House UK Limited
are natural, recyclable products made from wood grown in
sustainable forests. The manufacturing processes conform to
the environmental regulations of the country of origin

Printed and bound in the United Kingdom by
Cox & Wyman Ltd, Reading, Berkshire

ISBN 0 7493 2085 0

for the Belles

Acknowledgements

For historical background, I'm indebted to *Belles of the Ball* by David J. Williamson, published in 1991 by R & D Associates, Devon.

My thanks to Paul Pierrot, who introduced me to the Belles; to Mark Bright, for his interest and support; and to Andrew Longmore of *The Times* for keeping me sane in small towns in Sweden. The next Lapin Kulta's on me.

I must also thank Deborah Orr at the *Guardian*, Paul Newman and Helen Birch at the *Independent*, Nick Pitt and Richard Wigges at the *Sunday Times*, Paul Simpson at *FourFourTwo*, and Pete Silverton at the *Mail on Sunday*, all of whom gave me space to write about women's football.

It was Michael VerMeulen, however, who got the story first – he usually did – and his sudden death in August 1995 was a hideous shock, and a dreadful loss for all who worked with him. Abundantly intelligent, massively energetic, he was an outstanding editor who championed his staff and his writers in their trade with a vivid passion, and an unfailing generosity. The atmosphere in the *GQ* office was, because of Michael, always lively, warm, and welcoming; he was the making of a great magazine, and of its many imitators, and is sorely missed by us all.

I had thought that getting anyone interested in women playing football would be hard, if not impossible. It was entirely typical of Michael that barely a sentence was out of my mouth when he said, 'I love it. Three thousand words.' That ebullient decisiveness is how I'll remember him, and it was for Michael that I first wrote about the Doncaster Belles.

You're washing the pots, doing the ironing, working all week, and you're thinking about Sunday afternoon. Outside of health and family, it means more than anything – and I'd like to think it gives them confidence too. Kaz and Gill, they've been half-way round the world, and what would they have been without football? Gill Coultard, she was a rogue, she'd probably be in trouble, her brothers have been – she'd be going nowhere, anyway. Like too many women in pit villages, three or four kids, grossly overweight, down club every weekend, nothing in her life. Or what would Kaz have done? Go round Goldthorpe and Barnsley getting drunk on a weekend – and that's the summit of your life as a young woman? So I'd like to think they could look at this game and think, You can give me something. You can give me a name in life.

Paul Edmunds,
manager of the Doncaster Belles

Contents

impressions

Cooling towers shut down and steamless, dead on the flat horizons under sodden grey clouds. The clubhouse a brick box with boarded windows, barbed wire round the roof. Old men in cloth caps and spectacles, faces sallow and craggy under silver hair, fingers nicotine yellow, murmuring appreciation in the drizzle; younger men in nylon leisure suits whooping, cheering; dumpy women with lined faces and determined, don't-put-me-down make-up smiling, minding prams among kids in soaked trainers and thin jackets. Paul seething along the touchline before them, stern-faced, never satisfied, yelling for *quality, options, get it in the box*.

Gill in the tackle, a low centre of gravity like Maradona, sliding in with her foot to the ball immaculate every time, up like a shot to come away with it again and again, opponents in the Molyneux old gold clumsy and baffled on the turf in her wake. Joanne's bob rising in an arc of curls against the leaden sky, back straight, two foot higher to the header than the challengers around her, dropping the knock-down to feet, yellow shirts tearing forward once more. Tina like a wraith dancing, twisting, thin and lithe and gone. Joanne putting Kaz through to open the scoring and Kaz with her arms up, grinning, *that'll teach you to kick my mates*.

Nicky taking a purely beautiful second, looking up from the mêlée twenty-five yards out to chip the keeper, the keeper falling backwards, one hand flailing high in empty air. Kaz charging down the sideline, the woman in her wake hanging on her shirt, stretched out behind her like she's running for a bus but the bus is long gone, the cross whipped in fast and low, Joanne sidefooting home for number three, then doing the Klinsmann victory dive ebullient through the penalty area mud, arms out and eyes wide.

Paul smiling, loving it now, 150 souls laughing around him at the cheek of her lighting up a Yorkshire winter's day; saying contentedly, 'She'll not slide as far as him, mind. Not the same shape.' Then someone fouled again and Paul back in manager mode shouting, 'In the back, referee, *in the back*. What is it here, two falls and a submission?' Channy, hair up rakish over a blue bandanna, pelting in another sweet, on-the-button corner; Kaz heading home for the fourth.

Half-time: mud-caked legs, livid bruises, bright blood running on Joanne's knee. Sheila clipping bandages, Rob pouring tea, Paul praising, urging, spurring, 'They're after a bit of flesh, aren't they? A bit of international flesh on their studs, that's what this lot want. So look after yourselves, eh?'

Telling Tina it's the best forty-five she's had yet. Gail on her crutches with her quiet smile laughing, telling Tina not to go passing to that Kaz no more if she wants a goal for herself, ''Cause you'll not get it back off her, not up there. Greedy bag. You gerrit in.'

Kids playing on the pitch waiting for the restart. Ann trotting out grim, resolved, muttering, 'Hard, in't it? Studs up all the way.'

Flo elbowed in the midriff. Tina taking Gail's advice, scoring number five, more Klinsmann dives, grinning women sliding through black muck. *You kick us, will we take the piss here or what?* Kaz brought thudding down as she lines up to shoot, Sheila up and out with the magic sponge; two minutes and she's back, saying Kaz is OK. 'All she wanted were a bit of sympathy.'

Joanne thumping in a free kick from twenty-five. Yellows

running back to restart, then wondering where the ref is. He's teetering on an office chair in the goalmouth with a ball of string and a reel of tape, trying to hang the net back up. Joanne turning to the sideline, arms out, a brilliant, blazing smile as wide as the Humber on her face, saying, 'I burst the net. *I burst the net.*'

Doncaster Belles 6, Wolverhampton Ladies 0 – and it should have been 7. Tina got pushed two-handed in the back, crashed over in the area for the most obvious penalty you ever saw in your life – but the ref didn't give it, did he? 'Cause it's only women's football . . .

The mat in the hall outside Nicky's council flat left upside down so the bloodstains won't show. The look on her face when the bank say they want their fifteen hundred back, and never mind how she lost it.

Debbie in nerve-raddled hyperdrive after she gifted Arsenal two goals, hands fluttering over her kitbag like hummingbirds, putting things in, taking things out, zipping it open and closing it again, not knowing where she is, abruptly standing and running off, leaving the bag spilling over on the floor in the echoing space under the concrete stand, red-faced, red-eyed. It was all right them saying never mind, it wasn't her fault – 'cause it was, wasn't it?

Joanne walking into the terraced house in Stoke with the 'To Let' sign outside, picking up the last things in her lunch break. The mail, a cassette rack, books I'd loaned her – most of the rest had been nicked. Saying grimly, 'I'm getting better now. I *am* getting better now.'

Jonesy waking up on Kaz's sofa after the Christmas social, her first big night out as a Belle, wondering how she got there, then fainting at work in the supermarket later that day.

Channy putting a note to herself into the computer at Elland Road to ring Paul, then forgetting to ring him anyway.

The time last season she turned up and said quietly to Lou, 'Between you and me, who we playing today?' Lou laughing out loud, telling everyone they'll never believe what Channy just asked. Channy saying, 'I'll not ask again. Next time I'll just guess.'

Kaz training with the fifteen-year-olds on a Saturday morning – she'd kick a ball with anyone, Kaz would – and they loved her for it, so they had a whip round. Kaz finding four cans of sweet Woody in her bag after, feeling so touched she could have choked.

The language: talk about someone's baby with these, the way they smile and say, 'Ah bless.'

The smell of pickled onion flavour Monster Munch.

The pain on the faces of the injured; Ann lying twisted on her side, gasping, Sheila running out and Ann telling her, 'Me right cheek's numb.' Sheila starting to work on her face and Ann laughing, 'Not me face, it's me arse.' Back on the bench Gail asking Sheila, did she rub it for her then? Sheila grinning, saying, 'Did I 'eck. Told her to get up and get on with it.'

Flo at her bench in the pottery, spinning the casserole lids fresh from the press, the machine whining and thumping, white dusty water trickling from her sponge as she tidies up the handles, not thinking in the noise, just dreaming of Friday night dancing, Sunday afternoon playing. Jumping on her bike after knocking off, tearing through the traffic to the five-a-side with the lads; them saying, 'She's ever so elusive. She has the speed, not just in her feet, she *thinks* so quick, much quicker than us. You forget she's a girl. The only time you remember's when you run into her and get a bra in your face.'

Ann bent double on the sideline at Rotherham after two hours of football, hands on her knees, face burning, nothing left to get up and get on with, the tears mingling with the sweat as they run down her ember-red cheeks. The gentlest fingers in the world can't rub the pain away that day.

They're footballers, absolutely typical footballers – not like the untypical few who make thousands a week, but typical like the tens of thousands who play every weekend because they love it, who pay to watch the best when they can, and who wonder when they do what it must be like to run out there before the crowd – to be one of them in dreamland, instead of one of us sat here bawling.

Typical footballers – catch them lying round the house, like as not they'll be doing it in a track suit. They read the tabloids; they get Sky if they can afford it. They're not much for books, most of them – the stories on their shelves are told in trophies, not in words.

They like cars and mobile phones; they're expert in the arcana of consumer credit agreements, of sick notes and insurance claims. They like a weekend out in Blackpool; they like lager. True, Debbie's a lemonade girl, and Micky says, smiling, she's not a drunken mum like some of these – but drinking or not, you'll not get them apart on a Friday night. I remember Lorraine in the Dolphin, thirty-three now, a Belle since way back, looking fondly at the young ones, Jonesy, Kilner, Helen, Des, stood in a circle on the dance floor after time was called and the music stopped. They were still singing, recycling the last song among themselves in the suddenly bright and emptying pub, a Take That song, 'Back For Good', softly running through it with their eyes closed. Lorraine said, 'Look at them. They're not bothered about anybody else in the place, are they? 'Cause we stick together, us.'

A laugh and a joke at the game, a beer and a bop after, all for one and one for all – typical footballers. Except that they're women.

1

Opening Day

Sometimes the manager felt like packing it in. Wednesday nights training, Sunday afternoons playing up and down the country from London to Liverpool to Southampton, the phone on the go every evening with fiddle-faddle paperwork and fixture foul-ups and everyone's little knocks and crises – it wasn't as if he got paid for it, and didn't he have a life too?

Didn't he have his own training to do Tuesday, his own games to play Saturday? Because, OK, thirty-seven now – but we all know there's nothing beats playing, don't we? When you play it's you, you and the ball and the next man to beat – but when you're the manager it's only them, and all you are is the guy in the dug-out with the hoarse throat and ragged nails.

And then, as if teaching full-time wasn't absolutely enough, teaching in a part of the country where the old work was all gone, where the mines were closed and there was nothing to replace them bar tossing burgers in the Leisure Dome, where kids came to class from homes stripped of hope or ambition, and it wasn't just reading and writing you had to teach some of these, it was how to use a knife and fork – as if all that wasn't enough, weren't there other things he wanted to do?

He had a five-year-old daughter, Laura, he could have done with seeing her more. He had his Open University degree, that little private slog of additional ambition. And he had his other ambitions – to run a marathon, to do a parachute jump, to learn a foreign language and a musical instrument . . . but you should have these goals, he believed. You should aim for these things because it didn't matter how obvious it was, it was still true and it always would be that the more you put in, the more you got out. So you shouldn't moan, you shouldn't let people down, you should stick at things – and that was one reason why, though he sometimes felt like packing in, he didn't.

All the same . . . ten years he'd been with them, six years he'd been manager, they'd won the Double last season and after that, what more could he do? Before this eleventh year began, he got to wondering if there was anything left he could tell them, anything new he could say – if it wasn't time for someone else to come on board with a fresh point of view.

But the trouble with that was, who would? He had this idea of an assistant manager, someone to come in alongside him and get the feel of the set-up, get the respect of the players, get primed to take the reins and let him go – but then he'd ring round people he knew in the game and they'd say they'd come on a Sunday afternoon, and on a Sunday morning they'd call back and cry off. They had to go see a car, or a dog, or fix the garden, and no matter the arguments he put to them – that these were the best in the country, that he'd coached a dozen internationals in one session, that he'd walked out at Wembley with these – the truth still was, in their hearts, they didn't want to know. They'd rather run some Sunday morning pub team than this lot, some women's team. Women's football – that was the lowest of the low, that was.

But let them think that – Paul Edmunds knew different, he knew better, he knew what it was like to see Gill, Joanne, Kaz and the rest on their game. So, sure, sometimes he felt like packing in – but then he'd remember how these girls, these women, these old stars ascendant and these new ones rising, how as people and as players they were just too bleedin' good. And when he remembered that he thought, never mind commitment, never mind sticking at things because that was what a person ought to do. It was also, simply, that he liked them too much to let them down.

On 24 April 1994, the Doncaster Belles won the Women's FA Cup. In the past dozen years they'd got to the final every year bar one, and they'd won it six times; a month after this latest win, they wrapped up the '93–'94 national league title as well.

Even as they enjoyed the Double, it was during that spring that Paul Edmunds had his doubts about going on. He faced the prospect come the autumn of starting all over with everything the same, with a team that picked itself, with no target but to win once again what had been won the year before – but in the summer things changed, the challenge suddenly became more demanding, and in this little-known quadrant of the country's best-known game, he found there was still a job he wanted to do.

What happened was simple: he lost three of his best players. For some years goalkeeper Tracy Davidson, centre-half Louise Ryde, and left-wing Janice Murray – an unemployed accountant, a police officer, and a furniture upholsterer – had travelled 500 miles a week back and forth between Merseyside and Doncaster to train and to play. Now they decided it had got too much; they signed for Liverpool instead, the club the Belles had just beaten in the FA Cup Final – and it wasn't a shock.

Every summer you wondered who you'd keep; as the women's game grew bigger and other clubs grew stronger, the sport naturally became more regionalised, and good players didn't need to go 125 miles any more to find a decent club. In Liverpool the three he'd lost had a good, well-organised team close to home now, so there it was – but paradoxically, even as he regretted the loss of their talent and experience, and the personal loss too, their departure made the new season more interesting, it gave him something new to aim at. Defending pole position with the same old faces had seemed a hard, static sort of prospect. Now, however, he had to start building a new team, he'd have new, younger players coming in – and there was little so good for a restive teacher's mind as new pupils in the class. He couldn't say how they'd do, how they'd blend – but the future looked exciting again.

Nicky Davies, a Welsh international midfielder, transferred off her own bat from Ilkeston Town in Derbyshire, seeking to better her game, a woman who struck him as impressively determined. Keeper Debbie Biggins, eighteen years old, a girl he'd had his eye on for a while, moved up a division from a Bradford club called Bronte; striker Tina Brannan, after some havering and wavering, took the plunge and stepped up two divisions from Huddersfield. Other girls came in from the reserves, notably Clare 'Des' Utley, merely fifteen years old – a centre-half who, if she stayed fit and keen, would play for England one day as sure as the sun shines on the Sahara. But whether they could all play together now, of course, remained to be seen.

First omens were good; pre-season, the Belles warmed up by winning the annual Reebok tournament. But still, he couldn't get them together like a professional men's squad, he couldn't run them up and down hills and in and out of game plans all day; they had their jobs in the shops and their shifts in the factories, they had their August holidays coming, they'd earned their two weeks of tan and beer and beaches. So when 4 September came around, opening day in the FA Women's National Division, and the Belles kicked off their twenty-fifth season against the Millwall Lionesses, Paul Edmunds still had no real idea at all whether this new outfit could do the business like the old Belles or not.

That Sunday morning, like all Sunday mornings, was his daughter's time, Paul and Sheila and their little girl lying late in bed, savouring a few idle hours. But by eleven, when he'd dressed and washed up the breakfast, knowing there were three hours to go before the referee blew his whistle, all thought had turned to the afternoon, and the nine months running away beyond it.

A boyishly handsome man, with bright blue eyes under curly ginger hair, he stood over the sink in his bungalow a few miles east of Doncaster, and he wondered whether playing three forwards would work. Outside the sky was cloud-streaked, windy, scurrying patches of blue. He knew that in Stoke Joanne and Flo would be setting off about now; he knew Gail in Hull would be getting quietly ready, nerveless, while on the other side of Doncaster in Bolton-upon-Dearne her best mate Kaz, quite the opposite in temperament as in geography, would be white-faced, stomach churning with tension already. He knew everyone, from Stafford to Leeds, from Castleford to Burnley, would be thinking about this one thing as he was now – thinking about two o'clock coming round, about boot on ball, about togetherness and conflict after the long, dead summer, and all with that butterfly mix in the belly of the first day's dreams and fears.

Of course, he told himself he had it in perspective now. In his twenties he'd been a pro for three years with Leicester City and Bournemouth – a winger, a fast man, though by his own admission not a hard one – before injuries put paid to his career. He remembered Joey Jones bringing him down at Wrexham when he was clear through on goal – thinking wryly it'd be a red card for that now – and the crack of the bone in his wrist as he fell. And then other pulls and tears, all that time on the treatment table, wondering if they'd have you again next year.

He hadn't got into it the normal way, on schoolboy forms, cleaning boots as an apprentice. From the mining village of Askern he'd got away to college, and in Sunderland he'd studied to be a teacher. He'd played for Great Britain in the World Student Games, and it was there that Leicester saw him – and going into it that way, even then he thought he had it in perspective, knowing he had a career he'd studied for, another life he could always fall back on.

But all the same – when the season began as a pro it was your life, your career, your money, everything, there were men around him with their families' security hanging on one mistimed tackle. Then, when he was let go by Leicester, there were those weeks sitting by the phone until Bournemouth came for him, the future stretching away empty – and when Bournemouth let him go in turn, he couldn't face that again.

Whereas now, if they lost every game this season, he'd still be paying the mortgage. Now, there wasn't that same intensity, it wasn't blood and life, and what mattered always, above everything, was to enjoy it. To enjoy it, win or lose.

Three hours until the whistle blows, Sheila in the sitting-room packing the first-aid kit, and you can tell yourself that. Only once you're in football, you don't *ever* want to lose. And then the butterflies come, to the pro and the Sunday player alike, and the manager with his hands in the sink wondered how Des would do, fifteen years old playing centre-half against grown women, and how Tina would mesh at the front with Kaz and Gail, and whether Skiller's knee would ever really mend, and all the ways he could somehow get things wrong, and then the Belles could lose.

It was unthinkable. Last season they'd played twenty-seven, won twenty-five, drawn one, lost one. They'd conceded only nineteen goals and scored 170, a strike rate of over six goals a game. They'd finished four points clear of Arsenal, and along the way they'd beaten Millwall three times, 6–1 at home and away in the league, 9–0 in the FA Cup. So now it was Millwall again and he told himself, We like playing these. They go out and play, and they let you play too. But they still finished fifth; he could have had easier opposition on the opening day. And then, new players, a new system . . .

It was midday. He went out on the gravel drive to get the match balls and the kicking balls in the big red bag from the garage; he loaded them in the blue Fiesta with his and Sheila's kitbags. They drove in intermittent sunshine into Doncaster, stopping on the way to leave Laura with Sheila's parents. Sheila's mother asked him as they were leaving, 'Will you win today then?'

He said, 'We'll know about that at a quarter to four.'

Third Division Doncaster Rovers played at the Belle Vue Ground and, uniquely in women's football, the women's team played on their town's league ground too. Across the road from the considerably more sumptuous racecourse, Paul and Sheila pulled into a wide dirt lot before the main stand, a red wall of brick and breezeblock topped with grey tin. The players were arriving early for their first duty of the season, the team photo call; Rovers' juniors were still in the dressing-room after a training session, so the Belles had to change in the grandiosely named Executive Suite, a thin strip of a room with a little bar and a few tables. Bags and track suits jumbled awkwardly on the floor between the furniture – but they'd known plenty worse. A while back they'd played on a colliery welfare club's pitch and after matches, being women, they weren't allowed on the snooker tables.

They went out on the pitch to get their pictures done; they knelt on one knee on the rich green turf for individual shots, then assembled round a bench, five standing behind it, five sitting, five on the grass before it with the League trophy, the

FA Cup, and the Reebok Cup. They wore their yellow and blue spanking new for the new season, a policewoman and a bank clerk, a shop manager and a social security officer, girls from school and college and women from factories, people who made gas valves and casserole lids, all nobody particular all week, all somebody special today. Two photographers hunkered down before them. Elfin blonde, five foot four, drop-dead pretty with a husky voice like sugar melting, Flo said, 'Can I get my tits out then?'

Other faces smiled – that Flo. And Paul would tell anybody who listened (not that many did, or even asked) that you'd see them larking about, you'd see them taking the piss, and you'd think they weren't serious, *and you couldn't be more wrong* . . .

Flo grew up in Chell Heath among the six towns of Stoke-on-Trent, the youngest of six children. She was an accident (or maybe not) after the father of the other five had cleared off, and she never knew her own dad; he came to see her once when she was two weeks old, and he never came again. By the time she left school at sixteen she had a truancy record as long as your arm, she was courting some feller, she was in the pub every night; she went into the potteries to put handles and lids on dishes and bowls for Wedgwood and she thought that was all there was, just work and beer and some feller.

Then she saw a thing in the programme at Port Vale about a women's team and she thought she'd have a go. She found she was quick and she was fierce; she quickly moved up through two better clubs, playing up front and scoring goals by the hatful until, with the second club, she played against the Belles in the FA Cup. Paul liked the look of her; he signed her, turned her into a defender because he wanted her pace at the back, and at the end of her first full season she found herself playing before 1,670 people in the FA Cup Final, live on Sky.

The Belles won 1–0 and it was rugged, relentless, and when at last the whistle went to end it she thought she was going to drop, legs molten, face burning, lungs heaving, eyes unseeing. Then she looked up and as she stumbled off there were all these people taking her picture, girls all about her, some little lad saying, Can I touch yer? Can I touch yer? And she thought, You think you're nothing. *But I feel like I'm summat now* . . .

They went into the dressing-room. The walls were tattily clad in thin, pale wood; two striplights gave it a bleak, hard tone. Two signs in the form of car number plates said, Keep Fighting. There was the standard issue PFA health warning, a small poster: 'Elbows can seriously damage your health', with pictures of shattered cheek-bones and eye sockets. To one side the shower room had crumbling tiles and plaster in pale blue and white; it was tiny, a few phone boxes' worth of washing space. There was a single loo.

They settled on the benches round the room. Joanne got her hair back in a bob, Tina snipped at Debbie's fringe, Sheila strapped up Micky's ankle. Someone noticed she had a new sponge and she said, 'We had a purple one but you,' she pointed at Channy, 'you went and blooded all over it, didn't you? Splyeurggh.' The women laughed, tied shinpads and socks, screwed in studs. They could hear the Lionesses in the corridor, their voices and footsteps, as the smell of embrocation slowly filled the air. Paul stood back against the centre of one wall, watching, and when he spoke they fell silent, staring at the floor, listening in.

'Right. We've had an excellent season last season, and we're all wanting to do well again. We've got some new faces come to the club because they want success, and we're still *desperate* for success. So we've got to have that desire to win, whatever happens, whoever plays, we've got to have that *desire*. I want you to show everybody who's coming along, plus yourselves, that you *want to win the game*. So make yourself available, do your job, work hard for each other, talk to each other, enjoy our game of football – and I'm sure we'll come away with three points.'

He named the team, giving particular instructions to players in each area. The minute he was done Kaz said, 'Toilet', and dived for it. There were nerves everywhere in silent faces, but no one got nervous like Kaz Walker did. Just blow the whistle, get me that ball . . .

They went through a black door, down a brick tunnel painted garish red under the bright blue sky. Coming out of the main stand they faced a low-roofed terrace on the far side, with two open little terraces behind the goal at each end. All were empty. Coffee cups and burger wrappers from yesterday's Rovers game still blew across the concrete. Belles chairman Robert Kantecki, one of life's eternal optimists, gestured behind them and said, 'Good crowd. Good crowd.' They were so few you could count them – forty-seven. Others filtered in before kick-off, until there were forty more. But Linford Christie was running at the Don Valley Stadium in Sheffield, and 6,000 were watching Doncaster's newly promoted rugby league side play Ellery Hanley's Leeds down the road – and then, women's football. It's not a *real* game, is it?

Back in the dressing-room when they'd warmed up they were noisier, breathing harder, talking more. Paul paced among them saying, 'Make sure you've got rid of the jewellery, ear-rings, rings, necklaces, take it all off. And listen in as we're getting ready, listen in for two, everybody. Starting from the keeper, we're looking for Ann and Nicky wide. If they're marked up, kick it as far down the field as you can. Midfield, stay with your runners –'

A cheap buzzer sounded, a loud, unsteady electric goading. 'Corners. Joanne takes 'em both sides. Micky near post, Kaz six-yard box, Flo coming late far post. Corners against, Nicky and Ann posts –'

Flo was grinning her head off. Sure, she came in late far post. Trouble was, she always had her eyes shut . . .

The buzzer sounded again, twice. Paul wound up as quick as he could, scrambling in his last instructions before the void opened up where his grip was all gone and it was down to them. He said, 'Got to be hard out there, got to go for it. First tackle, first challenge, first time you get the ball, take them on. Frighten them.'

But captain Gillian Coultard was taking over now, clapping hands, saying, 'C'mon lasses, plenty of talking.' She went among each of the four new players, Nicky, Tina, Debbie, Des, slapping shoulders, telling them to have a good one.

They were on their way out and Paul was still talking, pushing, releasing. He said to the emptying room, 'You show 'em. You *show* 'em.'

For twenty minutes it was even, the remaining seventy it was a rout, it ended 7–1, and Kaz Walker got five of them. 'It's them boots she's got on,' said Micky Jackson, 'they're Bergkamp's.' Micky was off in the dug-out by then, a tall, composed bank clerk with a tan lump on her shin as big as your hand, swelling rapidly purple.

Joanne Broadhurst wasn't right either. She did score a goal – an audaciously exact lob over the keeper from thirty yards – but she felt light-headed, like she wasn't there, like it was all going on around her and she couldn't touch it. Sheila worried about her, this had happened in training, she fretted that Joanne had something grim like glandular fever. Others, more sanguine, wondered what she'd play like when she did know where she was.

But she was unnaturally quiet coming off. The team jester, an invaluable spirit, any other day after Kaz Walker hit five she'd have led them singing that, like Blackburn Rovers, the Belles were walking in a Walker wonderland – but she was too tired for that today. It was great to be back playing but she was drifting somehow, she wasn't all there, and she kept herself to herself. There was two hours' drive back to Stoke still to come, there was her private life in a pig's ear when she got there, and she had a fork-lift truck driver's course starting Monday. Someone else could tell the jokes today.

They came off in pale sunshine, the first chills of autumn lurking in the late afternoon. Before they showered and went up to the Executive Suite for cheese-and-onion sandwiches, sausage rolls and pork pie and strong tea, Paul praised them up, well pleased to win so thoroughly with four new players, Nicky scoring on her debut, everyone playing their part.

But he was disappointed to give away a goal, because there was always something, and you weren't ever perfect. Gail's finishing – come training on Wednesday, he'd give her one-on-ones for half an hour. There was Kaz got five and Gail had missed at least as many and in other, harder games that could be costly. And he turned it over in his mind, this move, that slip, each tackle, each pass, each chance that went astray – but then, still and all, 7–1. That'll do. We can only get better . . .

Across the corridor, meanwhile, the Lionesses were quiet. Among them Lou Waller, five foot three of pertly pretty England international, nursed a wrenched and tender knee, hobbling, worried, badly rocked back, wondering what you did about the Belles. With admiration, without malice or envy – because there wasn't an ounce of mean in her body – she shook her head and she thought, Belles. They're *lethal*.

2

A Reet Game

In 1969 a teenager named Sheila Stocks was asked by a friend if she wanted to join her selling Golden Goals tickets at Doncaster Rovers. Always a Rovers supporter, she said yes – after all, you got in free. So they watched the games, half a dozen girls clutching pads of raffle tickets, and they decided they fancied having a go themselves. With friends from school they bought shirts, and one of them designed a badge – they were the Belle Vue Belles back then, so the badge had the letters BVB twined through a bell – and they played five-a-side, seven-a-side, eleven-a-side, any game they could get.

Then her dad found out there was a league, the Sheffield League, and when they joined it Sheila Stocks hit Cloud Nine. She'd always liked kicking a ball about but to be in a league, to have your games actually *mean* something – that was special, that was serious, and from that moment she really thought they'd arrived. After all, they were good enough – they could play against lads and get the ball off them, they could get past them and shoot – so why shouldn't they have a team and a league of their own?

They played around South Yorkshire until the Sheffield League folded, then went further afield to Nottingham and Derby, because the next nearest league was down there. They started entering the Women's FA Cup – the first competition was held in 1971 – and found themselves travelling as far as Devon and Cornwall. As the Seventies went on they grew and they learned, and they enjoyed it so much that before long they thought they should all of them be playing for England. But Sheila knew they'd been naive then, and it was fourteen years before they could say for sure they were the best.

Once they did reach the top, winning their first FA Cup in 1983, they stayed there; when the Women's Football Association organised the Premier League in 1991, putting the best ten teams in the country for the first time into a national competition, they won that too. The second season they lost it to Arsenal, the third season they got it back – and now the men had moved in.

The WFA never had any money and suffered persistent bouts of fractious infighting – so when FIFA decreed from Zurich that all football of every kind, at every level, should be run in each country by a unitary body, it seemed a positive move that the Football Association in Lancaster Gate, the men's long-established and well-resourced authority, should take over.

But Sheila was only one among many who, in fact, had considerable misgivings. Would the men understand or recognise what the women had built up? Would they take them seriously? Or were they taking over, as she privately feared, just to keep them in their place? Still, like everyone else, she was prepared at first to give the FA the benefit of the doubt, and to welcome the possibilities they represented. Did they not have the experience, the organisation, the clout, the money? Could things not be better run now, and the women's game be better promoted in its own right?

Time would tell – and meanwhile, as its fourth season began in September 1994, the ten teams in the renamed FA Women's National Division were the Belles, Red Star Southampton, Liverpool, Leasowe Pacific in Birkenhead, Ilkeston Town in Derbyshire, Arsenal, Millwall and Wembley in London, plus the two newly promoted sides from the northern and southern feeder divisions, Wolverhampton and

Croydon. There were regional leagues nation-wide below these top three divisions, 158 teams entered the new season's FA Cup, and in all it was reckoned at least 12,000 women now played football around England at over 450 clubs.

The Belles alone ran teams at Under-12, Under-14, and Under-16 levels, as well as the senior side and reserves, and from every club people pushed out into schools and communities trying to move the thing forward. Sometimes, in some places, it was hard; in south-east London Lou Waller, working for Millwall's community scheme, often felt more like an unqualified social worker in a track suit than a football player. But push out they all did, and in schools especially girls were taking to the game in big numbers. People were starting to realise this was serious, that FIFA ran a Women's World Cup now; at home, first Channel 4 and then Sky started broadcasting the Women's FA Cup Final – and people felt the wall of prejudice they'd been pushing against for so long was at last showing a few promising cracks.

Of course, twenty-five years ago, when she scored ten goals in her first game for the Belle Vue Belles, Sheila Stocks never dreamed it would grow as it did. Yet here she was, on a Wilfreda Beehive coach rumbling down the M1, girls catwalking down the aisle in the season's new gear from their kit sponsors Xara, Tina putting on a Manchester United video to universal catcalls of Yorkshire derision, Joanne selling badges for a hospital charity, Paul at the front scribbling on the team sheet – and it seemed a long, long road to this from Saturdays working in the sticky bun shop, Sundays playing in the Sheffield League.

But then, somewhere down that road it had come to rule her whole life. It started with her mum and dad – Mum doing the kit and the teas, Dad doing the finance – so then the club and the game were inside her home and taking over until it reached the point where, whatever else she did, qualifying as a teacher, getting married, Sunday and the Belles was as much inside her as her heart, her blood and her bones. She knew anybody who wasn't involved in football wouldn't understand that, but that couldn't be helped; anybody who had been, they'd know, they'd recognise that special feeling that goes deep beyond words. It was a benevolent bug, a permanent sector of your soul under occupation, a perpetual rhythm winding round to every kick-off, and every week when that whistle came it was a desperate desire to win every time – because people say it doesn't matter if you don't win, but oh my it does, it's *everything*. If you lose . . . oh, it's all right people saying there's another day, you'll learn from it, keep your chin up. But when that final whistle blows and you've lost, you feel as if your whole world's caving in.

In 1983, the same year the Belles won their first FA Cup, Sheila Stocks looked out the window from the class she was teaching, and saw a man with curly ginger hair going by outside. The head said he was an ex-professional footballer who'd come for an interview and he'd got the job, and she liked the sound of that. They had a friend who went as a go-between; she asked Sheila what she'd say if Paul asked her out, and she said she thought she'd say yes. So on the Friday after work he told her it had been costing him a fortune, his dry-cleaning bill, and she wondered what on earth he was on about. He said, 'I've been trying to impress you. Haven't you noticed?'

From the beginning she watched him play in the mud-and-muck-in leagues for Grantham, then for Burton Albion, these days for Armthorpe in the Northern Counties East Premier, but to start with he didn't go to watch her. He didn't know the women's game and he feared they'd be terrible, that he wouldn't know what to say. Then, in the spring of 1984, he saw them beat Southampton in the quarter-finals of the FA Cup and he found he was impressed – impressed enough that when the next pre-season came around and he wanted to get fit, he asked if he could train with them. What he found when he did, however, didn't impress him at all.

In fact, he thought what they were doing was rubbish. She told him, 'All right, you know all about it, you do it.' So he became Belles' coach, and took over as their manager four years later. They'd married by then, in 1986; Laura was born three years later and, Sheila would tell people now, ever since he came on the scene her career had gone backwards. She'd say it laughing, knowing she was forty-one, that she'd played twenty-four years, that this year finally she'd hung up her boots. But for this tall, lean woman – one who speaks straight as ever Yorkshire did, a woman you got the feeling that if she were teaching you, you better learn something or else – for her to accept that she wasn't first choice and captain of the club she'd helped found any more, as the years went by and the baby came, hadn't been easy at all.

They argued; she wanted so desperately to play. But he looked at it as the manager – and to think he had eleven better than her, that was truly hard to stomach. When she'd not get picked she'd say nothing in front of the team, then they'd go home and have volcanic rows, until they were struggling not to let it come into the marriage and destroy it, and sometimes it came a bit close. More than once he'd say, Look, the marriage is more important, I'll pack in – and then she'd think, Well, he's more important to Belles than me now, it should be me that packs in. And they got through it – but still she felt, if she couldn't leave Laura with her mum and dad so she could come on the away trips . . . to stop being involved, it'd be like someone cutting her arms and her legs off.

*

They left Doncaster at nine in the morning; Micky Jackson told Paul as she was getting on the bus that her shin hadn't mended, and he was well pleased with that. At sweeper, with only two defenders in front of her instead of last year's three, he rated Micky in many ways the side's most important player – and now he'd have to change it all around. On top of that he had a filthy cold; Sheila said it was staying in his wet kit after training on Wednesday, but Paul said that was medical myth. First week back at school, he said, the kids always gave you something. He'd been in bed all day Saturday.

They were an obstinate pair, but they knew how to laugh at each other. When he was playing she'd shout Paul, Paul, and he'd be running up and down the wing not seeing her, not hearing her. Then he'd come off and she'd shout again, and he'd still not connect. She said, 'If you don't knock him over he doesn't know you're there.' He'd come back from a game and she'd ask what colour kit he'd played in, or who they'd played, and he wouldn't know. 'He just turns up and plays. I say to him, No wonder you didn't last long as a professional.'

And did the Belles care what colours they played in, did they care about their yellow and blue? 'Oh yeah, not 'alf. We have to look and feel the part. Can't be raggy-arsed rovers, us.'

On Tina's video Cantona scored, and Sheila smiled. 'Bit like me.' On the speakers the crowd roared, and Sheffield Wednesday fans among the Belles loudly jeered.

Oblivious to the noise as he juggled names on the team sheet, Paul, planning a debut now he'd lost Micky for a fetchingly pretty eighteen-year-old from the reserves named Sarah Jones, remembered his own debut for Leicester. It was away to Sunderland at Roker Park, the third biggest crowd of the day, thirty-some thousand in the ground. There was a minute's silence for some reason, and he stood looking at the wall of people in the main stand thinking, 'Fuckin' 'ellfire. When I get the ball they'll all be watching me.' And he was really, really frightened.

They kicked off, the ball went forward, the next pass it came wide to Paul. He stood there waiting for it, seeing it come in slo-mo, and he felt 30,000 people on his neck. He was thinking, it's going to go under my foot and they'll laugh, and there'll be eighty-nine minutes and fifty-five seconds of my debut still to go . . . so he got it down, laid it off to the full back, and ran away quick as he could, heart pounding like an earthquake. And then, after that one first touch, he was OK, he lost them. 30,000 people, and he didn't even know they were there.

They drew 0–0; his home debut the next Saturday they beat Shrewsbury 2–1, and he scored. He remembered taking the corners and the stands cheering as he put it down to take it, and knowing that was directed at him; it was a special feeling. It was worth a few injuries to have thousands of people call out your name – and he thought it was a crying shame that these women, playing Wembley Ladies this afternoon, playing anybody any Sunday, would probably never know what that feeling was really like.

Belles had played Wembley three times; the first time was in the FA Cup a few years back, and they beat them 17–2. Paul said, 'Sounds awful, doesn't it? But actually it was a really good game, and I could see they had something going for them. They were young – and they've grown up now.'

Wembley got into the top flight last season. Belles beat them 5–1 away, 2–0 at home, and Wembley finished fourth; along the way they beat Arsenal, helping Belles get the title back, but Paul liked them for more than just that. He got on well with their manager John Jones, respected the man's ambition for his team and admired their discipline. Jones was formerly a Royal Navy PT instructor and his side were well organised, they had a spine of naval steel; this was a manager with direct, icily hard blue eyes, and his programme notes told what he wanted under rigorously ticked-off bullet-point headings. He wanted Skill, Fitness, Concentration, Spirit. And, said Paul, 'When he sees the names on my team sheet he'll be thinking, Who are these? They're all over the place. He'll be telling his lot, This is our chance here. We can do these.'

He was pulling captain Gillian Coultard back at sweeper, giving little Jonesy her start at left back. 'She's a nice girl,' he said, 'a smashing girl, and she'll be frightened to death. She'll be feeling like I were at Roker Park.'

As they went out to warm up I asked her how she felt. She smiled shyly and said, 'Am I allowed to swear? 'Cause I'm shittin' meself.'

The dressing-room was a square box with a bare concrete floor, artex-type swirled white walls, a plasterboard ceiling. Paul told them it'd be hard, no bones about it; he said to get the ball forward fast, cause there wasn't a defence in the league could cope with our three up front, if you just give them some service.

'Hey, Gaily,' Joanne grinned, 'you going to score this week? Target's white thing at the end, sort of square-shaped.'

Kaz said, 'Don't get on her,' and gave Gail a big hug.

But Gail Borman didn't know what nervous meant. She smiled quietly and said, 'Do I look worried?'

Kaz said, 'Talk to us, Joanne. Talk to us in midfield, tell us where to go.'

'You go where you like, you do.'

'Just talk to us, all right?'

'All right. D'you want to go out next week?'

'Nah. I've got summat on.'

Coultard said, 'Don't you be frightened, Jonesy. You enjoy

yourself.' Thirty-one now, seventy-five times an England player, the Bryan Robson of the women's game, if you had to have a makeshift sweeper you'd be pushed to find one better than Gill Coultard.

Paul told her quietly if she won the toss to kick off playing right to left so he'd have Jonesy on his touchline, near where he could talk to her. He didn't mention Des, though – fifteen years old, one game under her belt, and he was confident in her already.

They went down three rough concrete steps, over dirty rubber matting between teetering wire fences to the pitch. The ground was Vale Farm, Wembley FC's home in the Diadora League, an unfinished place of bare brick and dirt with one small roofed stand. A few handfuls of people were dotted about, not enough to bother counting. The whistle blew, and John Jones said firmly that he was optimistic.

He'd barely shut his mouth when Tina Brannan scored. It was four minutes gone, 1–0, and Wembley were looking at their dug-out as if to say, How many players have they got on here? On sixteen minutes Brannan got tipped over to win a penalty. Broadhurst spanked it in so hard that when the keeper dived the right way and got a hand to it, she had her arm knocked back like straw for her pains, and the score was 2–0.

'Heads up,' yelled Jones, 'heads up.' And they got them up, too, and slowly, surely, remorselessly, they pushed the Belles back. Coultard was taking it off people's toes in her penalty area now, Jonesy was bedding in, Des was standing up, Flo was racing everywhere.

'Regroup,' shouted Edmunds, 'think about what we're doing here.'

Gail fell, crying out in pain, clutching her right knee. Sheila was out like a shot, Paul straight after her. The referee asked if there was a stretcher; after a long while she got up on one foot, came off hanging on Paul's shoulder. 'Nice and steady,' he told her, 'nice and steady. Keep it moving, keep it moving.' Carefully he steered her over the grass, keeping her away from a rougher patch of sideline.

She said she didn't know what happened. 'Did I have the ball? I can't remember. All I know is I heard a big creak, all in my knee. It were quite bad, you must have heard. I don't usually go down, me.' She was white, hobbling. There was a bit of life coming back into it but she was frightened, the way she'd heard it twang, really frightened.

On the field the Belles were ten, and Paul had no subs. Micky's shin was a no-no, and Skiller's Gazza knee was still acting up. He shouted 'Goalside, everybody,' as Wembley surged and drove, winning corners, Kaz Walker back defending. They fought through to half-time, and in the dressing-room it was gritted teeth and exhaustion.

Paul told them, 'Hey, well done. 2–0 up's not bad, 'cause they've had the ball as much as we have. But you can see it's going to be hard, you've got to work for each other now.'

Sheila rubbed ice on Gail's knee. She said she might try it again and see; Kaz told her to save herself.

Paul kept at them. 'Try and keep it, eh? I know it's easy for me to say, I'm not playing, but keep *hold* of it. And Jonesy, you've had a very good game by the way, but listen.' He gave her an urgent quick lesson on where to stand inside her player, 'Not outside, not level, *here* – and you'll beat her for pace every time.'

'Let's keep our concentration,' said Coultard, 'we've had a giddy five minutes there.'

They stared at the floor, hot, red, worn, up against it now, and for a little minute there it felt bad, never mind the scoreline, because the forty-five minutes coming looked brutal and dour. And then they lifted it. In a pause Joanne said, 'There's nowt wrong with you, Gail Borman. You're just trying to get out of them shuttles at England training next weekend.'

'Here,' said Kaz, 'am I holding your hand for nowt then?'

Gail smiled, wan. 'I weren't kidding, honest.'

'Sniper!' yelled Kaz. 'Sniper!' She acted Gail's fall, jelly legs, wails of pain, crossing herself frantically.

'Funniest thing I ever seen,' said Joanne, 'that Kaz Walker at Millwall. I heard this great big clatter and I looked round and there she is gone right under bench in dug-out. Flat on her back. Ee, she says, might as well 'ave a drink of that pop while I'm 'ere.'

There were gales of laughter, young girls smiling, Tina saying she can't concentrate out there, she looks at Kaz and Joanne and she wants to giggle all game.

'Hey,' said Paul, 'they've got to score three here. And they're not going to, right?'

'Over the top,' said Kaz, 'over the top every time. 'Cause they panic at the back when we're going through.'

But they didn't, actually; they were big and fast and stern, and the next forty-five minutes you couldn't take your eyes off it. Gail went on, and limped straight off again; Paul sent Skiller on with her dicky knee, and she stood up with the rest of them against opponents determined to get back in it. The managers paced the sideline, gnawing lower lips; in the eerie, crowdless silence the soundtrack was the taut, staccato bawling of the dug-outs, the thump of boot on ball, the cries of breathless women. The tackles flew in, Wembley made substitutions, Paul had none to make, by the end Kaz and Joanne were both limping, and all through it the game went end to end with a vengeance, corners, shots, clearances, last-ditch interventions in both boxes. 'Good job it's an England weekend up next,' said Sheila grimly, 'we'd be lucky if we could turn out six next Sunday.'

Paul smiled once, the one time late in the game when Coultard left the back. 'Hey, Gill. Not daft last five, eh?' He smiled because Wembley had broken back, Coultard wasn't there, a strong, grown woman was bearing down with only Des in her way and the youngster stood up, took the ball, left the Wembley player in a heap.

Injury time was eternal. Tina Brannan, Nicky Davies, Ann Lisseman all looked shattered. Joanne would give Tina balls to chase and she'd go after them with her head rocking, only her mind making her move when her legs couldn't do it, but she still forced a save at the death – and then it ended 2–0, and Paul in the dressing-room was jubilant, fierce, overwhelmingly proud.

With his voice half gone he told them, 'I'll tell you what, I'm absolutely delighted. We've played with nine and a half players, backs against the wall, and we've showed a lot of character today. Magnificent defense. Jonesy,' and he stepped forward to point her out, 'in ninety minutes of first-team football you've aged twenty years. You could have played ninety games in the reserves and not learnt like today. You got better, and better, and better, and better. Hey, they took her off, her you were marking – they took her off, didn't they? You had a *reet* game.'

Outside while they were changing he said, 'A battle like that, that'll do no one any harm at all. But then, look what we've got – Gill, Joanne, Kaz. That's some spine, isn't it? Kaz, what a game – she's headed it more in our box than she has in theirs.'

But then Kaz Walker, though still only twenty-five, was having more and more influence in the club all round. At training on Wednesday, he'd had a sixteen-year-old they'd been bringing on, bags of talent, and he wanted to keep her – but she was worried about how much you had to put in to be a Belle, worried she'd not be able to grow up and have a drink on a Saturday night. So it was Kaz he sent to talk to her. You get to play for England, Kaz told her, you get to go around the world – but it doesn't mean you can't have a drink.

In the packed little clubhouse the drinks were mostly halves of lager. Wet-haired from the shower, the women scoffed platefuls of sandwiches and pork pies, crisps and cake. Among them Tina Brannan's face was still magma-red with exertion. The club she'd played at before, Huddersfield, were in the Yorkshire & Humberside League, two flights down from the National Division – Belles Reserves play in it – and she said the difference was night and day.

She said, 'It's a hundred miles an hour out there, it's a killer – but it's good, it's making me so determined. I've been training all week and I'm still not fit, but I love it. If I'd have played for Huddersfield today I could have scored five or ten, and I wouldn't have come off tired. But I'd rather score none and be as tired as I am today, and get more out of it.'

I asked how many she'd scored last season that had got the interest going in her, and she said it was 104. I said – as you would – you what?

'That's why I left. It's embarrassing. And I definitely won't get 104 here. But as long as we're winning, I don't mind if I don't score at all.'

Sarah Jones was tired too and, quietly, she was pleased with herself. She said, 'I enjoyed it. It were hard at first, first half I didn't really know what I were doing. But he's had that word with me at half-time, told me what I were doing right and wrong, where to stand, and I did better then.'

Paul said later, 'She probably did better second half 'cause she were out on the other touchline then. Away from me shouting at her.'

In the clubhouse she dropped her little bombshell. She said, 'I thought I played all right, actually. 'Cause I've never played defence before. In reserves I play up front.'

A reet game indeed.

3

It's Only Women's Football

'They used to say if you wanted a centre-forward, you shouted down a mine shaft and up one came. But if you shout down the shaft nowadays all you get back is echo. You want a centre-forward nowadays, the place you shout is the dole queue.'

Paul Edmunds

Kaz Walker worked in Income Support for the Department of Social Security in Rotherham. Her office was a four-storey brick box close by the town centre, a sloppy planner's mess of a place liberally marred with Seventies concrete crud. At four on a Friday afternoon, while the security guard loitered mistrustfully behind dirty glass doors, she came out smiling, wearing jeans, a lumberjack shirt, a white denim jacket. She had short blonde hair and a square, strong, pleasing face, bright with personality. 'Ee,' she said, 'I like me Fridays.'

The job was intensely stressful. Twenty-five years old, she'd been at the DSS seven years, but the seven months since she started doing Income Support had been something else. For the privilege of taking home £670 a month – which she thought, uncomplaining, wasn't bad for an office job round there – she had people screaming at her down the phone all day long.

She dealt with people wanting money, people she'd promised would get their benefits, people who were desperate – so they weren't coming at her in a nice frame of mind, and the amount of abuse she got was unreal. But then, the amount of work she had was unreal too, they could have doubled the staff and not kept up with it all. She'd be in there knowing she had all these people to pay, she'd know she wasn't ever going to get to them all, she'd be on and off the phone, pick it up, put it down, pick it up, put it down, people screaming, I ain't got me money, where's me money, people just *screaming all day* . . . and she was quite easy-going, Kaz Walker, she wouldn't ever have thought she'd get stressed out about her job. But this'd get to anybody.

So she thought about football all the time – not just playing, but what she'd do for training each night when she got home. If she'd had a real pig of a day she mightn't bother, on a bad day it'd do her more harm than good – but otherwise she'd do a half-hour running Monday, Thursday and Friday evenings before tea, then another half-hour after on the exercise bike, or on the step-up machine. Wednesdays the Belles trained together and then Tuesdays were different – Tuesdays, grimly, she did two hours of weights on the multi-gym in the spare room. Dean had bought it for her last Christmas; when she'd seen it she'd smiled and thought, That's nice, in't it? Bless him. He's bought me pain for Christmas.

But her and Dean, they'd learnt to live around football. She'd always played, he'd always been a supporter – Manchester United, Barnsley, Belles – and that was that. Sometimes, if she had a bad game, he'd get it in the neck; she could get dead moony then, she could get a reet face on. And pre-season was bad too, he'd keep his head down then, Kaz getting bored and all twitchy, sat watching *Waltons*, praying for September. But you got used to it. At first he did complain a bit, when she was always off playing, Sundays away, England weekends, snatches of another life in other countries. But from the start she'd played and it was either that or . . . or forget it, basically. So he said, with his gentle smile, 'That were sorted out early on.' Besides, he said quietly, 'It makes no difference. I don't go out with her 'cause she's a footballer. I go out with her 'cause she's Kaz.'

On Fridays when she was done running, they'd have their night out. She liked to go out with him then and she liked to get drunk, and after all those people yelling all week she reckoned she had to. She'd train before they went, because she felt guilty she was having a drink – she didn't drink any other day of the week – but Friday was her day and she loved it. They'd go out local where they lived, where they knew everybody round Bolton and Goldthorpe, they'd go round all the pubs and there'd be family there, and they were at school with most of the people they'd see; it was a small community and a close one, and it kept her sane for the working week, it kept her steady and knowing where she came from, and knowing also why all those people on the telephone were screaming. It kept her sympathetic because, she said, 'You have to be, don't you, coming from here. Half of who we know's unemployed.'

West from Doncaster, through the low, rolling flats of south-east Yorkshire, the first thing you saw as you came into Goldthorpe was the colliery on your left, a big pub on your right. Both were closed, the windows of the pub boarded up with ply. Kaz and Dean lived in Bolton-upon-Dearne down the hill from there, in a square of worn brick semis round two tattered tennis courts. The courts, the pavement, the school buildings, the shops and homes all look burdened, structures breaking down at the edges.

In their front room angel fish hung in the aquarium, and a Sky dish hung on the wall outside it. Dean was five years older than Kaz; they'd met nine years ago when she was out ladding it on a Saturday night in Barnsley and they'd been together ever since. He'd left school in 1979 on a Friday, went down pit the next Monday; it closed, he was transferred, the next one closed, and after the strike he gave it up. He went to college for a degree in sociology and psychology, spent a year dying of boredom as an accountant with Leeds Health Authority, so then they agreed to knuckle down for another year on her wages while he got his teacher training. Now he was an infant teacher, working with five-, six-, seven-year-olds, especially kids with learning difficulties, at the school a quarter of a mile off from home that he'd gone to himself – and, like Kaz's job, teaching there put him face to face with what had happened to where they lived.

The first year after the pit shut wasn't too bad, people had their redundancy – but then the money slipped away and the problems grew. Kids coming to school wouldn't have books, so he'd find some for them to take home, then when they got home they'd not have pens. And you'd notice the crime creeping in, the vandalism, things breaking. Kaz said, 'It's got progressively worse. There's not a lot of money knocking about here. But it's where we live, in't it?'

She grew up in Goldthorpe; her dad was a builder who went off when she was seven, and her mum brought the kids up on her own. She had an older brother and sister, and it was her brother who started her kicking a ball, when she was four or five; she followed him everywhere, she went where he went and he played all the time, so she played too. So now, of course, he said he'd taught her all she knew.

But kicking it about with the boys stopped at the age of eleven; under the FA's Rule 37, organised football was single sex only after that. Not everyone agreed with this – but while Kaz thought you could maybe raise the mixed age limit by a year or two, she thought the principle of gender division beyond that was sensible. Five foot eight herself, ten and a half stone, she'd not have it said she couldn't hold her own, but a lot of women would get knocked all over the place, and what for? Because the point was, they didn't *want* to play with lads. Would Sally Gunnell run against Linford Christie? What would that prove? Women's football was a totally separate thing, with their size and strength it was physically impossible to match grown men – and she just wanted, instead, 'To play in us own right'.

Doing so, of course, they still got the idiots leering, asking if they swopped shirts after the game, saying if they played girls they'd hammer them – but it didn't bother her any more. It did do at first, she wanted people to take it serious – but they weren't worth talking to, people like that. They weren't going to change their minds, were they? So you just ignored it.

She said, 'You always get them having to compare it, how fast or how good it is – but we've done well, when you look at what little facilities or backing we've had. So rather than just saying, Oh, you're not as good as men, why not look at how good we are as women? And then, a lot of the time, you'll see a men's game on the telly and be honest, it can be absolute garbage; the only reason it looks exciting is the atmosphere from the crowd. Take out the crowd, and it's people playing that fast they're giving the ball away all the time, and is that exciting? So us, we play a different game, yeah – but don't tell me it isn't physical because of that. It hurts just as much when I go in for a tackle, doesn't it?'

I asked if she felt they were invisible, unconsidered people, and she said, 'Not really, not round here. People know I play for England and they're pleased about it, you don't get a lot of things like that round here – but otherwise I'm not bothered what people think. I love playing, I don't think I could enjoy playing any more than I do already, so I'm not going to stop, am I? And it makes no difference whether people watch or not.'

But it must get her down to think they were the champions, the FA Cup winners, and they walked out into empty grounds? She said, 'Yeah, but what can you do? I wish people would come – but people like their Sunday dinner, don't they?'

And only one thing remained that still really irked her. If no one else took it serious, so be it – but when referees didn't, that made her mad. She'd be fouled and the ref'd just say, Oh, leave it, let it go – or if they were thrashing someone he'd start favouring the other team, as if they were schoolkids, and needed looking after. She said, 'I hate that – and you get a lot of it, unfortunately. But there's just this stigma all round, isn't there? That it's only women's football.'

When Kaz was fifteen, she lived a few doors down from Karen Skillcorn; at the Belles they asked Skiller if she knew any other girls that were playing round her way and Skiller joked that she did, 'But I'm not fetching her, 'cause she's better than me.' She took Kaz along and she'd been a Belle ever since.

The Belles just had the senior team then, and among a raft of England players Kaz got on as a sub here and there – until the centre-forward got pregnant, and then she was in. She remembers going on in her early games frightened to death, absolutely petrified. 'I were just running about, don't even think I kicked ball, I were that excited.'

Then, on her debut for England, playing away against an Italy B team, still only a teenager, she scored with her first kick. That was a thing to remember – and it was then she realised she really wanted to do this. Before, she'd not been fit, she didn't train, it was just a laugh, a social thing, a drink after the game. But it got more serious after Italy.

She had thirty-odd caps now, fifteen or sixteen goals for her country – she didn't know for sure, the women didn't keep track of their stats with the stamp-collector's precision of the men – and football had come to mean a hundred times more than her job. It had changed her, too; as a teenager she'd been wild and rough-edged and out drinking all the time, yet now she was the one Paul asked to speak to a promising teenager who might be a bit wildly inclined herself. She still found that amazing, that someone could want to use her as an example, and when he'd asked she'd been a bit shocked; compared to what she used to be like, she'd never have thought anybody'd ever ask her to have a word with anyone.

But then, she thought, if there hadn't been football, God knows what she'd have ended up like. One of these housewives with twenty-five kids, one of these baby machines they had round here – dear God, what kind of a prospect was that? And when she thought about her job, she knew she'd rather be the one getting screamed at than the one that was doing the screaming.

The more you put in, the more you get out – and so, in women's football, all the time it was getting harder, and all the time it was getting better. It used to be they could run out and put away ten or fifteen goals every game – once, absurdly, they won a Cup tie 46–0 – but with the national league, and other clubs coming on, there weren't many walkovers now.

The Belles were playing Leasowe, and they were in a bad way to face them. On top of the three they'd lost to Liverpool, the knee injury sustained against Wembley by Gail Borman, Kaz's partner for club and country, was the worst, shredded cruciate ligaments, and she was out for the rest of the season. Joanne Broadhurst's knock on the ankle in the same game was a stress fracture and she was out too, in plaster for four weeks. Of those who did start, four others were injured, including Kaz with a dicey ankle; given the casualty list, Paul said privately that if they won anything at all this season, they'd have done very well.

In the professional game, of course, you got casualties too – but you got other problems for your money that the women had yet to encounter. I watched the game with Mark Bright, and he'd had a horrible week at Sheffield Wednesday; after a poor start to the season, a sensational story in the *News of the World* quoted an unnamed mole alleging mutiny in the Hillsborough dressing-room, of players wanting Trevor Francis out and Chris Waddle in for manager. They'd been left wondering who Francis thought the mole was, who'd start the next game, who'd end up on the transfer list, who was going to blab the next unguarded comment to the next loitering hack; they were living in that febrile, paranoid, sealed-off little pocket of hyper-discomfort that's a professional club when the goals and the points aren't coming – so Bright thought the Belles might cheer him up on a Sunday afternoon, and they did.

He'd seen two women's games before, so he wasn't surprised at the quality – but all the same, as a fearless and physical Leasowe attacked the injury-racked and out-of-kilter Belles, his comments betrayed an unforced, involuntary admiration. He saw pace, vision, close control, commitment, the lot; he compared Micky Jackson to Alan Hansen for her composure, Flo Lowe to Des Walker for her speed of foot and mind, he liked Tina Brannan's quicksilver pace and her unselfishness, and he was impressed with Ann Lisseman, her determination, the way she dug in at the back.

But it was Coultard and Walker who really caught his eye. He thought Coultard was brilliant, holding together a cobbled and buckling side – the amount of ground she covered astonished him – and when she scored Belles' opener he said it was all she deserved. Nor was he surprised when

Walker got the second; she was, he said, 'A complete player. She's got two good feet, crossing or shooting, she heads it well, she's strong, she's fast – and you don't see many strikers who work that hard either.'

I asked if there were things he'd improve on; he said it wasn't his place to criticise. I said, people say the women are defensively naive . . .

He smiled. 'Naive? Not in any way. They could be tighter about offside, maybe – but no. I see the little things that go on in the professional game, nudges, obstruction, running across people, rushing the keeper, protecting the ball when it's going out of play – they're doing all that. Making it hard for people to get free on the ball. Then the commitment in the tackle's been excellent; the referee could have been a bit firmer at times, I've seen studs showing here. There's been things that in the men's game would have been a yellow card.'

He said, if he'd not already seen women's football, 'I'd be very impressed. You'd think they'd not know how to kick the ball, that they'd toepoke it, they'd just run about giggling – that'd be a lot of people's idea, that it's only women – but not a bit of it. They're sidefooting it, they can hit it off their laces, off the outside of the foot and the inside – and more than that, they can see the pass before they hit it, that's even more important. It's not always executed well, but it isn't in the Premier League either – but that Skillcorn, look, she's turned and sprayed one wide thirty yards in one movement, cleared two defenders, and it's placed so perfect that if this was *Match of the Day* and you were highlighting a midfielder, you'd pick that. It was a really good clipped pass, it was dying as it reached the player, the Mitre was spinning backwards – just perfect.'

He said, 'I'm not looking at it as women here, I'm looking at it as football. And you can see that these people just love to play.'

I'd thought he'd come along to do me a favour, so I could see what a professional made of the women's game. But later he said, 'Oh no, I'll come again. It's refreshing. I'd like to see how they get on.'

Debbie Biggins made an exceptional, pure-instinct save from two yards as the final whistle blew; the game ended 2–1 to the Belles, and Biggins kept them in it for their third win in three. But if Mark Bright had enjoyed it, Paul Edmunds hadn't. In the dressing-room he tried to be positive, he tried to sound pleased they'd got three points, and then he shredded them.

'You sit down, every one of you, and you think what needs to be done, 'cause we've been awful. We've started bad, and we've got worse. There's people have come off, they haven't gone into a sprint for ninety minutes. But football's not about having the ball and looking pretty, it's about working hard to get it, there's nowt just happens, it's about *hard work*. So we need some winners here, and we'll never achieve *anything* until we get them. We need people who are going to *die*.'

Bright smiled. 'Managers aren't often happy, are they?'

In the Executive Suite he and Paul talked after the game, and Bright signed autographs on match programmes for the nervous and smiling younger girls as he did so. Flo came to ask how he thought she'd done and he told her she played like Des Walker, nipping in front to nick the ball off the attacker all the time, driving them mental.

She grinned and said, 'D'you want me autograph then?'

Later, he told Kaz she played like David Hirst did at Wednesday, that mix of art and muscle, and Kaz grinned too. She said, 'I score more goals than him, mind.'

4

Managing People

Ann Lisseman wanted to play football, catch bad guys, and save the whale, not necessarily in that order. If she could have had one dream fulfilled, it would have been to swim with a whale – a dream which, when she first heard it, Joanne Broadhurst mulled over before saying, 'I suppose I might go down the beach with a lager and wave at one.' But then PC 5615 Lisseman was a more serious person, and an ambitious one too – taking exam after exam to become a detective, a sergeant, a woman on top in a very male world.

Because in the police the sexist, the racist, the homophobe, they were still all there. She said sometimes it was horrible, they could be the world's worst; when you got the policeman that looked down on you as a woman, you didn't half get a hard time. It came in little comments, in condescending behaviour, in the way they treated you – 'only a girlie'. They'd say the women should have a women's department, just get left with kids and rapes. They'd leave the magazines on your desk . . . that attitude was still there, it was there every day.

So why did she do it? She did it because she'd always wanted to, since they came with the careers talk when she was fourteen at school; she did it because they weren't going to stop her – and she did it because it would change, because it was already changing, because she could see it being addressed and getting better all around her.

And then, she did it because away from that residue of neanderthals, you couldn't beat it. It was a job where most of the men around you, you were that close to them, they didn't look at you any different; you were one of the guys, you did your job, you put people away. You picked something up from nothing, you worked hard, you found out who did it, you got the evidence, you got a fair result – that was brilliant. Or it could be just as brilliant when you dealt with someone from the public, someone who'd probably never met a police officer, never been in a police station, and they'd been robbed, or they'd had their car pinched, so you treated them right and they went away thinking the police were OK – that could give you a pretty good feeling too.

She worked in a Crime Support Unit in Birmingham city centre, a team responsible for an urban area including the hardest parts of Handsworth, an area with more crime than the whole of Warwickshire. They worked serious and serial crime – armed robbery, murder, anything that needed numbers quickly. The week before the Belles played Wolves she was on observations in Soho Road, where a lot of women in a predominantly Asian community wore gold, and it was robber's alley down there. They'd snatch chains, they'd run by people grabbing their bags, they'd pick on old ladies collecting their pensions, people seventy, eighty years old, they'd give them a good thump and take their money. One of these days, she thought grimly, one of them'd have a heart attack, and then she'd be dealing with a murder.

They'd picked up four juveniles that week too, four from a gang of six they reckoned were on a string of burglaries; they were fourteen, fifteen, the youngest was eleven. Eleven years old . . . it was weird, but you got used to dealing with them, it wasn't a surprise any more. And some you got in, you'd think they might have a chance, it wasn't like all criminals were bad people, there were some you felt sorry for – but one of these, she knew she'd be seeing him again. It went from being a schoolkid taking fifty pence off another kid, they

called it taxing, taxing someone for your bus ride, it went
from that to attacking lone people in a gang, to using knives,
to armed robbery, doing petrol stations and that, and they
weren't more than eighteen, and it just got worse, worse and
worse, more and more weapons, knives, pickaxes, scaffolding
poles, firearms. Just lately two teenagers, they were having an
argument and one pulled a knife and the other one pulled a
bigger knife, and he chased him down the road and stabbed
him in the back and he died, and why? What was the matter
with it? Sometimes, she thought, the world was going totally
crazy – so when Sunday came she forgot about it, because
she had to. At least once a week, she just had to.

She was twenty-nine years old, five foot four ('nearer five
foot three and a half, really') and she weighed nine stone. In
plain clothes she'd gone after a thief down the street one
time, brought the guy down, been wrestling on the pavement,
and luckily a pair of bobbies were nearby so they came to
help. When they searched the guy, they found a dirty great
knife. She said, 'You think afterwards, Flippin' hell. Oooh,
Christ almighty. That was a bit rash, wasn't it?'

She said, 'If you thought about it too much you wouldn't
do it. Going in places, arresting people . . . but it's in the back
of your mind, I suppose, to be careful. You stop people, you're
very wary now. You watch what they're doing with their
hands.'

She had a colleague stabbed a while back. She said,
'You're never scared at the time, and you're always scared
afterwards.'

'I had four deaths in a week once, that was horrendous. When
you get a sudden death or a suicide, that's always tragic.
Particularly when members of the family find them, that's
not very nice. Anything to do with bodies,' and here she gave
an odd, helpless little laugh, 'I don't like 'em. When I was late

getting to the hotel that evening before the Cup Final last season, that old woman, what a *waste*. She's gone through it, two world wars, lived in a tower block, got her routine, doing nobody harm, and someone's come and killed her. For no reason, no robbery, nothing. Just like that. And you think, that could have been my grandma. And then you have to forget it, you have to get on with it.

'I think the worst . . . there was a chap who passed away on a bus. Seems sort of insignificant, doesn't it? Until you meet his wife. And you have to take her up to the mortuary to identify the body . . . oh. Oh,' she said, a sort of small moan, a sound of genuine pain, 'Oh, I hated it. She was on her own, crying. She asked me how he died, making sure he didn't suffer, making sure he had his dignity. Then she said, "I was just waiting for him. I had his tea on the table." And it brought tears to my eyes, imagining her waiting.'

I asked if she ever thought about packing it in and she said, 'Yeah. But we all don't want to go to work some days, don't we?'

On a Sunday she took her mind off it with the Belles, and at work they were great about it. She'd never once been mocked or criticised for playing; when they could they'd swap shifts around for her, or ease up and give her a few hours off, and on a Monday they'd always ask how she'd done. 'Even', she smiled, 'the ones who might give you gyp in other ways.'

They knew she was good, because she'd sometimes played with them on an office team against other police sides, and they'd take her along like a secret weapon. They'd not say anything and she'd see the other lot thinking, Yah, they've got a girl on their side, what's that? And she'd go past them and they'd not know what to do then, would they? But she didn't do it any more – it got rough and some of them weren't that good, and (more likely out of clumsiness than malice) you could too easily wind up with a broken leg; it wasn't worth it.

Besides, sometimes you did get malice. Some men, they *can't* be beaten, can they? Not by a woman. It terrifies them, the very idea, so then they kick you, and you know damn well they mean it. Or there was one who came to circuit training and in the sprints he ran next to her, and she beat him – and then he was banging his fist on the wall, his head too, going, Oh no, a woman's beat me, a woman's beat me. Dead serious. He was absolutely distraught that this woman had beaten him at running. What a knob, you know?

Later, talking about a manager she'd had at a previous club – her opinion of men in the women's game was in general pretty low – she talked about him ranting and swearing and she said, 'Some men, they seem to need to dominate, don't they? They don't think about *managing* people – they don't think about people's feelings, they don't think about the consequences of what they say. And how's that going to get the best out of you?'

She grew up in Malvern, the oldest of four; her parents both worked at Aldermaston, her father was an amateur player and then a referee, and from when she was young she always went with him. She started playing on a boy's team, then when the rules said she couldn't do that any more, the manager found her a women's team in Worcester. She'd get the bus there and back every Sunday to play for this lot and they were rubbish, they'd get thrashed 15–0 every week. But she still went, and it progressed from there; she played on a few other teams, then went to Solihull Borough, in the Northern Division one rung below the Belles; they played the Belles a few times in cup competitions and Paul signed her three years ago.

With the three players gone to Liverpool, and the injuries, she was starting games now, but it hadn't often been like that; a grafter while others shone, she'd been a perpetual sub. She knew other players were better than her, so fair enough – and sometimes too the pressure of work, of studying to get qualified for promotion, would be so great that she'd not be able to train like she should, and then her fitness would suffer, and she knew it. But it was frustrating not getting on, and Stafford where she lived wasn't exactly down the road from Belle Vue, and sometimes – like last summer – it would cross her mind to leave. But where else could be as good as the Belles?

Other teams she'd been on, they'd say they wanted to win, but they'd not do anything to help themselves. They'd get blasted on a Saturday night, then they'd wonder why they couldn't run round on a Sunday. Or they'd have training once a week but they'd not do anything else, fitness-wise, they'd not be at their full capacity, and she wanted more commitment than that – and if there was anything that summed up the Belles it was commitment in their work, commitment in their attitude. Besides, players like Kaz, Gill, Joanne, they weren't just good, they were exceptional, they were such class, and you wanted to train anyway to keep up with them, you wanted to work hard – otherwise you just looked stupid.

She kept the commitment in perspective. She ran two or three miles every day that she could, did circuits once or twice a week in the local gym, went two hours each way to training on a Wednesday when shifts allowed it – but she wouldn't move to Doncaster to make it easier, she wouldn't muck her career about. She said, 'It's not *that* important, is it? I'm sorry, but it isn't. I love football, OK, but I don't live for it. I haven't got a job that allows me to.'

On the other hand, if the football wasn't there, 'It'd just be like a big hole. It'd be horrible.' And because she loved it that much, not starting, being sat on the bench, it wasn't any fun. She knew someone had to do it – but she didn't feel Paul was always quite fair, and one element of her nerves on a Sunday morning was always to do with whether she'd turn up and not get a game, and whether, if she didn't, he'd bother to tell her why. He was better than any she'd had in the past – but if she didn't start, or if she did and he took her off, she wanted to know why, and what would it hurt to tell her?

She didn't know what he was thinking sometimes. You only found out if you were in when he read out the team, and that bothered her. Last season she'd got that fed up . . . but she wasn't going to leave. She didn't want to let people down – and then, she didn't like to be beaten. She felt she'd worked that hard to get her fitness back up, and after Wembley he'd said she wasn't fit, and she came from there really pissed off, she'd run her bloody legs off for him that game. So now she saw him as a challenge. Not start her, start her and take her off – she'd be damned if she was going to quit on him.

The Belles didn't play for three weeks; their game in Ilkeston was called off because of a waterlogged pitch, the Sunday after that was an England game. But it meant the injuries cleared, and they had Joanne back – her plaster had come off a week early – so with the exception of Gail Borman, they were near enough themselves again.

With Belle Vue unavailable, they played Wolves on their training ground, the Miners' Welfare pitch in Stainforth. The pit was shut, as was the coal-fired power plant across the fields, the cooling towers hulking grey and lifeless under a drizzling sky. There was a rough little clubhouse of worn brick and rusted metal, with barbed wire round the roof. Club helpers doled out tea and coffee from big urns. The Belles squeezed into a tight little dressing-room and Paul named the team, and Ann was starting.

It took them twenty minutes to get back into shape against a big Wolves side who had little to offer beyond muscle, lard and bottle – but of those, they had plenty. Some of the tackling was brutish and Sheila, jogging out to tend one clattered party after another, was angrily surprised to learn that the ref (seeing this was only women's football) hadn't bothered checking studs before the game. People were getting opened up out there. Afterwards Ann had a ballooning purple calf, stud marks raked through the skin. With grim satisfaction Paul said, 'It'll toughen them up. Got Arsenal next Sunday, haven't they?'

And the Belles stood up to it. On twenty minutes Tina Brannan skipped through a motorway pile-up of a challenge by the corner flag, some centre-half the size of a redwood lunging helpless through her slipstream as she whipped in the cross, and Coultard was horizontal in the air over the penalty spot, the diving header punched in, the keeper all ends up as it flew away off her legs, and after that you knew it was only a matter of time. With Broadhurst back, the best midfield pair in the country took charge, by half-time Belles were 4–0 up, and by the end when it was 6–0, Wolves were falling over all round the park, playing ten in their goalmouth, just a bunch of big bodies, nothing left.

Ann was substituted with twenty minutes to go; Paul sent on a Canadian girl they'd just signed named Bianca Wilkinson from the town of Mission, British Columbia. Ann sat on the bench, shrugging.

Afterwards Coultard reminded them about the monthly committee meeting; if there was anything bothering them, anything at all, as players' rep they should go to her. Flo said, grinning, 'I can't score a goal.'

'Can't sort that out in committee, lass.'

It was the standing joke – everybody scored but Flo. This game, on a corner, she'd come screaming in far post to meet a flick-on, dead cert to notch one, and it spun away wide.

In the pub down the road where they had their tea and sandwiches she sat with Chantel Woodhead, and described how the ball had come too fast off her shin. Channy smiled sweetly and told her, 'Because you're crap.'

'Least I don't need winding up. You need winding up before you'll move, you do. Dozy cow. Cloud Nine, that's your address, in't it?'

Across the room at the bar Ann said quietly, 'Well, I started, didn't I? Look on the bright side. Starting's a bonus.' Then Paul came and had a word with her, told her she'd done all right; he'd taken her off because they were winning and he'd needed a proper look at this Canadian girl, needed to give her enough of the game. So when he'd gone Ann said, 'Bless him. Thanks very much. I've come off thinking I've been subbed, oh God, what have I done? And now I know I didn't do anything wrong. I can go home happy now.'

Home happy to study *The Police and Criminal Evidence Act 1984: A Guide for the Practitioner.* She had another exam for sergeant coming up in a month.

5

Overdose Time

'The more she gets the ball, the better we play.'
Paul Edmunds on Joanne Broadhurst

Forty-five years old, the son of Poles who came to Yorkshire after the war, Robert Kantecki was a big teddy bear of a man who discovered sexism in 1991. The Belles that spring were in the FA Cup Final against Millwall, and they didn't have the money for the bus or the hotel; they approached a friend at the rugby league club, he approached Kantecki, and Kantecki wrote the cheque. He did it because it dismayed him that a side could be that successful and yet, being women, could attract no local backer.

The following season was the first for the national league; a week before it began, he agreed to be their sponsor and chairman. Another obstacle then arose that really engaged him, left him reeling between disappointment and disgust. For the opening game he went round local schools giving out free tickets to the kids, and one of the headmasters wouldn't let him do it; lasses in the kitchen, lads playing rugby, that was that man's way of thinking. Kantecki said, 'I could not understand it. My girlfriend, Julia, she'd told me about sexism, but I'd never thought about it – so meeting it like that made me extremely dedicated.' They ended up, him and another guy, handing out tickets by the school gates like drug pushers. 'Even just four years ago,' he said, 'people thought women playing football were weird bastards. Freaks. So you could say I saw a challenge.'

He was no tycoon. His company, Centurion, employed thirty people supplying tools and hardware to the DIY trade, he had a printing business, nice house, drove a Merc – but finding five grand and more each season to subsidise the Belles was no small wedge. More than money, also, the time he and Julia put in meant he neglected his business – but it meant the Belles could develop a youth policy, to get a solid footing for the future, and he felt now he could look at that with satisfaction. He said, 'With so many people it's just, What can I get? But you should give back too, and I've done something I've loved here. And I can't ever sponsor Man United, can I? But I bet if I could, it wouldn't be as much fun as this.'

Fun – that was the essence. He'd started because he thought women playing football deserved better, but as he came to know the Belles it became a matter of the heart. By now, he certainly wasn't there for any marketing notion that putting Centurion on the shirts of a team who mostly played in empty grounds was worth five grand; he was there because it was like having a whole new family, and you could see that the affectionate way they took the piss out of him made him beam.

No one took the piss with a quicker tongue than Joanne Broadhurst, and Kantecki adored her for it, relishing every Sunday the tonic of her humour and enthusiasm. Before the Belles played Wolves on 16 October he said, 'She loves it so much, she'd play on a broken leg.' After the game, it turned out she had.

She'd taken the ankle out of plaster a week early so she could be ready to face Arsenal; she'd called Sheila, said she had two legs again and could play against Wolves, and that way she'd have a game under her belt before the big one. Sheila replied that she'd been laid up for three weeks, and how could she be fit? Had she done any training? Joanne said, 'Yeah, I ran down the shop for me fags.'

The Thursday before Wolves, the consultant told her this stress fracture had to be treated like a proper break; he wanted her back in his surgery next Monday and when he put the plaster on again, this time it was staying on for six weeks. So Joanne went to Stainforth, said nothing, and played anyway. She wanted to try it out, wanted to see if it would stand up; she knew in her heart it was madness but the idea of six weeks out – missing Arsenal, Croydon and Liverpool along the way – was intolerable, unfaceable, the spiritual equivalent of a jail term.

After the game it was bad. She screwed up her courage to tell Paul, still not wanting to believe it, still imagining there might be some way this wasn't happening – and he told her to face reality, to get the plaster on and get mended before she ended up in a wheelchair. But after losing Gail Borman, he said, to lose Joanne as well was shattering.

She drove home to Stoke, and in the morning she couldn't walk. The consultant found a big swollen bruise inside her shin above the ankle; he looked at her and said, 'Have you been playing football?' She told him she'd bumped into a chair – and I'll bet that doctor just rolled his eyes to the sky. Even three days later, after the way Wolves had played, both legs were still patched grey and purple, and the short deep cut on one knee was a solid scab. That doctor must have thought to himself, a chair? She's bumped into everything in the furniture warehouse here.

But the thing with Joanne was, the girl couldn't help it. She said, 'I just want to play, I love football more than anything. If it were a practice match with the reserves I'd want to play, I'll play with anybody, I *need* to play. It's what I've always done, all my life – and then it's our team, Doncaster Belles, best mates together, and playing for us against anybody's just such a good feeling, it's everything I want in my life. When I'm at work I'm thinking about the next time I'll play, or about what football's on telly; I'm thinking football the whole time, in my body, in my mind. So being injured's just like . . . everything's gone. Can't do anything. Just sat here, just like . . .'

There weren't words for it. Marooned in an armchair she waved her hands about, fidgeted, fiddled with the drawstring of her England shorts. Take Gascoigne, add in a brain, subtract the whingeing and the petulance, and there's Joanne Broadhurst – a total football junkie, beached, stuck at home with a pile of videos, Sheffield Wednesday, Maradona, 501 Great Goals, nothing in her head but the day she could kick a ball again.

I asked if we could turn the spin drier off, it'd bog up the tape; she hopped into the kitchen on her crutches and yanked out the washing. 'There,' she said, 'my pride and joy.' It was a Wednesday shirt, the away strip, with an eight on the back and the name, Waddle. 'My hero.' She carried herself with a slouch in the shoulders like he did, and on the pitch she made chances like he did too.

She was twenty-six, and she was five foot four – though when she played she looked taller, as if the flow and weave of moving with the ball at her feet gave her extra magic inches. I asked what she weighed and she said, 'I dunno. I've lost about a stone. Can't you tell? Don't answer that.' Earlier she agreed that, no, when she dived across the turf, she'd not slide as far as Klinsmann; she jiggled her chest with a grin and said, 'Stout, me.'

The quick, knowing gags popped from an expressive face that could cheer up a room like an open fire – but she could be as temperamental as she was attractive. She was in a relationship just then that was heading for the rocks if it wasn't already on them, the injury was making her short-fused and edgy, and her semi-detached partner later spoke of taking a clobbering from the crutches one time, when Joanne's mood had swung down too abruptly. But when she wasn't off balance and she mocked herself like this – stout being a flirtatious exaggeration – she had a touch of Kathleen Turner about her, that kind of reckless, broadbrush sensuality. Ask Ann Lisseman if she had other interests, and she'd tell you she liked to cook a good meal for close friends; given the same question Joanne said, radiating mischief, 'Sex.'

Her first manager was her dad; he'd played semi-pro for Chesterfield, then managed Sheffield Ladies, and she started playing for him when she was twelve. It could be difficult, having your dad for a manager; she said, 'We used to have a lot of arguments, 'cause he used to shout at people sometimes. See, you can slag men off in a changing room and it doesn't matter, that's what they're used to. But the shouting and swearing and getting on your back, some women'll get upset, they don't like it, they'll get their heads down, and then they don't play. So my mum used to say he had to approach women different, if he wanted the best from us – and if someone shouts at me now I'll ignore them, it goes over my head, I've learnt. But back then I just used to walk off pitch, go home.'

Then the house would echo with doors being slammed – and it puts a new spin on trouble with a teenage daughter, doesn't it? Massive sulks and silence sessions 'cause you've said the girl's not pulling her weight in the five-a-side . . . and they got on better now, but he hadn't wanted her to go when she went to the Belles, when she was eighteen years old, and I imagine it was hard for him, like she was leaving home. She

said he'd built a good side – but in those days, if you wanted
to be the best, the Belles was the only place.

In the meantime she did Leisure & Recreation at college,
spent a brilliant summer working at Pontins – getting kids
playing football all day – then got a job in a Sheffield hotel.
The hours and the money were lousy, so when Flo heard
there was work going in one of Royal Doulton's distribution
warehouses in Stoke, she took it. Women's football's a small
world, they help each other out a lot this way, and around the
country as a result little pockets of players work and train
close together. Kerry Davis of Liverpool and England
worked in a sports shop in Stoke, Flo's old teams in Leek and
Crewe were nearby – so in different combinations, according
to who could do what when, they'd run together, train
together, put in an hour at the gym.

For Joanne, now she had her licence to drive the fork-lift
(the only woman so qualified among dozens of men at Royal
Doulton) the move had proved a good one. The warehouse,
to use an appropriate cliché, was the size of a football field;
fork-lifts whined and hissed down the aisles under pallettes
racked high towards the dim tin ceiling, and the staff hefted
and stacked the tons of fancy china on to lorries in the
loading bays, china for export to Europe, America, Asia. She
enjoyed it; it was physical work all day, loading forty-foot
containers on your own, talking football every tea break,
playing on a warehouse team with the men, and the money
was good too; depending on overtime she could top £200 a
week, and in the run-up to Christmas there was overtime
galore. So being injured now was double bad – not just no
football but no work, no overtime.

To get over it she was going to London to see some mates,
and then she'd be there come Sunday for Arsenal. She had to
show the flag – but she wouldn't enjoy it. She'd watch anyone
play; if she was driving down the road and she saw a game

she'd pull over, she'd watch kids, she'd watch fat, beery bastards playing rubbish on a Sunday morning, she'd even watch Sheffield United – but not Belles, she hated watching Belles. She said, 'If you're not playing and you see them getting ready you feel so nothing, you feel so crap. Then they're out there and you're not, and that's horrible.'

When she first went on her warehouse team against another side of men, the other lot stood off her to begin with. Then she beat a few and scored and they didn't like it, and one lad in particular started going to kick her, hold her shirt, jump in with the sliding tackles. Her side defended her, and before she knew it they were close to fighting. Another time, she got butted in the back of the head. Men . . . she shook her head. 'It's a shame. They spoil it, don't they?'

She was playing once with Kerry Davis against a YMCA team, and one of them showed Kerry his studs. She told him to leave it out and he said, all snidey, 'What's up then? You fancy her?' The look on her face describing this sorry guy, his fragile ego, his ineffectual fear and violence, was beyond contempt into indifference. She said, 'I don't know how men think. But they know they can hurt you, and there's some that try to.' She shrugged. 'I walk away. Don't want my Wednesday shirt getting dirty, do I?'

Wednesday were everything; she'd been going with her dad since she was nine, ever-present through the darkest days of relegation to the nether regions. Now, on Saturdays before Belles played, she'd go home and if there was a game at Hillsborough, her brother-in-law always had a ticket for her. She'd watch them, and she'd dream of being a professional.

Paul said she had no idea what it entailed, no idea of the pressure; he said, too, that the way she didn't look after herself, the irresponsible, the desperate, the positively zany way she played through injuries would have any manager in the professional game climbing up the wall. Mark Bright said playing against Wolves like she did was surely one of the loopier things he'd heard – but Joanne just shrugged. Maybe, she said, she didn't know what it took – but the problem was, being a woman, she'd never have the chance to know, would she?

A documentary recently made for the BBC about the Belles had ended on Joanne, and the tone was well caught, wistfully elegiac. She was shown alone in an empty ground under an empty stand keeping the ball up on her foot, on her knee, on her shoulder, holding it on the back of her neck, rolling it down and keeping it up again. As the leather softly thunked on boot and skin, a little soft-shoe football drumbeat, she said quietly on the soundtrack, 'A lad I played with at school, he got to play for Sheffield Wednesday apprentices – and I were better than him. That annoyed me, 'cause I wanted to be a professional.' She gave a sad little laugh before going on, 'I just wish I could be like they are, earning all that money for something you love doing. 'Cause a lot of women players could be that good, and earn as much as they do, if they were given the chance. But they're not, are they?'

When she was a kid she'd watch Wednesday training; she said she'd love to train with them now, because at Hillsborough or on the box she saw them doing things with the ball and she'd think, 'I can do that. But how do I know? So you wish you could kick around with them, just to compare yourself. 'Cause I can say I can do it but unless I'm there, how will I ever know how fast they are, or how physical? And I'd love to find out. It'd just fascinate me to see how good they really are.'

But then, she said, facing up to it, if the women's game ever did go professional, by that time she wouldn't be there anyway. She would, instead, still be spinning her fork-lift round the warehouse, stacking china in lorries, hoovering up the sports pages in the tea break; then maybe someday she'd be a sparky old lady watching the young girls play, remembering her own time long ago – and in that unknown future, maybe then they'd be paid for it the way Joanne Broadhurst never was.

I left her checking whether her Waddle shirt was dry yet on the radiator; I went home and listened to the tape, and when I saw her next I asked the obvious question: Didn't it ever make her think she'd been born the wrong sex? She answered straight away. 'Yeah, sometimes. If I'd been born a man, maybe I could have had a chance. I can't say if I'd have made it, but at least I could have tried.'

So she'd put up with being a man? She smiled; she might not know what went on in their heads, but in the men's game she knew what went in their wallets, and she could certainly put up with that.

We were on the sideline watching Arsenal and the Belles going hammer and tongs, a fast, fierce, no-quarter contest; she shrugged, half an eye on it, swinging on her crutches, wishing she was out there. She said, 'You are what you are. And as long as I've got my football, I'll be all right.'

Arsenal. They're 'boring, and lucky, and dirty, and petulant, and rich, and mean' – and that's an Arsenal fan talking, that's Nick Hornby in his splendidly melancholy *Fever Pitch*.

Arsenal. Even the name's boring, a nasal, sibilant clottage of stubby little North London syllables. You think of Arsenal, you think of Tony Adams with his arm up to the linesman looking for offside. He probably walks into the bar, said Paul, with his arm up like that.

But Arsenal, really. By tradition everywhere they're the side you love to loathe, the 1–0 kings, the automatons of graft, eleven cogs in a lustreless machine – and the women are just the same.

The Belles hated Arsenal. They were only founded in 1987, they were upstarts, big city bigheads, and they were just *Arsenal*, unsmiling, ruthless, professional, fun-free like no other women's team. In '92–'93 they beat the Belles 2–1 before 17,000 at Highbury during a benefit for the boxer Michael Watson, and the result gave them the league. So after the game, said Joanne, 'Us Belles were all singing, messing around – we were disappointed, obviously, but it's a game, we'll have another chance – and them, they were just stood there. If that had been us we'd have been out partying, we always stay together when we've won something – but them, they went home.'

But there's more to it, of course, than just Arsenal being Arsenal, five across the back, only scoring at set pieces. The Belles hated Arsenal because, in '92–'93, in that second season of the women's national league, Arsenal won everything – championship, League Cup, FA Cup too. So then, said Joanne, 'They were going round saying they were tops now, that Belles were past it, when we'd been up there ten years – and you don't suddenly become top team in one season. So we showed them, didn't we? We won it all back.'

But even as they did, Arsenal were still the only team last season to beat them, and the only team to draw with them too – 2–2 at Belle Vue, 3–1 down in London. I'd seen that London game, the only time I'd seen Belles lose – and since then I'd heard quieter voices amid the bravado say how Arsenal were Belles' jinx team, how they'd got to them psychologically, how they were the team in that bad year who'd taken it all away.

And now it was Arsenal again – top-of-the-league Arsenal away in Potter's Bar without Borman, without Broadhurst. I went into that Sunday filled with gloomy premonition, and everything that could go wrong did.

★

Flo couldn't drive; normally Joanne gave her a lift, but now Joanne couldn't drive either. So I set off at seven from home in North Wales, drove sixty miles to Stoke through the dawn mists and rolling greens of Shropshire, through tractor-slicked mud and silage on the country roads, through the red-brick villages with their yew trees and dark ponds, through Overton and Burleydam and Audlem and Woore. Then I wound round the tangle of the Potteries and at eight thirty I parked outside Flo's house, a thin, Sky-dished two-up, two-down on a narrow Hanley backstreet with a chippie and a pub and a corner shop.

I was early, the curtains were drawn, and I felt like death. The previous forty-eight hours I'd driven to Devon and back for a christening; my kids, excited about the journey and the family gathering, hadn't slept much, and neither had I. So now here I was at the wrong end of a cold morning in a little Hovis-ad road all cobbled alleys and ginnels, nothing down me but a pot of tea and two Marlboro, bowels in a knot, head thick as a muddy blanket, and Arsenal still two hundred miles down the road.

I left Flo sleeping and walked down the hill into Hanley shopping centre; at a paper shop they told me McDonald's might be open. I couldn't find it. I wandered empty, rain-smeared pedestrian precincts afflicted with a growing, tautening, unstoppable dawn desire in my belly to evacuate two days' worth of motorway sandwiches. At last, buttocks clenched with grim and panicking determination, I stumbled in under the yellow arches, limped wincing to the counter, and begged through gritted teeth for directions to the toilet.

It was in a mother-and-baby's changing room. I collapsed on to the seat in an ecstasy of relief, read the sports pages, looked around – and there wasn't any loo paper. I was reduced to rummaging through a binload of yesterday's soiled nappies for remnant scraps of unused baby-wipe and tissue; it was, I thought, an Arsenal kind of day . . .

I got take-out coffees and some dreck in a bun, crawled hollow-bellied back up the hill to Flo's house, knocked on the door; she let me in and pointed at the clock. 'You dozy pillock,' she said. 'Didn't you know the clocks were going back?'

She could have been in bed an hour longer and so could I. It really was an Arsenal kind of day.

Passing Stafford on the M6, Flo perked up; she'd seen two magpies. 'Two for joy,' she said, 'so we'll win. Either that, or I'll score a goal.'

But she was snuffling and snorting, she felt a cold coming on. 'It's going to be hard breathing today. Hope that Marieanne Spacey hasn't got her running legs on, 'cause I won't catch her if she has.' She'd marked Spacey before and she'd done all right, but it hadn't been nice. 'She grabs you, does all snidey things, pushes you in the back and that. You have to watch her. But she's good on the ball, dead tricky. I enjoy a challenge, mind, if I'm feeling fit. But if you're not – she can piss on you then.'

So was it different playing Arsenal, compared to all the others? She said, 'It's harder, yeah. Sometimes they only have one forward, that's why they don't score much, it's all set pieces. Though now I've said that they'll probably score five coming through us, and I'll end up getting a right bollocking.' She grinned. 'I can't let 'em get past, can I? Don't want Paul screaming down me neck. But then, I'm *determined* not to let 'em in, even if I have an 'eart attack, 'cause I *hate* losing, especially to Arsenal. When we lost that time last season I got a right lump in me throat, I had tears in me eyes. That BBC lot come up to me filming, and I couldn't speak. Oh, I were *sad*. 'Cause me 'eart's there, in't it?'

I asked if they were dirty, these Arsenal, and she said, 'Oh yeah. Not clumsy dirty like Wolves either, they're better at it. Especially in defence, it's all pull, pull, shove, shove. That Gill Wylie in the middle, she's evil, man. If you've got ball and she's coming in, you know you'll be fucking flying then.'

Then she thought about it a while. She was rough-edged, Flo, never had the easiest childhood, and the casual observer could easily have put her down for just a larrikin, a late-night clubber, a not-give-a-damn larkabout. But behind the bubble and cheek she was bright as buttons, and she didn't blame Arsenal; she knew, even maybe admired a little bit, why they were the way they were. Seeking to explain it she said, 'At the back they're just a hundred per cent commitment. So you can call it dirty – but you get past them, they'll bring you down 'cause they're doing it for their club, 'cause they're Arsenal, and they'll just not have you getting past. If it's what they've got to do, they'll do it, no different to Arsenal men – and I can understand that.'

But they were up against these without Joanne. Flo shook her head, said it was bad. So I asked how she'd feel herself if it were her in plaster for those six long weeks, and she smiled. 'Wouldn't be able to dance, would I?'

Then the smile vanished; she'd seen another magpie. She said, 'Oh fuckin' 'ell. Don't need that. One for sorrow. We'll lose now. Two magpies and another makes three. So we'll lose 3–0.'

When you think it can't get worse, it always does. Wilfreda Beehive got the squad and their travelling companions into the services at Watford Gap, and Paul gave me the injury list. As well as Gail and Joanne, Ann Lisseman was out; the calf kicked by Wolves had swollen up hugely, she'd been in hospital and nothing was broken, but the swelling wasn't going, and now they were talking about a blood clot. As for the eleven who would play, five of those weren't fit either – Kaz, Channy and Debbie Biggins in goal were all carrying dodgy ankles, Skiller's knee still wasn't right, and Micky Jackson had a back pull. All in all it was like Wilfreda Beehive shouldn't be going to Potter's Bar, she should be making for the nearest out-patients instead.

Paradoxically, Paul said it made him less fraught. As we set off for the last stretch south he said, 'It's one of those rare occasions where I honestly don't know what might happen before we start. With a full complement of fit players, I'd be more nervous – but now, I simply don't know. So the first five minutes'll tell me a lot, it'll tell them a lot too – but in some ways the backs-to-the-wall thing makes it easier, because expectations aren't that high.'

With Joanne out, he was giving teenager Tracy Kilner from the reserves her first start alongside Coultard in midfield. He sighed and said, against this lot, she'd learn what it was all about today.

The ground belonged to Potter's Bar Town FC; it was down a pleasant, tree-lined street of large, set-back houses, and the little clubhouse was smart and solid, with Sky TV in a tidy bar – none of your colliery village plywood and barbed wire here.

The bags thudded down on the concrete; the Belles packed in tight round the benches. Paul named the team and as he spoke Kilner stared at the floor, white-faced, chewing her nails, all but visibly trembling. She was looking at the Arsenal side on the back of the programme, the international names, until Coultard leaned over to her and ran her finger down the list. She said, 'Don't let these frighten you. 'Cause they're *shit*.'

Paul told them, 'It goes without saying that today's an important game. But don't get it in your heads that this is the be-all and end-all of the whole world, this one match today. It's one football match, that's all it is – whatever the circumstances, it's eleven of them and eleven of us, and what it's about today is who wants to win the most. So you go out there with a heart as big as a dustbin lid, you roll your sleeves up, all muck and nettles, north of England against these soft Cockneys, and we'll do 'em. 'Cause they've never done a hard day's work in their life, these, they've never been down pit for a shift, have they? So let's make sure we don't give them anything at all, *not a thing*. And it don't interest me who's in their team – what interests me is who we've got in here and I'm telling you, we'll be all right. We'll be *all right*.'

When he was done Gill said, 'Hey. We're quiet in here.'

Beside her Flo piped up, 'That's 'cause I'm concentrating on taking me necklace off. I'll be back to me normal self in a minute.'

Players were diving in and out for the toilet as Paul and Gill demanded ninety minutes of work, ninety minutes of character. Flo took her turn diving out and as she went she muttered, 'Ninety minutes of sheer hell, more like.' But when she came back she went to Kaz first by the door, then the next girl, then the next, demanding of each, 'How much do you want to win? How much do you want to win?' holding their heads in both her hands.

Gill told them, 'If we go out and battle like we can, that's 2–0 before it's started. So c'mon, eh? Let's get out there.' She gave Kaz a fierce long handshake and as she led them out Paul, in Joanne's absence, quietly, superstitiously spoke the Broadhurst mantra, the thing she always said, the last words they always heard as studs clattered on their way out the door: 'Enjoy yourselves. Stay on your feet. Watch the line.'

Barely five minutes into the game, twenty yards out, nervous Tracy Kilner struck a blistering shot that came back off the post. And if that had gone in, it might have been a different day altogether.

★

Here was a classic Arsenal fan for you: a weird little old geezer with silver hair and fancy togs, a paisley scarf and a pale-brown, sort-of-velvety bomber jacket. He shouted, 'C'mon reds. They're not a wonder team, so worry them.' I mean, *worry them* – if that's not an Arsenal shout, I don't know what is.

Arsenal scored after fourteen minutes, they hit the post twice and they had the better of the first half. But after the turn-round the Belles had the wind behind them, Arsenal had the sun in their eyes, and as the Belles got back in it they made chances, they levelled – or did they?

Ten minutes into the period, Kaz flicked a free kick on for Tina gliding through two defenders in the D; the keeper came, Tina rounded her, it looked like she'd gone too far, the ball drifted close to the near post but, twisting, she spun as she fell towards the goal line, and she just got a foot to it. The ball crept across the face of the goal, crossed the line, bumped back out and away off the far post – and the goal was disallowed by the linesman, the referee meanwhile having wandered off to Narnia. Or wherever.

Tina swore afterwards it had definitely crossed the line; after the whistle, Arsenal manager Vic Akers also said the Belles should have had the goal. Later, his players told him it hadn't gone in so, naturally, he believed them and changed his mind – but either way, feeling robbed and angry, the Belles were energised, and for fifteen or twenty minutes they got on top.

Then Kilner came off injured, Nicky Davies ditto soon afterwards. In goal, Debbie Biggins's ankle went – but with both subs used by then, she had to play on anyway. The same went for Coultard, who took a clout in the hip, and for five minutes after could only stand in the centre circle limping and wincing, struggling to get back in it – and as the clock ran out, Arsenal took remorseless advantage. Any time they got anywhere near they were firing bullets, and they were near all the time; it was only Debbie standing up on one leg who stopped them getting more than the two late goals they did get. So, as Flo's magpies had prophesied, it ended 3–0 to Arsenal.

In the dressing-room Paul told them, 'We're obviously bitterly disappointed, no one more so than me, but if we look at it, we were unlucky there. So you've got to look back and say, What are the positive things that come out of it? 'Cause we've had a lot of good individual performances. Micky at the back, Debbie in goal, Gill, Skiller, I could go all round the team, you've all done ever so well. And look, that's one loss, that's all. Play them at home, we'll beat them, 'cause we'll have eleven fit players next time and they're not that good, are they? They're not that bleedin' good. So the scoreline doesn't reflect how well we've played, and you've worked ever so hard, all of you, you've played through pain, and that's what I'm pleased about. Now, training for those that are fit, seven o'clock Wednesday.'

Which was all fair and good, and I can't think what better he might have said. But after he'd gone from the dressing-room, Flo said, 'We were dead quiet, dead upset. It was overdose time in there.'

Paul and Sheila had to run; they'd been invited to the annual Awards Dinner of the northern branch of the Football Writers Association in Manchester. In recognition of their trophies and promotions, awards were given to Alex Ferguson for Manchester United's Double, to Burnley's Jimmy Mullen and Port Vale's John Rudge, to Shrewsbury Town's Fred Davies, Chester City's Graham Barrow, and to Dario Gradi of Crewe Alexandra. Then there were Special Awards for Billy Bingham for his two stints with Northern Ireland, and for Paul Edmunds for winning the Double with the Belles.

It was, said Sheila, wonderful, marvellous, brilliant. She looked around and it was like a different world, rubbing shoulders with Ferguson, touching the FA Cup, seeing their own trophies right up there alongside it. She said, 'After all these years, to have the women's game accepted by the men like that, to achieve that – it were absolutely brilliant.'

It made up for losing – and besides, do the Belles *really* hate Arsenal? No, not really. Hating Arsenal's somewhere between a philosophical dictum and a natural-born thing, and at Arsenal they must have got used to it a million years ago. Besides, women's football's too small and too friendly for hate. At that conceptual level, that level of Platonic footballing essences, you can say you 'hate Arsenal' – but then you see the individuals get together and you know they don't mean it, you know it's only words. You see Kaz and Gail have a chat and a laugh with Marieanne Spacey before the game, international partners; you see Kaz waiting on a goal kick to come her way, leaning a casual arm on Gill Wylie's big shoulder beside her, the two of them smiling – and you know they both know that if they kick each other somewhere down the line it's only in the cause, it's only in the game. Or there's the Belle and the Arsenal girl who dived out behind the clubhouse after the game to share a spliff together, 'cause what the hell – they don't get paid for this, and what's to hate?

In women's football they train, they work, they run their legs off, and they enjoy themselves, win or lose – because otherwise, what on earth would be the point?

Although, having said that, when I drove Flo home later I'd never seen her so down all year. She said, 'That could be the league gone, that could.'

6

Falling to Pieces

Statement of the obvious: a football team exists to play football. If they're winning, they want to play again and keep winning; if they lose, they want to play again and put things right. But between the weather and the demands of the England team, clubs in the National Division now found Sunday after Sunday going idle. In a season steadily more disrupted, the Belles went two more weekends without a match – and then, on the third weekend, were obliged by the FA to play a match they didn't want to play anyway. Held over from the previous season because they'd run out of Sundays last spring, the match in question was the League Cup Final – and the team they had to play in it was Arsenal.

The Belles were furious. Aside from the fact that they no longer had the team from last season who'd won their place in this game, so that the fixture now seemed empty of meaning, they'd been under the impression that it would at least be played on a date to be mutually agreed between the two clubs – whereas it had instead been sprung on them on the last day in the world they'd have chosen.

Given their general mistrust of Arsenal, they suspected immediately that Vic Akers had swung it this way to capitalise on their injury list. But Akers, in fact, like many in the women's game, held an opinion of the way the FA was running it that sank lower by the day, and he said of the committee meeting that determined this match, 'They just threw a date at me out of the blue. I said I don't think the opposition would be too happy with it, but that was that. Decision made.'

So at a quarter to nine that unwanted Sunday morning I drove away from home with the headlights on in thick murk and pouring rain and I thought, I don't fancy this; I'm not up for this at all. It's only a game, it's not even part of the right season, it doesn't mean anything . . .

But what does football mean anyway? What's all this about? In a world where there's a good number of more serious things we might be thinking about, the game's become so all-pervasive that my son, not yet five years old, was already coming home from school with the vague idea that Ryan Giggs was 'world champion'. And then, here we'd been thinking the whole circus was back in the groove again – bye bye hoolies and hello Sky's wallet, hello Man U in the embryonic Euro Super League, hello Klinsmann and all the other foreign glamourboats parading under the grand new stands – hello, after the sordid troughs and serial tragedies of the Eighties, to an unrecognisable entertainment business of a game swirling with pots of money, fountains of style. But it didn't last, did it?

Athletic Bilbao put out Newcastle, Trabzonspor put out Villa, Trelleborgs put out Blackburn, Man U got mauled in the Nou Camp and Gothenburg, Ardiles and Atkinson and Walker got the sack, *Panorama* alleged Venables was bent, the *Sun* alleged Grobelaar was, and a lot more people alleged George Graham was too. The game all of a sudden looked about as bright and new as Paul Merson's liver, the nonsense engine was jammed into overdrive on front page and back, op ed and editorial, a bawling vortex of moral panic – this, remember, with Cantona's kung-fu and the vileness in Dublin yet to come – and all over a bunch of grown-up boys kicking a bag of air between two sticks. And I love football, OK – but are we mad? Where is there respite? Where did reality go?

In the *Independent*, Maggie Brown wrote one of her regular 'I hate football' pieces. The game, she said – more or less correctly – was 'a form of male soap opera, a window on a strange world where drama, dirt, deals and a certain type of brilliant but limited physical talent mix and swirl around'. But then, she concluded, 'Perhaps change is in the air. I've just had to spend £28 on football boots for my daughter.'

And that, of course, is why I drove on down the road after all. Money and TV might be turning the men's game into soap (with astonishing amounts of lather) but in the women's game you still get real people, playing the real game and nothing more. You don't have to take out a second mortgage to watch it, you don't have to buy any merchandise, you don't have to listen to Jimmy Hill at half-time, you don't have to worry whether anybody's bent, and you don't have to watch criminal idiots chucking the furniture on to the heads of small children. It is instead romantic, it's attractive, it's a laugh, it's got its head on its shoulders instead of its snout in a brown envelope, and if your lot lose you're not obliged to believe that the world's come to an end – which, given the state the Belles were in, was probably a very good thing.

The game was at Cambridge United; compared to what they normally get, the dressing-room was palatially spacious. A smart painted sign said 'Welcome To The Abbey Stadium' on squeaky-clean brick walls, freshly coated creamy white. Paul looked about him and said, 'Shall we have a five-a-side in here then?'

It felt extra roomy, however, because he only had eleven players. On top of the injuries Tina Brannan hadn't shown up in Doncaster, and Flo hadn't been at the services where she was supposed to meet them on the way down. Mind you, Paul hadn't wanted to be there himself; he'd planned to send them off to an easy league game against lowly Southampton under Coultard, and have the day off christening his best mate's new baby – and here they'd sprung last season's leftovers on him instead.

Flo arrived, breathless; the friend who'd been driving her had got lost in Northampton. She said, 'Did you think I weren't coming then? Would I let team down, me?'

Paul groused that he'd have to change the team sheet. 'Jonesy, put 12 on. You can breathe again now. Here, who's knackered my pen? All the way from Majorca, this was. Not for you lot to clean your studs with.'

A local reporter came in to check names against numbers. 'Who's 4?'

'Me,' said Flo. 'Sexy one.' She was bubbling; to her amazement, she'd been called up for the next England training session. 'I were quite shocked. And I better shape up, 'cause I've been drunk for three weeks.'

'When were you ever sober?'

'Who's the minute's silence for, anyway?'

'Burt Lancaster,' said Kaz.

'Right,' said Coultard, 'let's get fucking stuck in, eh?'

They didn't; Arsenal mauled them 4–0. Nicky Davies went to hospital, concussed after a clash of heads; some of the others played like they should have been joining her. Flo and Des did well, but they had to; Arsenal were swarming all over them, strong and hard and confident. Standing by the dug-out Paul seethed and griped and muttered to himself, or at the linesman. 'Offside, linesman, hey, number eight, *offside*.'

I said it did look like they'd not played for three weeks. He answered, 'Looks like some of them haven't played in their lives. Hey Skiller, we're in *yellow*. For God's sake, she's twenty yards off them. Game's happening all around us, and we're just standing there watching.'

It was a dispiriting afternoon, illuminated only by Marieanne Spacey's extraordinary thirty-five yard rocket for Arsenal's second goal, by Kaz at half-time saying of one somewhat portly Arsenal defender, 'She should be selling pies somewhere, her,' and by a vivacious gang of Belles fans from Hackney. I went to ask how come Hackney had a Belles branch, and it turned out they were Hackney Ladies FC. They supported Belles, they said, because some of them came from up north, because Belles played good football, no rough stuff, no cheating, because Belles loaned them a keeper at a tournament once, and because in their own division they played Arsenal reserves and they hated them. (As you do.)

One of them was also a nurse, which came in handy when Nicky Davies was stretchered off. She wasn't unconscious, was the message, but she was right out of it, she wasn't there at all.

Later, one of them shouted after an Arsenal foul, 'This is football, not boxing.'

In the dug-out Paul said, with a wry little smile, 'We'd have lost by a knockout by now if it was. Makes you wonder if you're in the right place, doesn't it? Still, if you're expecting commitment from players you've got to show it yourself, haven't you?'

I said I wished Joanne were fit. He said, 'Not as much as I wish she was.'

When it was over and they'd picked up their losers' medals, Kaz, walking back to the dressing-room, threw hers to the supporters from Hackney. The woman who caught it had a look in the case, then made to throw it back; Kaz shrugged and gave a little smile, gesturing gently that she didn't want it. She was very close to tears.

And with the new players coming in the Belles were, as Rob Kantecki said – both a truth, and a euphemism – 'in transition'. But he said, in four years, he'd never seen them lose two games on the trot – and I wondered whether what I was seeing here was transition, or disintegration.

Four days later, Paul was more depressed than I'd ever known him; in ten years, he said, he'd never seen a Belles performance like it. 'It was like watching a mirror image of the Belles I used to know. In the past I've sent them out and I've always known that if they played, they'd win. The other team would never look like scoring and even if they did, we'd always score more. Only this time, it was Arsenal who looked like that.' So he was dreadfully low. The more he turned the game round in his mind, the less he could dredge up any confidence that he could turn the team round on the pitch. Even patched and mended, maybe even with Joanne back, how could they hope, playing like that, to match Arsenal next time – or, come to that, to match Liverpool, who would likely be as strong themselves?

But the thing was, he thought, it was just something in people today. Take Tina Brannan – she plays five games, the fifth they lose, the sixth she doesn't turn up. Why? Because she'd asked for her forms back, so she could transfer back down two divisions to Huddersfield. It baffled him – one loss, and you pack it in? At training he'd asked Kaz what she thought, how someone could do that, and Kaz said she reckoned maybe Brannan had sampled the top flight, and decided she didn't fancy the graft it took. Maybe she fancied an easy life knocking five every Sunday past rubbish teams, and having everyone tell her she was great. And all right, he said, no one's getting paid for this – but where was the commitment? Why have that talent, and piss it away?

That talent, any talent, the more you worked at it, the more you got from it, the more fun your life was. Only people now, they didn't seem to want that, they didn't seem to know that, they didn't seem to care. And it was all very well saying it was a new era, it was transition, that it'd always be hard throwing reserve players against Arsenal – but Jackie Sherrard, a veteran Belle with a broken-up knee, had told him there were days she couldn't bear watching the reserves any more now either, she had to go walk her dog instead, because at that level too she couldn't see them making the effort.

When Paul was a kid growing up in Askern, everyone knew when you left school you had a job to go to down pit. So if you tried to get out like he had, if you went to college and aimed to better yourself, no one knocked you for it. Maybe if you came back from your first term away as a student and went for a beer in the club, they might notice your accent had ponced itself up a bit, saying 'Saturday' instead of 'Sat'dee', and they might take the rise out of you for that – but for what you were trying to do for yourself, no one would knock you for that.

But now there were no mines, there was no work, and everyone knocked anyone who tried anything at all. He'd see it in school, people saying, What d'you want to bother trying that for? Go to college? What's the point in that? It won't get you nearer any work, will it? 'Cause there isn't any . . . so the kids came in lazy, they sat in front of you like puddings, and the parents came in with no respect, no ambition, all motivation drained – and one of his colleagues who'd watched the Belles floundering against Arsenal said to him, Oh boy. You have to deal with it at school all week, and now you have to deal with it in your team on a Sunday too?

The following Wednesday, a lot of them didn't turn up for training. Last season, when they'd been beaten by Arsenal he'd told them, 'We don't sit around in little corners in twos and threes in this club throwing blame about, we get together, we work together, we win again together.' So they had, and they'd gone on to take the league and the Cup with a collective *élan*, a family *joie de vivre* that was infectious and resilient. But it seemed that was gone now; it seemed twos and threes was all they had.

So it was easy to say that I enjoyed women's football because the skill was there, but the fishbowl psychosis of the professional game wasn't – and it was easy for Paul to say that because it was amateur he had it in perspective, he knew his mortgage didn't ride on it. But he still sounded that evening like he was spinning inside in a bleak, dark torment, like a big piece of his world was simply falling to pieces.

About this time, Sheila had a kid come to school with his birthday card, a kid nine or ten years old. He asked her, Did she like it, and she said yeah, it was very nice.

He said he'd chosen it himself. His mum had given him the money, and he'd gone to the shop and he'd bought it himself. And she thought, What's going on with people now?

7

Aren't We All Mates Together?

Happily, you don't have to play Arsenal every week. Recovering from their nightmares, the Belles went to Millwall and won 4–1; they beat Truro 6–0 in the FA Cup, and then – with Joanne back out of plaster – they played Leasowe on a December swamp in Birkenhead, and beat them 4–1 as well. Then they had their Christmas break – and when the first Wednesday in January came round, on a freezing evening with the ground bone-hard, over twenty turned up at Stainforth for training. They were, it seemed, themselves again – and they needed to be, because their first game of the New Year saw them back in London, facing Wembley in the next round of the FA Cup.

At Vale Farm, John Jones believed absolutely that his team could win. They might have lost to the Belles four times out of four – but they were good enough, strong enough, disciplined and determined enough that there was no reason at all why they should lose a fifth time. And, he said, look out for Kelly Smith wearing seven. She was only sixteen, he'd only lately brought her into the seniors – but he wanted me to know, we were talking dynamite here.

He sat in their dressing-room, red Wembley shirts hanging clean and pressed off the hooks, his formation newly drawn up on the marker board – for the tactically minded (and for those who think women's teams don't know what they're on about) it was an intriguing 3–1–3–1–2. Outside the sky was grey, the pitch was heavy, slick mud sticking to your shoes off the sideline – and John Jones looked at the afternoon coming and he said, OK, of course you respected opposition like Coultard, Walker, Broadhurst. But that didn't mean you had to fear them.

At Wembley, he said, they didn't fear anyone – and whatever happened, when it was over, no one would be able to say they hadn't given it their best shot. They'd give anyone a clean, hard game and they'd shake hands afterwards, and more people should come and see them do it, and in the future he believed they would, because – in clubs like these two, playing muddy little places like Vale Farm – this was where the spirit of football lived.

He was right. What followed was one of the most exciting games I've seen in my life – and 150 people that afternoon, all yelling and screaming and cheering by the end, all utterly absorbed, can count themselves lucky to have been there.

The Belles were held up; Flo was half an hour late getting to Watford Gap. Maybe she'd been busy arranging the stickers on her tracksuit; 100% Gorgeous Horny Devil, they modestly announced. As for Joanne, there was no sign of her. Paul looked about him as they squeezed into the tiny dressing-room, fretting, wanting to start his team talk, but Kaz was on the loo. While he waited, Flo wedged herself down on to the bench beside Kantecki; with a grin she told him, 'Move over, fat git.'

Paul told them, 'It's going to be very difficult. They're a good, fit, organised, well-drilled team. But most of you have experienced FA Cup Finals, and winning them, and you'll be thinking to yourselves, I want a bit more of that. I know I do – I'd like to see my ugly mug on TV again and it's the only chance I get, Cup Final day. So what I don't want come April is to be sat on my settee watching some lot of Cockneys playing it, I want *us* to be there. And so do you. So I want to see us determined to hold on to that trophy – 'cause it's *ours*, and nobody's going to take it off us.'

But outside, while the Belles loosely warmed up as they pleased, and Wembley in notable contrast worked together sternly, noisily, regimented, he watched Joanne strolling round the back of one goal, arriving just thirty minutes before kick-off, and he shook his head. He said, 'What am I doing here? What *am* I doing here?' He riffled on his clipboard through the slips and papers and forms of the new FA officialdom, the team sheet in multiplicate, and he sighed. 'Media copy. Who gets that then?' As if anyone ever covered women's football . . .

Out on the pitch with her mates – Des, Kilner, the young ones sticking together – Sarah Jones tried not to fret. She'd had her debut here, she remembered going white as a ghost when he said she was starting – but she'd started another game since, got on as a sub three times, she was getting used to it, and there was always Kaz to look up to; Kaz always had a word for you. You'd see her be so nervous too, and she still always played that good, and you'd not mind so much being nervous then yourself. So maybe if they went well – didn't Belles always go well in the FA Cup? – she'd get a run-out today, and that would be something. Because it was still amazing to her to be part of this; to be a Belle, to play with England players, to play in the last sixteen of the FA Cup . . .

She'd started playing when she was five, when her little sister was born, and her mum said she didn't want any more kids. She thought now maybe her dad started kicking it about with her because he didn't have a lad, and to find as she grew up that she was good at it, she really hoped that was nice for him. She'd become a Belle at fifteen – and then, disaster. She lost two whole seasons – one to a year's ban because she misunderstood the age rules and played for the Under-16's when she was a fortnight too old, the next to a broken leg in the opening game. You lost your impetus like that, it got hard to be bothered – and she only came back this year for the sake of being with her mates, thinking there was a long way to go yet, and she'd be back in reserves.

Then they gave her the forms, signed her as a senior, she started that game here September – it was unbelievable. To be in the National Division, to be counted among the top of your kind in the country – you felt you were somebody then. She'd go back to her course at Wakefield College on a Monday and all the lads would ask her how Belles got on, and did she play, and how did she do, and it just felt *special* . . .

So being on the bench was OK, she was only eighteen; some of these others were knocking on, her time would come. She sat in the dug-out, and she waited to see how the biggest game in her life so far might go. Then she watched that tall Wembley seven, that Kelly Smith, skinning Nicky Davies, and she thought, Flippin' 'eck. She's a bit good . . .

Kaz scored in the seventh minute; the corner came in and there she was, a yard taller than anyone else. I thought, here we go. 1–0.

But this Kelly Smith was a revelation, she was tearing down the left leaving bodies in her wake, one, two, three, four, she didn't care how many, she just went – and four minutes later Wembley equalised, Ayala Liran bundling in Smith's shot as Debbie Biggins parried it. After that, Wembley ruled the field.

Paul couldn't believe what he was watching. That seven was taking Nicky to the cleaners – and Skiller, Mickey, did they care? They were walking about out there. He shouted, 'Hey Skiller. Go in as if it's going to chuffin' *hurt* you, eh? What is it, if it's not dropping on my foot I'll not bother?'

A cold wind gusted under gathering grey clouds; the little

crowd dotted about the tatty stand, stood on mud banks and broken concrete, murmured appreciation as Smith, again and again, went slicing towards the area. Paul groaned, 'Where are we? We haven't won a ball yet.'

Smith was even beating Coultard now; she had everyone foxed, the Belles area was a chaos zone. Wembley surely had to score, bar Debbie in goal there wasn't anyone seemed to know how to stop them – but the keeper gathered shots, free kicks, crosses, everything that came she claimed it, and the Belles hung on.

In the dug-out, off her crutches after surgery now, Gail Borman was having trouble staying sat down. 'Hey,' she shouted, 'let's get stuck in. D'you *want* to win it?'

Maybe Flo and Des did, they were running about like they'd tackle trucks, those two, and Des got booked for her pains – and Kaz, you could always rely on Kaz, she was doing more in her own area than she was in theirs. But the rest of them? Paul snarled, 'There's some of these haven't fuckin' woken up yet. They want to stroll through it, they don't want to work. Her, look she's not broken into a fuckin' trot yet, never mind sprint anywhere. I mean, do I know these? Since I've been at club I've not seen so pathetic a performance. Hey, you. Never mind holdin' your bleedin' head, get chuffin' *tackling* somebody.'

At half-time he spun round and marched furious into the dressing-room; he stood waiting for them, hating every second going by until they were all in and he could get after them, try and turn them around. The door was barely shut before he started, and all the time as he spoke his voice slowly ratcheted up until he was shouting, leaning forward, arms out and fingers pointing, disbelievingly angry that the Doncaster Belles could ever play so badly. He said, 'After they've equalised I couldn't wait for half-time, 'cause it's just gone from bad to worse. In my time here that's one of the worst halves I've seen. Now that's not going to make you feel any better, I realise that – but for everybody watching it doesn't look as though you want to win it, it doesn't look as though you're bothered. And I can't see inside people's heads, so I don't know – but we've got to show a bit more commitment than that, 'cause we haven't got enough people working hard to win the game, it's as simple as that. Nicky, are you injured?'

'I've had a stitch from ten minutes in . . .'

'Jonesy, get your gear off. Right side of mid-field – and that seven, if anybody hasn't noticed, she's all left foot. So Jonesy, you've got nice pace, you stay with her, show her inside.'

Jonesy looked white, Nicky Davies looked like she'd been hit. But he'd taken her off and that was that, he was racing on, asking them all who they were, what they had, what they wanted. In the most telling of phrases he demanded, 'Aren't we all mates together? Don't we help each other out?'

Because it was *abysmal* from the sideline, it was *embarrassing*, and they'd got out of jail, they were lucky to be one-all here, so they better roll their sleeves up, 'cause they'd disappointed a lot of people that half. And that wasn't going to happen second half, was it? They were going to go out and work hard and win this game. 'Cause some of them weren't even out of bleedin' breath yet, they'd not hardly bleedin' run anywhere. And he didn't mind at the end of the day if they'd given their best and got beat, fair dos – but they hadn't given their best, had they? So they'd go out there now and they would, 'cause that first forty-five, *it wasn't good enough*. It was the bleedin' FA Cup this, it wasn't some Mickey Mouse Cup, *it was the bleedin' FA Cup*. And some of these in here hadn't won anything in their lives, so they better go out there and win this 'cause he wanted winners, he didn't want people who'd have others win things for them. *So come on, eh? Everything's got to be better, all of us. We do it together, every one of us . . .*

He was shouting, yelling that they should be what they knew they could be, and Gail was chipping in, and Rob, and they were all clapping hands and urging and demanding, and Gill was beating a hand to her chest and shouting, 'In here, lasses, in here. We've all got to want it in here. We've got to dig a bit deeper, we've got to graft for what's in us life. And if we put the effort in, we'll get something out of it. But if we don't we'll get *nowt*.'

'Yeah,' said Flo, grinning. 'Let's screw 'em.'

Sheila told her quietly as they went out in a roaring clatter, 'Like Billy Whizz, you. Good half. Keep going.'

Wembley won two corners; Flo cleared it, cleared it again. Kelly Smith cut past Jonesy, shot just wide; another Wembley strike hit the post. A bunch of kids behind Debbie's goal chanted loudly for the home side, and all around the little ground people were shouting, cheering, applauding. Kantecki stumbled out of the dug-out saying, 'I've got to stand. This is too stressful.'

But at the other end Joanne was beginning to make chances, and Kaz was beginning to get on the end of them; for half an hour now the game became a frantic swirl, the Belles hauling themselves back into it – until, with twelve minutes left, Kaz Walker towered above the pack in the area, and thumped home another header from a corner. 2–1 Belles.

John Jones was on the touchline roaring, 'Let's fight now. Let's *fight*.'

Gail shouted, 'Last ten, Let's keep going 'til the end.'

But Kelly Smith was keeping going too. 'Jonesy,' Paul shouted, 'Jonesy, tuck in. *Tuck in*.' And beside him Rob, Gail, Sheila, they were all pacing, bawling, hoarse, as Debbie saved another shot from that lethal sixteen-year-old. Again Smith went, she left Jonesy, she was into the area, Jonesy went for the ball, stretching, Smith was tumbling, Joanne, enraged, was acting out the dive for the referee's benefit right there next to her, but Jonesy didn't see that, she was crashed to a stop on the turf and she knew the ref was going to give it even as she lay there, she didn't know if she'd got to the ball or not but she knew Wembley'd got a penalty with five minutes left, she knew it was because of her and she wanted the earth to swallow her up. She looked towards the bench, petrified, raddled with remorse, thinking Paul must be screaming at her, thinking his head must be exploding; thinking she'd never get picked again.

He wasn't screaming at her; he was muttering in a private rage about diabolical officials sent down by the Lord to try us. Beside him Rob asked, 'Has he give it because he thought it was appropriate? A pen for falling over? Disgraceful. Disgraceful.'

On the pitch Joanne told Jonesy, 'Never you mind, she dived. She dived.'

Flo put an arm round her, grinned. 'Eh, Jonesy. Were you on the piss last night or what?'

And Gill told her to get her head up, and she tried to, but it didn't matter. That nine, that Ayala Liran, she put the kick away past Debbie and it was 2–2, and the Wembley bench and the crowd were all cavorting and whooping, and she thought now Belles had to play another half hour, and it was all because of her.

She got a grip and knuckled down, and she went off after that Kelly Smith again.

They collapsed in a circle round the Gatorade bucket; a circle of mud and untied shinpads and cramps and pain. Sheila and Rob worked on weary legs. John Jones shook Paul's hand and said, 'Good ninety. Good ninety.' Then they went at it again.

In the first minute Gill Coultard went down in a nasty collision, and Sheila was out there a long while. Eventually Gill was up and testing the leg, hobbling; it was a bruise on the bone, on the lower shin. Sheila came back and said, 'If I'd told her to come off she would have. So I told her she were all right. 'Cause we need her.'

'Kaz Walker,' said Paul, watching her run herself into the ground, still smiling as she did it. 'Kaz Walker. Our only hope.'

And then it was 3–2 to Wembley. I didn't see how it happened, I only saw John Jones leaping about bent double on the sideline, both fists clenched, screaming *Yes yes yes* . . .

Behind him Wembley's coach, spinning on the spot a bit himself, said to one of their players on the bench, 'Did he show a bit of emotion, or what?'

'Shit or bust now,' muttered Paul.

In the darkening evening under the lights the atmosphere was electric, the tension ferocious. Every soul in the crowd was shouting, every player was chased beyond exhaustion, and Jonesy was thinking *Christ, oh Christ. Belles out of the FA Cup this early for the first time in a dozen years because of me* . . .

Back at sweeper Flo was thinking it was like the fuckin' Alamo, this. She was thinking, they just keep coming, these, what have they got, nineteen on here or what? And she was thinking, me and Des, we've had all these up our arses for two hours 'cause there's some in front of us don't seem bothered today – but she knew Kaz was bothered, and she was thinking something else too. She was thinking, we're not going out here, no way on this earth. She was thinking telepathy, she was throwing her mind and her heart and her whole soul up the pitch, she was thinking, *Kaz Walker, you, you're going to score another goal here* . . .

There were five minutes left. Down the right Gill Coultard burst through two tackles, looked up, crossed. Kaz was on the edge of the area, the ball arcing over, and she spun and volleyed first time from thigh-high and it just sang through the air into the angle of post and bar, too hard and too fast for the diving keeper, and the score was 3–3. As the Belles bench ran screaming and punching air to the touchline, as the Wembley bench stood stunned, as all the yellow shirts ran to embrace her, Kaz Walker raised her arms to the sky, eyes burning, smile wide, a radiant illumination of joy in the floodlit white twilight. Stood jubilant in the D she told her mates, 'I fuckin' *love* football, me.'

On the bench Gail shouted, 'Deep breaths, Channy, deep breaths. Keep breathing,' and Sheila fell about laughing.

Paul shouted, 'Keep breathing, Channy, Gail says that'll help.'

Then it was done and they stumbled into the dressing-room, everyone embracing everyone, clapping hands, a torrent of laughing voices, the air thick with mud and sweat and relief.

Ann, collapsing on to the bench: 'My fuckin' legs have fallen off.'

Sheila, grinning enormously: 'That's what I call a cup tie.'

Flo, staring at the floor: 'I don't want another fuckin' one like it.'

Joanne, standing, arms wide: 'Well done girls, eh? Great game.'

Gail, quiet and smiling by the door: 'I'll make final yet.'

Sheila, raising more gales of laughter. 'Channy, *breathe* . . . oh, but I nearly fell in bucket when that third one went in.'

Paul: 'I've aged fifteen years, my hair's gone grey, I've got stomach ulcers – don't you ever, *ever* do that to me again. But hey, we showed a bit of character, eh? Whatever they say about us, we don't fuckin' lay down and die, do we? But I'm pleased for you, well done everybody, all thirteen of you,

excellent. And hey, just think, all those poor sad people sat at
home watching Man U on telly – when you, you've been
playing, *you're part of it.*'

And Joanne started them singing:

> We're off to the FA Cup Final
> We'll really put on a show
> We'll show 'em a brand of football
> They really want to know
> We're representing Donny
> We're proud to do or die
> Wembley won't be doing it
> 'Cause they'll never qualify . . .

It was a stupendous afternoon, one of those games that calls
up all the big adjectives – titanic, heroic, epic. But it was also
honest, free of malice and cheating; the way the managers
shook hands and vied to out-praise each other's teams for the
local reporter from cable TV summed it up. The one thing
wrong with it was the crowd – two of the best teams in the
country laying on a feast, and only 150 there to see it when
it deserved ten times that many, a hundred times . . . but
there you go. It's only women's football.

Still, they were used to that. Nor was it the reason why,
twenty-four hours after his team had taken part in this
enthralling game, Paul Edmunds announced to the management committee of the Doncaster Belles that, come the
end of the season, he was resigning.

8

'Purely Sex Prejudice'

In 1895, a pioneering organiser of women's football with the splendidly apt name of Nettie Honeyball played in a North v. South fixture at Crouch End. The North won 7–1, but whether they were any good or not, the *Manchester Guardian*'s principal interest was in what the ladies chose to wear; the North sported 'red blouses with white yolks, and full black knickerbockers fastened below the knee, black stockings, red berretta caps, brown leather boots and leg-pads'. Getting over this sartorial excitement, however, the paper's reporter doubted whether, once the novelty wore off, women's football could ever regularly draw crowds.

World War One proved him wrong. Women doing the men's work in factories saw no reason why they shouldn't play the men's game on football fields too, and teams sprang up all around the country, from Bath to Sunderland, from Huddersfield to Glasgow. By far the most successful side were Dick Kerr's Ladies, from the eponymous munitions plant in Preston; playing matches for war relief charities during and after the war, they raised over £50,000 in five years.

To begin with, it was literally a shoestring operation. One of their players, Alice Stanley – a sprinter who would later hold the British title over a hundred yards – had no boots when she went for a trial, and had to play in her working shoes. 'They took quite a battering as you can imagine. My mother went up the wall when she found out.'

By 1920, Dick Kerr's Ladies were nationally known. With the Football Association looking kindly on the charitable efforts of the women's teams, and granting permission for them to play on league grounds, Dick Kerr's played before 18,000 in Cardiff, 20,000 in Hull, and 23,000 in Edinburgh, where they beat a representative Scotland team by the somewhat embarrassing margin of 13–0. In all, they played thirty matches that year, winning twenty-five, drawing two, and losing three.

Of the draws and losses, one of each came against a French side of typists, students, dressmakers and factory workers. They toured for a week in April, playing Dick Kerr's at Preston, Stockport, Manchester and Chelsea, drawing a total of 61,000 to the four games; gate receipts went to the National Association of Discharged & Disabled Soldiers & Sailors. Before the return tour in October, Dick Kerr's wrote an open letter to their hosts, and the tone evokes both the mourning of that time and some cheery British pluck: 'We come to France with feelings of friendship towards France unsurpassed by any sporting organisation which has yet visited your shores. To many of us there will be a touch of sadness in our visit, insomuch as many of those near and dear to us are taking their last long sleep along the various fronts we shall visit. Needless to say we are out to win all our matches . . .'

Dick Kerr's returned home unbeaten after playing in Paris, Roubaix, Rouen, and Le Havre, the series again having drawn some 60,000 spectators. On Boxing Day, they then wrapped up their year with a game against St Helen's at Goodison Park; 53,000 came to this single fixture, at least 10,000 more were turned away, and over £3,000 was raised for charity.

Women's football at this point might have entered the popular culture. 'The Football Girl' had a regular magazine column in *Football Special*; comic strip heroine 'Nell O'Newcastle' had her own ripping yarn in the fourpenny *Football Sports Library*. Published in 1922, the pulp novel *Bess of Blacktown: A Mill Lass Footer Yarn* was widely read; a tale of kidnap, corruption, love and the long ball, it featured, among other obstacles the women had to face, a melodramatically brutish mill boss named Peter Henneker:

> 'What I say, I mean!' he cried, thumping the top of his desk. 'I forbid anyone in my employ to run a girl's football team!'
>
> 'You can't – you can't prevent us,' declared Bess. Peter Henneker sprang to his feet.
>
> 'You have your choice!' he snapped maliciously. 'Either you give up your rubbishy football, or you leave my employ!'

But many owners, in fact, had seen the benefits of sponsoring works teams pretty quickly; apart from the fact that healthy, happy workers were more productive, a winning women's side with your name on it was good publicity. By 1921, there were about 150 women's clubs around the country, and their charity games regularly pulled crowds topping 10,000. Their very success, however, was their downfall. With the war over it began to stick in male craws, and since it was becoming harder to argue that the women couldn't play, it was instead said more and more that they shouldn't – that football was unsuitable for their fair featherlight frames.

The captain of Huddersfield Atalanta, one Mrs Barraclough, vigorously rejected this: 'If football were dangerous some ill-effect would have been seen by now. I know that all our girls are healthier and, speaking personally, I feel worlds better than I did a year ago. Housework isn't half the trouble it used to be, because there is always Saturday's game and the week night training to freshen me up.'

Since the unsuitability argument wouldn't wash, those men who felt threatened turned to another line of attack. During 1921, rumour began filtering into the FA that women were being paid to play or, worse, that gate receipts meant for charity were going astray – and though these charges were apparently unsubstantiated, they represented a damaging attack on the principal justification for the women's game, a slur on the vehicle they'd found to drive them through the wall of male prejudice. Dick Kerr's manager, A. Frankland, protested robustly in *Sports Pictures* that neither his players nor his club had taken a penny piece for playing – but the FA had the weapon they required. On 5 December 1921, they passed the following resolution:

> Complaints having been made as to football being played by women, Council feel impelled to express their strong opinion that the game of football is quite unsuitable for females and should not be encouraged.
>
> Complaints have also been made as to the conditions under which some of the matches have been arranged and played, and the appropriation of receipts to other than charitable objects. The Council are further of the opinion that an excessive proportion of the receipts are absorbed in expenses and an inadequate percentage devoted to charitable objects.
>
> For these reasons the Council request the Clubs belonging to the Association to refuse the use of their grounds for such matches.

In fact, when Dick Kerr's played St Helen's at Everton, of £3,115 raised at the gate, the expenses received by the two clubs totalled only £28 – less than one per cent. But even if someone somewhere had cooked a ledger or two, the first paragraph of the FA resolution said it all; in the absence of hard evidence, the rest was smokescreen. The women might have done their bit during the war, they might even have got the vote – but as far as the FA saw it, when it came to football, it was time to clear them off the pitch and get them back to making tea. That, certainly, was how it looked to the captain of Plymouth Ladies, one Mrs Boultwood: 'The controlling body of the FA are a hundred years behind the times, and their action is purely sex prejudice.'

But the FA held all the cards. Dick Kerr's Ladies had their swansong the next autumn on a tour of the USA; they played three men's teams, losing twice in New England, and drawing 4–4 with a Washington eleven. The 'fair kickers' were given decent coverage in the *New York Times* and the *Washington Post*, then returned to a country in which there was nowhere they could play. Deprived of decent grounds to stage their games, the women were stifled; those few who played on did so in unattended silence.

In early 1994, director Paul Pierrot was researching a documentary about the Belles for the BBC; at a Rovers game, he was approached by the lady who made the tea. Her name was Jenny Gill, she was seventy-six, in the Thirties she'd been a centre-forward with Woodlands Ladies, and no one at Belle Vue had known about it. Pierrot took Gill Coultard to Jenny's neat little bungalow to film them talking together; they sat on the sofa and Jenny said how when she first saw the Belles, she wanted to run out and join in. She said Rovers weren't so good. 'They ought to come see these lasses. Might learn something then.'

Gill asked, 'Was it hard in them days?'

Jenny smiled, remembering. 'One woman I tackled had thirteen stitches down her leg.'

'Out of the same mould as me then. So did you have a sponge man running on?'

Jenny snorted. 'Not likely. I'm not having him sponge *me* down.'

In the back room her husband Jim played Blackpool dance tunes on his electric organ. He'd first met Jenny after he'd seen her playing; he laughed and said, 'They were kicking each other to death, it made our day. But the people that mattered,' he sighed, 'them that carry the little cases – that's a different story.'

The little cases at the FA didn't rescind their ban on women playing at league grounds until 1971 – even now, only the Belles played on a professional club's turf – so it wasn't surprising that in the memory of the older women still involved those fifty years of banishment, and the continuing disregard ever since, conjured a deep mistrust of the men who run football. Women, thought Sheila Edmunds, were always second-class citizens to these people – and nothing the men had done, in the eighteen months since the FA took over the national side and then the league, led her to believe that they thought any differently today.

She was far from alone in feeling this. For thirteen years from 1980, Linda Whitehead was the first and last full-time paid official of the WFA; she lost her job in June 1993 when Lancaster Gate took over and, she said, 'A lot of people felt very bitter. Everybody was keen at first for the FA to become involved, and the WFA did have a lot of problems, so we appreciated them coming in – and it wasn't what they wanted to do, it was the way they did it, they just rode roughshod all over us. They wanted to do it in their own time, in their own manner, and the grassroots feel they've been left to one side – that the FA's only interested in the national side, and that otherwise the women are way down the heap. But then,' she said, 'they don't just act this way in women's football, do they? It's the same with the men's amateur game. The FA, they're just a law unto themselves.'

Elsewhere, the feeling was the same. Echoing Whitehead, Vic Akers at Arsenal described the FA's takeover as, 'A steamroller job, an absolute steamroller job. Right from the off they came straight through us. Whatever we had, it wasn't going to be good enough for them.' He described them as 'blazers', in a tone that near enough made an item of menswear into an oath. He said, 'They think everyone else is an idiot, that's just the way they are. But they've been in charge all this time now and I've never seen any plan whatsoever of what they mean to do for the women's game. I haven't heard anything at all, not even in a conversation.'

What he'd heard instead, at one of the committee meetings, was the FA's coaching boss, Charles Hughes, the High Priest of Direct Football, 'Trying to tell me the basics of the game, how to play it. And you can imagine, I nearly had a bit of a dust-down with him – 'cause the women's game isn't about smashing the ball all round the park, the women want to *play*. And I'm wondering just how conversant he actually is with women's football. Does he know the results on a Sunday? But I try to talk about this and the chairman says, "Excuse me, but Mr Hughes is speaking." And I'm thinking, Just a minute, I'm speaking here too, aren't I? But,' he sighed, 'you can't get through to them. We've got no clout with them at all.'

The *modus operandi* of Hughes's coaching department was once described to me by an FA insider as 'Stalinism, only more centralised', and in the way they ran the women, that seemed apt. Belles' secretary Alan Burton said, 'They want to dominate, to be instrumental in every decision. I want to be able to talk to other secretaries about a game, a venue, a kick-off time – but every little decision has to be made through them, and it frustrates you. It loses a lot of the inter-club relationships, and it's spoiling the atmosphere.'

★

Millwall's secretary got a glossy video in the post about drugs, and how the FA were going to start testing in the women's game. 'So now I know', she said, 'that if a girl gets a cold she can't do Lem-Sip. Fine. But wouldn't a glossy video promoting women's football that I could take around the schools be a little bit more useful?'

During the first half of the Belles' twenty-fifth season, however, efforts by the FA to promote women's football seemed minimal, to put it mildly. England's women were then engaged in a European Championship quarter-final, a two-leg fixture against Iceland; a fixture that was crucial because if they won, they'd qualify for the Second Women's World Cup in Sweden the next summer. So I rang Vic Wakeling at Sky Sport, since they'd televised the last women's FA Cup Final, to see if he had any plans for this Iceland tie – and though he was talking to the FA about the rights to the women's game, he said no, he had no plans for the Iceland matches, because no one had told him they were happening.

As for the national team itself, the man appointed by the FA to manage them had never played professional football, had never previously coached women, and had acquired the bulk of his coaching experience – twelve years of it – in that well-known bastion of football and feminism, Saudi Arabia. On top of that he had a full-time job anyhow, as the FA's Regional Director of Community Development in the North. His name was Ted Copeland, and when I asked if he was exactly the best qualified man for the job, he shrugged and said simply, 'If you can coach, you can coach.'

I was later privately assured that, given the attitude of other senior coaches in the FA to women playing football, he was (within that circle) the best choice available. Certainly, he was committed; he believed the players were skilful and dedicated and he wanted to help them improve. He said he saw it as a challenge, and you got the strong impression that the chance to work regularly with a team on the field, any team, made a welcome change from driving his desk. He wasn't, after all, getting paid any extra to do this (which hardly suggests the FA saw it as an important job) but still he'd taken it on.

While he may indeed have been a good coach, however – and a number of players did say they were learning from him – whether he was also a good manager was more open to question. By his own lights, he saw himself as trying to raise standards – standards of preparation, of diet and nutrition, of behaviour, as much as standards of play – but the way he went about this struck the players as ineptly draconian, and more and more of them came to view England duty as a chore, not a pleasure. It was, it seemed, alarmingly easy to get in trouble with this bloke.

In August 1994, heralding the new season, the *Guardian Weekend* ran a piece about the Belles winning the league the previous spring. Five thousand words across two double-page spreads, with a wonderful lead picture of Kaz bursting through a tackle – the magazine's editor, Deborah Orr, said admiringly, 'She just looks so *strong*' – it had to be the biggest, most positive piece of coverage the woefully underfunded, undersold women's game had ever had in a national paper. Unfortunately, however, I made the mistake in this piece of presenting the Belles as they are – vibrant, earthy, ribald. In one passage, touring the worn back streets where Flo and Joanne lived in Stoke, the sprawl of bottle kilns and pot banks, of terraced houses and council blocks, I'd followed them as they went looking for a new car to get them to their games, after Joanne's old one was stolen and trashed:

On used lots in dingy 'burbs slippery salesmen talked down at them like they were children, like they wouldn't have money, like they wouldn't know cars. On a windy hilltop they found a white Nova with hubcap trim and go-faster stripes ('Right posey,' grinned Broadhurst) and Lowe lifted up the covers to get at the metal round the spare tyre in the boot, and started pressing down hard. She said, 'They go through at the back sometimes, these Novas.'

Broadhurst snorted. 'How d'you know that then? You been shagging in one of these and your arse went through and hit the floor, did it?'

Copeland wasn't amused; he rang Joanne and gave her an earful, said she shouldn't talk to anyone without his permission, talked about them bringing the game into disrepute, and demanded an apology in a tone she described wryly as 'not very friendly'. The next training session, she wasn't called into the England squad.

The Belles thought it was nonsense; Kaz said of Joanne, 'She's one of the best players in the country, she's playing the best football of her life, and she didn't even get in his sixteen. I don't understand that. For me, she should play.'

Joanne was unhappily resigned to it. 'He only picks boring bastards, he doesn't like personality. So what can I do?'

Paul told her not to change, to stay herself – but he was angry because, while she put a brave face on it, she was clearly upset. He said, 'Copeland phones individuals, he never rings me. He's never once called me to ask about the form or fitness of my players, never once, and I don't like it at all. It's out of order, totally out of order – and saying we're bringing the game into disrepute, really, it's farcical. If it wasn't so serious it'd be funny.'

Belles players used to love going away to play for England; now, said Sheila, they came back from Copeland's sessions 'demoralised'. The tone was joyless; from Copeland's assistant Julie Hemsley they endured regular, po-faced reminders about 'remembering who they represented'.

Flo sighed. 'It's not like we're running down the street with our tits hanging out, is it?'

Kaz said, 'They wouldn't treat the men like this. And OK, it needed to get more disciplined – but there are extremes you can go to, all the unnecessary, niggly little things, and it gets people annoyed. 'Cause you can be disciplined, but you can still have fun. And they've got to understand that we're amateurs, that it should be a bit more light-hearted, that you should be able to have a drink after without worrying you'll get your head chewed off. 'Cause if you can't celebrate winning, what's the point? What's the point of winning if you can't enjoy it, and you can't show that you enjoy it?'

Joanne had played for England eighteen times; the words she used to describe Copeland's training sessions were 'disheartening' and 'depressing'. At another club, the manager told me of a young player who went to her first England training weekend – and rang home in tears from the hotel on the Saturday night, saying she wanted to come home.

Kaz said, 'I will play for England, of course I will. It's the greatest honour. But it's not comfortable, and I don't want to be involved with the gentleman himself. I'll be nice, I'll do what he says – but I'm not that interested any more.'

On 8 October in Reykjavik, England beat Iceland 2–1. In London, trying to get a report on the game into *The Times* – England, after all, were now just one game away from the World Cup in Sweden – journalist Alyson Rudd found she couldn't get any information from the FA, and ended up having to wake some poor Icelander from her bed for the details.

At the end of October, Iceland came to Brighton for the return leg; again, England beat them 2–1. Rudd was there for *The Times*, I put a report in the *Independent*, Sky and *Breakfast Time* both gave it an item, and that was it – England's women qualified for the World Cup, and that was all the coverage the FA could muster. Working on the sports desk at the *Daily Star* that evening, Arsenal's Vicky Slee saw nothing come in on the wire; she only heard the result when a team-mate rang her.

As for how England would fare in the World Cup, reality arrived with a rude shock in December; at Watford, in the first leg of the European semi-final against Germany, England were destroyed. The Germans gave a masterclass, they won the game 4–1, and Kaz barely got a touch in the whole second half; she stood on the half-way line, and she watched the Germans play.

In the stand, Vic Akers was seething. Why wasn't Copeland playing a sweeper? Why was he playing a forward at left-back? Why, when Arsenal had beaten every side they'd played and conceded fewer goals than any other club, were only two of his players in the team? Why was Marieanne Spacey on the bench? Who was picking this team?

In 1993, after Arsenal won the treble, Akers had taken his side to Germany, guests with nine other German teams in a summer tournament. Over there, players trained four times a week, the thing was serious and organised; it was, he said, 'The most eye-opening experience I've ever had as a coach.' Arsenal came tenth out of ten – and, he said, 'If anyone had thought to ask me what was coming, I could have told them. But they didn't, did they? And now we're getting a thrashing and I'll tell you, the Germans aren't even the best in Europe. You think these are good, you wait 'til you see Norway.'

In short, the prospects for the World Cup looked grim. As for Copeland, I asked what he was doing playing a forward at left-back and he said, 'We've lost three left-backs.' So I asked him to name them and he named one, then he struggled to name a second, and the name of the third escaped him entirely. I thought, no wonder you've mislaid them, if you don't even know what they're called.

On 3 January Paul Pierrot's film about the Belles went out on BBC1. It was a romp; it showed them playing, training, working, clubbing, going ten-pin bowling, winning the FA Cup, drinking and dancing with the trophy, getting back to business in the league the next Sunday and winning that too. The players liked it, it was fine, that was them on there, that was the way they were – they all liked it, with the exception of Gill Coultard.

A remote person, not too sociable with the others, not one for being out drinking, football was everything to her and it had been for nearly twenty years, since she first went to Belles from the colliery village of Thorne at the age of thirteen. Now, into her thirties, she knew Sweden was her last shot – and she was worried sick what Copeland would think about the film, and whether it would affect her place as captain of England.

So, the evening after the Wembley cup tie, the management committee of the Belles met in a back office at Robert Kantecki's Centurion warehouse. They talked and worried about this book, the film, their image – and all the while Paul sat there thinking, What have we got to be ashamed of here?

After three hours, bored to death, he announced his resignation. He did it because ten years was long enough, it was time he saw more of his daughter – but he also did it because all this fretting what people thought of them, all this bother about the FA and Copeland and how they were supposed to behave now these people were running things, all this nervy, small-'c' conservatism – that wasn't his idea of what the Belles were about for a minute. He did it, in short, because it was getting so it wasn't any fun any more.

9

A Lovely Ninety Minutes

It was one-fifteen on a Saturday afternoon in Hanley, the rain pouring down so heavy and dark it was nearer night than day. Flo's cramped sitting-room caught what dim light was going through the single back window from her bare brick yard. A porcelain figure stood by the team photo on the mantelpiece; she had one armchair and a sofa, a small low table, TV, video, a sound stack, and barely room left to walk in. By the door leading upstairs she stood looking at her mates crashed out horizontal in the gloom, leaving her no place to sit; they were dressed but immobilised, still dead in the head. They'd been down the Wine Vaults in Newcastle-under-Lyme, gone clubbing after, got back late; Flo grinned and thought, Can't handle their ale, these.

But they'd have to stir, it was time to get busy. Donny was two hours away, the Wembley replay was kicking off early tomorrow in case it went to extra time, Joanne's car had been pinched again – they burned it out this time, bastards, barely round the corner from her place – so now Joanne was in Sheffield, and Flo had a transport problem. She kick-started her suffering mates, doled out change to the one that was broke, and hauled them down the five steep red steps from the front door to the narrow street.

She'd had a knock on that door the other day, a little lad, maybe ten years old, cute-looking, one of a gang she knew, the kind like as not that'd lob a brick through your window as soon as spit – for a lark, like. But they'd lost their ball over the wall into her yard so she said she'd go fetch it, and he stopped her. He said, 'Ey. You were on telly. You're a Donny Belle, you.'

She said she was, yeah, smiled, turned to go get his ball, and behind her he asked for her autograph. She laughed, thought he couldn't be serious, but he was, he meant it – and she was used to signing the odd programme at games for kids on the touchline, but this was stupid. Only it was special, too – and it had to be thirty times now, in the fortnight since the programme went out, that strangers had come up to her in pubs, in the kebab shop or the street and they'd grab her, they'd seen her, they knew she was a Belle. One time, she'd been watching Sky's Monday night game in the pub – broke, she'd had to cancel her own subscription – and during the game half a dozen lads must have come up, said they couldn't believe they were talking to her. It made her go red 'cause she knew she was only her, she wasn't famous – but it made her feel good too, getting recognised.

So she knew some people weren't best pleased with the programme, thought it made the club look rowdy – but that didn't bother Flo. It didn't bother her either that she thought sometimes she looked like a knob in it, posing, lying on her bed in her shorts like the director told her to, saying how bad she wanted to beat Arsenal, or taking her track-suit trousers off in her bathroom after the five-a-side with the lads from work, showing the camera that knock on her ankle. She remembered the crew filming that, Dave Sound and Dave Camera, them ragging the director, saying he was only after that shot 'cause he liked her legs, and her saying so he should like them too. Best legs in team, weren't they? Everyone said so.

The knees and ankles were red, inflamed, flakes of dry white skin peeling, like on her elbows and knuckles too; psoriasis on all the joints, since she was twelve years old.

Sometimes when she played it cut up and cracked, and then sometimes it would bleed – but it wasn't bad, it didn't often hurt, and she didn't care people seeing. Nor did she care people seeing her on telly out clubbing on a Friday night getting shitfaced, or dancing in the dressing-room, or sneaking a quick Silk Cut on the disco fire escape after they'd won the FA Cup. That was just her, you got what you got – and they should have a programme about women's football every week, and if it meant she looked a knob every week, fair dos.

Back when they were making the film, when Paul had learned she smoked the odd cigarette, he'd sighed – they were amateurs, he couldn't tell them how to live. Then he'd smiled and said, 'The way she's playing at the minute, she can smoke wacky baccy for all I care.'

Of course Copeland wouldn't like it – but she couldn't be getting bothered what Ted Copeland thought. That England session when he'd called her up before Christmas, she'd ummed and aahed, nervous, then she'd rung him too late, missed the deadline, and she hadn't gone – and he'd been nice enough on the phone about it, encouraging, talking about next time. But if or when a next time came, she didn't think she'd go then either. Sure, she'd love to play for England – but not if it was all long faces, not if it wasn't any laughs. The time she'd been before, she'd felt like she was back at school, them treating you like a kid all day. And maybe they thought they were being dead professional – but it wasn't professional, was it? She wished it could be – but it wasn't, and it wasn't going to be either.

So Sweden, those two weeks of the World Cup – more, with getting together beforehand – the fact was, she couldn't afford it. She'd bought the house a year back for twenty-seven thousand (pence, her mate said) and it was the best part of a week and a half's work every month to pay the

mortgage. And they were good about her football at work,
they'd switch their shifts round to fit in with her; last season
when they'd played all those Wednesday night games at the
end, when the fixture list got more piled up than Stoke in the
rush hour, they'd always let her do an early on match days,
start at six, be gone at two, so she had time to get ready for
the evening. Her boss, Frieda, she was good, said she didn't
see why Flo should be penalised if she wanted to play; the
works Sports & Social even sponsored her kit.

But if she went off for half of June to be an international
they weren't going to pay her wages, were they? And
England, they gave you £15 a day for being away; you
weren't going to pay the mortgage on that, were you? Now
maybe if the atmosphere in the camp had been more
enticing, maybe if you didn't feel you were going to get
nagged all day, maybe if you didn't worry that if you went to
Copeland's England you'd get the confidence dented right
out of you . . . maybe then she might have gone, and let the
mortgage worry about itself. But that was how they were, and
if you looked at what mattered in her life, it wasn't England,
was it? It was Belles.

When she'd first gone to them two years ago, she'd been
nervous as a kid. From the likes of Leek and Crewe, haring
round up front knocking five a game past duffers without
hardly drawing breath – it was a step up, wasn't it? But people
like Kaz, they put you right – Kaz was dead down to earth,
she spoke her mind, you could talk to her, she hadn't got a
big gob like some. And Paul got her sorted, he knew what he
was on about, he made her a defender, made her see what she
could do, so she was confident now; she felt she was a starter
every game, she had something, she mattered. She felt she
could even be useful now, talking to Des at the back there,
trying to help her along. For fifteen Des was class, Des was
going to be seriously good, she wasn't scared or skinny like

some of the other young ones – but still, fifteen was fifteen, and she'd get caught the wrong side of her player sometimes, or stood square, so the player could leave her – and then Flo would have a little word.

It was an amazing position to be in, when she thought about it – but to be a Belle, to be in football, it was amazing all round. She had work, money, relationships, the back wall of her bathroom so raddled with damp it was falling off into the yard, a wagonload of hassle all week – and she had ninety minutes on a Sunday when she didn't have to think about those things, when she was dead good at what she did, when no one got past her, and it was all she really cared for in the world. She said, 'All the problems you have, you don't think about none of them. So whatever else happens, I have a lovely ninety minutes every week.'

When she was a kid, growing up on a bleak, windy rise in Chell Heath, they used to have scheduled battles with the kids from Norton, teenagers turning up to clout each other with sticks over who owned the bridge between the two places. One of her brothers had a hole kicked in his chin once, a steel toecap job; their dog chased his assailant down the road, chewing holes in the seat of his trousers.

She came out of school at sixteen with no exams, no nothing, and went straight into the potteries; she did two years at one place, then six more years since at the Eagle for Wedgwood. It was a great warm warren of old, brown-black brick and cobbled yards, a humming labyrinth of ovens and lacquer, machines pressing and printing, hundreds of thousands of pieces of chinaware moulded and cooked, coloured and glazed, shunting cautiously on belts and trays towards the department stores of the world. The shop she'd been in lately at the front end of the process, it was loud in there, the dust press going thump hiss whine, thump hiss whine, plates and dishes and casserole lids coming out by the trolleyful, and a fine grey-white powder settling down on to everything. You couldn't hear yourself think; it was a good job you didn't need to.

Now they were shutting that shop down, moving her on to piecework by a million quid's worth of new caster machine, a great tangly robot of wires and steel that made teapots; as they came off she'd fettle and tip them with a sharp little knife and a sponge, tidying up the edges, washing off any muck, cleaning out the spout. It'd be better, the machine was further off and a lot quieter – but it'd be worse too 'cause her money would drop, specially at first, before she got up to speed. At the minute she took home £170, £180 a week, and it was tight enough on that.

So if there hadn't been football . . . getting pissed and making teapots, she thought, would have been about the size of it, the start and the finish, with no out but two weeks of Spanish package every summer. Whereas now she was a Belle . . . it had been like seeing the light. She might not score goals any more, not at the back – only own goals, anyway – and scoring goals, that beat sex, it was the best thing in the world, you saw it in the back of the net and it was just, *yaaaaaaahhh* . . . you lost it for a minute then, off to a different world, a dead nice feeling inside. But still, if she didn't have that now, she had something better – she had a new set of mates, she was her own person, she had a place where her heart was and that place was the top team you could be in. And the only trouble was, getting there.

She went to a bar she knew, asked her mates if anyone could drive her, and no one could; at the counter she worked the phone, ringing cousins, friends, Ann Lisseman in Stafford, and no one could. She rang the bus station, and there was a bus at nine thirty in the morning to Sheffield; the ride was two hours, then Joanne or her dad could maybe fetch her – and she could see every carless Sunday being this way now, getting moithered, real hassle. She thought sometimes she'd not bother going any more 'til she'd done that crash course and got her test, found some old car so she could drive herself – but however much hassle it was, not being there would have been worse. What if something went wrong, what if they lost and she'd not been there? She'd hate herself. That time her mate couldn't find the way to Cambridge to play Arsenal, that had been horrible, sat in the passenger seat wanting to strangle the driver for not knowing where she was – and you just had to be there, didn't you? Whatever way you could find, you had to be there – 'cause you knew they'd be there for you.

Well, some would, Kaz gave it everything, Des didn't stop, Channy always tried – on the days she was all there, anyhow, when she hadn't gone wandering in her head someplace. And Joanne never shirked it – she wasn't really fit again yet, but she wasn't happier anywhere than on a football field, and she didn't ever pack in.

But some others at the minute, they seemed to think it'd just come natural. Against Wembley, they didn't bother getting back – or if they did try they didn't bloody catch them, did they? So her and Des, they were on their tod in there, two hours non-stop in a tide of red shirts – and she couldn't walk the next day, she had to go home early from work and have a sleep, she couldn't walk properly again until Thursday.

Still, they'd win the replay. She could see into the future, like she did when she knew Kaz would get the third at Vale Farm and keep them in it, and she knew this second go at it they'd beat them. She was absolutely *convinced* that they'd beat them . . .

Stainforth Miners' Welfare, Sunday, forty-five minutes to kick-off; the horizons of the flat land were strips of icy turquoise beneath a low, featureless roof of grey cloud. Big pools of water lay on the running track round the pitch; a bitter wind whipped across the chill and empty fields. Rob Kantecki and Alan Burton worked their way down the sideline, hammering rusty metal poles into the wet earth with broken half-bricks; when they strung red and white ribbons of plastic tape from them, making a flimsy crowd barrier, the wind caught the tapes, bowed them out taut and set them flapping, a hard rattle slapping on the keening air. Paul paced about the clubhouse, restless, vexed, wondering where Flo was, watching Joanne stride quickly across the field from the road. She'd been to Sheffield bus station to fetch her and she'd not been there, and Joanne was angry. 'Why didn't she come and stay at my house? She knows she can do that.'

Ann said, 'She rings me yesterday. Why yesterday? Why not in the week?'

Paul sighed, gnawed his lower lip. John Jones came to shake hands, and wish him good luck. 'Well,' he said, 'I won't wish you *too* much luck.'

Paul laughed, somewhat grimly. He said, 'I think we rode all ours last week.'

'Cause it was really looking brilliant today. No sign of Flo, and then Channy'd totalled her car on the way here. She said she was all right, it was only the car was done in – but she was complaining of chest pains.

They squeezed into the bare little box of a dressing-room, stepping gingerly over the carpet of kitbags. They were thoughtful, tense, not talking much. Paul told them quietly, 'There's been a lot going through my mind since last Sunday, we were that poor – and only six people came to training Wednesday, which isn't good enough either. But it's important to give people a second chance, to let them show that last week was just a one-off – so after much thought, I'm putting the same thirteen out, in the same positions. Assuming Flo turns up.

And what I want you to do is say to yourself, you're going to prove me wrong. 'Cause I have doubts about you now, and so do some of them supporters out there. So it's down to you, each one of you, to perform a damn sight better than last week. Don't look at anybody else, look at yourself, inside yourself, be honest with yourself – and do better, eh?'

Nicky Davies looked wanly relieved. Last Sunday after the game she'd been close to tears, stood alone while the others had their tea, barely able to speak – taken off after forty-five, run ragged by a sixteen-year-old. All her form seemed gone, she'd been pathetic, she didn't know who she was. Now she had another chance.

Gill said, 'Let's get stuck in a bit more, eh?'

Joanne chanted the mantra: 'Stay on your feet. Enjoy yourselves. And watch the line.' Then she added, 'And if that left foot gets it, *definitely* stay on your feet.'

'Fucking hit her first minute,' said Gill, smiling. 'That'll do it.'

They laughed, went out to warm up – and there were twenty minutes left before kick-off when Flo came running from the road, grinning nervously. The bus had been late; Joanne's dad had brought her. So Paul patted her on the back, ushered her towards the dressing-room, turned back from the clubhouse and looked up helplessly at the sky, half amused, half exasperated. He thought, I wish she'd sort herself out – but by God, he was pleased to see her. And she'd never let them down yet.

He told them, 'We've never lost a home game. Never. Not in the Cup, not in four years in the National Division. So you go out and show people you're still the best team in the land. 'Cause it's not often you get a second chance in this life, is it?'

Skiller headed wide in the first minute, Kaz had a shot in the second minute and didn't miss by much either, in the third minute Nicky Davies had the ball in the net. The ref disallowed it, it came off her arm as she ran in – and up the other end from the free kick Kelly Smith hit the post. The ball bounced out, hit Debbie Biggins on the arm as she dived, and she just managed to squirm over and grab it before it rolled back over the line. You get some action in women's football . . .

Kaz scored after thirteen minutes, 1–0, and after that it was anyone's game, another wonderful game, with no malice on the pitch and no ugly abuse off it; it was taut, tension-racked, fast, foul-free, 200 fans from both clubs all yelling and cheering, and Nicky Davies had Kelly Smith locked up all right this time, but still Wembley weren't rolling over here for anyone. They had Des clearing over the bar from two yards out, they hit the woodwork again, Flo was in the breach every time, Channy was up and down like a train, Gail was grinning, shouting at her to keep breathing, and at half-time they were buzzing, everyone talking, smiling, grabbing tea and Gatorade as fast as Kantecki could pour it, all knowing they were back nearer to themselves again.

In the hubbub Paul said, 'What's the matter, Des?'

'Got a pull.'

'Keep it warm, get some Deep Heat on it.'

'I have.'

'Get some more on it.'

Kaz sat, fists clenched, looking about her, from one face to the next. 'Come on, eh?'

Paul told them, 'Let's start this half like a house on fire.'

'Hey Channy,' said Gill, 'wild thing. Get in there.'

'Good job, Nicky,' Paul said, 'good job on the seven, you've done well. But mind the ref, he'll not give us owt, so don't start chuntering at him, eh? Just yes ref, no ref.'

'Three bags full ref.'

Sheila smiled and said, 'Just score another goal, for God's

sake. Gail's doing my head in on bench, can't you calm her down?'

Joanne grinned. 'The great Gail Boring.'

'She never scores in Cup Final anyway,' Kaz laughed.

Someone farted. Gill gasped, 'Oh fuckin' hell.'

'Ee,' Kaz told her, 'stop swearing, you.'

'A few more like that,' Paul said, 'they'll not come close to mark you then.'

'Come on,' Gill told them, 'let's get out there. 'Cause I can't flippin' breathe in here.'

The time slipped by, the tension racked up. Channy's dog wandered on to the pitch, and Gail grinned. 'She's got the dog going to left-back to cover for her, when she goes down the line.'

Paul wasn't amused. He said, frowning, 'Club's had one warning for not looking after dogs already.'

Sheila came back to the bench, said she thought Micky'd broke a finger. She'd strapped it up, told her to stay out there, but she didn't think she needed telling. Watching, her own fingers were wound tight together, clenched white. 'Worse than last week, this is,' she muttered. There were twenty minutes still to go. The crowd edged forward, Rob and Alan's tape all pushed aside into tatters on the ground.

Kaz did an overhead, one foot wide. Gail smiled. 'Ooh aah Kaz Wack-ah.'

Paul still wasn't amused. He said, 'We look absolutely knackered here' – and he was hoarse, both fists punching down curtly through the air, and Belles were defending now, all defending. 'We don't think, we don't use any brains at all. Hey, *hey* – get the ball up this end, eh?'

Last ten. He sent Kilner on for Nicky Davies; Nicky'd run herself into the ground minding Smith. He told Kilner, 'See that seven, that's yours. Get right up her back. Don't go bombing up field, you stick to her. And when you get it, just kick it up there. Not daft, eh?' He patted her on the shoulder and told her as she went, 'Stick one in top corner while you're at it.'

Last five; Belles were caught offside, and Wembley's keeper came out to take it. The kick was a dud, Skiller pounced on it, freed Kaz; Kaz looked up, all alone thirty-five yards out, the keeper frantically back-pedalling, way off her line, and all the bench were on their feet screaming, screaming, 'Chip her! Chip her!'

Calm as you please Kaz paused a fraction, weighed it, looped it up and over in a long, slow, sweet, spot-on-the-button arc into the far floor of the goal, 2–0. Heaven, relief like a flood tide; people leaping, hands in the air, the crowd a rippling strip of happiness in the wind. But Paul said, 'It's not over yet,' and Wembley got one back in a crashing scrum in Belles' area in injury time, Debbie and Ann all in a tangle, 2–1, and then the whistle came and people were streaming on to the pitch in a dancing throng of embraces. Then, somehow, spontaneously, they were lined up in a little alley by the clubhouse, warmly applauding both teams as they came off – and Nicky got in among them, gave Ann a hug, said of Wembley's late goal, 'You trying to give me a heart attack?'

Among them Flo was singing, arms pumping, *eeh-ay-eeh-ay-eeh-ay-oh* – and no one else was joining in, they were too shagged out. She grinned and shrugged and said, 'I'm singin' with all me mates.'

10

The Wrong Trousers

Channy couldn't work Flo out at all; the girl was off her head, she was like somebody possessed, she was so *extra* all the time. Channy liked her all right, she made you laugh and you needed that, specially with Joanne being a bit quiet lately – but she was crazy too, she was an absolute nutcase.

How could you get called for England and not go? To Channy's way of thinking it was unfathomable. She supposed, if she didn't want it that bad . . . but how could you not want it? She knew Flo liked her nights out, she knew her mates in Stoke were important to her – but did she doubt her ability, or what? Channy couldn't sort it out for a minute.

Still, she wasn't complaining. England had a mid-week friendly against Italy in Florence, and Flo not going training meant Channy'd been called instead – so while Flo scampered off from Stainforth to get the bus back home, Channy headed south with Kaz and Gill to the England base in Maidenhead. And playing for England, wasn't that what anybody would want? To represent your country in anything, tiddlywinks, anything at all, wasn't that the ultimate? The way Channy thought, if Flo didn't fancy it, that was her right and her business – but for herself, it was as big a reason as any for playing. Indeed, if she didn't have England to aim at, sometimes she wondered if she'd bother to play at all.

Twenty years old, she was a strong, stocky figure, standing five foot three, with her weight around nine stone – it varied, she didn't take much notice. She'd taken enough notice of

herself to get highlights put in her hair the week before
England went to Italy, mind; after Belles won the Wembley
replay and Gill told her she'd had a reet game, Kaz said she
should get her hair flashed every week. But beyond the
banter, if Channy couldn't work Flo out, the rest of them
couldn't work Channy out either. Quiet, unflappable, with
brown eyes in a pleasant oval face sometimes watching,
sometimes wandering, they couldn't tell if she was ever
bothered about anything. Was she gormless – or was she just
very, very laid back?

Channy didn't mind what they thought; she knew what
she was doing. She'd turn up and ask who they were playing
today, and they'd look at her like she was thick, like she
wasn't all there; they'd nudge her and grin, tell her to wind
up, Channy, wind yourself up. Joanne'd look at her and say,
'Ball, Channy, ball – round white thing, eh?' And that was
OK, it was a laugh, it was only surface stuff; if they ever did
get to her, she'd let them know all right – but they didn't
because the truth was, she really *wasn't* bothered, not like
some of these were. So she'd go out and do her best, she'd
work hard not to let people down, she wanted to win – but it
was only football, wasn't it, and what was that?

It was nothing, it was a game, it was trivial. There was so
much going off in the world, people dying of cancer, wars,
and you'd see people getting really upset over football and
you'd think, What? How could you get those big emotions
just for a game? She did remember a match once, some FA
Cup tie, she'd got that adrenalin buzz off it, she'd seen
everybody's faces round her and suddenly it hit her, Christ,
I'm up for this, this is *serious* – and something clicked then,
her stomach went; she thought, God, *come on here Chan*. But
she couldn't remember what game it had been and it hadn't
happened again. Nor did she think about football all day,
she didn't dream every night about diving headers and

twenty-five-yard screamers, it didn't enter her head. She'd drive to the ground on a Sunday with the music blasting, singing along – and she'd only remember it was a game she was going to when she got there, she'd only start thinking about it then. Sometimes, Gill'd show her up in training, she'd be going through the motions, run forward, head it, run forward, head it again – then Gill'd take her turn and she'd be at it like a whippet, *whoosh whoosh*, and Channy'd watch her and think, Right, yeah. That's what you're supposed to do. Better tune in here.

And then she would 'cause she looked up to Gill; Italy would be the England captain's eightieth cap, and how could you not look up to that? Besides, coming from the same direction, Gill from Castleford, Channy from the other side of Leeds, they'd often share the ride to training, and she knew Gill a bit now, she could read her face – so if she did something wrong in a game she'd see Gill look at her and she'd know, OK, next time I'll do better.

She was the model, Gill, everyone knew it, even the ones who thought she was a stay-at-home square; you simply had to respect what she'd done. When Copeland said, after England qualified for the World Cup, that his captain, Gill Coultard, was the example every young girl should look to, he could have been describing precisely the way Chantel Woodhead thought.

So, with that model, Channy knew what she was about. They could rib her that she was a space cadet, that she wasn't all there – but she was there all right, she was there 'cause she had a chance to play for England, and anybody sane, if they were good enough, they'd want to have that goal. She was there for that – and then, she supposed, she was there for her dad.

Her dad was a hides and skins broker; somewhat like Channy, he was short and strongly built and a reserved kind of character – but when he watched her play, which was most Sundays, you'd always hear him shout for her. He didn't let her near his work and she didn't want to go near it; it wasn't like an abattoir, but she didn't fancy seeing the ears getting cut off things, the muck and snotters inside the fresh leather before they salted it. She lived with him, instead, through football; a Leeds season-ticket holder, he'd been taking her to Elland Road since she was eight.

She was the youngest of three daughters. The oldest, seven years her senior, was never interested – but Lisa, two years older than Channy, loved to kick a ball from as far back as she remembered. They lived in a bungalow tucked into a wedge-shaped road junction by Farnley, between Leeds and Bradford; you got to it up a dirt track through a field they owned, and they owned the next one along too. They kept animals there – rabbits and guinea-pigs, three goats, two sheep (well overweight, Channy thought, Lisa was spoiling them) and two lambs Lisa'd saved from the slaughterhouse. There was enough room that every summer since they were kids all the lads would come over and they'd have a kickabout across the sloping grass, and Lisa was always first in there.

Channy wasn't bothered, she'd rather watch. Lisa'd nag her little sister that she should play with her; her mum would say she didn't have to if she didn't want to but then her dad would tell her, You go on, you get out there. So she did, and now it turned out she was better than Lisa. They'd both been England Under-21s, back when the WFA still ran such a thing, and Lisa did still play; she was with Huddersfield, two flights down from Belles. She was maybe more skilful too, more fancy on the ball – but she was dainty, she was slighter, she didn't put herself about like Channy could. And then, she was animal-mad, she spent a lot of time looking after theirs in the field now, so she wasn't going to put in the hours and the effort like Channy did. But then, Channy – never mind if it was only a game, if she sometimes thought there were other things she might be doing on a Sunday – the fact was, with England calling, she didn't think her dad would let her stop playing even if she wanted to.

In their early teens, the two sisters spent a few years with a team in Bradford – but when the National Division was formed, Channy moved to Bronte. She thought, if she was going to get kicked every week, if she was going to get her knees scarred to bits, if she was going to write off any chance of ever walking down a catwalk, she might as well get kicked playing with the best. And for someone who people said wasn't all there, the move was pretty calculated – aiming to be a Belle, she picked Bronte for a year's experience to help her get there. Learn what the top's like first, she thought, don't go off the deep end with Belles where she'd not get a place, or not be up to it if she did – and then move on when she'd done that first year's study.

Bronte got relegated and the team there fell to bits. Sammy Britton and Rebecca Lonergan went to Arsenal, Isabel Pollard went to Millwall, Channy went to Belles; those four, they'd been a gang, and there were others at the club who hadn't liked them much anyway. Coming back on the bus after a match they'd lost, the dissension broke into violence, one woman trying to throttle Channy, she had her fists round her throat, Channy couldn't get her off, and all she saw then was Sammy's fist flying past into the woman's face, her glasses flying off, mayhem . . . and you didn't get that going off at Belles, did you?

Channy was a left-back by then, but she wasn't sure about it. Like anyone in women's football who was good, she'd started up front, or at least in the middle – so early on at Belles she said to Paul, I'm not a left-back, I've got more to offer than that. And he said, Let me tell you something, Chantel Woodhead.

She thought, Oh God . . .

First, nobody is guaranteed a place in this team. Second, nobody, *nobody* picks and chooses where they play.

Oh yeah, I didn't mean it like that, I meant . . . and she was thinking, Oh God. Whoops. Oh no.

He told her she was good there, she was good running on to it, and she was good for the team in that role. He hold her if she stuck at it she'd be England left-back yet – so you go for it, Channy. And seeing she was going to Italy now, she supposed maybe he had a point.

For a person who said she wasn't bothered about football, there was precious little in her life that didn't have to do with it – and she'd have gone pro tomorrow if she could have, no question. She was on the treatment table at Leeds once and Carlton Palmer was there too, moaning about how many games they had to play, Wednesday, Saturday, Wednesday, Saturday – and she looked at him and said, 'Where you going now then, when you're done in here?'

'Home,' he said – like, where else would you go?

It was midday; when she was done, she'd be back in the store sorting orders 'til five, or later – and these people, she thought, sometimes they didn't know how lucky they were. A while later, before Crystal Palace played Liverpool in the Coca-Cola semi, someone asked Palace manager Alan Smith about the pressure – and he said his players were highly paid professionals. He said they should go work in the National Health if they wanted to know about pressure – and why weren't there more people in football like that?

She'd been going to Leeds since she was a kid and now she had a job there; she'd done two stints at Elland Road for work experience on a sports and recreation course at college and she'd liked it, she'd asked them to keep her in mind, and they did. She started out in the shop, selling shirts and souvenirs over the counter – but by then Leeds were back in the big time, champions under Howard Wilkinson in '91–'92 – and the big time in football was getting very big indeed.

The new East Stand rose over the M621 like the side of an aircraft carrier, a massive bulk of pale grey; it had a shiny new shop in the concourse among the fast-food bars, past the hanging multi-screen TV beaming glib'n'gibber Sky chat pre-game. It was glossier by far than the tat old shop at the other end of the ground, banked up around the back with a huddle of Portakabin offices – but when the new shop opened, to Channy's relief, they didn't send her over there, marooned away from the other staff. They kept her in the old shop instead, shut it down except for match days and set her running mail order from there instead.

Business was heading off the graph. It wasn't Man U – where over a third of their monumental turnover was now merchandise – but in '93–'94, while Channy was winning the women's equivalent of Man U's Double with the Belles, Leeds United turned over nearly £250,000 in mail order alone. This season, they'd reached that figure already, with nineteen weeks still to go – and it was being run day-to-day by a twenty-year-old shop assistant, on a shop assistant's wage. But that was English football – a ramshackle, post-Victorian operation, scrambling, thrilled and bewildered, through a sudden torrent of new money into the satellite age . . .

A year back they'd given her a computer, and a book on how it worked – no training. So she read the book, she went to the accounts department for help, she set up all the files and the records, she put Leeds United's mail order on computer, and she'd needed to; in the run-up to Christmas they took £40,000, the phone was off the hook with orders and queries and complaints, they'd taken Lisa on to help her, then a YTS lad as well, and by December she'd packed in having a social life, it was work, sleep, work, sleep, work – and sometimes she wondered what she was doing here. They were winning, sure, she was on top of it and she liked that, she wanted to stay and get it running really good, and her boss was decent, he was thankful. Still, all this, and she was taking home £120, £130 a week . . . what a mug. Don't thank me, she thought – put it in my wage packet.

But they don't notice you, do they, if you're nobody? And it wouldn't be just Leeds, it would be the same in every football club there was, everywhere you went – if you had no money, or you had no status, then people didn't see you. It bugged her; she wasn't one for cursing or getting angry, but there were times it really, really bugged her. She remembered some club do, getting introduced to some big noise, some director and his wife, this is Channy from mail order, and them saying Hello, no more, turning away. So whoever it was told them, Channy's in the England squad – and their heads swivelled back all right then, like, Oh, *she's somebody after all* . . . and she thought, Get lost. Just get lost.

Still, some were good. The physio, Geoff Ladley, if she had a knock or a pull he was always attentive, he always had time, he helped her a lot and she appreciated that; if she didn't have him to tend her, where else was there to go? Then the players were all right, they took an interest; Strachan was dead nice, he got her a pair of boots off his sponsor, near a hundred pounds' worth, and that was a big help. Then Gary Kelly or Carlton Palmer, they'd always ask how she was doing, they took it serious, they never took the mick – or Gary Speed, he was dead good-looking, he'd come and ask after Belles, and Lisa's legs'd turn to jelly. That made her smile.

The gaffer, Wilko, she was less sure about him. Last season she'd been thinking who might sponsor her kit so she went to his office, knocked, went in, and he was busy; there were a couple of the coaching staff in there, and he looked up and barked, 'Yes?'

Nervous, she asked if he had a minute, there was this thing she wanted to ask – and he went, 'Why? What d'you want?' And his manner was that abrupt, it was off-putting – so she thought, it don't matter, and she left it. Then one of the coaches came after her and she said what she'd wanted, only she wasn't going to grovel for it, there was no need to be tret like that – and it got sorted out then, they had a whip-round, she got sponsored. But it hadn't left her warming to him.

Then later, he did start acknowledging her; she was left not knowing what to make of him. One time recently, after that film about Belles was on telly, she'd been on the treatment table and he'd come in – he was talking to David O'Leary about his injuries, and whether or when he might stop playing – and she was thinking, Oh no, I shouldn't be here, I shouldn't be hearing this. Then Wilko said, 'Who's this?'

She was dreading it. He said, 'You kept a low profile in that film, didn't you?'

She said something quiet like, 'Yeah. Bit rowdy, aren't they?'

And he told her it was all right, he enjoyed it. What he liked was the way they were all so naive, so honest – like when they lost and the camera was on them, you could see them actually feeling the loss, not for the cameras, not acting, but natural, really feeling the loss like it came from inside. It was a good film, he said, and he liked that manager they had, looked a caring guy – and he was stood there saying this, and Channy couldn't believe it. She thought, maybe he was all right after all.

On the other hand, she knew Copeland and his mob wouldn't be happy about that film a bit.

The Italy game was the first time England got together since the film was screened. Kaz, Gill and Channy headed south, sure that when they were there they'd take flak for it – and if they did, Kaz was ripe and ready this time to stand up to it. What you saw in that programme, she'd say, Belles getting pissed after they'd won the FA Cup, that was team spirit, that was why they won, and they should have a little bit more of that round England – 'cause with England the way it was at the minute, she was just stood about with a reet face on, and that wasn't her at all.

What was her, instead, was playing for Belles and having nights like that after; nights like that were why she played in the first place. She didn't get paid for it and she didn't play for trophies, she gave chuffin' trophies away – and you played that many games down the years that you'd not remember too many – but you'd remember your nights out with your mates, you'd remember your good times, and that was why you did it, to be together like that. And that's what she'd have said to Ted Copeland, if he'd asked.

He didn't. She heard from others that the film wasn't approved of, but no one said anything to her face. Instead, she took a little ankle knock to the physio and they declared her unfit – unfit, her who'd scored five goals against Wembley in the previous ten days. But they dropped her anyway.

It got worse; they took the captaincy off Gill. Here she was, Copeland's model player – and he told her four hours before the game she wasn't captain any more, and he told the team as he sent them out from the dressing-room. Channy couldn't believe it – and he gave her the first half, so she got her first cap – but apart from having a laugh with Kaz and a few others (when no one was looking) it left her with not one thing about the trip that she enjoyed.

Pre-Copeland, she'd got in the squad for training a few times as a teenager, when Barry Williams from Sutton ran it, and it had always been fun. But this . . . in Italy the bus pulled into the hotel, and these dirty great gates swung shut behind them, and they thought, Right. We're in prison now. The doctor was OK but the rest of them, they were so miserable all the time, they spoiled it for everyone. 'Cause you knew what you had to do, you knew you were representing your country, you knew you were there to give your best – and then they niggled and griped, they were on your back, and it really was like being in prison.

Match day, she was hanging about chatting, chilling with people, and they all had their shorts on and Channy was cold, so she went and put a pair of her trousers on. They were striped pants and OK, maybe they were a little loud, but they were hers, they were nice. So then Hemsley called her and she told her, 'Chantel. You are provided with a track suit, it is there for a reason – wear it.' Words to that effect. And Channy thought, You what? What a thing to say, what pettiness – and she had to go and change, when she was preparing in her head for the game, and it was just . . . it was just so *silly*.

As for Copeland – she thought, as a coach, he knew his stuff. She didn't feel she had as many options in front of her as she did at Belles, with the way he played, but she could see what he was getting at. But as a person . . . well, he'd given her the first half, it was a friendly, he'd told her someone else would get a crack in the second and fair enough. Then after the game, Hemsley called her to his room. 'Chantel. Ted would like a word.' So you had to follow her down the corridor to his room like a kid in school thinking, Oh God, what have I done?

He was reasonable; he said it wasn't a grilling, he was just asking how she thought she'd done – so she said she didn't think she'd played too well, and if there was a reason for that it was fitness, she wasn't really fit enough. 'Cause what else could she say? That learning he'd taken the captaincy off Gill as they went out to play had affected her a lot? Channy didn't like seeing anyone upset, and she knew how bad Gill must have felt, she was really, really disappointed for her; she was left walking out thinking, I don't believe this, this is a disgrace, this is *disgusting*. No wonder she played half rubbish. For the record, they drew 1–1 – but in the circumstances, so what?

It wasn't, said Kaz grimly, a good week for Donny Belles – and it got worse. They were scheduled to play Wolves away the next Sunday, but half the north vanished under a blizzard and the game was cancelled.

With Arsenal coming to Belle Vue next Sunday, it was a great way to get prepared – only then Arsenal cancelled too. And what was going on here? Paul said, 'We're going into mid-February, and since September we've played seven league games. *Seven*. It's a nonsense, isn't it? Weren't they supposed to be running this thing better now?

Three weeks after they got past Wembley, Belles' next game was the FA Cup quarter-final. They were playing St Helen's Garswood from the Northern Division, one flight below the Belles – and forty-five minutes before kick-off Flo, yet again, hadn't made it.

It was one late arrival too many. In the dressing-room, Paul told Channy to stop playing with her dog and tune in; he read out the line-up, started Kilner in the middle and said Flo could wear twelve – if she got there. Because he couldn't have it any more, it was upsetting him, it was upsetting the other players. They couldn't get ready not knowing if she was coming, or whether she'd be playing if she did come, or who else might be playing if she didn't – and if it was a long way to come to sit on a bench, whose fault was that?

Meanwhile, Joanne was ribbing Channy. 'Hope you're dressed properly.'

'I can't believe', Kaz sighed, 'she's got bollocked for wearing striped trousers.'

'Focused,' Paul told them, 'you've got to be focused. That's the in word, isn't it? You, Debbie, you get focused on coming for everything. Got to be daft to be a keeper, that's what they say – so you've got everything going for you, haven't you?'

The ref was knocking on the door to call them out when Flo ran through it; a cousin had brought her. Breathless, she started scrambling into her strip as the team filed out; Paul watched them go then said to her, heavy with angry irony in the empty, kit-littered room, 'When you're ready, Flo.'

Behind his back as he left she mouthed at him, *Fuck off*. Gail Borman, near walking back to normal now, loyally present at every game, went to sit with her as she changed. Hurt, frustrated, flapping about with boots and pads, Flo said, 'Bollocks to it. Fuckin' attitude, when I'm struggling to get here. That's it. After today, that's it.'

At half-time, Belles were 3–0 up – Micky got a header and a penalty, Gill put one in from fifteen – and as they went out for the second half, Paul caught Flo in the corridor and gave her a hard, fierce embrace. He muttered close in her ear, 'Don't you worry. We'll get you on in ten minutes.'

Flo grinned, shook her head. 'Nightmare,' she told him.

'Yeah,' he smiled, 'you are, aren't you?'

Ten minutes into the half he sent her up front with Kaz, let her have a runabout up there; the last thing he needed was Flo unhappy. And she didn't score – but she got a sniff of the other end for a change and she came off smiling. But then, they all did – Belles won 4–0, Joanne got the fourth – and before they changed, Paul made a point of singling out Coultard. 'Gill, outstanding in there, got in there like a good skipper does, wins us a penalty, scores the second – and we're away then, aren't we? Outstanding.'

Not good enough to be captain of England, mind – and not good enough to be player of the match, either. Someone nominated Channy's dad for that instead; the game was a dud, played in a gale, and he spent more time chasing after balls blown miles out of touch than anyone did playing football. Still, when you've made the semi-final of the FA Cup, who cares how?

Of the eight teams in the quarter-finals, three others beside St Helen's were from the lower divisions. With standards rising everywhere in the women's game, Leyton Orient, Bristol City and Huddersfield Town all made it this far, regional league sides who'd all beaten National Division clubs along the way.

In the other quarter-finals, Arsenal thrashed Orient 8–1, Huddersfield lost 4–3 in Bristol, and Liverpool–Croydon was cancelled; the pitch in Kirkby was a swamp. They'd have to play it next Sunday – when Belles were supposed to be playing Croydon in the league, which they now couldn't do. They'd be idle yet again – but Channy, meanwhile, had more immediate problems. She was sad, really sad that Huddersfield had lost; she'd badly wanted to play them in the last four 'cause if they'd met, she said, smiling, she could have broken Lisa's leg.

But worse than that, with the away game against the Germans coming up, she'd been dropped from the England squad. Hemsley had rung her – not Copeland – and said she wasn't fit enough, which was maybe fair enough. But then, Hemsley said, that was only part of it, and she brought up the dress code.

Channy asked her, 'What are you telling me? That I've been dropped because of what I wear?'

The dress code, Hemsley told her, reflected her attitude.

'So it looks', said Channy, 'like I've been dropped for wearing the wrong trousers. And what can you say to that? But it doesn't make you feel like going again, does it?'

★

At Liverpool, Tracy Davidson and Jan 'Psycho' Murray decided they weren't going to play for England any more. 'The management leave a lot to be desired,' said Davidson, 'and if you don't enjoy it, what's the point?'

Paul said, 'It doesn't surprise me. It disappoints me, but it doesn't surprise me. But these people, they should be looking after reception children, not grown women – because they don't treat them like adults, they don't give them any respect at all. And we have to pick up the pieces when they come back disappointed and slapped down. Mind, in some ways it's a motivation for them, they come back thinking, Thank God that's over, let's have a decent game of football – but in most ways, it's detrimental to what we're trying to do here.

'And I think they better sit down and ask themselves why people don't want to play for their country any more. It should be the biggest thing that's ever going to happen to you, to play for England should be the pinnacle – and at the moment, it's not. So either they change their own ways, or they bring someone else in, someone who knows about women's football – someone who knows about managing amateurs, too. Because I don't think they realise what these people put in, all the things they give up, and how much they want to enjoy their football. And if you say to them, you can't have a drink after the game, you can't wear that pair of trousers, you can't eat that sausage for breakfast – well, they'll say they don't need that, won't they? And that's what they're saying.'

He said, 'This is our national sport, among women it's the fastest growing sport in the country, and something's going wrong at the top. And it needs sorting out sooner rather than later, or we can forget about winning the World Cup. It'll just be an embarrassment.'

11

Play with a Smile on Your Face

After the Croydon cancellation, Belles were scheduled for a second attempt at playing Wolves away, and that was cancelled too – so when they played Southampton at Stainforth on 5 March, it was their first league game for eleven weeks, and it showed. They didn't have Flo, she was waiting on X-rays for a back injury – but against this lot, they should have been walking it in the net all game whoever was fit.

Paul told them to play with a smile on their faces, then spent the whole game with a grim glower on his. In the first half they were absolute rubbish, in the second half they were worse; he was disgusted. It was a standards thing – they won 4–1 – but where was the use in that if they couldn't make a pass from one yellow to another? They weren't sharp; they'd get the ball and before they did owt with it they wanted to look at it, wash it, peel it – and play like that against Liverpool next week, they'd get murdered.

When he left the dressing-room, Gill Coultard exploded. What was wrong with them? Their attitude stank. She took it out on Debbie Biggins, she'd let in a soft goal against a garbage team like that and she'd had a smile on her face? What was that? Debbie tried to defend herself, said she were smiling 'cause she were embarrassed . . .

Coultard said she didn't go a hundred miles back and forth to play with people had an attitude like that. And where was everybody at training?

Debbie pointed out that Coultard herself – unlike Debbie, who came a considerably greater distance – hadn't been training for some weeks, to which there wasn't really an answer, and Coultard stamped from the room. She was in wobbly mode, it had been coming ever since Copeland took the England armband off her – but it came sooner or later just about every season. Sheila, who'd known this distant, gritty, brittle soul for near on twenty years, since she first turned up aged thirteen out of Thorne, a rough-house scamp, always fighting, took her aside to say she was out of order, going after an eighteen-year-old girl like that – but she didn't think it likely she'd got through to her, she went home expecting tailspin, and sure enough they got it.

As the Liverpool game approached, on the Thursday Coultard huffed at Micky Jackson that she'd be turning up at quarter to two, keep everyone waiting on her for a change. She talked about retiring; then on the Friday night, in the pub on the North Bridge where the young ones liked to go out, get their spirits up for the weekend, she announced that she was signing for Liverpool. There weren't too many had a smile on their faces then.

In Stoke at twelve thirty that day, the staff of the Royal Doulton warehouse knocked off for their half-hour lunch break. There was no smoking in the building, so lunch for most was clocking your card in the machine by the door, stepping out past the little brick and glass security box, and lighting up. The patch of pavement by the barrier where the wagons came in towards the loading bays was carpeted with butts.

Joanne stepped through the smoky pack in her England shirt, and walked away under what felt like the first blue sky of the year towards the parking lot behind the big brick barn, past the looming forty-foot containers docked in the bays.

She'd finished filling one of them that morning, pallette-load upon pallette-load of trays and dishes for America, and it was a good job it was hard and heavy work, 'cause she wasn't getting much training in. The way her life was going, she wasn't getting much of anything in.

First the car got burned out. Then her place got burgled while she was playing Wembley at Stainforth, they got her telly, video, CD and cassette player, her tapes and CDs, her cheque-book, bank card, driving licence, passport, the whole onion. She was alone in the place by then, her lover gone, and it scared her, she didn't fancy being there when they came back for another bite – so she moved back to her mum's and dad's place in Sheffield, she had nowhere else to go, the 'To Let' sign went up outside, and it was like her life was just emptied right out. She borrowed a mate's car, got up at six every morning, crossed the Peak District for work at quarter to eight; she knocked off at quarter past four and with the traffic it took her longer getting back, two hours or more. It was mega-depressing.

And then there was England. She knew she was good enough, she knew she was way better than some of these he was picking – but she'd not been called for nearly a year. And she'd have given blood and soul to play in the World Cup, there was nothing she could want or dream of more in her life than that, and never mind what Copeland was like, she'd have gone to Sweden if Vlad the Impaler was running the team – but he didn't call her, and he didn't tell her why. She thought, with a wry smile, Well, they say he's approachable – so I'll call him. Just give me a reason, that's all, *just give me a reason* . . .

She got in her mate's car, used her half-hour break to whip round to her old place. There were still a few last things to collect. And she was getting better, she told herself, she was bearing up – but a smile on your face? Wasn't it all bad enough, without your captain going barking as well? Wasn't football the only thing that kept you going, and didn't they need Gill to keep going with them, not to lose her head and go blathering about retirement? 'Cause Liverpool this Sunday, hey – didn't they have to show those three who'd left them to wear Scouse shirts instead, Lou, Davo, Psycho, didn't they have to show those three defectors a thing or two now? Only when she thought about them, she didn't half miss them.

Half eleven that night in the sitting-room of a tidy little semi in South Sefton, just north of Liverpool, and no smiles on any faces here either. A tall, lanky, blonde-haired fifteen-year-old boy sat on a sofa, his left eye ballooning pale violet, so swollen it was nearly closed, his right ear red and puffed up, the bridge of his nose a great rounded grey bruise, maybe broken. He fidgeted, talked uncertainly, tried to be exact; he looked pale, still shocked.

Lou Ryde sat opposite him, taking him gently through it, slowly getting a page and a half of bare, unemotional statement out of his halting account; across every little falter she helped him, while the boy's father stood tense by the door and his mother knelt on the floor upset, helpless, wanting something done. Lou's colleague Ronnie sat on the sofa by the boy with another form, chipping in requests for names, numbers, addresses. The boy's mother said plaintively, 'It's only the second time we've let him out. And this happens.'

He'd been with a group of his mates, walking across a bridge, about nine fifteen, nine thirty, and another group of lads were coming the other way. They'd gone past them, someone had looked at someone else – just looked, that was all – then these others had turned around behind them, they were coming back from behind them asking what they thought they were looking at, one of them was calling him a lanky twat, giving it all that, and next thing a fist was coming over his shoulder and he was down. He got up, they followed him, hit him again, two of his mates got fat lips – and they hadn't done nothing, they were just walking. And these others, they'd be sixteen, seventeen – but no, he'd not recognise them, he'd not know them again, it was dark, they'd come from behind.

Softly Lou pushed him a little, was he sure? He wasn't protecting anyone here?

His father said one of his lad's mates maybe knew one of these others, said he went to the same school as his boy did – but it was a big school, the boy said, he didn't know them. Maybe his mate might. His mother knelt fretting; the room was stiflingly hot, the air thick with silent pauses.

Ronnie and Lou went through the formalities; would he be prepared to go to court on it, did he agree with the statement when she read it back, did they accept that the police could access medical records to back up any case that might arise? Ronnie told them not to bother going to hospital tonight though, they'd still be waiting there with tomorrow's birdsong, best leave it 'til morning. Both officers were courteous, quietly efficient, professionally concerned.

When they got back in the car Lou said wearily, 'He knows.'

'He bloody knows,' said Ronnie. 'One of those others is from the same school as him, and he's telling us he doesn't know who he is? Get on.'

'He definitely knows,' said Lou. And as far as catching anyone went, it was a waste of time – but if it made the boy's mother feel any better that they'd been round, then there was point enough.

It was gone midnight; they'd be in the car 'til seven. The next night, Saturday through to Sunday dawn, she'd do the same shift – then go home, shower, change, get in the car, let Barry do the driving and head for Donny to play her old team.

A stocky, attractive blonde with bright, impish eyes, Lou Ryde was Donny born and bred, from Edenthorpe; her mum worked for the Coal Board 'til redundancy came, and her dad was with ICI. She'd left for Merseyside four years back, partly because the South Yorkshire force had a height restriction then – five foot six, when Lou was five four – but in Liverpool five four was good enough and she'd always wanted to be a policewoman. But she'd also left because of a man.

It had come to a head when Belles were playing an FA Cup Final at Nottingham Forest. She'd thought he was all right, they'd gone about together with Kaz and Dean – but he didn't come to the game. So on the way back she called, said they'd won, they were going to a pub in Armthorpe, free drinks, they'd be filling the Cup all night, and was he coming? He wasn't.

The lift she had, it was easier to drop her at her mum's place before they went out, than to go round the far side of Donny to Conisbrough to her house. She called him again from there and he said, 'What you doing going there instead of coming home? Shows how much you think of me, that does. You think about football more than me.'

She told him, 'Don't be silly. I can't get home, this was my lift, that's all. So are you coming or not?'

'No. And if you aren't outside the door of that pub by ten o'clock when I come to fetch you, I'm going. You can find your own way home then.'

She thought, Stuff you – but it put a damper on the evening, didn't it? And Dean, he was lovely, he put an arm round her shoulders and asked her, 'What's up?' So she blubbed and she told him, and he said, 'We'll soon sort that out.' Tia Marias, brandies, you name it – sozzled, she got absolutely sozzled.

But at ten, early yet, she was still clear enough in her head to remember to go out the door and see him. And she wasn't going home, no way, they'd just won the FA Cup, so she told him, 'Come in and enjoy yourself.'

He wouldn't. She was stood there with the car door open and him at the wheel saying, 'I'm fed up with you always going off to football. You can't think much of me, if you're always buggering off here, there and everywhere else all the time.'

'So what d'you want me to do about it?'

'If you don't get in this car right now, that's it. You can choose. Football, or me.'

'That's easy then.' She shut the door and went back in the pub.

They put the house on the market, and she went back with Skiller one day to get her stuff. Skiller was big, she'd look after her if he was there – but he wasn't and nothing else was either. All he'd left was the curtains and a dining set he'd missed in the kitchen. Her mum said she'd never liked him anyway, and she asked her, 'Why the bloody hell didn't you tell me in the first place?' She moved to Liverpool soon after.

Summers, when she was a kid, she played with lads in her road while ten o'clock every night. At junior school, she played on mixed teams as long as it was allowed – then at secondary school, no chance. They had you in a skirt and a frilly leotard, they had you prancing round the gym to some stupid music, and why? Because you were a girl, they thought you wanted to do that? So she lost the horrid kit, deliberately, got an E for games – and went on, never mind football, to be British Tae Kwon-do champion for seven-odd years. E for games indeed. When Belles won the double last season she'd

Opening day, 4 September 1994.
Back row, left to right: Sheila, Rob, Des, Skiller, Debbie,
Micky, Kaz, Paul. *Middle row, left to right*: Gail, Nicky, Tina, Ann, Flo.
Front row, left to right: Kilner, Jonesy, Gill, Joanne, Channy.

Scoring against Wolves:
Joanne and Tina do the Klinsmann dive.

Kaz Walker: 'A video-fit of the perfect centre-forward.
Quick, strong, brave, scores goals.'

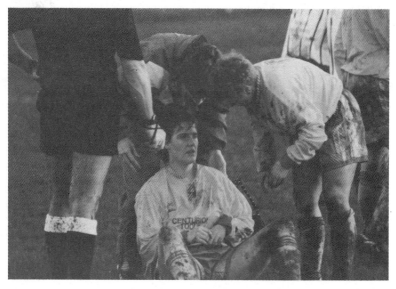

'I've never been this injured in me life, me.'

Gail at Wembley, before and after the knee went.

The Edmunds family.
Paul says he'll mow the back garden soon.

Channy bangs the drum on her twenty-first.
'Maybe I'll mature as a player now.'

Jonesy getting fit in pre-season.

Nicky Davies.
'We're all knees, us. Haven't got a decent knee in club.'

Des Shepherd on the
turnstile at Armthorpe,
and helping to bring
Skiller off after the
knee went at Croydon.

New Belles Jonesy
and Des after Croydon
kicked Des's ankle.

Joanne Broadhurst. 'She's a beautiful footballer.
The more she gets the ball, the better we play.'

Sheila to Flo: 'I'm not a miracle worker.
If you haven't trained on 'em, I can't make you run.'

Debbie Biggins:
Joining the Belles was like 'falling into a whole new family'.

Gill Coultard with England manager Ted Copeland.

been Player's Player of the Year, a rock at centre-half in the country's best team.

Now, she missed them badly; she knew Tracy and Psycho both did too. They'd seen that film on telly and by the time it was ending Psycho was crying – all those years of your life there, all those years a Belle – and they wanted to get in their cars and head straight off back down the M62. But it wasn't practical, was it? And there it was. Liverpool were a good team, good people – but it wasn't the same.

She missed Paul too. At Liverpool she had a woman manager now, Angie Gallimore, and of course in some ways she was more approachable; if you had gutache 'cause you'd just come on, you could tell Angie why you weren't your best in training, and she'd not have brought that up with Paul. She thought he was probably a shy man anyway, not really a fierce one – but he could put some fear in you when he wanted to, and it wasn't a bad thing. 'Cause then, when he told you'd had a good game, you knew he really meant it and you were so made up then, you got so much confidence off it.

So she knew how he'd be talking in the dressing-room before they played on Sunday, and she knew how the Belles were Liverpool's jinx team and she was dreading it. That killer instinct you needed at the back – how was she ever going to put that into marking Kaz?

Early in the game they were stood together, waiting on a Belles goal kick. Kaz put a hand on Lou's shoulder, smiled, and told her, 'We miss you, you know?'

And Lou thought, Oh Christ, shut up, you. I could be meant to tackle you any minute here.

But then, the first five minutes, she'd keep catching herself going to mark red shirts instead of yellow ones anyway.

The Friday night, there was her and Ronnie in one car, another copper on his own in another, and the three of them

covering twenty-six square miles of the Copy Lane sub –
52,000 people. They had a support team in a van, and Bootle
could always throw in bodies if something heavy went off –
but otherwise, it was down to the three of them. They were in
Cavalier 1600s, Instant Response Vehicles – just how instant,
said Ronnie, 'Depending on how far away you are.'

At eleven they had a video briefing in the Constables'
Writing Room, a square grey box with maps on the wall of
Litherland, Netherton and Sefton, Maghull and Lydiate,
Aintree and Weddicar. The maps were dotted with colour-
coded markers for Burglary Dwelling, Burglary Other, Auto
Crime by day and by night through February and March;
there were plenty of dots. There were mugshots, faxed or
photocopied: 'Identity Sought'.

Ronnie said, 'Who you playing Sunday then?'

'Donny,' Lou told him. 'Over there.'

'You'll get battered then.'

The sergeant ran the video; it was a relaxed update on
local bad guys, delivered to camera by an officer in shirt-
sleeves at his desk, with rough cutaways to shots of each
named suspect in turn. One was 'our favourite' for a spate of
night breaks on the Ford estate, another was marked down
for recent offences in Lunar Drive. 'He's out, and he's active.'

The third had stabbed someone, allegedly over the poor
quality of the drugs he'd been sold; he had a bad coke habit,
he did service stations and he was now thought to have a
handgun. 'He can be a very, very violent person – and our
fourth subject, he favours robbing with knives and he could
be working with this character, so take care. These are not the
world's most stable people. Now, while on the subject of bad
people, this next one's assaulted the ageing mother of a
colleague during an aggravated burglary. He's escaped twice
already, he's missing and he's wanted and he won't come
quietly.'

The three constables watched the video, stony-faced, as the roll-call continued. There was another burglary suspect, and evidently someone else thought the same 'cause he'd had his windows put in last week – then there was the news that it was club-breaking season again, with two lads arrested on the roof of the Holy Rosary in Aintree, going in for the fruit machines. And there was news on the next generation: 'A right little team forming up in Litherland, these two lads and another nicknamed Cret doing burglaries, motors, with three more running mates getting together with them.'

The video ended on news that next Friday was Marty's last day. 'Anyone that liked him, or just wants to see the back of him, come along for a drink. Thanks for listening, and good luck.'

Before she'd gone on shift, Lou'd been training on the astroturf at Prescot Sports Centre, the Liverpool squad kicking lumps out of each other in a practice game. Before that, she'd been ironing her uniform shirt and she'd said, 'If I had a husband in the police, I'd be worried sick. If he was on nights, I doubt I'd sleep. But when it's yourself – you don't think it can happen to you, do you? And there's been a few times . . . we had a call, a lad threatened at gunpoint. So you screech up, bail out, run after them, and you don't think. You just do it.'

After the briefing, Ronnie opened the boot of the Cavalier to check their kit. 'Ah, key,' he said, satisfied, 'one of the best keys in the world, this.' It was a sledgehammer. They had body armour in there too.

A normal Friday night, they'd be busy through midnight with the pubs chucking out – drunks fighting, domestics – then you'd be quiet for an hour or so, until the clubs started emptying. Then they'd get drugged kids falling about the place, and more people punching each other. On their turf they had a tall, glossy, neon-splattered tower called the Paradox, and a shabby barn called the Kiss on a pot-holed road in an industrial estate.

Ronnie threw the car into the street, putting in a test call, giving their call sign, Romeo One-Five, letting them know they were Status One, available for calls. Straight off they were sent to a closed-up house, the owner in a geriatric ward since Christmas, the door and a few windows boarded; the neighbour'd called after someone passing lobbed stones through a couple more of the windows. Somewhere else – Bootle, Crosby, Kirkby – the radio crackled talk of an assault, two males.

Ronnie sat in the car in the dark, narrow street while Lou spoke with the neighbour. He said, 'Days, you get youths mucking about – just crap, really. But nights, you might get a decent job. Car thefts, large-scale disturbances. Bit of adrenalin then. What I don't like, you get an awful lot of domestic violence. Some of that, you go in, they're trying to kill each other, you separate them, then they both try and kill you. So you take them down the station and they've joined the police river then.'

I said, 'Must make you shake your head.'

'Bang it against the bloody wall sometimes. Still, it's brilliant when you get a result. The other day we got two, in a stolen car, with a bunch of stolen goods and a load of coke. One of them, he's twenty-three – looks forty – and he's been inside, he's out again, he's straight back to work. But it's like a job to him, selling drugs to kids – scum. Whenever you arrest him he's got money on him, £500, whatever – and he's on the dole. And dickheads like us are paying taxes to give it to him.'

They drove around the empty night, through Aintree, round tattered estates, past Ashworth where they keep Ian Brady, swinging regularly by the Kiss and the Paradox. Kids came and went in little groups at the Kiss, dead young, girls in minis barely reaching their thighs, lads in shirt-sleeves; never mind that it was freezing. 'Dope and E and acid,' muttered Ronnie. One time there, we passed a boy stumbling down the broken pavement, clinging to the bars of the fencing round the factories. Ronnie said idly, 'Going home by rail, is he?'

He was forty-four; when he was fifteen he'd been on the books at Liverpool, but his knee got torn up. 'The physio was Hitler's daughter. I'd hear her clanking down the corridor, I used to be in tears before I'd even seen her.' He still played now, just kickabouts; when he'd come to Copy Lane he'd organised a five-a-side team to play other stations, or anyone else who was game. He played cricket too, for Halsall in the Southport & District League. 'We're that good,' he said contentedly, 'we've got an Australian coming over to play for us.'

But football was the business, wasn't it? When Lou had the temerity to suggest you didn't have to support Man U to acknowledge that they did play great football, that brought on a comically overplayed spasm of Scouse hacking and retching – the very idea . . . and, they both said, policing the Grand National might be a 'mare and a half. But every copper they knew was putting in for shifts at Anfield come Euro '96.

We went around and around, but no one was thumping anyone tonight. On an unlit lane between big, flat fields they stopped to throw their blinding sidelights over a car parked ten yards off on the grass – me, I hadn't even seen it – and a man's head blinked up through a flailing of limbs on the back seat, so they left them to it. 'What I want to know is', said Ronnie, 'where's her head then?'

Later, PC 1058 Louise Ryde was out of the car in the Paradox parking lot watching cabs come and go and we were talking football again, and out of the blue Ronnie said of her, 'Bloody good player, you know. Bloody good player. Our five-a-side, we've got two women on it – and we're beating other people, no problem.'

Eight hours later, ten o'clock Saturday morning under a dismal, grizzling grey sky, Nicky Davies stepped on to a high-fenced five-a-side court outside a sports centre in Burnley, a squat complex of stained square boxes in red and grey brick. Stubby terraces rolled over the rims of the rises all about; veins of snow lay over the tops beyond. On the court, boys, six to ten years old, the Junior Clarets, watched this small woman with her short black hair coming on; they mostly wore Burnley strips, home and away, but one was Blackburn, one was Leeds (like as not Channy sent it) and one was Jean-Pierre Papin in the Bayern Munich kit.

When the kid in the Blackburn strip took a throw-in a yard inside the line, the coach already on the court ticked him off. A ginger-haired girl watching on crutches called out, 'What d'you expect, him wearing those colours?'

The coach was Roy, a policeman. As Nicky came on he said, 'This is Nicky. Nicky is an international footballer. So if she tells you today is Sunday, it's Sunday – and you listen to what she tells you, OK?'

She said later it did help, that, men setting her up in front of the kids, getting their attention. But of course, after they'd done it, she couldn't make any mistakes then, could she?

She ran defence, jogging along the back line of one of the teams, getting boys marked up on attackers, encouraging, cajoling. 'Don't dive in, don't dive in . . . hey, good lad. Good tackle.'

The kids came off bright-eyed, told their mothers and fathers waiting to collect them that they'd scored, or they'd nutmegged a grown-up. Nicky said of Roy to one of the kids, 'Widest legs in football, him. Put the ball through his legs, you could run through after it.'

Roy said to the girl on her crutches, 'Hey Angie. What happened to you then? Fall off your bar stool?'

'Look who's talking, state of you last night.'

'Yeah. Which dumb bugger's idea was it to organise training this morning anyway?'

Nicky'd moved to Burnley from Nottingham in November, to do a year on the Training For Work scheme with Turf Moor's Football in the Community programme. You got your dole money topped up by £10 a week for doing it, but that didn't matter; just being in a professional club was what mattered, being around football all day. Saturdays with home matches, they were the best; coach Junior Clarets at ten, be back to Turf Moor for the Saturday Club by twelve. Her and the other trainees, they'd have up to forty kids come in, paying £9 a head, they'd run coaching and games for them in a huge old brick barn of a gym behind one side of the ground, give them packed lunches, sit them in a block in the stand and mind them while you all watched the game together, then their parents came to get them off you after. And, true, it did look like Burnley were getting relegated – but every other way it had turned out they were dead nice people, and a good thing too. The stuff that had gone on in her life just lately, if she hadn't had these around her to turn to, she wouldn't want to think how she might have ended up.

She was twenty-seven, five foot two, just over eight stone; she had gorgeous eyes of the deepest brown, pools of melted chocolate in a round, neutrally pretty face. It was a don't-notice-me face, not readily forthcoming – there were things that had happened when she was younger that had left her uncomfortable even sitting beside a man on a sofa; there'd been a time when even hugging her mum had been hard. Even now, if she went out, others might wear skirts, but not her. She always wore trousers, she was always ready to run – and if she couldn't run, she'd hit.

Then she came to Burnley and she fell in love. It was like lightning, something she'd never in her life have expected to happen to her, falling electric from the blue. He'd started at Burnley as a volunteer the same day she did, they got on fine for two weeks, then she gave a party for the kids at the club, he came back to her place for a cup of tea after, they got talking, he took her out for a meal – and she found herself so comfortable, so warming to him, that before she knew it she was spilling all her life story.

He got arrested that weekend. He told her his ex-wife and her new boyfriend had started it, they'd set on him, and she believed it, stood there listening in shock as she found herself tumbling head over heels – and whoop, before she knew it he'd moved in, they were living together, and him promising the earth every day. He talked about holidays; she'd say, yeah, she'd love to – what about Cornwall? And he'd say, don't be stupid, we're going to Barbados, or America – then he was on about a car, said he could spend twenty-five grand on a new one for tax purposes. He had her trying new cars, test-driving them – and she was falling, falling all the while. They were engaged in three weeks.

About that time he said he'd lost his filofax on the train, all his credit cards, and he started borrowing off her. She didn't notice, she was too busy taking him down to her mum's in Nottingham for Christmas, the two of them spoiling him rotten, buying him presents, taking him out – but when they were home again in the new year and she started asking when the money was coming back, it never did, and one thing after another started falling in place.

He'd talked about playing rugby, and he didn't; he'd talked about doing football coaching, and the club found out he hadn't. He'd been borrowing her car, and another trainee's car too – and he didn't have a licence. Then the invitations for the engagement party, he was supposed to have ordered them and he hadn't. So she rang his dad and the walls began caving in for good.

His dad said he didn't want nothing to do with him. Up until ten days before the party, the way he'd been playing it, his mum and dad were paying for it; his mum was out buying them that holiday in Barbados for their engagement present and she'd love Nicky to bits, his mum would – Nicky'd seen him talking to her on the phone, and she always sent her love.

His dad told her his mum had been dead for two years and at the funeral he'd ripped off the caterers. Nicky went to see the ex-wife – and it got worse, and worse, and worse. The guy'd stolen his own chidren's video games, he'd been in and out of jail – so she called it off, a week before the engagement party. And in January she'd bit back the tears after the game at Vale Farm, stood apart from the others after she'd been substituted, not because she hadn't been able to mark that Kelly Smith, but because the way she'd been sucked in by this compulsive liar, the way he'd mugged her soul, she couldn't have marked a bowl of porridge.

He came round to try and talk her out of calling it off; he must have had the cab driver in his spell too, he had the guy chase her in his car, nearly run her off the road. She made it to the police station – and they gave her the full nine yards in there. Prison sentences going back ten years, fraud, deception, robbery, beating up a sixty-two-year-old man in front of his family, participation in a prison riot . . . you name it, he'd done it. And she stood there thinking, he's broke my heart and I've give him fifteen hundred quid for doing it.

In the weeks since then, it didn't go away. Presents he'd bought her, she'd learn they'd been bought on stolen cheques; the engagement ring came from money he'd got fencing a hot car. And she got calls and letters, three or four a week, saying he never loved anyone the way he loved her. She had to open the letters too, in the vain hope there might be some of her money coming back. Then, two weeks ago, he came round in person.

She'd got a council flat in a cul-de-sac high on a hill above Turf Moor, a one-bed place on the first floor of a modern terrace. You went in a little hallway, there were two flats off the hall downstairs and open concrete steps with a mosaic finish going up to the landing and her door. He came up the steps, knocked on the door and she wouldn't let him in; he got heavy then, mouthing off, kicking the door, saying she didn't know what she was doing and she must still love him. Biff was there with her, one of the lads from the club, telling her to leave it, forget it – but she said, No way. I'm going to punch his lights out. So she went out and she hit him and she hit him again, and he said, I'm glad you did that, I feel better now. And Biff was saying, Ignore it, leave it, if he carries on we'll just call the police.

But he was still stood out there on the landing saying he'd done nothing wrong, he couldn't understand it, she didn't know her own feelings – and she was stood inside in amazement, thinking, he doesn't see what he's done. Was that possible, that he simply didn't see what he'd done? And the rage was building inside her and he was kicking the door again, shouting that he wasn't going.

She told him he was going all right; she told him if he didn't, she had a weight-lifting bar and she'd use it. But he carried on and on, so she opened the door and she whacked him round the head with the iron bar; he went down like a sack of potatoes, blood splaying on the mat and on the mosaic. He was moaning for her to call him an ambulance, call him an ambulance – and she didn't think 'til the next day what she should have done then. She thought, she should have stood over him and told him, 'You're an ambulance.'

Later it looked like the police thought the only offence

she'd committed was not hitting him hard enough. When they got him in court, it took forty-five minutes to read out the charges; they gave him two years' probation and compensation orders to repay the bank, the club, the hotels and the shops he'd conned. Her own money, they couldn't make him pay that back – that was domestic. And when it was done he said he'd be back for her yet, he'd see about her smashing him round the head like that. She told him, You try – and she knew it wasn't over yet.

So now, with Liverpool coming up, she couldn't credit Gill Coultard going round saying she had problems. And where did she think she was getting off, telling the young ones she was signing for the opposition? Nicky'd heard it all from Debbie Biggins, and she couldn't believe it – the woman had a job, a steady home life, she'd got five numbers on the lottery, she played for England, she was going to the World Cup, what more did she want? Problems? She should come to Burnley, try some of hers on for size.

Born in London, adopted at birth, Nicky'd grown up in Nottingham since she was six. She had an older brother who played for Clifton All Whites, got offered forms at Leeds and Wolves – he never made it, one of his knees went – but she was as good as him and her dad, a draughtsman at Plessey, he just loved to watch her play. When she was twelve, he took her down to the club that's since become Ilkeston Town – and when she was thirteen, he died.

They diagnosed cancer in the January and in the March he was gone. Towards the end, they made him a bed in the lounge – her mum wanted to care for him at home, she dropped to six stone doing it – and the last three days were the worst. Nicky said, 'He died for three days in front of us. He was the most fantastic, perfect bloke you could ever hope to meet. He never lost his temper, he was totally brilliant.

And losing him . . . I haven't got over it. It'll be fourteen years a week on Saturday, and it still feels like yesterday.'

When she got her first Welsh cap in 1993 she dedicated it to him, and she framed the shirt for her mum – it meant the world, that did. But back when he died she'd packed in playing for more than two years, and by the time she was leaving school she was heading fast off the rails. All her mates fell away, not knowing what to say to her; her mum got in with another man, and she didn't like him. She left home at sixteen; on and off for the next few years she ran with a gang, getting pissed every night, doing meters and shops to pay for it; her first week in a probation hostel, she learnt how to pick a lock. In another place she put in her landlord's windows after she caught him using binoculars to watch the girls that were renting from him – and more than once she was banned for driving without insurance. Driving, she loved that second only to football, and it brought her no end of trouble – but in Nottingham there was a traffic cop called Tyrall and a constable called Tony Arrons, and they got right on her back. She thought, now, she could say that they'd saved her.

They'd say to her again and again, You can play football – so get out and do it. All right, you won't get paid for it like the blokes do – but you could make something of yourself, so why don't you? And along the way, the odd driving offence got let slide . . . then there was Alan Young, the Community Officer at Notts County, he'd helped too. She got coaching qualifications there, got a regular place on the team at Ilkeston and started straightening herself out. 'Well,' she laughed, 'I started working on it.'

The Saturday Club kids cannoned about the echoing bare gym; Nicky and some of the other trainees, Biff, Dean, Sonic, went running among them. She had a smile on her face. Later she said, 'I was an idiot. And you look back and you feel bad, you regret it – but you know what life can be like, too.

And when I'm with the kids now, especially the Special Needs kids, the ones that are getting abused, the ones getting in trouble – you don't want them ending up where you've been, do you?'

She'd gone to Belles to better her game, and to begin with it looked good, four goals in six games – but with all she'd had going off, her game hadn't got better, it had got worse, and she didn't think she'd played like she could do yet, not once. Paul would tell her she was Ryan Giggs in training, but she never was on a Sunday – and the Belles had rallied round her, Kaz, Flo, Joanne, Rob, Paul, they'd all have a word for the new girl, they'd all lift her, they were sound as a pound.

The only one she couldn't work out was Gill – she thought, she's the captain, and she doesn't talk to you? She did do once; early in the season Nicky'd given her a lift, they'd been in the car forty-five minutes, and she'd been human then – but there'd been nothing since, barely a word, when she should have been there, she should have been helping. And now, this signing for Liverpool – what was that? Nicky didn't fancy playing without her, never mind having her on the other side, she was that good – but if all she could do was bring a sour face in the dressing-room, maybe they'd be better off without her all the same.

Still, Nicky shouldn't have been playing against Liverpool herself; she shouldn't have been playing another game all season. She had a stretched ligament coming away from the bone in her right knee – which, after Burnley had beaten Oldham 2–1, and the gleeful kids had been gathered up by their parents from the stand, she took down to the physio's treatment room.

He was a delightful man, Andy Jones, a smiling barrel plonked on a pair of matchsticks. Nicky went in with Angie, the redhead on her crutches, and she reminded him that his team for the Comic Relief tournament she was organising were playing in togas. He expressed disappointment – 'I'd been hoping to wear a Mr Blobby suit' – while he sat Angie's foot in a bucket of ice, got Nicky laid down on a couch, then wheeled over a small, featureless metal cabinet sprouting glass bulbs on the end of flexible arms, a kind of laughable terror machine out of Fifties sci-fi.

He said, 'Can I ask you a personal question? Do you have any metal or plastic in that leg? No? OK. No pacemaker in your heart? No hearing aid? Good, thank you. Because this machine would melt the stuff in your leg, stop your hearing aid and make you deaf, and stop your pacemaker and make you dead. So I'd rather know first.'

It was electrical heat treatment. He set it up and told her, 'Don't move. You'll feel a gentle heat. If you feel anything worse, don't move, and don't panic. And if I'm not here, scream.'

After the deep heat, he rigged her up on an Interferential Therapy Unit – another little cabinet, this one with small pads on the end of wires that he strapped on tight around the knee under bandages. 'You should feel a tingling,' he said, 'like pins and needles.' It was a pain reliever – it bombarded the nerve ends until they were good and confused, so that if she had pain in it later, the pain stimuli to the brain would cut out, overridden. He said, 'This is effective, if she has a brain.'

Chris Vinnicombe came in, a Burnley player, clutching a bottle of Mumm – he'd scored. Seeing Nicky tied up there he smiled and said, 'Frying tonight,' then he turned up the dials.

She arched her back, writhing and laughing on the couch. 'I felt that up to me ears, you bastard. No, Chris, don't. Noooooo . . .'

Outside the room Andy said, 'She shouldn't be playing, not in an ideal world – but we'll try and coax her through. It's important to her to be playing just now, her heart's more important than her ligament at the minute. And what's happened to her . . . we've all been very shocked. It's a cliché to say a football club's a family, but this one is, and we've all tried to pull for her, I'd really hope we've been supportive – 'cause she's been a big boost round here. She's a lovely lass.'

I'd said earlier that he had a professional squad to look after, and he didn't have to treat her (never mind Angie, who wasn't even a player) and he'd shrugged and said, 'I'm here anyway.' He had, in fact, been treating her every day for three and a half weeks.

The morning of the game Micky Jackson got up eager to play, eager for Belles to stick a few past Davo. She had a bit of a chesty cough, but she didn't think it was anything – then she made herself some breakfast, it caught in her throat, she started hacking and she ended up heaving sick, retching so bad she put her back out. One minute you're eating toast, the next you can't walk. She rang Paul and he told her to bring her kit anyway, he'd need her on the bench – and she thought about the game, and she could have wept.

In Blaxton, Paul and Sheila sat by the phone, waiting for it to get worse. As usual, the night before, Flo'd finally managed to find herself in the same place as a phone, and her back was still bad; she wouldn't be coming. Now Micky was out, there was Nicky with her knee, and Kaz had the big toe on her right foot so swollen she could barely kick a ball – and as if all that wasn't bad enough, three hours before kick-off they still didn't know if they had a captain or not. Alan Burton had called to say Gill would be there by quarter to one, but who knew? Sheila said grimly. 'Depends what colour track suit she turns up in, doesn't it?'

Paul thought the behaviour of his captain was . . . well, it was certainly bizarre. He shook his head, the woman needed help – but they'd long ago resigned themselves to Gill being difficult. The youngest of eight, with her mum dead a few years ago, she'd never got on with her dad, and apart from one sister she wasn't close to her family – Belles were her family instead, Alan Burton was near enough an adopted father to her – and she had a need to be the centre of attention in this family, to have her importance in it regularly acknowledged. And God knew, she was important – as a player. But as a person . . . this signing for Liverpool, it was fantasy, craziness. Just in practical terms it was a nonsense, from Friday night to Sunday morning you'd never get the paperwork through. It looked, in short, more like the footballing equivalent of a suicide attempt, a scream for attention – get everyone on the phone to her saying, No, Gill, no, don't leave us, don't leave us . . .

Paul said, 'It's transparent. Everyone can see it – except her, of course. And she comes in in a foul mood, face as long as a yardstick, and people think, Oh God, here we go again. But she's a very mixed-up individual. And you can say the club would be a happier club without her – but the team would be a worse one, because she's a very, very good player. But I tell you what – if I were a psychiatrist I could earn good money trying to work her out.'

Still, for a league game potentially crucial to where the title went, it was great preparation, wasn't it? Paul had called Lorraine, the reserve team coach, told her to give Jonesy the first half that morning, then bring her off and send her round to the seniors. And Kaz's toe . . . well, at least with Kaz Walker they were sound. She'd called Friday before she went out, said she hadn't kicked a ball – but, said Sheila, 'I'll bet she were bopping on it after she rang.'

She'd told Paul, 'I'm playing. Even if it's broken I'm playing. And if it gets that bad I can't walk, OK, bring me off – but I'm playing.'

Paul told her to have Dean carry her round the pubs on piggyback that night, and he'd see her at the game. But now, he sighed, 'Do I really want to be here? Do I really want this? Lovely sunny day – I should be out in the back garden, not going to Stainforth not knowing what eleven I'm sending out. And I'm annoyed, I'm angry. There's people letting good, honest people down here. Gill – well, it's not good, but I don't think she knows what she's doing, and Copeland's badly hurt her, that's definitely a lot of it. I'm actually more annoyed with Flo; there's no reason for her to be late like she has been, to be so disorganised, never to call 'til a Saturday. No reason at all.'

Sheila said, 'We thought since she came here, she were getting her life more together. But now, she better watch it – or she'll be going back down the hill where she came from.' She grinned and told Paul, 'I told you you should have signed me for another year.'

She got Laura ready to go out; she was going to an ice-skating show in Sheffield with her grandparents. She was, they said, the member of the Edmunds family most likely to enjoy their Sunday afternoon. 'Never mind,' Sheila said. 'We'll get a draw. I feel it in my water.'

Paul shook his head. 'We'll get beat today.'

Liverpool had three current England players; if Davo and Psycho hadn't decided they couldn't be bothered with Copeland any more, they'd have had five. They had two others who'd played for England in the past, and at centre-half they had Lou Ryde. And they'd not played Arsenal yet – but apart from drawing 1–1 at Wembley on the first day of the season, they'd beaten everyone else they'd played. They'd done new England captain Debbie Bampton's Croydon by 3–0 twice; they'd put seven past Ilkeston, ten past Southampton . . .

Ah well. It was a glorious afternoon, the sun gleaming in a

bright blue sky. The running track round the pitch was still a quagmire of long, streaky puddles, but it was almost warm; it was spring at last. Nicky arrived with her knee strapped up by Andy Jones that morning from calf to thigh; Snoops, her sparky Jack Russell, went splashing in the muck. 'Come on, Snoops,' Ann Lisseman told him, 'get your kit on.'

Paul carried out the little benches with the peeled white paint for the home and away subs, one on each side at half-way; Rob stood in the goalmouths on a chair, stringing up the nets. In the clubhouse Sheila told Ann, 'Need you to stay on your feet today, when Psycho goes hurtling up wing.'

Ann laughed and said, 'Thanks for that. I was perfectly all right 'til you told me that on the phone yesterday, and me stomach's never stopped twitching since. I put the phone down, me hands were shaking – I had to have a brandy. I thought, that Sheila, I'm not speaking to her ever again. Making me all nervous and gitty.'

Laughter echoed round bare concrete. Channy turned up in shorts and shades and Sheila told her, 'Where d'you think you are, Ibiza? Look at the state of that. Hey, Channy, did you bring your tennis racket?' She was wearing the away shirt, not the home one; Sheila told her she was dropped, bad dress-code attitude.

Lou turned up with her mum. She told me, 'You know that Kiss club? Kicked off good style, literally five minutes after you left us. Ten of them fighting, pissed out of their heads. So we threw 'em all in the van, and all the girls are screaming, No, no, don't lock 'im up. But they're all swearing at you, and what do they expect? Busy last night, too – a couple of assaults at the Paradox.' She'd got off at seven, lain on a cushion in the back of the car on the way over and now she felt sick. She was trying to force a Mars bar down, but it wouldn't go, and she gave it away.

Gail arrived; Ann told her she was playing last man, Kaz

could carry her round the penalty area on her back. Gail smiled quietly; she said, 'I can jog. And I can hit it with my left foot.'

'Hey, that's not bad,' Paul told her, ''cause you couldn't before. I'll have to get an operation like that.'

It was ten past one; Gill, Joanne, Debbie Biggins, and stand-in midfielder Claire Large still hadn't arrived. The Liverpool squad were walking over from the road like an army – how many teams had they brought, then? – and behind them, now, came Gill Coultard with Alan Burton. Paul said, 'Here comes Captain Courageous' – and she was wearing her Donny Belles track suit. He went to see her, put an arm round her shoulders, a little bracing, had a short quiet word. When he came away he said quietly, ' She's nearly in tears. But she's here.'

In the dressing-room she sat silent, head down, motionless, leaning forward, fiddling with her watch. Everyone else was buzzing, bubbling, high on nerves. Rob was rubbing his hands together, smiling, twitchy. 'Hey,' he said, 'I'm excited.'

Joanne grinned and told him, 'Doesn't show. I can't see no movement there.'

'Right,' said Paul, 'we've had to make a few changes today.'

Gail asked, 'Does that mean I'm in then?'

'We're getting that desperate, you nearly were. But look, it's a lovely day and we didn't do ourselves justice last week, so let's put on our shirts with a bit of pride and put that right, shall we? 'Cause we're all mates on the field and we've got to help each other out. It's going to be tough today – but they've never beaten us, these, and we've never lost a national league game at home. So let's keep both of those records today, all right? Three points here and we're still on for the league. Off you go.'

Gill went out first, alone. As she went out the door, Gail ruffled her hair. She said nothing, her face showing nothing at all.

On the touchline, before she warmed up, Nicky said she
was going to have a word with her. She was surprised how up
people were, how confident they were acting, even if they
didn't feel it – but she needed Gill onside. Gill was the
captain and Nicky wanted to tell her, look, I'm trying my best
– I haven't had the best season, OK – but help me out, will
you? *I need your support* . . .

The way it turned out, she didn't need to ask for it. They
warmed up, they went back in, and Paul fired them up. 'No
ifs and buts and whys and wherefores – let's go out there and
do it, because we can do it. Penalties – we haven't got Micky,
so who fancies it? Joanne?' She nodded, no problem. 'Right,
Joanne's got penalties. Best of luck, everybody.'

Joanne said, 'Come on, girls, Stay on your feet, watch the
line, and play with a smile on your face.'

'That's a new one,' said Paul. 'This season's motto.'

They went out in a rising clamour of studs and clapping
hands, and before they did anything else on the pitch, Gill
called them together in a huddle. She told them what had
been said last week, it was past, that was over. They were all
together now, it was ninety minutes now, it was blood and
guts now, but they were Belles, right? And they could win
this, and they were going to.

They looked at her and they thought, all right. Then,
quietly, as they peeled away to line up, she went across to
Nicky. She told her she was a good player, a dead good
player, they all knew it; all she had to do was believe in herself
like the rest of them believed in her and she'd be right. Nicky
walked away from her feeling ten feet tall.

With Micky and Flo both out, Gill played sweeper. The
first clearance Belles made she roared like a bull, *Get out, Get
out*, voice echoing across the wide, flat fields as she charged
forward, throwing Des and Ann up the pitch in front of her,
Channy and Nicky wide surging on, and you could see

Liverpool back-pedalling, stunned at the noise of her, thinking, Christ, here they come.

On the bench, Micky Jackson smiled. She said to herself, I think the captain wants to win today – and Gill Coultard played a blinder. The one time all game Nicky Davies let Psycho go she got clear on goal, and Coultard made twenty yards like a rocket to take it off her feet in the penalty area, got up and brought it cleanly away. And of course, as the early battle went end to end, Paul grumbled – Joanne was taking too long on the ball, Kaz was turning like the *QE2* – but when Skiller got Belles' first just past the half-hour, chipping Davo from twenty yards, it was different class, he was made up, and he began to think then maybe his afternoon wouldn't be so bad after all.

Channy got the second on thirty-nine minutes, a blistering volley from twenty-two. Liverpool stormed back at them, Belles had a panic attack, Nicky let a ball roll out at Belles' end when she could have hoofed it upfield, Liverpool got a goal back from the throw with a minute to go to half-time, and Paul erupted. 'Fuckin' garbage, she does that, should have kicked it in bleedin' stand, no idea, what a fuckin' wank goal.'

Sheila tried to calm him down. 'Don't blame her, don't blame her.'

He yelled, 'Hey, *come on* – what we panicking for? Talk to 'em, Debbie. Fuckin' hellfire, what we *doing*?' Corners fell into Debbie's goalmouth; Paul was screaming for half-time. 'Hey, ref, are we changing round? Or are we playing full ninety one way?'

Sheila told him, 'Shut up, Paul, you'll get booked. You'll embarrass me.'

Back in the dressing-room Kaz said fiercely, 'C'mon. Can't let these tossers get back in it, eh?'

'First class,' Paul told them, 'first class, everybody,

absolutely brilliant. First to the ball, getting in there, winning the tackles, excellent. We've had an excellent forty-three minutes – and then the last two minutes, what we doing? Hey, I know it's after the event – but Nicky, you get the ball back there, you boot it ninety thousand yards into that chuffin' graveyard over there, OK? We're 2–0 up, they've got to score three times, all we got to do is kill the game – so you don't give them a throw-in back there, you kick it ninety thousand bleedin' yards in a field somewhere, make 'em fetch the bleedin' thing. But it's over now, and all we got to do is learn from it. 'Cause they've still got to score two now to beat us – so if it's a free kick, if it's a goal kick, if it's a corner, we don't run and get it, we *walk* to get it, we walk *everywhere*. We look, is there anything on early? – no. So we take our time, we slow things down, and we get a hold of this – 'cause they didn't deserve that goal, did they? They didn't deserve a bleedin' thing 'cause we've run 'em ragged all friggin' half and they're frightened to death, they are *absolutely frightened to death*. And we can win this, can't we?'

Loudly they all agreed that they could – and while they did, Gail leaned over to Kaz. When it was still 0–0 she'd been clear, maybe thirty yards out, and when she could have gone in on Davo, she'd shot limp and early; now Gail told her, 'Kaz. Take it in and curl it round her, eh?'

'Hear that?' Joanne grinned. 'Coach Boring says take it in and curl it round her. You got that? Good. Here though, what's wrong with Lou? She never played like that for us. But come on, eh? 'Cause when Arsenal see the score we win this by, they're gonna shit themselves.'

Kaz was holding the ball up on the touchline by the bench, a player came in on her, she got clouted on the instep and she fell down across the line. The ball cannoned back to her and, half scrambling up, still with two hands on the ground behind her back, from horizontal she whacked it thirty yards forward, then fell back again, wincing. Sheila told her, 'Well done Wack. Now get up and go head it.'

She got up, jogged forward, and got in the area as someone struck a screamer that Davo tipped up on the bar; it fell back out, Kaz went after it and a panicking defender brought her down, an ankle sandwich. She fell in slo-mo – 'like a sponge', said Sheila, thoroughly approving – and Joanne struck the penalty so hard and precise that Davo was left just standing there, her eyes on the line of air the ball had flown through. 3–1 Belles, eight minutes into the second half – and after that Liverpool crumbled, they were outplayed all over the park.

Not that it was perfect, mind. They won a corner, Channy ran to take it – and Paul shook his head. 'Do they listen to anything you tell them? She's running faster to take that than she has all game.'

Skiller made it 4–1 on seventy minutes, a header from a corner. Liverpool went up the other end, crossed it in, it arced over Debbie's fingertips, there was a striker heading it in from barely a yard out – and Des, just turned sixteen, leapt on the line behind Debbie to head it straight back out again. 'Magnificent,' said Paul, 'she's magnificent.'

When she went down injured Sheila ran out to see to her and she told her, 'Brilliant header.'

Des said, 'I didn't head it, it just hit me.'

'I don't care. It didn't go in, did it?'

There were ten minutes left. Paul sent Jonesy on for Nicky Davies; Nicky'd had Psycho locked up all game, she'd had her best game of the season, and Paul told Jonesy to do the same. 'All you got to do is stop eleven playing football. Just stop eleven, OK?'

When Nicky got to the bench he said, 'Excellent game – I've only brought you off to break it up at the end here so don't worry, you've been excellent. But take that strapping off now, OK? Let your leg move.'

Out on the field, Channy was sprinting to take another corner. Before Paul could say anything Sheila told him, 'Never mind. At least she's remembered you told her to take them.'

The ball came in, got cleared, and bounced off Joanne's . . . how shall I put this politely? Joanne's abdomen. Paul, smiling: 'Control those, Joanne.'

And then, in injury time, an instance of purely lovely football, just as good as it gets. Kaz's new striking partner Vicky Exley, a transfer from Sheffield Wednesday, took a ball played sharp out of defence to hold it wide on the line. Gill was roaring like a stoker from the back like she'd been doing all game, *Get out, Get out*, and Belles were all surging forward – and as they came, Exley fed Joanne with a slide-rule ball through two back-pedalling pairs of Liverpool legs. Kaz up ahead was on a peeling run, curling away with the whole defence lost, heads spinning, where she go? – and Joanne fed her on the button, twenty yards inch perfect along the deck, bang in her path so she didn't have to break stride. So she collected it and, clear on Davo, with Gail smiling as she watched, she looked up, took it in, and curled it round her. 5–1 Belles.

After the whistle Gail said quietly. 'I can't wait to get back.'

Rob told them in the dressing-room, 'Drinks are on me.'

Joanne thanked him, 'Cheers, big knob.' And she sang,

> Arsenal watch out
> The Belles are about
> We've just had Liverpool for breakfast
> They thought they would win
> And five went in
> And suddenly Liverpool were nowhere.

Kaz said, 'I don't know where we get our character from sometimes. But we must have some, eh?'

Across the room from her Gill said happily, 'I've never seen Psycho so shit frit in all me life.' She had a bigger smile on her face than she'd had all season.

12

No Fairy-tale Today

With Arsenal up next in the FA Cup semi-final, there couldn't have been a better time to put five goals past Liverpool. Elated, with her back mending and antibiotics clearing the chest infection, Micky Jackson rang Paul three days later and said she wanted to come training, even if all she did was watch. He told her not to be daft, to stop at home; the weather was bleak, she'd do herself no good at all.

At Stainforth that evening it looked like everyone else had come to the same conclusion; of the seniors, only Kaz and Channy turned up. Large, Kilner, and Exley were there, and five other reserves, and that was it; in the bare box of the clubhouse Paul looked weary, let down. With a hint of bitterness he asked, had I brought my boots? Outside, meanwhile, spring had lasted five minutes; half-way through the session, a chill wind started chucking down sleet at forty-five degrees, the sodden air flashing and glinting in the dim training lights on their stubby poles. Kaz packed in early; she said, 'I'm struggling with me toe, it'll not be right by Sunday. Still, I'll be playing – and we've got to beat them one of these days, haven't we?'

Debbie Biggins arrived; she was interviewing at Rovers the next day for the Training For Work scheme. She lived in Skipton, worked part-time in a tea-shop in Keighley, but she was over to Donny twice or more every week now and she couldn't afford the petrol; besides, the brakes on her old Renault were giving out. She talked cars and football with

Helen Garnett, a reserve player with a stress-fractured ankle who'd braved the foul night for the sake of watching her mates train; Garnett told a weird story about her goldfish getting electrocuted, and her saving them with mouth-to-mouth resuscitation. While she talked she kept the ball up on her crutches, hopping and stumbling about on the concrete. All the time she'd been injured she'd been doing it, she'd even bent one of the crutches, and she was well-practised now; the ball stayed up 116 times. Watching her, Debbie said, 'We're going to win on Sunday. I've just got that feeling.'

Paul came in, drenched, and sat down with Kaz; she took her trainer off to show him the toe and it was badly swollen, a lilac bulge. He told her to keep ice on it all the time to get the swelling down, to go home and do nothing, nothing at all. She grimaced. 'I can't bear sitting about doing nowt.'

As she left he said fondly, 'There's nobody like her. And player for player, we can match them – but not if nobody comes training we can't.'

A few miles north-west towards Wakefield, in the TSB next to Asda on South Elmsall High Street, posters showed smiling faces proclaiming imminent prosperity: 'Mum's saving for my future'/'We've put money aside to feel secure'/'I'm building my nest egg'/'Say *Yes* to great mortgage deals'. Across the street between the posters you could see K Fabrics, Hair By Clare, The Flower Shop, S Vodden Family Butcher and Capricorn Travel, Hinitts Bakers and a shuttered place called Rumours. Up the road a little way, The Korner (Now Open!) was barred and shuttered as well.

Frickley Colliery was a mile from South Elmsall; as they'd done in Askern a few years back, they closed it in the week before Christmas, 1993; around three hundred jobs went. Season's greetings to you too . . . for six months, fifty or a hundred stayed on to do the salvage work; by the summer, that was it.

At the bank, Micky Jackson watched the redundancy cheques come in, and then she watched them dwindle away. Some were sensible, some weren't; too many of the younger ones blew it, new cars, holidays, no thought. And there'd been anger and bewilderment, before the emotions faded like the money into numbness and red ink. Those that did get jobs were laughing – but plenty didn't. Now, there was the industrial estate in South Kirkby nearby, and not much else, and Micky worried how long the branch would stay open. If they could shut down bigger ones in Sheffield or Rotherham, what chance did South Elmsall have? Just this week, Netto'd taken over Asda, and there'd likely be more jobs go there too . . .

In the staff room on the first floor a flip-pad on an easel showed the results of the branch's 'mystery shopper' test. Every quarter the high-ups had someone anonymous get on the phone to them, or come in person, and on most of the counts – were they courteous, were they prompt, did the branch look smart? – South Elmsall rated a hundred per cent. (One of her colleagues laughed, 'So Micky must have been off that day.') But if things didn't pick up somehow across the next twelve months, it mightn't help too much. Business-wise, what's a hundred per cent of nothing?

Seven of the eight staff were women; they'd watch Micky play when they could, and now and then she'd be featured in the bank's newsletter. The eighth, a man, started work a few weeks back; when he found out she played he asked her, 'How long d'you play for, then?'

Mickey smiled. 'Two forty-fives, same as you.'

She was twenty-six years old, five foot eight, and she weighed ten stone; attractive without ostentation, she wore her dark hair short, round a quiet smile in a dusting of freckles. She was, in the jargon of the day, South Elmsall's 'Senior Customer Service Officer'; to you and me, she was the assistant manager. She'd gone into the bank as a YTS straight from school at sixteen, and she'd been there ever since; a responsible, steady woman, she hoped one day to have a branch of her own.

She came from Birkenhead; her dad was a lorry driver, and her mum worked in the Cadbury's factory. She had a sister five years older, an accountant in a hospital, and a brother eighteen months younger, an alarm engineer. Her dad played on local weekend teams; she'd gone to watch since she was four or five with the other players' kids, and when it became obvious her brother wasn't that bothered, her dad started putting all his encouragement into her. From twelve, she was on a five-a-side team, going to youth club tournaments round the country; when she was fifteen, they found out at Bebington Ladies, the club that later became Leasowe, that women played eleven-a-side too – for two forty-fives, no less.

A year after she went there her dad started managing them. In his late thirties by then, with two bad knees, if it hadn't been for Micky he might have gone into managing a lads' team – but he was always pushing her on, he always wanted her to do well, and the fact that it was women, he never said anything, he just did it. After a few years, he'd pushed her on well enough that she made the WFA's England Under-21 squad, and she met up there with Skiller, Kaz and Joanne. Then Leasowe played Belles in the FA Cup – and she was surprised, everyone said they'd be a big-headed lot, walking around high and mighty, and they weren't like that at all. They were normal, you could have a laugh with them – only they were so good at what they did, and when she started spending the odd weekend in Donny, and they asked her to join them, it was exciting and it was tempting, really tempting.

For months she said no – it was too far to travel, she liked her job too much to risk it, and she was worried what her dad would think. But on the other hand, she was nineteen – and she was thinking, if you're going to leave home, you may as well make a good go of it. Normally you'd go down the road, you'd not go further than the next little town – but when she asked at the bank they were good about a transfer, it turned out easier than she'd thought, there was a branch in Worksop she could go to – so she did and her dad went mad, absolutely mad. Looking back, she knew she'd hurt him – deep down, the only reason he did what he did was for her, so to uproot and leave, that was hard.

Six years later, the storm past, the father and daughter made up, Micky got what he must have hoped for all the time he'd been behind her as a kid – in spring 1994, she was called up for England. So there it was, the dream, to be part of an England camp, playing Spain in Bradford – which, to her boundless disappointment, turned out under Copeland and Hemsley to be an absolute farce.

They had twenty-two players there, and she thought if you busted a gut in training, if you did really well, you were there with a chance of making the squad for the match – but in a practice game it became apparent to her that that wasn't actually the idea. He had the England eleven playing the other eleven, and you were trying to show what you could do, breaking up their attacks, getting the ball off them – and before you could start any attack of your own he'd stop the game and he'd give the first team the ball back. She felt like she was there to be used – like she'd taken three days off her job, a job she cared about, just to be a body for Marieanne Spacey to run at.

Off the pitch was worse than on it. She was rooming with Channy and the hotel made a mistake with their alarm call one morning; they called at ten to eight, instead of seven thirty. Thinking they had time, they lay back in bed, then she looked at the clock; Christ, it was gone eight, they scrambled into their kit, tore downstairs, they were five minutes late for breakfast – and Hemsley dressed them down for it. Micky tried to explain, said that their call had been late, but she wouldn't listen – and Micky was stood there thinking, I'm not some kid, I'm a professional person, I'm responsible for people and money, and what am I doing taking this? So later, since Hemsley wouldn't hear it from her, she had one of the hotel management go to her and apologise for getting their call time wrong. Whereupon Hemsley came over and told her, Don't you ever embarrass me like that again – and Micky looked at her and thought, What a big woman you are.

The morning of the game, spare bodies like Micky were told they had to carry the players' bags. She thought, I've took three days off work to carry Marieanne Spacey's bag? She sat with Flo at breakfast and they thought, Well, we're not playing, we'll have scrambled egg and sausages – better get something inside us if we've got to carry those bags – and they got bawled out for that, too.

Bad as it was, she thought she'd go again; it was England, wasn't it? And he'd told them the same twenty-two would be called again, so she went back to work and booked another three days off. People in the branch were excited for her, said maybe next time she'd get in – hadn't he said in training she was playing like Beckenbauer? But evidently he was just being sarcastic – because a few days before she was ready to go again she got a letter telling her she was dropped. No call, just a letter.

She felt, at work, she'd been made to look a right pillock, never mind being messed about – so she rang Hemsley and she said to be treated like that was disgusting. Hemsley said it was the admin and Micky told her, Sod the admin, couldn't one of youse have the decency to pick up a phone? Oh, said Hemsley, her and Ted weren't completely organised yet – and Micky thought, You what? You've been running England six months now . . .

The reason they'd dropped her, she was told, was she didn't have a left foot. Soon after, Arsenal came to Belle Vue, they went 2–0 up and Copeland was watching. Belles got a penalty and Micky put it away, 2–1; then Belles got a corner, there was a ruck in the goalmouth and Micky slid in and scored the equaliser – with her left foot. On top of that she'd had a reet game, cleaning up at the back all ninety – so she tore into the dressing-room, changed as quick as she could, and steamed upstairs to the tea-room. She wanted to tell him, No left foot, eh?

When she got there he'd gone. And now, even if he did call her again, Micky Jackson, like Davo, like Psycho, like Flo, had no desire to play for England ever again for as long as those people were running it.

There was another thing about the FA that bothered her: money. The obvious choice after Sheila's dad got poorly, she'd been Belles' treasurer for three years now, and keeping it going was a regular scramble. If it had been just the first team, at a pinch they could have survived. If you played at Rovers, you might get a hundred quid or more at the gate; you'd get another sixty or eighty selling programmes and raffle tickets. Against that you'd have maybe fifty to pay out for the officials, twenty for the sandwiches, fifteen on laundry for the kit – so you'd come away a bit ahead. Even when they didn't have Belle Vue (which was all too often) and they played at Stainforth where you couldn't charge entry, you'd at least hope to break even. Then there was thirty-five quid per player from their kit sponsors, a hundred a game from match sponsors – more often than not one of Kantecki's companies – and you'd raise more again at the Christmas social and at the end-of-season club awards.

But buses for away games were three hundred quid a time, sometimes nearer four hundred. Then there were the reserves, the youth teams; without Kantecki's money, none of that would have happened – and after four years, never mind losing Paul, Rob was packing in now to concentrate on his business. So, OK, it was down to them to get out there and find another sponsor, it was down to them to run their own thing – but all the same, here was the FA saying they wanted to promote women's football, and what were they actually doing?

They gave you the odd small subvention; they gave you back fifty pence a mile for your away games, not including the first hundred miles. But when the Belles played Liverpool at Scunthorpe in the FA Cup Final in April 1994, and 1,674 people came through the gate, and the game was broadcast live in its entirety on Sky, neither the Belles nor Liverpool received a penny. In the men's amateur game, at the FA Vase or the FA Trophy finals, the clubs in those got a piece of the gate – so why not the women?

To add insult to injury, the two clubs were given just thirty tickets each. And it would be the same thing now, this semi with Arsenal at Rotherham United's Millmoor – Belles would be out a few hundred for the bus, Arsenal likewise coming up the motorway, the Cockneys were staying overnight beforehand as well – and yet however many came, neither club would see a thing from it.

But then, expecting anyone to turn up and make this game viable might have been asking too much anyway. The Monday before it was played, in the Public Affairs Office at Lancaster Gate they hadn't even written a press release.

Joanne rang Paul on the Thursday, said she was fine, she'd be there – but she'd heard from Flo that her X-rays weren't good, she was still on the sick, and she didn't think she'd be coming. Paul said that was a shame; he didn't want to change a winning team, but Vicky Exley was cup-tied and he'd fancied making a straight swap, giving her Exley's place up front next to Kaz. An hour later, the phone rang; it was Flo, and she'd be there. After all, it would have been pure fairy-tale for Flo to score in this one, wouldn't it?

The day before the game she got the bus over from Stoke, and stayed the night with Kaz and Dean; during the night, she dreamed they won 3–2. It was a last-minute winner; Flo crossed, Kaz knocked it in, she jumped in the air with her arms high and wide – and in the air she started turning into Paul Furlong. Flo ran to hug her, give her five, and found that Kaz was now black, bald and male. She shook her head and said, 'Dead weird. But I always dream before big games, me – and I've never dreamed us losing yet.'

While she was dreaming in Bolton, in Blaxton Sheila was polishing dust off the big wooden case with the WFA Cup in it. Over a dozen years it had become almost like a piece of her furniture and she hated giving it back, it made her stomach turn over. The day before, they'd put Laura in an England shirt Joanne had given her and Sheila must have taken eighteen pictures, her little blonde girl smiling with the Cup and the league trophy. 'Still,' she said, 'hopefully we'll not be without it too long.'

They dropped Laura at her grandparents, then drove into Donny past the racecourse, down grand old Bennethorpe with the Victorian lamp-posts, down South Parade to the Waterdale car park. The squad was gathering round the bus; Rob was fretting that his coat was filthy. 'Never mind. I'll wash it for the final.'

On the bus Flo sat behind him, worrying about her back. She had a curve in the spine, they were sending her to a specialist – but she was on the sick, and she was more worried about that. If the telly came today, and someone from work saw her on it, she'd be sacked. So why play? She said simply, 'Me 'eart.'

It wasn't, I suggested, just a tiny bit to do with her getting a chance up front? She said, 'Nah. I'd have played anyway. Last Sunday were 'orrible, sat watching clock all afternoon. I rang round that evening, no one were in, I didn't find out while Monday – it were dead bad waiting. But I were made up when I heard. I thought, Thank God for that.'

From the back Kaz shouted, 'Hey, Flo. Had my boot polish gone off?'

She called back, 'Fuckin' manky, weren't it? Scruffy cow. Here,' she said, getting up to scamper away down the aisle, 'let me get back there, beat somebody up.'

Micky watched her coming, Belles' mad elf. She thought, God knew what went on in her head – but she brought them together, didn't she? And if you ever tried to change her, she'd not play the same – though if it ended up that she couldn't walk, she'd not play again anyhow.

At eleven thirty the bus rolled up to Millmoor; they'd been told to be there ninety minutes before kick-off. The sky was slinging down freezing sleet; the parking lot was a rubble zone, a dereliction of pot-holes and bare brick and debris, the wall round the back of the main stand topped with shards of broken glass. But first impressions were misleading; as they unloaded their bags the sun came out, and a pair of smiling stewards came to pick up the kit and start carrying it in for them. The younger girls couldn't believe that; they made big surprised eyes at each other, as if to say, Are we special then? They followed the stewards in under the stand, the ribbed concrete ceiling sloping up above them, the space echoing with the shuffle of their trainers, and Des said quietly, 'You could get lost in here.'

'This way,' one of the stewards told them, 'you've got lucky dressing-room.'

Maybe they say that to all the girls . . . but not really. One of them had said to Rob, 'You Arsenal?'

Rob smiled and said, 'With accents like these?'

So the steward told him, 'Right, you're at home then. Not giving it to no Cockneys.'

Rob wandered round the dressing-room, past the toilets into the bathroom; neatly tiled in red and white, the bath was team-sized, deep and gleaming. He went back and told them, 'Hope you brought your rubber ducks.'

Joanne grinned and asked him, 'Hey, big knob. You excited today?'

Paul told them to go look at the pitch, have a walkabout. It was sodden, grassless, really heavy. Flo muttered, 'I'll have cramp in five minutes on here.'

'Be like playing on Blackpool beach,' said Kilner. 'Did you bring your goggles then?'

Rob looked at the stud marks dug into the mud along the touchline. 'See these sparrow prints? Yorkshire sparrows. Ey oop, that's *mah* breadcrumb, pal. Don't get birds like that down London.'

And they'd been told to turn up ninety minutes before kick-off, but with an hour to go there was no sign yet of Arsenal. Back in the dressing-room Paul told them, 'Put programmes down, 'cause I'm talking now.'

'What programmes? We haven't got any.'

'No. We haven't got any opposition, either.'

Gill said grimly, 'Do they get special privileges then?'

'I hope they get fined. Now listen in. Are we going to polish our boots, Wack? Are you with us, Channy? Right – there's people looking a bit nervous, so don't worry about it, it's only a game of football, and if you play like you did last week we'll be OK. But those senior players who've been here before, they should be encouraging those who've not, 'cause I don't want us going out there with any fear at all. I want us proving a few people wrong, just like we did last Sunday; I want us proving we're still the best team and getting a few more people eating humble pie, like them sat up in that stand, the dignitaries of this FA establishment. 'Cause Cathy Gibb phoned me midweek, that woman who writes for whatever it is, she said that were a good win last Sunday, that surprised a few people; she said before that, Arsenal thought all they had to do today was turn up. And the FA, they'll be even more worried – they thought they had it all worked out, Arsenal winning here, Liverpool beating that lot down in Bristol, an Arsenal–Liverpool final, country's two best teams, it sounds good that, doesn't it? It's a decent tight final then, isn't it? So they'll be shitting themselves now, absolutely shitting themselves, 'cause whoever wins here goes on and thrashes Liverpool – and it's not what they worked out, that, is it?'

He had people laughing all round the room. He told them, 'They expect us to get beat, eh? So we prove Arsenal wrong and we prove the FA sat up there with all their badges wrong – and listen, there's a few in here can do themselves a power of good in front of those people today. They don't have to prove anything to me, or to anyone in this room – but it seems some people still need a bit of proof, don't they? So today's your chance.'

He read out the numbers, and told Gill she was staying at the back. He said wryly, to more whistles and cheers, 'After last week's promising performance, I thing we might eventually have found a position for Gill. I've been looking for a place where she might play reasonably well.'

'After all these years,' Kaz grinned.

Gail smiled. 'Haven't tried her in goal yet.'

When he came to putting Flo up front with Kaz, that

raised more hoots and whistles too. Flo looked around them, red-faced and bubbling, and barked out, 'What you laughing at, you lot?'

Sheila was working on her legs; she told her, 'You do realise, Flo, I'm not a miracle worker. If you haven't trained on 'em, I can't make you run.'

'Never mind, I'm naturally fit, me. Got fit when I was little, when I had to bomb off after smashing people's windows.'

Paul told her, 'They'll be laughing on the other side of their faces when you've banged three in, won't they? And we're going to win today, aren't we?'

And they laughed, they shouted, they were going to win – but he could see Kaz with her bad toe in a bucket of ice, and when he sat down in the dug-out and the ref blew his whistle, Paul Edmunds felt so bad he thought he was going to throw up right there.

The game was weird. Four hundred came, if that; four hundred at Stainforth and the place would have been buzzing, but four hundred here was a mausoleum. The little old stadium felt hollow, tinny, a place of isolated shouts, a sunlit void host to scurrying ghosts over the cloying mud. You thought, who sees this? Who cares?

Hunched under the perspex roof of the dug-out, Gail Borman cared. With Arsenal not getting out of their half in the early minutes she was twitching on the bench, bawling her head off. Paul said to her, 'You were never this noisy on pitch. You going to be like this all ninety?'

There were ten minutes gone; Des won a tackle, slipped the ball on for Flo. Flo gave it to Joanne and went haring off ahead, Joanne put it over the top for Kaz, Flo was tearing into the area, Kaz laid it out in front of her, a defender came flying in from behind, Flo went down with her ankles pulled out from under her, the ref put his whistle in his mouth, Belles' bench were all up pointing at the spot – and the ref gave a goal kick. The defender hadn't touched the ball then – and we all looked at each other. How could that be?

Paul yelled, 'Referee. When they're brought down it's a penalty.'

Sheila snapped, 'Shut up, Paul.'

'You shut up.'

'D'you want to watch it from stand? 'Cause that's where you'll be if you don't stop gobbing.'

Two minutes later, Marieanne Spacey missed a sitter; four minutes later, Kaz scored. Someone shouted from the stand at Paul to sit down; he turned round with a grin and said, 'You'll be tired of saying that by the end.'

Sheila said grimly, 'I'll bet Kaz can feel her toe now.' Paul told her to have the ice bucket ready and again she snapped at him, 'I have. What d'you want me to do, follow her round pitch with it?'

But by the half-hour, Arsenal had their heads down, they didn't want to know; Akers was on his feet, tearing his hair out. Not for the first time, Des tackled Marieanne, left her lying in a heap; Gail shouted approval, then muttered more quietly, 'Get her out of the game, that's it.'

While Marieanne was down Joanne came for water. 'Hey you,' Gail told her, 'stay on your feet.'

'And enjoy meself. Rob – you excited yet?'

The game started again; Paul shouted, 'Keep 'em going, Gill. Push across, Wack, five's struggling, get on the five.'

'There's a few of them struggling.'

Arsenal's keeper, Pauline Cope, was out of her area, yelling at her team-mates so loud everyone in the place must have heard it, 'Oi. Get fucking hold of it.' What – no red card for foul and abusive language? And Marieanne kicked the ball away when Belles got a free kick – what, no yellow?

Gail said happily, ' They don't fancy it, do they?'

And then they were level – the ball hoofed forward, Debbie coming for it, an indecision attack, stuck in limboland not on her line or off it, Sammy Britton bearing down, thanks very much, a neat lob, 1–1.

Gail sighed, 'What a shit goal to give away.'

Soon afterwards Sheila had to run and see to Channy on the far side. While she was out there she told her, 'Clatter that Marieanne one more time, she'll be off.'

An Arsenal coach on that side heard her and he said, 'That's a good tactic, that is.'

With feeling, Sheila told him, 'We didn't used to play like that, until we came across you lot.'

In the dressing-room Kaz sat with her foot in the ice bucket, urging them to lift it – but it was flat, they couldn't believe it was 1–1. Joanne said, 'That were a penalty, weren't it? He shit himself, didn't he?'

Flo shook her head, angry and sad. 'I didn't dive, I swear. She didn't touch chuffin' ball.' As if to say, what do we have to do to beat these?

'You dive next half,' Paul told her, 'he might give it you then. But look, Deb, that goal's gone now, it's history. So get yourself organised, 'cause if they don't score again we can't lose, can we? And their crowd didn't have much to shout about, did they? Those five they brought.'

Channy asked Kaz, 'How's your foot, love?'

She was wincing, gingerly pulling her boot back on. 'Absolute nightmare. But look, they're rubbish at back. Just give us some balls, eh?'

Joanne told her, 'You blast 'em, Kaz.'

'Nah. I'm a new woman, me.'

And three times she'd get free on goal, three times with her throbbing right foot she'd try to place it, and three times

Pauline Cope came to smother it. There would, it seemed, be no fairy-tale today.

Mixed with the mud was sand, your foot would just sink in it. Channy kicked one ball, said her standing foot disappeared underneath her. And there were heavy legs all round; on the far side Micky went down with cramp. Sheila ran across to deal with her, she was with her an age on the sideline, time was ticking, ticking, and Paul was roaring at her, 'Sheila, get her back on. *Get her back on.*'

Kaz went by the dug-out and asked him, 'What we doing, Paul?'

'How do I know? They don't tell me, they've been over there ten minutes.' Arsenal were attacking, attacking ten players all the while. Sheila came back, and he looked daggers at her.

She shrugged and said, 'I told you, she had cramp.'

'So was she going on or coming off?'

'I'd have told you if she were coming off. Stop panicking, you're worse than them on pitch.'

The time crawled by, the game raddled with tension, punctuated with disjointed shouting. With ten minutes left Micky came off hobbling, the back of one calf swelling violet. Kaz bundled it in from a corner, 2–1 but no, the ref disallowed it, some foul we'd not seen. The bench stood in the orange-brown muck, disbelieving, then slowly Paul turned back to sit down. He said to Gail, 'It's much easier playing, in't it? Bloody murder in here.'

Gail said she was shaking all over. So was Des, after Sammy Britton elbowed her in the temple; so was Gill, after a ferocious shot thumped off the top of her head and knocked her out. A stretcher came, she went behind the goal, sat on it, got up again. Kaz sat in the centre circle and thought, Ah, she's all reet. She just wants a cup of tea.

And you've got to enjoy it, haven't you? Cope told Kaz she was a big fat knacker, and Kaz grinned. Or her and that Kirsty Pealling trying to mark her, they had a chat. Did Kirsty mind when Copeland didn't pick her? Nah, said Kirsty, not bothered. Gill Wylie looked at them and said, Hey, you two. You going to concentrate here or what? Then it was extra time.

Arsenal won 3–1. The second one Debbie couldn't help, the third was a disaster – a high ball falling easy in her hands and she dropped it, gifted it to Marieanne. As the time played out, Kaz wanted to run back there and kill her, all butter gloves and lettuce feet; once it was over she wanted to hug her, say never mind, she were a dead good keeper for all that, she were only eighteen.

Micky sat on the hoardings by the dug-out and looked at the dictaphone like it was an instrument of torture. Not now, Pete. When she said there'd be another day, they'd still got the league, the lump in her throat was so big the words barely got past it. Was she crying? She said, 'Maybe later.'

It was raining, the sky turned flat grey. Ann Lisseman came off, stood bent double on the sideline, and she wasn't waiting 'til later for the tears. Inside, in the silent dressing-room, they could hear an Arsenal girl acting out the Meg Ryan fake orgasm from *When Harry Met Sally*, screaming Yes! Yes! Yes!

Paul was held back by Sky. In his place Gill said, 'Get your heads up, lasses. You can be proud of yourselves today.'

Sheila told them, 'They didn't deserve it, did they?' She added bitterly, 'FA'll be pleased though.'

It had been, said Vic Akers, the real Final – and Ted Copeland was there to watch it. But he didn't come and talk to anyone after, not to the managers, nor to the players from either side in his England squad. Paul shook his head. 'An enigma.'

★

Flo cadged a cigarette and limped away with her half of lager, to sit hidden on a little stairway leading up into the stand. She had pain all down her back, on down through her left thigh to below the knee. She said, 'I think I had one little tear. I thought, Flo, don't do that. Must have been the wind blowing. And I best leave it out now 'til I see the specialist, it's never been this bad, I can't walk. But it was a penalty, wasn't it? I didn't dive, I wouldn't do that. Well, I probably would – but I didn't then. She kicked me flying. And she said she didn't touch me and I went, You fuckin' did, you little shit. Does your 'ead in, don't it?'

On the bus back to Donny, Paul said, 'The only good thing about today is it's a short journey home.' And he was angry; he cited an instance when an Arsenal player was down, Debbie had the ball, she'd thrown it away over the sideline – and once the girl had been treated, an Arsenal player, instead of throwing the ball back to Debbie, had thrown it away over the goal line. That way, Debbie'd have to kick it back into the game off the floor, instead of out of her hands, and they knew she wasn't so good at that, didn't they?

Or another time, Belles had been attacking over the half-way line, the ref stopped it for an injury – and instead of letting Belles put the ball back into their defence from the drop-ball, so they could keep their possession and start again, as you would even in the men's professional game, at the drop-ball the Arsenal player had competed for it.

He snorted, 'Sportsmanship? I hate it, I hate everything they stand for. The only thing, the *only* thing they want is to win. And if that's the way it's going to go, they can have it.'

Back at Waterdale, he watched Flo hobble off the bus; he said sadly, 'I don't think we'll be seeing her again.'

Kaz went down the aisle with Dean and Paul told her to

do nothing, no training, nothing at all. She looked stricken. 'I can do weights, can't I?'

'No, you can't do nothing. Dean, you'll tell her, won't you?'

Dean smiled. 'I try to. But you can tell I'm a forceful character, can't you?'

Kaz turned up at Stainforth three days later – as did a lot more people than a week before, still angry, still disbelieving – not to train, but just to be with her mates, to go around and around the post-mortem with them. Of her toe she said, 'I've smashed its head in, haven't I? But what can you do? You leave it all week, and then Sunday you smash its head in.' She was limping, she couldn't wear a proper shoe; at work she had it up on her desk for air all day. At the DSS they were, she grinned, sick of the sight of it.

Even so, she couldn't keep away from a ball. If she couldn't touch it with her foot, then fine, she'd go outside and keep it up on her head and her knees instead. She stood under the lights in the cold, clear night, the ball bouncing, gleaming, while on the pitch the Belles trained – and among them was Gail Borman. She did the warm-up, the running, the star jumps, the press-ups, the sit-ups; when it came to working with the ball she bailed out and went to run the far sideline on her own, alternating sprints and jogs, looking slim and trim and quick. She said the physio reckoned she'd be kicking a ball again next week. It had been seven months.

At the end of the session, Paul pressed the rest of them through a sequence of races, three players at a time doing shuttles, up and down and back again along a line of markers, turn, sprint, turn, sprint, turn. As they ran he shouted, 'Go right round your markers, don't step over them, don't cheat, don't kid yourself. You can't kid yourself on a Sunday afternoon.'

By the end they were wiped out, flat on their backs under

the stars, heaving for breath, each gasp a little surge of mist on the air, each attempt to speak collapsing in a pained little moan. While they lay there he squatted down on his haunches and told them, 'Well trained, everybody. Now, Sunday morning, it's eight o'clock at Waterdale and remember, the clocks change Saturday, so you've got an hour less in bed. And we're playing Croydon, they've got half a dozen England players. So,' and his voice was heavy with irony, 'they must be a very good team, eh?'

13

Going Down Like Flies

Gill didn't come training. The next night she rang Paul, said she'd not be playing Sunday either; she had a headache. She wasn't so concussed she couldn't go to work though, she wasn't so concussed she couldn't go out for a drink at Kilner's birthday party. Paul couldn't believe it – he'd had Joanne play on a broken leg, he'd had Flo turn out against Arsenal with a bent back and the doctor telling her not to go out of doors, he'd had Nicky playing for weeks on a knee she should have left alone to mend for the rest of the season, he'd had Kaz scoring goals with a toe she could barely walk on – and the captain had a headache?

He said, 'All right, Gill,' and put the phone down. There were only a few weeks to go, and he couldn't begin to tell the state she was in; they could still win the league, and he didn't want to say something he'd regret.

On Sunday morning, as the bus pulled out of Waterdale, Gail Borman was more stern. She said, 'He should drop her next week against Wolves, teach her a lesson. Have her turn up, then put her on bench. And we'll beat these today, too – show her we don't need her.'

Paul came down the aisle to ask her, 'You fit enough to do sponge?' He'd left Sheila and Laura in bed, the two of them flu-laden; with Flo gone and Gill crying off, any more casualties, he thought, he'd be picking subs out of the crowd. And this patched crew were heading down the M1 now to play a team led by Copeland's new captain Debbie Bampton, with half a dozen others who'd got in his squad; two of them, Alex Cottier and Donna Smith, had won selection after they'd transferred from Julie Hemsley's club in Brighton.

Kaz shook her head. 'It's embarrassing, in't it? It's absolutely ridiculous. That Cottier, our Stanley's better than her.'

Stanley was Kaz and Dean's dog – and the Belles weren't short on motivation today. In the dressing-room Paul told them they were fancy Dans, these Croydon, they'd want to dance about on the ball all day looking pretty. 'But you get roped into 'em, they'll not live with you then, they won't like it. And they're not England players 'cause of who they are, they're England players 'cause of who they play for – so there's individuals in here should be looking round saying, Hey, I'm better than these, I should be in that England squad. 'Cause you should be.'

From the looks on their faces, he didn't need to tell them – and, after getting up in the dark to spend five hours on a bus, after Croydon scored first, after Des quit the game at half-time with her ankle badly bruised and ballooning, after Claire Large was knocked unconscious and got up and played on, after Skiller came off on a stretcher with her Gazza knee pranged again, the Belles beat Croydon 3–1.

Joanne said afterwards that when Large was down and blacked out, Bampton was nagging the referee to get on with the game. Angrily Kaz said to her, 'Hey, you can have three points, you, so long as Claire's all right.' But that, said Joanne, was your new England captain for you.

She'd made the second goal for Kaz, she'd scored the third herself with a sweetly placed chip from eighteen yards, curled inches inside the post – and, a little while back, she'd made that call to Copeland. He'd told her her ability wasn't in question, but her attitude was. She was left shrugging, thinking, What can you do?

★

The dressing-room afterwards was a casualty unit. Skiller was in bad pain, pale, sat on a bench with her foot up across an overturned wire wastebin, her knee wrapped tight in a cold, wet towel, her face a picture of lurking fear that after four years struggling to get back, she might have torn it all up again. Ann and Channy had groin pulls, Des had a bag of ice strapped to her ankle with a scarf; Kaz was pulling her boots off, wincing. She said, 'We're going down like flies, us. But we still chuffin' win, don't we?'

Paul told them how proud of them he was – and for all the pain, there'd been players out there smiling all game, just loving playing football. I remember Joanne going to take a corner, spinning the ball on one fingertip as she walked, studying it with a kind of raptness, an absolute involvement. I remember Kaz coming to the sideline while an injured player was treated, sticking her hurting foot in a bucket of water, boot and all, head thrown back to drink while she stood there, and people looking at her, thinking, What on earth's she doing? But she said, 'I don't care what people think. I do first thing that comes into me head, me.'

I remember when they'd gone in front, Paul shouting at her to tell them to break the game up – and she looked at him with her arms wide and a big grin, her eyes a broad panto-mime of incomprehension. She said, 'What does that mean?'

I remember Joanne brought down tumbling in the area, and Jonesy smashing her head on the roof of the dug-out as she leapt up to point the finger, to claim the penalty. As the ref demurred she stood there rubbing her skull, embarrassed; Paul rolled his eyes and told Gail, 'Hey, physio. One of our subs is injured.'

I remember Gail shouting to Channy as the second half began, 'You're on this side now, Channy, you've got me on your back. We're at Croydon, OK? And we're going to win.' Always best to remind Channy where she was . . .

I remember Paul calling to Claire Large to mark six, so she went and marked ten. Paul shook his head. 'She never were very good at maths.'

And I remember Kaz, all talked out about England on the bus back home, satisfied she'd got it off her chest to Paul about how morale in the national side was the lowest she'd known it, laughingly indifferent now to the water torture of having to watch endless Charles Hughes coaching videos, or to that Hemsley on the bench – this woman shouting at you in a game, 'Run!' So you stood there on pitch and you thought, Thanks for that, Julie. Run. I know what I'm supposed to do now, I'm supposed to chuffin' run . . . the stories went on and on up the motorway, a laughing cascade of disbelief. They'd had them in some room like a class of kids, banging on about diet and nutrition, asking if they could name a fat. So Kaz's mate Clare Taylor stuck her hand up and said, 'Jo Brand.'

I remember Kaz getting bored of all that, 'cause where's the point worrying? I remember her turning and calling out to Debbie Biggins, 'Hey, Deb. Are you eating plain crisps? Ooh, I hate people who eat plain crisps. Says a lot about your personality, that does.'

I asked what she favoured herself. With a look somewhere between gleeful relish and absolute contentment she said, 'Pickled onion flavour Monster Munch, me.'

In the game they'd just played, they'd gone behind after six minutes. So they'd looked about them and they'd thought, England players, these? Now Ann Lisseman said, with a dirty great jubilant laugh, 'Where were they?'

Paul said, 'I don't know. I couldn't pick them out.'

In the clubhouse, none of the Croydon players came to talk to them after; they went and skulked in some other room. Belles climbed back on the bus laughing, thinking, Thanks for the hospitality. Skiller laid herself out on the back seat, Des spread her injured leg across two seats, Kaz rested her foot over Gail's knees; there were bags of ice all round. When they got back to Donny at ten Skiller and Des went to hospital, and they were there 'til gone three the next morning.

In Croydon the bus set off, and a portable rang. Helen Garnett answered it; she said, 'Hello. Is that the England manager?'

But none of them thought the result would make a difference – and if it did, in Channy's case it mightn't help anyway. She'd talked to her employers – Leeds United, a Premier League football club – about getting time off should she be called again for England, with the World Cup coming up. They'd not been helpful; they'd said what she did, after all, it was only a hobby.

Modern times: in Hull three days later, I stayed in a pub whose owners turned out to be gay. Plonked down amid a confusion of roads through old port warehouses and cold stores, it looked a dump from the outside, but was redecorated with lavish floral gusto within. The owners' living-room was cluttered with exotic birds in big cages, and aquaria glinting with tropical fish. Handwritten signs on the doors downstairs firmly proclaimed that the pub was drug-free.

The landlord, a substantial, powerfully built man, wasn't someone whose injunctions on that or any other matter I'd have chosen lightly to disobey. When I brought in a dansak from the take-out down the road, and he said the fiver I'd got back in my change from there was a dud, I didn't argue. On the television, John Major was reported to be claiming he wasn't finished. Handing me back my dud note the landlord growled, 'What, is the demolition job not done yet?'

Beside me at the bar, a lad who'd come from work at the bingo hall looked at the worthless paper in my hand and sighed. He said, 'There's millions of 'em about. We get 'em every week.'

Morning came bitter cold under a pale, clear sky, the pavements sheened with a crunching carpet of ice. I drove to the Royal Infirmary, Hull reminding me of Portsmouth where I grew up, a town of low horizons bombed out by the Germans and the planners who came after them, left disorganised and piecemeal, a bitty randomness of tower blocks and green spaces and old brick.

In amongst it, the hospital was maybe fifteen stories of looming grey shoebox; soon after eight, as she did three mornings every week before work, Gail Borman drove her company van into the car-park and walked up two flights to Physiotherapy. She always walked, she never took the lift – had to keep that knee working . . .

Knee ligaments, above all the anterior cruciate, the ACL – it was the injury you dreaded. If that thing ruptured you knew you were lucky if you were back inside a year, and when you were back, in your head you'd always wonder if you could ever be the same. It wasn't a thing your body could mend by itself, it had to be replaced – with synthetic material, with a dead person's ligament, or with other material from inside your own knee – and in Gail's case they'd gone for the latter.

Crudely speaking, the tendon connecting patella to shinbone's a vertical rectangle, a kind of tough elastic strip; you can cut out a central slice of that and, all being well, it'll repair itself, scar tissue sealing over the upright little letter box hole you've made. Then you use what you've cut out to go in where the snapped cruciate used to be – and it was a procedure Gail had, not unnaturally, been dreading. Other Belles who'd been through it spoke of two or three days afterwards in severe pain, and no one on the medical staff was inclined to try and minimise that possibility.

Six weeks after she'd fallen at Wembley in September, Gail

waited to go into theatre. There was a lad there who'd had the same thing done and she could see him hovering, wanting to talk; he was a chatterbox, the nurses said, they tried to keep him away, but he got to her bedside soon enough. Was she having the shot in the arm, or was she getting an epidural? Oh God, she thought, didn't you only get one of them if you were bad with a baby? But this lad had had an epidural, it had took them three goes to get the needle in his spine and he had to tell her every detail.

They wheeled her in; she asked the anaesthetist if it was arm or back, and it was arm. She thought, That's all right then, looked at the clock and was gone. However long later, she woke up – and she could barely feel a thing. It was sore, but not much, it wasn't bad. She was always a tranquil person, not one for nerves – but now people asked her, Did she have a nervous system at all? Maybe not, she told them – and if she didn't, she smiled, then she was glad.

After that, the hard part started. She had two months off work; she was on crutches in a brace to allow it a little movement, that was better than plaster and your muscles wasting – and they told her her progress was good. You couldn't say there was a norm exactly, everyone was different, but she was some weeks ahead of how people generally went. By New Year, she was getting in the gym; now, in late March, every Monday, Wednesday and Friday, she was working on it for the best part of two hours.

Early, the gym was near empty; a high-ceilinged hall with a polished wood floor, it had wall bars, weights, benches, couches, cycling machines, a jogger and an isokinetics machine laid out around the walls. She stripped down into shorts and sweatshirt, and sat on a couch to do some stretches; when she was ready, she got on the jogger and started running. Where she ran on the machine, she could look out over a bare vista of a church spire among low roofs of terraces, small warehouses and abandoned buildings beyond the car park under the icy sky.

There was still a slight limp in her movement. Her trainers thumped softly, steadily on the belt whirring beneath her, the machine whining quietly as she ran. After ten minutes her face was shading red; after fifteen the sweat was popping on her cheeks and forehead, her breath low and tight, her eyes still, staring fixedly ahead. After twenty she stopped and lay down. The counter on the machine clocked 2.5515 miles, 316 calories burnt. She said, 'I could stop at fifteen minutes, I could leave it at that. But I keep looking out that window and I tell myself, Sweden '95. Sweden '95.'

She didn't think she'd make it, but she was damned if she wasn't going to try.

The senior physio for orthopaedic out-patient rehabilitation was Geoff Plummer, a tall man thirty-four years old who'd been there thirteen years; in the afternoons, when the gym was taken over by the neurologists, he ran a clinic of his own, and he'd toured with the Great Britain rugby league side.

He had four ACL's at the minute – Gail, another woman who'd done her knee jumping off a stile when she was out walking, a lad who played football, another who played rugby. And the people who tended to get this injury, they were generally motivated types, they'd want to get back to their sport; more often than not a physio'd be holding them back, not pushing them on, and you did get a few, there was little point them coming if they weren't prepared to take your advice, they might as well go to a garage.

Gail, he said, seemed sensible on that front, but it remained difficult to say precisely when she or any other person could get back. In the nature of the injury, when the muscle strength and the movement were recovered, there was still the head to be mended, the confidence to be regained to go out there, to twist and turn and kick a ball and take a tackle. So, I said, given the normal time frame, she'd not be back this season.

He said, 'I didn't say that. Realistically, unless she's very confident, it's probably not worth pushing for the last few games. But once she's had the go-ahead the decision rests with her; she does seem a confident person. And the way she's worked . . . her attitude, and her regard for her general fitness, are excellent. She works as hard, certainly, as any man I've seen; having worked with professionals, I'd say she has a very professional attitude, that she's very single-minded. I'd say she's a shining example.'

The shining example was on the isokinetics machine. She sat in the seat, her right thigh strapped down above the damaged knee with its five inches of livid violet scar, the lower leg lifting and lowering a padded bar. The machine worked the leg against resistance, with a counter measuring angular displacement, and a light running across a dial to gauge the range of movement. As she worked, doing batches of ten lifts against the weight – she'd do 250 in all – her hands were pressed white against the seat, her face clenched taut. Finding that the machine was set on a higher range than she normally used, Geoff adjusted it down a bit; he said, 'You like the other one, it makes you look better.'

She grunted, 'None of it's easy.'

The machine, Geoff said, was a baby as far as the science of isokinetics now went, but it served them well enough. It wasn't fully functional, though – you could work on it, but they'd patched it into a new computer and the software transplanted from the old one hadn't taken, so you couldn't calculate the significance of the work you'd done. When it was up, the computer could compare your damaged leg against your good one – in terms of muscle strength, exten-sion, flexion, torque – and they'd been waiting two weeks for the software people to get on it. Early in the month, her bad knee had caught up to eighty per cent of the good, and by the end of the month now it should have been past ninety per cent, strong enough to kick a ball – but he didn't want her trying until he knew for sure and the wait was frustrating.

In the larger scheme of things, of course, a software glitch hardly signified the collapse of the NHS. On the other hand, if it weren't for a donation from the WRVS, they'd not have had the machine at all.

There were showers, but when she was done she didn't have time to use them; it was past ten already and she had to get to work. She splashed on cold water and deodorant, and drove to the office; it was near the town centre in a twisting warren of one- and two-storey warehouses, a neat little office building with space for a few cars in front off the narrow street, and the Providence Inn and the Green Baize Snooker Club on a cobbled square around the corner.

A few weeks off her thirty-second birthday, she'd been at Rutherford's over fifteen years. Out of school with a few CSEs, the second of eight children, she'd worked a short while packing cucumbers in a greenhouse, she'd been on the dole, she'd thought about the army – then a six-month YTS came up as an invoice typist, and she'd stayed ever since. The company distributed hot-drink vending machines from Scarborough through Humberside to Lincoln; they were a family business thirty years old, turning over about a million, employing twenty, and Gail ran the office.

Her boss, a large, straightforward woman named Mrs Mason, invited me in, said not to mind the poodle under the desk, and that she didn't mind Gail's football either. She'd always played, and as it became more serious with Belles and England over the past few years, they'd come to live with it, to give her the spare van, to let her have the odd piece of her paid time off. Of course it wasn't ideal, Mrs Mason would have preferred not to 'carry the computer', as she put it, for the two months Gail had been recovering from the operation, or for the weeks she went away with the national side – and it did cause a little friction, there were one or two who grumbled. There was a lad in a band who'd been heard to mutter, how come he couldn't get time off for what he did? But Mrs Mason was pretty blunt about that. He didn't play the drums for England, did he?

Besides, time was short, Gail wasn't getting younger; they wanted her to have her last chance. And they were a small firm, they could slot things around her – she described it as an obligation. I said, technically they had no such obligation; she replied, 'It isn't an obligation, it's just what we do. Because she's a very good worker.' All the same, other employers might say they were being generous – and Mrs Mason shrugged. She said, 'They do. But they put the men to shame, don't they? They're like football used to be, before the big money went into it, all the fouls and the temperament you get now. Mind you,' she laughed, 'she ought to watch what she eats.'

In the little office outside, under shelves of files and ledgers, Gail was organising her elevenses. She got coffee from the company machine; she pressed the two sugars button, then added another half-spoonful. She said, unabashed, 'Got to get those 316 calories back.' Then, from the drawers of her desk and her bag on the floor, she laid out a bottle of vitamin C tabs, another of multi-vitamins and minerals, a can of Coke, a catering mini-pack of three bourbon biscuits, a Mars bar, and – they must have some secret striker's ingredient, these – a pack of pickled onion flavour Monster Munch. She smiled and said, 'Don't tell England.'

Den, the warehouseman, said, 'That's just the morning, you should see the afternoon. It piles up that much, all you

can see is her little nose poking out.' But she was, Gail said,
five foot four, eight and a half stone, and it never varied – and
there must be diet companies world-wide who'd love to know
how that's done.

Gail was lucky; when she'd first had the injury she'd gone to
see her consultant privately, the man was keen on sport and
sympathetic, and he'd organised her operation on the NHS
double-quick. In Doncaster, however, Skiller's experience
had been less happy altogether. At the hospital after the
Croydon game, she'd waited with Des for four and a half
hours, and other people were getting seen to ahead of them;
she'd sat there and thought, If I'd told you I'd done it falling
downstairs, would you see me quicker then?

   She was a big woman, five foot eight and eleven stone, and
a handsome one; at work, in the Doncaster branch of
Supercigs, they called her Lineker, and the resemblance was
marked. Twenty-seven now, she'd been a Belle since she was
sixteen; neither her father, an electrician down the pit until
they shut them all, nor her mother had been interested in
football – but growing up in Goldthorpe, from as early as she
could remember she'd always played in the street. When she
was a teenager, she played with five lads in an impromptu
six-a-side league; they all had Spurs kit and they played on
the school field, sometimes Kaz from two doors down would
muck in, and they were as good as the boys, easy – but they
weren't allowed to play with them officially, and she didn't
know women played eleven-a-side anyway.

   Then she was on the bus one day, and she read a story in
the paper over someone's shoulder about Belles going to
Holland to represent England in some tournament. There
was an item about women playing on local TV, too, and they
gave out Linda Whitehead's number at the WFA; Skiller
called, Whitehead sent her contact numbers, she went

training with the Belles, and it was like finding your place in the world, the best thing that ever happened to her. Back then, she remembered, they used to travel to away games squeezed on to wooden benches in the back of Jackie Sherrard's dad's works van, and they'd all try and sit as far off from Kaz as they could, reeling away from the stench of the pickled onion Monster Munch.

Now, a decade on, converted to the pickled onion brand herself, she couldn't imagine playing for any other team. She'd guested for Micky's dad once when he took Leasowe to a tournament in Sardinia, and it wasn't the same; they were all bickering at each other on the pitch, and you never had that at Belles. So to be injured, not to be part of it – it was a perpetual, nagging frustration, life without playing no more than a flat line.

She ruptured her cruciate in the spring of 1991. Dean was doing the sponge then, so he strapped it up and it felt numb, like toothache – but when she took it to the hospital they said there was nothing wrong with it. She went home, that night the knee swelled up bigger than her head, it was bleeding inside, boiling hot, and it hurt like hell. Still they said there was nothing wrong – so after a few weeks, with the pain and swelling gone, she started jogging on it. She couldn't feel anything, so she went to play; the first time she tried to kick a ball, the leg collapsed beneath her. They'd said there was nothing wrong – but when they opened it up they found the cruciate had disintegrated completely, there was nothing left of it but scraps.

By the time she got to see the consultant, she'd lost two months already; it was another six months on the waiting list before he could operate. It was a wretched time to be out; that autumn the national league began, they were playing good teams every week now, not cantering about knocking fifteen past rubbish, and to miss out on that was horrible.

Then, after six months, she was at work and the phone rang, and it was the hospital wanting to know why she wasn't there for the operation. She wasn't there, she said, because she'd had no call or letter from them telling her to be there – and the operation was postponed for another three months.

They did it at Mexborough; when she woke up, the pain was intense. They'd put plaster on from ankle to thigh, it was pressing down on the knee, she couldn't move it at all; when she took it to be cut off in Doncaster two weeks later they laughed at it, said it was a right mess, and it was, it was a disaster. Immobile in the casing, the knee had sealed up inside, clogging with scar tissue. The physios couldn't get it to bend; in the end they had to put her to sleep again, then crunch and wrench it all loose.

Not that she really knew what was happening; if one of the doctors hadn't shown her a diagram, she'd not have known what they'd done to her at all. But as soon as you mentioned sport, especially football, they didn't want to know, did they? They looked at you like it was your own fault; when she'd first taken the injury in and told the woman at reception how she'd got it, the woman had said to her, 'What are you doing playing football? It's a man's game.'

There was a year of rehab; she got back to training in February 1993. Towards the end of that season, a sunny day at Millwall, Paul sent her on for the last ten; they were winning 3– or 4–0 and he told her not to do anything, to keep out of the way, but the feeling as she ran out was unbelievable, her stomach completely turned over. She only had a few touches – but then the whistle went and everyone was shaking her hand as if she'd done something brilliant, and brilliant was exactly how it felt.

Even so, she wasn't right; she could still sense it and it was in her head all the time, the niggling worry, the fear of the tackle. She played through the next season, on and off – but it was only this year that she'd felt her confidence fully return. Four years after the knee went, two years after being more or less mended, just on the Friday night before Croydon she'd been saying to Lorraine, the reserve team manager, how she felt great, how she was back. In the dressing-room before the game, when Paul was telling them they were better than those England players, he'd singled her out, said she'd been their best midfielder these past few games – and he didn't praise people often or loosely, so when he said something like that you knew he meant it, you felt really boosted.

So she went out to play, and towards the end of the game Kerry Davis fell on her leg. She felt it go beneath her, she felt the pain, she heard the crack and she thought, Oh Christ. Here we go again.

Micky looked after her on the bus back north, keeping ice packed tight around the knee. Skiller said if it was gone she wasn't having it rebuilt again, she was too old now, she wasn't going through four more years like that. Finally, at two thirty in the morning, a doctor got round to her and said nothing was torn, it was just the medial ligament had been strained. He told her, 'You look a bit down. Are you disappointed I'm telling you it's not ruptured?'

She said, No, she was relieved – but she was down because after what happened the first time, she couldn't confidently believe him. True, it wasn't swelling like before – but her replacement was a plastic one, like catgut, and if that snapped it mightn't swell like broken tissue would anyhow.

Five days later, she saw a consultant. In the interim the knee had eased, she could walk on it, and she was cautiously hopeful. A nurse put her in a bare little room on a couch, left her notes on a small desk to one side and pulled a curtain across the end of the room. The consultant came in, scanned

the notes for a few seconds, then turned to examine her. He
didn't look at me. Thinking I should at least introduce
myself, I said why I was there, that I was writing a book about
the Doncaster Belles. He said, 'What's that?' Then he looked
at the nine inches of vivid gashed scar on her sunbed-brown
knee and said, 'What was that for?'

I don't know what he'd read in the notes, but he didn't
know she played football, he didn't know she'd had the
cruciate replaced, and his manner didn't suggest he much
wanted to. He worked on the knee, testing it through the four
directions of movement, firing questions in rapid staccato.
How did it happen? Did it swell? Did you carry on playing?
Could you walk? Which side does it hurt? Can you walk on it
now? He was with her a little over five minutes; brusquely he
concluded, 'It doesn't look too bad. You've got a bit of
arthritis in there, there's quite a bit of grinding. But I can't
see you've done any damage, there's no ligaments torn. We'll
put an elastic bandage on it.'

If I hadn't called him back that would have been it, he was
already on his way through the curtain. As he went I said,
'What about her playing?' I meant, of course, when could she
get back in a game, but he didn't take it that way; he understood me to be asking whether she should be playing at all.

He said, 'Candidly, if you play football, you accept the risks.
And she's got a half-buggered knee, it'll not get better through
playing. But that's the trade-off, isn't it?' Then he was gone.

Unconvinced, Skiller went to a physio who knew the
Belles for a second opinion; he told her if she worked on her
quads and hams, she'd be all right to play in a week or two.
Naturally, she hoped he was right – and she said of the way
Belles kept winning, even as players fell injured one after
another, 'We're up there, aren't we? And we want to stay up
there. So you don't give no excuses. You get on with it.'

★

That was on a Monday; the day before, she and Des had sat
out Belles' away game at Wolves. Des had strained her ankle
ligaments, there was a chance she'd be out for the rest of the
season – and although Gill was back, in the first half the
Belles were disjointed, disorganised, incompetent. Wolves
had to win to avoid relegation and they were making a scrap
of it; over Willenhall's smart little Noose Lane ground,
beyond the Watery Lane industrial estate, the sun might have
been shining on the tin barns and warehouses, but on the
pitch only Joanne shone, spraying passes round the field with
casual precision, dancing through tackles with an airy
deftness. The rest of them, they didn't look like they knew
each other's names, and at half-time they barely deserved to
be 1–0 ahead.

Paul was as angry as I'd seen him. 'I said let's start nice and
bright, and what happens? Kick-off, Channy, you're half
a-fuckin' sleep, she runs past you, she could have crossed it
first minute – that sums us up, that. Half a-fuckin' sleep, it's
pathetic, it's like watching under-11s at school. Gill gets the
ball at the back and we all go *gneeeoooww*, all she can see is
backsides disappearing in the distance; nobody comes short,
nobody thinks, we all just run, we run all over the place, and
why? Can't you talk to each other?'

The dressing-room was bright with shafts of sunlight
through opaque high windows; the Belles looked at the floor,
steam rising off their bodies. He told them, 'I could go on for
fifty more minutes, but really – would you look at who you're
playing against? They're all playing in bleedin' training shoes,
they're that chuffin' wide, they're sixteen years old, and
they've had a better half than we have. So you look at your
player and you think, I'm going to give you a fuckin'
nightmare this half. 'Cause player for player they shouldn't
be in the same league as us, and they're making fools of you.
So who's got a bit of pride in here? 'Cause pride, that's all

they've got, these – they work hard, they try hard, and it's all they've got. But I'll tell you what – it might be good enough to beat us, if we don't show a bit of it ourselves.'

Belles won it 5–1; Joanne got two of them, playing as well as she'd played all season, magic dust in her boots, the full jinking repertoire running cruel rings round no-hopers. She came off grinning – and things in her life had been that bad, she said, she'd gone on the sick, the doctor had put her on anti-depressants. But she wasn't taking them, was she?

She'd had a letter calling her to the next England training session; they'd asked her, what was more, to tell them her size so they could get her a blazer. So Joanne didn't need no sunshine pills, she was the happiest woman in Noose Lane; she was, it seemed, going to Sweden after all.

14

You're Only Playing a Name

The Owls were playing Leicester. In jeans, sweatshirt, bomber jacket and Kickers, Joanne came through the crowd filtering into the South Stand at Hillsborough on a warm, bright blue Saturday, smiling, her face as warm as the day, like outside of an England shirt this was the best place you could be. She'd been coming nearly twenty years, it was only ten minutes' walk through the park from her parents' place, and here she was – despite the fact that the Saturday before, the way fans do, she'd sworn she'd never come again.

They'd got beat 7–1 by Forest, Wednesday's worst home defeat in history; for the first time in her life, she'd left before it ended. It was 4–1 when she went, maybe twenty still to play; she heard the other three go in as she walked home. Forest, especially Brian Roy, they'd been that good the Wednesday crowd were applauding them, and they'd been calling for Trevor Francis's head. She agreed, the man was messing up – but she didn't like it 'cause it didn't help, did it? She knew what it was like to be on the wrong end of a hiding; to get the crowd on your case as well, it could only make it worse.

In the aftermath Francis dropped half the team, including Mark Bright; she thought it was ridiculous. But Wednesday were in such a state, hovering like half the Premier League over the relegation trapdoor, that panic was pretty much the order of the day. On her way into the ground she met a bloke who worked with her sister and he asked her, 'Did you bring your boots then? We could use a player or two.' She smiled; whatever the state of it, it was some dream, wasn't it, to play out there. She could have done, once; a few weeks after she moved to Belles, her dad's side played a Cup game here – but she'd made the move anyway. It meant more to be a Belle, didn't it?

We were high in the South Stand; a block of bright sunlight lay across the bottom of the Kop and when they clapped in there, from where we sat the hands all flashing, fluttering, looked like a cloud of butterflies. That was where she normally went, behind the goal; she'd stood in there as a kid with her dad, back when it was a great uncovered bank curving to a point way up behind you – then later she'd had a season ticket with her mum in the North Stand. It was all pens and fencing then, the stands were wood, great poles blocking your sightlines – so it was better now, but she did wish you could still stand. You had mates when you stood; you wouldn't know them from anywhere else, but you'd always meet up in your spot on the Kop, you'd plot your away trips there – whereas now, buying tickets to sit, who knew who you'd end up with?

But it couldn't stop her coming. Hillsborough was her second home, up or down she always came, she got a buzz just watching them run out – and she watched this game rapt, rising from her seat involuntarily as chances came and went, fists clenching ready to acclaim a goal. She was a quiet fan, not a screamer – women screaming bugged her, too often they didn't know what they were screaming about and it only made men think they were right, that women didn't know football. But herself, she knew the team inside out.

Ingesson was a donkey, Bart-Williams was the world's slowest black man, Sinton was a waste of money, Pearce was a good, old-fashioned centre-half, kick anything that moves, Atherton was the most improved player of the season, she

rated Walker and Sheridan, and Waddle was God. He had the
ball now and she was murmuring to herself, *go on, tek him on*,
and he put someone in and the header shaved wide, and she
sighed, 'Brighty'd have scored that one. Still,' she grinned,
gesturing to the press box behind us, 'wake a few of them up
in there.'

It was like Belles playing Wolves, a nothing game in nice
weather; Wednesday won it 1–0. As they fumbled their way to
the points she looked out over the shining pitch and sighed,
'I'd love to play on there.' But when we went in the players'
lounge after, I have a feeling she may have revised that wish
to try herself out against professionals, to train with them
and see how she fared. She looked round the packed room
and grinned, 'Christ. They're all so *big*.'

But what did that matter? She was an England player
again, and all was right with the world. Back when things had
been falling to bits she'd barely been able to train, but she
was running again now, getting out in the countryside from
her parents' place, and she felt fit and good and ready.

On the other hand, the squad Copeland had picked did
mystify her. There were six from Bampton's Croydon, more
than from any other side; Arsenal had five, Liverpool and
Belles three each, Millwall and Wembley one apiece, and the
twentieth was Karen Farley, an ex-Millwall player now with
Hammarby IF in Sweden. And Joanne wondered – very far
from alone in this – how come? Croydon had been beaten by
Arsenal twice, by Liverpool twice, by the Belles, by Wembley
and Ilkeston too. It was a nonsense – and some of the
instructions that came with it were nonsense too.

'Players should travel to meet the team wearing smart
casual dress (and) are also reminded to bring with them their
toiletries.' What did they expect them to do? Turn up in rags
and not wash?

Sheila told her, 'You go there, you live by their rules, you do what they say, you keep your mouth shut. And when the World Cup's over, you tell them to shove it.'

'She plays for England, her' – and the only trouble getting picked, it got people so proud of you it could be downright embarrassing. Joanne would say to her dad, sure, she'd come and watch his lot play – so long, she'd smile, as he didn't go introducing her to all his mates. Dean's mum was the same with Kaz; they'd be out somewhere and she'd virtually be telling strangers on the street.

As for Channy's dad, Channy's progress was simply the brightest thing under the sun. She thought he must have give up hope, the third child coming and her being another girl – but since she'd gone to Belles he was like a new man, he was on the bus for away trips, he'd be on the sideline shouting all game, 'Channy's free, give it to Channy.' And people'd laugh at him, but it was like having new mates, he loved it; he loved it so much he'd got her mum coming too, and her mum didn't even like football.

They spoilt her, specially Sunday mornings; she couldn't have been more comfortable. She'd lie in bed as late as she could get away with and he'd be running her bath, telling her mum to cook lass her breakfast – but preparation, he said, preparation was everything. He'd say he was her coach, he'd take her running; he used to play himself, of course, and he'd go mad if she got an injury, telling her she were soft. When her ankle was bad he'd say, 'I've had more injuries than you'll ever have, I used to sit with foot in beck – so you get it in that bucket.'

And Channy'd say, somewhere between unwilling and bemused, 'But it's cold, Dad.'

They'd go down village for a drink, and everyone knew her – Paul Woodhead's daughter. He'd say, 'You know Arthur, don't you? Arthur used to carry my boots.'

Arthur'd say, 'I did, aye. Reet player, your dad was. We'd have two balls, one for him, one for the rest.'

Channy'd be thinking, Lord, I only came out for a drink – but her dad was at bar saying, 'You know our Channy, don't you? Got an England cap, she has.' And he was that proud, she couldn't mind it – though maybe it was a bit hard on Lisa. He was actually trying to make Lisa join Belles, and neither sister was too sure about that. They lived together, worked together – they had to play together too? Besides, Lisa said Huddersfield were a young team, they were going places. Maybe the manager weren't as good as that Paul sounded to be, he weren't never happy; if they got five he wanted ten, he didn't give out praise like Paul could – and the team had stars in too, Channy didn't like the sound of that. But all the same they were Lisa's team, and she thought she should stop with them.

Wednesday evening after the Wolves game, Huddersfield were playing Bradford, the Woodhead sisters' old club; at Elland Road the same night Leeds were playing Ipswich, and they were both meant to work. But Lisa was desperate to play so Channy said she'd cover for her, she'd work her shop in the East Stand in her place.

The police horses clopped through the crowd outside, milling through air thinly reechy with that special deathburger scent, the slimy pads of ground ear and nostril in a bun that will, surely, survive every effort at gentrification. It was a quiet night, only 28,600 came; in the main shop they pressed a couple deep at the counter, handing over plastic for shirts and souvenirs. Hunter Davies said in *J'Accuse* on C4 that the emblem these days of the Man U fan wasn't the scarf or the rosette but the carrier bag, and Channy agreed, she thought Leeds could go the same way – if they got their act together, anyhow.

In Lisa's shop, an electrician had been messing with the

motor that raised and lowered the metal shutter between counter and concourse; he'd left a plastic box of wires dangling and as kick-off approached, the security man couldn't get the thing to close. Channy watched, frustrated; they were still stuck there, fiddling with the chain and the catches on the motor, when Yeboah scored three minutes into the game. She watched the replay on a monitor on the wall, and sighed. When Yeboah came, everyone said he had the finest bum you'd ever seen; they said they couldn't believe they'd found someone with a bigger bum than hers. 'So,' she smiled, 'we've got a lot in common, really. Apart from he's black. 'Cause his bum's all muscle, and so's mine. I'd love to see him in a pair of Levis, mind.'

Finally we got in the stand; under a wispy evening sky the game was going nowhere particular, all English thud and blunder. We had one of those nine-year-old managers behind us, a piercing little shrieker yelling at the players not to be so soft, to get your tackles in, you plonkers. Channy grinned. 'I'm going to crack him in a minute.'

She wasn't like Joanne, though. She'd had her season ticket those teenage years, but if she didn't get in free with her job now, she wasn't sure she'd often pay to watch any more, especially not when it was cold – she couldn't understand people paying to sit and watch when it was cold. And then, this scrappy jumble we were watching now, 'Some of these wouldn't get in our team, these Ipswich. Some of these Leeds too, tonight.'

Then Rod Wallace skipped through two cumbersome challenges, fed Gary Speed, one touch, 2–0, the goal a diamond in the gloomy murk – and Channy, who said she wasn't bothered, was out of her seat yelling, pointing and cheering. When she sat back down I smiled, eyebrows up – you're telling me you don't care? – and she looked a shade embarrassed. She said, 'Habit, in't it?'

But scoring was the point, the whole point. Ian Wright, she loved him to bits, she had all his videos – he was so arrogant, the way he strutted, the way he celebrated, he made her laugh, the dancing, putting his hand to his ear to hear the cheering. 'Thinks he's God's gift,' she said. 'And he is.'

Out on the pitch, Yeboah stuck two more in. Leeds were rampant and Ipswich doomed, the crowd booming and jubilant as they chanted the giant Ghanaian's name, this ferocious amalgam of muscle and pace; Channy stood to admire him and said approvingly, 'The hit man.'

She said, 'I love scoring. Don't do enough of it, that's the only trouble. I want to play centre-forward, put Kaz left-back for a change, see how she likes it then. When he put Flo up there for Arsenal, ooh, I were sick.' But she said this smiling; I was left to wonder if the reason no one could work her out was that she lived in a permanent condition of irony.

'When you score,' she went on, 'you've got to celebrate, haven't you? I go mad, me, run about, arms wide – I want hugs, don't I? That one I put past Davo against Liverpool, lovely, I knew it were going in, saw the gap, let loose, and I *knew*, you just feel, *Yes, yes, get in*. Twenty yards, brilliant. And if anybody else scores I'll run and congratulate them – might take me ten minutes to get there, mind, by the time I have done I'll be the only one left. And Gill, she'll be back waiting to start with her hands on her hips. But I'll be twenty-one soon – so maybe,' she said, still smiling, 'I'll mature as a player then.'

In the meantime, she'd had her letter from England; she'd not been called again, and was on standby. She was delighted for Joanne; for herself it was a disappointment, even if it wasn't a surprise. But how did all those Croydon players get in? And now, she supposed, if they went for a drink, maybe her dad would only ever be able to say, 'She's got an England cap.' Just the one.

A few minutes before full time, she went back to the shop on the concourse. The security man came to wrestle with the chain on the shutter; a foot and a half up, the shutter jammed. Well, she thought, unless there's any limbo dancers out there, we'll not be selling more Leeds shirts tonight.

The Belles got a letter from the FA too – a letter from the Chief Executive, Graham Kelly. The documentary on the BBC, he wrote, had been regrettable in its content and timing, unacceptable for its language and behaviour, and a disincentive to parents and teachers. Kelly concluded, 'I need not emphasise to you the potential consequences for your club should such behaviour ever be repeated.'

I found it amusing that it had taken fully three months from the film's screening for the FA to get this hectoring twaddle in the post – but for the Belles it was a distinctly ominous missive and Alan Burton, the club's secretary, was incensed. A conservative man, not one to rush to judgement, in this first season of the FA's rule he'd none the less been growing steadily more disappointed and frustrated – but the way it was going now, who wouldn't have done?

It was 9 April, Belles had seven games left, and three of those they still had no idea when or where they were going to play them. The tardiness at Lancaster Gate in making any arrangement at all was getting him so mad that Burton – as I say, a polite and upright man – found himself losing his temper on the phone to the FA's administrator, Sue Barwick, swearing at her so she hung up on him. And he regretted it, that wasn't like him – but if they thought this letter from Kelly, this boggling squib of pettiness, was a more pressing part of running the women's game than getting their actual matches played, what on earth did they expect?

Paul's reaction was more pithy. 'In the fuckin' bin,' he said, angrily pacing the pitch at Belle Vue, 'only fit place for it is straight in the fuckin' bin. 'Cause if Paul Pierrot had gone round any of these other women's clubs he wouldn't have bothered making a film at all, they're all that boring he couldn't have strung five minutes together. But us, we've a passion for the game, a love for the game, we've some character about us, so he saw something here he could film – and they should be thanking us for that, they should be thanking Doncaster Belles for getting women's football on TV. Instead of which they stand up there criticising, when they can't even get their own house in order – it gets right up my back. That letter – spit on it and chuck it in the bin.'

But he was, perhaps, a little tense. Out of the FA Cup, to stay in with a shout of retaining the league the Belles had to beat Wembley today, Arsenal next week, probably win five more games out of five after that, with Des and Skiller now missing as well as Gail and Flo – and every week the mountain to be climbed looked taller and steeper, and the legs that had to climb it were more battered and bruised. He had, he said, never known a season like it.

In the dressing-room Kaz stared white-faced at the peeling ceiling among the ruck of kitbags, the clatter of studs. 'I'm absolutely starving, me. I could eat a cow.'

Paul told her, 'Goal hungry, you.' And he thought, never mind who we lose – as long as there's Kaz, there's hope.

When he spoke to them his voice was fierce, and their concentration absolute. He wanted application, he wanted desire, he wanted noise. 'It's their last game of the season, these, they want to enjoy it, and I don't want them enjoying it. I want them getting hammered.' Kaz laughed, and Gill with her, getting up to take them out. 'I want you *loud*,' he urged, and Gill smashed a ball against the wall by the door, the tatty wood shuddering under the slam of the leather, and they all grinned, made a great, high-pitched *whooo-ooooh*.

Kaz shook her head, smiling. 'She freetens me, her. Send her out on her own, let her deal with 'em.'

When Gill had the England captaincy taken off her in Italy, Kaz, dropped herself, watched her lined up to go out, and she saw the tears in her eyes and she wanted to say to her, Come here, I know, let me hug you. She'd say later of her captain, 'She can be a knobhead sometimes, but so can we all. And never mind that, 'cause she's a Belle. So she's your mate, in't she?'

Gill was making a face in the doorway, putting on a mock look of sizzling ferocity – but she had a smile in her eyes. She said, 'Am I going out alone then? Come on, eh?'

Wembley scored three minutes into the game. It was overcast, cool, there weren't thirty watching, and by the sound of the cheer most of them came from London. Paul's voice echoed round the shabby, empty old league ground, raging, 'Are we going to start now then?'

He paced and snarled, muttering, yelling, rolling eyes to the sky – and I don't know what it was with these teams, but for the fourth time they were laying on a feast. The game was punctuated by huge, ear-battering roars from across the road at the racecourse, a big crowd had gathered there for some jet-car rally, and the engines whined and screamed and boomed, but if they wanted action they'd gone to the wrong place.

Channy's dad looked intense, desperate. He was stood near Paul, but Channy was having a 'mare and Paul wasn't mincing words about it; Channy's dad had to move away, he couldn't bear to hear her getting laid into. Paul was kicking things, bits of take-out rubbish, chip wrappers and burger trays drifting by in the soft wind through the dust. Then, with twenty-four minutes gone, Micky laid a long one through for Kaz on the deck, she streaked on to it, no mistake from eighteen yards, 1–1, and Rob was bawling, leaping about – but Paul wasn't any happier. As the game went on and Belles made more mistakes he turned away from shouting at them and groaned, despairing, 'Might as well talk to me fuckin' self.'

Kelly Smith was causing havoc, beating Jonesy, beating Gill, firing shots wide, or into Debbie's midriff so hard she was near knocking her over – and in Paul's head, it was permutation time. Hang on here now, that's two points dropped. So then we have to beat Liverpool away and Arsenal here, and Croydon here, and Southampton at their place, and Ilkeston twice, and Liverpool have to beat Arsenal for us too . . . the prospect was so narrow now that, for the first time all season, by the dug-out he fell silent. Near enough his last words of the half were, murmured to himself, 'Going to have to be a one-man show again, Wack. That's what it's going to have to be.'

Two minutes into the second half, Wembley's keeper cleared a ball long and high from her hands; it came down close by the sideline in front of the dug-out. Kaz jumped for it, with a Wembley player challenging behind her; they fell together and Kaz went down, her left knee juddering beneath her. She clutched one hand to the knee, the other to her head; on the bench the cruciate brigade were blanching as one, Gail, Skiller and Jackie Sherrard, the three of them all up and running out with Sheila. Gail swore she'd heard something crack; she felt sick to her guts.

Kaz told her, 'You haven't heard owt, 'cause I didn't.' She'd only ever come off injured once before in all her life, concussed when she got a kick in the head at Southampton; every game sooner or later someone clobbered her, and every game she got up and went on. But she knew she'd done something now. It didn't feel right; lying there she bent it, thought, OK, she got up – and normally she'd just set off, but not this time. She found herself stood there thinking, it's going to give way, it felt like jelly – and it felt like there was something there that shouldn't have been, too, like there were marbles clicking around inside it. She looked and saw the fear on the faces of the other three, and then the fear struck her too.

A foul had been called; as Gill lined up to take it Kaz stood testing the knee, terrified, and Sheila knew it was bad. Any other day she'd have gone running up into the area to get on the end of Gill's kick – but she just winced, shook her head, hobbled off and made straight for the dressing-room. Gail ran to the clubhouse looking for ice; Sheila came back out and said, 'She's frightened to death. I think she's going to be sick.' There were eight weeks to go to the World Cup . . .

Meanwhile, here at Belle Vue, of the starting eleven that won the Double last season, only Gill, Micky, Channy and Joanne were left. Add in Ann, Nicky, Vicky Exley, three from the reserves and an eighteen-year-old in goal, with forty-three minutes yet to play against Wembley – it looked desperate. With cruel precision a Wembley supporter shouted, 'Come on, Reds, you're only playing a name.'

Paul sent Kilner on in the middle; Joanne went up front. Kaz got her track suit on and limped back to the bench. Jackie Sherrard urged her to get down the infirmary, now, this minute. Kaz told Sheila something loose inside the knee was obstructing the movement; Sheila thought it might be a cartilage job, that'd be an operation, but not a bad one. Kaz said, 'Shut up. Just shut up.'

On the pitch, Gill and Ann were running a thousand miles, Micky was a model of composure holding it together in front of them, Kilner was crashing into anything that moved, Joanne and Vicky Exley were scrapping for everything. Gail was screaming, 'Well in, keep going,' and Sheila was grinning and stopping her ears.

It was unforgiving, fast and clean. Paul said contentedly, 'They're doing very well, in the circumstances. Channy's been a disgrace, mind.' But then, that they were still in it was remarkable. He said, 'We're struggling in too many areas, aren't we?'

But when you're a Belle, and there's no one else to do it for you, you get up and you do it yourself. One time Jonesy took the ball skidding through two big women, they tried to sandwich her and she was gone, a skinny little slip leaving them behind with a set, single-minded look in her eyes like, *that's mine, get out of my road* . . . and since the Christmas social they'd been going out together on a Friday, these young ones, forging the bond, and now on a Sunday as the injuries racked up and they had to carry the load, they said OK, and they mucked in and carried it. With four minutes left Debbie made a fine scrambling save, got up with it – and were they thinking, let's hang on for the point? Were they heck.

She turfed it up the field as hard as she could, and Paul yelled at her to hang on, get steady, 'cause him, he'd have settled for the point all right – and it looked to me like she spun round on the edge of her area and mouthed at him to fuck off. Later she denied it, said she wasn't that stupid, she had a bit of brain somewhere – it was just, she said, every yellow in sight was screaming for the ball, 'cause if they weren't going to run to the last and try and win it, what were they there for?

So, under the cosh a long while, come the death it was the Belles who were attacking. Gill was pushing up, Jonesy ran thirty yards and nutmegged a defender to feed Vicky, she was brought down, the free kick was headed away for a corner, and another, and then a third, and Wembley's bench were roaring at them to get it out, get it out of there anywhere, anywhere. It came out, Vicky collected it, danced through a tackle, fed Joanne on the edge of the box – and she was clear. She went a few paces, the keeper was coming, she was thinking where to place it, she didn't hear the defender tearing in behind, crunch – it was a good tackle, the chance was gone, and the whistle blew, 1–1.

John Jones said, with a hint of a smile, 'We're getting closer, aren't we?' But he looked like he was thinking, If you couldn't beat them when they had half the team on the bench, when could you?

For Belles, it was still two points gone. In the Executive Lounge, giving Gill her tea, Betty Shepherd told her Everton had beaten Tottenham 4–1 in the FA Cup semi, and Gill groaned, 'No, don't tell me, I've got it video'd. I'm even more depressed now.'

Nicky said she wanted to die, her knee was totally knackered. 'After Arsenal next Sunday that's it, I've got to rest it.'

Paul asked Claire Large, 'Claire, you injured? No? Well, that's one fit then. What about you, Jonesy?'

Shyly, Sarah Jones shrugged. 'Just blisters, me.'

In one corner Joanne and Sheila were laughing together. Joanne said, 'Looks like you and me, Sheil.'

'Right,' Sheila told her, 'I'll do front, you do middle, Gill can have back. We'll tek 'em all on.' Then she sighed. She said, 'Going to be a non-event, Arsenal. Better pray for rain, eh?'

Channy stood apart, looking glum. She said, 'I were bleedin' useless. It's not for want of trying – you try to get involved, but it doesn't come, and you don't know what you can do. I did get a kick early, but that wasn't it, I'm not making excuses. It's just . . . I dunno. I were playing brilliant before I went to Italy. Since I came back from that, it's just gone.'

They didn't stop long, especially the young ones. Gail had taken Kaz to hospital, and they all wanted to get down there and be with her. It would, in the end, be six hours before she got home, and the news she took back with her was that it probably wasn't ligaments. Still, they'd told Skiller that too.

15

Proud of Them

Trying to find out what had happened, Ted Copeland couldn't raise Kaz on the phone; he rang Gill, and Gill didn't tell him where she was. She didn't tell him because Kaz was in Blackpool for Good Friday getting, in her own words, 'drunk as a tree'. All the Belles who could make it away from work were there – lasses only, even Dean weren't allowed – putting up in boarding-houses, hitting the Pleasure Beach. In the evening Kaz looked about her, she knew young Des was the sensible one, so she told her, 'I've hurt me leg, so you look after me, you. You mind me while I'm dancing.'

Nicky Davies couldn't go. She had the Saturday Club to run at Burnley for the game with Derby the next day, and she had no money anyway. The bank that morning told her they wanted their fifteen hundred back, no leniency about it – never mind how her conman ran up the debt, never mind that the the police called them to confirm it, never mind that near a third of it was charges by now, not original debt in the first place. But there's banks for you. She sat in her little flat looking out over the Lancashire hillsides, grey homes running down to Turf Moor five minutes below, the clock on the wall ticking time round the face that was a football field, footballs where the numbers of the hours were, Snoops snuffling about her feet, and she looked bleak, helpless, robbed.

All that, and Arsenal on Easter Sunday, with only four left fit out of last season's starters. Herself, she couldn't walk properly, there was a pronounced lean and stiffness in her movement – but she tried to walk straight when Paul was about, and she meant to play through this game if no other. It beat thinking about the bank, didn't it?

She drove to Turf Moor in her battered Panda; at the ground, the latest good news was that Burnley's mascot Bertie Bee had been in hospital. At half-time they were running an 'It's A Knockout Madhouse', a battle of the mascots, a string of dribbling, ball-stealing contests between Bertie and his assorted winged and furry star guests – Fred the Red from Man U, Forest's Robin Hood Squirrel, Billy Bantam from Bradford, Wednesday's Olly and Ozzy Owl – and while these preposterous padded creatures gathered over hill and dale, their host had gone and got himself a knock. In the office, someone said Nicky might have to take over the role: 'The littlest Bertie Bee ever.'

She said, 'I've been waiting for this moment. All me life.'

Debbie Biggins rang. She'd just started work on the same scheme as Nicky over at Doncaster Rovers, so she'd not make it to Blackpool either – but some of the young ones were staying on for Saturday night and Debbie was, Nicky said, so besotted at being a Belle that she'd drive the width of the country to drink lemonade with them, the night before the biggest game of the season, just to be part of it. So what she wanted to know was, could she stop over at Nicky's when the night was done? What, thought Nicky, and come knocking on my door at two o'clock in the morning? She shook her head; she thought, must be a goalkeeper, that one.

She went to coach the kids in the gym. Later, in the stand during the game, one of the mothers told her there was a little girl who copied everything she did, that at school she even mimicked her voice. Nicky smiled and held her hands up, softly chanting, 'Hero! Hero!' Then she stopped and said sadly, 'What would anyone want to copy me for?'

★

Across the Pennines at Rovers, Debbie wanted to go to Blackpool because, besotted or otherwise, at Belles she'd found a home – a home for which she had, indeed, left her own family home. Born in Keighley, growing up there and in Skipton, her parents split up when she was six; she'd stayed with her mum, she still saw a lot of her dad, but now she was a Belle she wasn't seeing much of either of them. With the new job sorted she could be in Donny all the time, sleeping on her new mates' sofas and floors; she kept bedding in the back of her car just in case, but she'd not had much call for it yet.

The car was two hundred pounds' worth of clapped-out Y-reg Mazda; her dad sold cars and he'd found her this one after the Renault she had before finally died on her. She said she loved cars, loved speed and control (she'd crashed the Renault four times on the way to its demise, so she may have loved the former a little more than the latter) and the state of her transport was one reason she'd moved, with a second being money. A part-time job in a tea-shop couldn't cover two or three trips a week back and forth, eighty miles each way – but then, it was more than just junk cars and no money, because Belles were more than just a team.

She hadn't expected it at all. Like several others, she'd not wanted to go there at first, they had that reputation of being so nose-in-the-air over all they'd achieved – and her first few encounters with them hadn't been happy. From twelve years old she played for Bradford, and before the National Division began, Bradford were in the same league as Belles; the first times she played them they lost 16–0 away, 13–0 at home, a total 'mare. Back then she didn't know who Kaz and Gail were, obviously, but she knew they were in her penalty area all ninety minutes whacking shots in her face. She remembered Psycho too, slinging crosses in all game – and worst of all, she remembered Davo up at the other end. She'd get a second for a breather, look up, and she'd see her leaning against post having a cup of chocolate, or walking some dog up and down behind the net. It were insulting, degrading – though on the other hand (being a keeper, and therefore daft) she'd also enjoyed it. You had something to do in a game like that, didn't you?

In the second season of the National Division, she moved up to Bronte; they got relegated, the next season was no fun either, so when Liverpool came for her at the Reebok in the summer, it looked a good idea. Only trouble was, rumour was swirling that Davo was going there too – and about ten minutes after she signed, the rumour turned out right. She couldn't see herself getting games then, and she didn't like the way they handled it – so, nervously, she went to fill the hole left by Davo at the big-headed Belles.

It was like falling into a whole new family, a whole family of people like you; the way they looked after her made it the best season she'd known yet. Even when it was bad, especially when it was bad, there was always someone gathered round you; when Gill threw that wobbly, laid into her attitude, Kaz came and told her, 'If you've got a bad attitude, you, coming eighty miles to train every Wednesday, there's no hope for the rest of us, is there?' She felt eight feet tall then, but Kaz looked after everyone anyway, and it wasn't just Kaz. When she let in those soft ones against Arsenal at Millmoor, every one of them in the dressing-room had a word for her, and the first one to tell her to never mind, get her head up, was Gill.

It worked in other ways, too – the way Paul always had her busy in training, or, when she got the job at Rovers, the way Rob spoke to the manager Sammy Chung; next thing she knew, she was training with the men. And, she was happy to admit, she needed all the training she could get.

Goalkeeping was the weakest aspect of the women's game; Davo at Liverpool, Higgs at Wembley, Cope at Arsenal, they were the only three who had any real quality and experience about them. Herself, she could stop a shot – but otherwise she was bog-eyed, she couldn't judge a ball in the air and even if she could she couldn't catch it, so she hated crosses and corners, and then kicking it, God . . . she had lettuce feet all right. Which, taken altogether, she smiled, was a bit of a problem in a keeper, wasn't it? And she knew she could work at it, she knew she could get stronger – but she needed every boost that came her way.

She got two. She'd been with England before, a year ago, and now Copeland had called her up again; he'd been all right with her the last time, encouraging her to do the best she could, and she was dead excited. Then, here in Donny, she'd trained at Rovers – and, with these hairy great first-team professional forwards crashing in on her, she caught three crosses in a row. She couldn't believe it – why can't I do that on a Sunday? – but she'd thought to herself that she had nothing to lose and a great deal to prove and it'd be nice to surprise them, all five foot seven of her, eight and a half stone, eighteen years old, clattering up in the air in the face of these monsters saying, Hey. That's *mine*.

So all she had to do now were do the same with those Arsenal – which was easy said, but she couldn't see Belles winning it, 'cause she couldn't see them scoring without Kaz. What Kaz didn't score, she created – and without her the prospect was grim, it was really, really difficult. She said, 'I'll see a lot of the ball so it won't be boring. But the more I see it, the more chance I've got of making a mistake, so I'm deadly nervous. And I don't want to feel like I did after Rotherham.'

The *Doncaster Free Press* sponsored the Arsenal game; sports editor Tony Harrison gave Belles a write-up every week, but what more he could do to get the town behind them he simply didn't know. They'd brought more silverware to Donny over the past dozen years than everyone else put together – but they were only women, weren't they?

Harrison was from Scarborough, a place, he said, 'Where people retire to die, then when they get there they forget what they went for.' Sport there ticked over, more or less; in Donny, by contrast, it really mattered, and everywhere he went people came up asking questions. What could we do about Dons? What could we do about Rovers? But though plenty knew they existed, very few ever asked about Belles.

Even without being women, they had so much competition. Set aside one of the best racecourses in the country, set aside ten golf clubs, set aside hockey teams for both sexes, set aside the cricket club in the Yorkshire League drawing hundreds on a sunny Sunday – you had the Panthers going well in basketball's Bud National Division, with the Dome to play their games in, you had the Rovers and the Dons, and you had 120 boys' teams, aged eleven to sixteen, in one of the biggest boys' leagues in the country. In a rich area, it'd have been some tide to swim against; in a depressed one, with the mines gone and the railway engineering battered, where economic success was taken to be a decrease in the rate of redundancies, and where the Dons and the Rovers themselves were both near belly-up broke as a result, what chance did the Belles have?

Harrison said, 'I don't think people appreciate what they do for this town. Before I came here I'd only ever heard of one women's team, and that was them. But short of grabbing people by the neck, what can you do?'

'I do have a sense of humour,' said Paul. 'It's just Sundays make me lose it.'

At Stainforth, there was a hangover from Blackpool; with half an hour 'til kick-off, half an hour before their last chance of keeping Arsenal's hands off the title, there was no sign of Kilner or Jonesy, and the Belles had no subs. In the dressing-room Joanne pointed at Vicky Exley and told her, grinning, 'Better not be pissed, you. Anybody sober put their hands up.'

PC Lisseman raised her hand. 'I'm a square, me.'

'I were definitely a circle,' said Joanne. 'But I'm reformed now.' And they were laughing; the state they were in, what else could they do? Sheila was strapping Des up – any other day, she'd not have played – and to make eleven, Paul had squeezed signing one last player from the reserves before the deadline, a thin, strikingly attractive blonde named Joanne Sharp. Lorraine, the reserve team manager, said she was fit and fast, a good wide player – but she was a nervous and surprised player, too, chewing gum, hands working in her lap. When Paul asked her to play she told him, 'I'm not that good. I'm not as good as first team.' But whether she was or she wasn't, in at the deep end she went.

Joanne Broadhurst didn't even know who Sharp was; as she went out to warm up, she asked Lorraine about her. So Lorraine told her, and she told her as well that Sharp was frightened to death. Joanne grinned. 'Just tell her to kick fuck out of ten.'

Back in the dressing-room Kaz stood among them urging, encouraging. To Des she said, 'Tek it steady, eh? Just tek it steady.'

Des shrugged. 'I won't come off. Got no subs, have we?'

Claire Large wasn't having that. 'You go off if you have to, you. Don't want a knackered ankle the rest of your life.'

Amid the ruck of them preparing Kaz looked about her, then said quietly to Gail, 'I don't know what to do with meself.'

'Just sit yourself down.'

'No, I can't. I'll stand back here. Where's that new Joanne?'

'On loo.'

'Ah bless.'

She went outside and found Arsenal's big defender, Gill Wylie, on her way to warm up. Wylie gave her a hug and Kaz asked her, 'You going to miss me then?'

In her broad Ulster Wylie told her, 'I'm gutted for you, mucker, so I am.'

As the players warmed up and the crowd gathered, Jonesy and Kilner arrived – and Jackie Sherrard gave the pair of them a royal flaying for their lack of responsibility, for throwing the load on to others that were injured. Helplessly the teenagers pleaded that they'd got lost coming back; Sherrard fiercely asked them, 'How can you get lost on the M62?' She was, of course, fearful about her knee, scared silly she'd have to sit on bench herself – but at least, with fifteen minutes to go, the Belles did have thirteen.

Channy shook her head and said, 'I don't know. Young people today.'

'I don't have to stress how important this game is. They've put us out of the FA Cup, they've beat us three times this season – so I want us to get at them, I want them to know they've been in a decent game. I'm not looking to lose it, I'm not looking to see how many goals they score – I'm looking to win, 'cause we owe them. And if you think back, they didn't deserve that Cup match, they were going nowhere in that. So we can do it today, if you just lift yourselves one more time – 'cause regardless of what happens the rest of the season, we desperately want to beat these. They're not my favourite people, and I hope the same goes for you.'

He put Claire Large in the middle, told her to mark Marieanne. When he used the word 'mark' he looked at her like he meant it, with a quiet little smile. You *mark* her . . . then he ran down the Arsenal defence; they couldn't play, they couldn't run, one of them had an arse that wide she looked like Red Rum from behind. Which was all very well, and they laughed – but he was only putting one up front, nineteen-year-old Vicky Exley on her own, with Joanne floating behind her. He told Vicky she had a hard game today, handling those three central at the back on her own, and Ann grinned at her across the room. She said, 'See you then, Vicky.'

He told them, 'We don't let ourselves down. There's a lot of people coming to watch and we don't let them down either, we show a bit of passion. We're not expected to win, there's only us in here expect that we can – but this league's not finished, not by any means. So we have grazed knees and grazed thighs, we have bloodied noses, we have the lot out there today; we need everybody to put it in, we need everybody prepared to be hurt. Let's have some winners, eh?'

Amid the noise rising up from them Gill said, 'Let's do it for Kaz.' In the corridor the ref blew his whistle to call them; as they filed out Kaz by the door embraced each one, ruffling hair, clenching her fist.

When they were gone Paul looked at the empty little room, their Sunday home littered with plastic cups thrown aside, tape and water bottles and tubes of cream strewn on the benches and the floor, the mess of bags and clothes and programmes. He sighed, and braced himself; he said 'It could have been worse. Not much, like. But it could have been worse.'

On a cool grey day, egged on by the *Free Press*, over 200 came. Paul filed through them to join Kaz and Gail and Sheila on the bench; red and white tape, strung taut off rusty metal posts, bent neatly round the back of it to make a little bay for them by the sidelines. Laura sat with Sheila, quiet in the noise of the crowd, clutching her blue school lunchbox with the pickled onion Monster Munch packed religiously inside.

Paul sat with his wife and daughter and said, hoarse, 'I'm going to be quiet today. I'm losing me voice.'

Gail told him, 'I'll do it, Paul.'

Kaz grinned. 'You haven't heard me yet. Ten years, mind, ten years, and I never missed a game.' She was almost writhing on the worn old bench, twisting, leaning forward. 'Christ,' she said suddenly, 'I've bit me tongue and we haven't even started.'

Wylie brought Joanne down in the second minute; Joanne leapt straight up, anger on her face, her leg raised showing the ref how she was kicked. Every time she went forward, Wylie was on her like a wolf – but Kaz was roaring for her and Vicky to get after the big Ulsterwoman anyhow, 'She's had it, her, she can't run.'

Gail said quietly, 'I could get round her.'

Quick as a whip, smiling, Sheila asked her, 'So? I've seen you go round her before, and you put it over.'

'Not now,' Gail shot back. 'I've got a new knee, remember?'

Kaz yelled, 'Hey, Vicky. That number nine shirt goes a lot faster when I'm in it. Get running, you.' Then a long punt arced up into Belles' area, Debbie Biggins came for it and Kaz visibly shuddered as Sammy Britton charged in – but Debbie climbed, and she caught it. Kaz breathed out again; she said, 'Bless. I thought she were going to flap, throw it in over her shoulder.'

She didn't – and you could see Belles wanting this all over the pitch. Vicky turned Wylie, shot, and Cope palmed it wide; Channy's corner dropped under the crossbar, and again Cope scrambled it out. When it came away, Ann rose to win it, left her player on the deck and ran forward, grinning, tongue out, *I enjoyed that*. Paul, Gail and Kaz were clapping, shouting, 'Well played, yellows, keep going, get on her, well in,' leaping to their feet as Joanne ran wide, cut in, forced another corner.

Kaz said, 'Ooh, I feel sick.' Then she was up again roaring, 'Anywhere near, Channy, have a shot.'

Gail jostled her, 'Get off bench, you. You're worse than me.'

Sheila rolled her eyes at the twitching, screaming pair of them. 'God help us if we score, eh?'

It was a passionate effort against the odds, a surging, collective urgency of will expressed in beautiful, lung-busting football – and with twenty-two minutes gone Belles did score, 1–0, Claire Large rising in the perfect image of Kaz to head home Channy's corner, and Kaz was all but dancing on the sideline on her gammy knee, thumbs up, her grin so wide her face was fit to split, and the noise from the ragged crowd rose on the gusty wind, and for a minute there that little pocket of South Yorkshire in the shadow of the abandoned cooling towers could forget all but the Belles.

'Excellent,' Paul said quietly. 'We've got the wind, mind.'

Still Belles attacked. On the far side Wylie brought Vicky down, you could feel the thump as she landed, feel the air punched out as dust kicked up off hard ground beneath the bodies. When Sheila'd seen to her she went on playing, but she was running with her right arm held stiff across her chest now, wincing. She'd banged the top of her shoulder; Paul roared at her to move it, keep it moving. Passing the bench as he shouted Joanne smiled and told him, 'She'd move it if she had a pint in her hand.'

Vicky stayed on, half-time came near, the Belles were still on top – then Channy took out their eleven a yard inside the area, heads fell in hands, and as the crowd hung silent round the tape, Marieanne Spacey stepped up to take the penalty. She struck it hard and chest-high to the right, Debbie dived the right way – and even in the moment of her saving it, even as the ball squirted back off one upraised hand, the crowd was erupting into shrieks and bawls of glee and panic all at once, the ball still bobbling about the area, everyone crashing in to get it, and Kaz was screaming, 'Welly the chuffer!' 'til somehow it came out. Then all the bench looked at each other and thought, Hey, this could be our day, this – as Debbie made another outstanding save, two hands darting high above her diving body to parry a fierce drive from Spacey.

Back upfield, Arsenal's Joe Churchman lunged desperately to keep the ball in play. In front of Belles' bench it nudged over the line, the linesman raised his flag, and Churchman, seething mad with frustration, simply wasn't having it. The linesman was just yards away as she yelled at him, 'It was never over the fuckin' line, you bastard.'

Isn't that a red card? But she didn't get one, and although the anger in Arsenal was obvious now, the tackles smashing in, above all Wylie on Broadhurst, again and again, the ref just let it carry on. Paul cried out at him, 'You haven't got a clue what's going on here, have you? Not a clue.'

In the centre circle Micky and Wylie squared up against each other, pushing shoulders with flat hands; as the ref blew for half-time Joanne ran straight to him, pointing at Wylie. 'It's her every time. She's going to break someone's leg, her.'

Wylie and Joanne came off shoulder to shoulder, snarling at each other. Gail sneered, 'You like to give it, don't you? You like to give it.'

Kaz went to her mates as they came off past the bench. 'Hey,' she said, 'behave yourselves, you two.'

Jackie told Kaz, 'You'll have to fight for your place back, you.'

Kaz wasn't losing sleep over that. She looked about the dressing-room as they swilled down water and sugary tea, panting, dirt-streaked, red-faced, and she told them, 'You better chuffin' win, I'm telling you. Hey Deb, though – Rudolf Nureyev. Anyone got a pie for Deb?'

Paul asked them, 'Shall we calm it down? We don't have to
go diving all over the place, do we? We don't have to show
how hard we are. Stay on your feet, let them get niggly, let
them do the rushing about, you steady it down – and if it's
near touchline at the back, kick it three fields away. Now
them – five's got a bad leg, she can't run, and have you seen
the six? She makes Joanne look quick. So get it behind them,
hit it hard against the wind, and I don't care if it don't look
pretty 'cause I want to beat these, that's what I want. Another
thing – stay off ref's back. They're all whining at him, let 'em,
and you fanny him about, eh? Well done ref, go on, thank you
ref, get him on our side – 'cause they're in his earhole every
two minutes, and it'll get so he'll not want to give 'em owt.
But look, excellent, I can't fault one of you, your attitude is a
hundred per cent brilliant – so just imagine what it'll be like
in here after ninety if we beat 'em, eh?'

The room was a seething racket of voices, an echoey box
of noise. As they went out Kaz hugged each player, telling
one after another, 'Goal from you, please. Goal from you,
please.'

Deb threw a suicide ball to Channy, she slid in, heard her
hand crack beneath her. After Sheila'd been with her she got
up, carried on, and it was throbbing; she went to take a throw
in and bungled it. She saw Gill looking at her so she said, 'I
can't tek 'em.'

'Why did you tek it then?'

Channy shrugged. 'I didn't know I couldn't tek 'em 'til I
took it.'

So now there were two running round with their arms
pulsing, held tight before their chests – and Spacey by then
had shaved the bar from thirty yards, Wylie'd missed by a foot
from the edge of the area, the whole period was being played
in Belles' half. Debbie made another fine, full stretch save,

tipping a looper from eight yards over the bar – but her goal kicks into the wind were going no distance at all, the Arsenal pressure was constant, Kaz was moaning and gibbering on the bench, and with twenty-five minutes to play Spacey equalised, curling a free kick round the wall from twenty-five.

Des limped off, unable to run any further; Kilner went on, but it made no difference. There were seventeen minutes left when Arsenal got their second; a corner dropped on Ann's knee at the near post and before she'd moved Wylie'd smashed right through it and her both, bundling it in, a rough, brave defender's goal to make it 2–1 Arsenal. Kaz groaned, 'Reet spacker arse goal off her knee, too. Makes you sick.' But it doesn't matter how they go in, does it?

They were fading now, scrambling to keep out a third. Arsenal were all power and muscle, Belles were all played out – and it was a miracle, after all, that with so many injured they'd stayed in the race so long. But after eight stuttering, on-off months of cracked bones and wrenched joints, the race was over now. When it finished, Paul told them he was proud of them; they could hold their heads up high.

Over drinks in the pub down the road, Tony Harrison made Debbie's day; he gave her Belles' Player of the Match award. She had, he said, 'Made some saves there any bloke would have been proud of.' The award was an engraved carriage clock; Debbie blushed, said she were reet embarrassed.

Kaz smiled at her, told her she couldn't be late for training now, then went into mock-worship mode. 'Touch me, Deb, touch me.'

Deb revealed that she had, the night before, had only one and a half hours' sleep, wrapped shivering in blankets with two of the reserves in the back of her Mazda 'on the coldest road in Blackpool.' Had to be a keeper, that one.

Seeing Nicky limping through the tables Paul told her,

'Hey, well done Nick.' With index and thumb held close together he said, 'You were that far off Player of the Match.' Nicky asked who got it then, so he told her it was Debbie.

'What,' Nicky smiled, 'for bleedin' standing there?'

'It were a clock,' Paul said. 'She dropped it.'

Nicky laughed, and there were Belles laughing all round the pub – but apart from Spacey and Cope chatting with Kaz and Gail, I didn't see many Arsenal there. In an amateur game it was the Belles, win or lose, who came out of it with a smile on their faces. Already they were organising a night out, to put the loss of the title behind them, and as Kaz and Gail limped away to Gail's van in the car-park, Gail said sternly, 'Never mind, eh? When we're back fit, us, we'll have 'em next year.'

Channy and Vicky, meanwhile, went to hospital; five Belles in casualty in three weeks. It turned out Vicky wasn't too bad, she'd sprained ligaments in her shoulder, but Channy'd broken a bone in the back of her hand. She wasn't too pleased; it took that long to sort it out that by the time they were done, it was too late to drive to Wakefield for a drink.

The Dolphin in Wakefield – 'shaky Waky' – was a pub with black blinds closed over the windows, a dolphin logo leaping in white across each blind; over the floor, blue dolphins swam in a red carpet. There were red lights in the ceiling round the bar, and a tube of lights flashing red-blue-orange along the bar top; around the room, and above the tiny stage by a dance floor not much bigger, u/v lights made anything white shine purple. At eight o'clock there were maybe twenty in, and the place was a quiet bubble of voices over the insistent pulse of the Euro-energy. 'Can You Feel The Love Tonight?', 'Don't Let Me Be Misunderstood', 'All I Want Is You.'

Posters listed coming cabaret attractions – Sugar Kane, Lizzy Drip, Tarts On Tour, the Dame Edna Experience.

Strippers to look forward to included Grease Monkey, Young Blood, and Vigilante. Lights flashed round the stage and the mirrors behind it as the place steadily filled, and the music from the DJ's desk in the corner grew ever louder, fluted voices floating over the thump and hiss of the drum machines. In the noise and the press some of the Belles began arriving, and among them Clare Utley and Sarah Jones looked entirely different.

Both from South Elmsall where Micky worked, between Donny and Wakefield, they'd gone home from the game to Jonesy's house; she'd spent half an hour diffusing her hair, then another half hour doing the same for Des. To play, they wore it pinned tightly back; now, it was flung loose in torrents of curls, moussed, lacquered, waxed and shining. 'If it's not right,' Sarah smiled, 'I'll not go out, will I?' She wore Kickers, jeans, a check shirt, a little necklace with three beads of wood on a black string; she looked stunning.

She had a boyfriend, a seventeen-year-old lad who went to college with her; he didn't watch her play Sundays, he was playing rugby league then himself. They saw each other Saturdays; Fridays she was out with the Belles. She said, 'He doesn't know where we go, he'd kill me.' Then she realised that was just a reflex statement, and amended it; she said, 'I don't suppose he'd be bothered. He's just never asked.'

Beside her in the crush Kilner pointed at Jackie Sherrard and said, 'Christ, when she had that go at us, eh? Scared me more than me mum does.'

Jackie smiled and said, 'But they respect me for it, don't they? The thing is, they've all got so much potential,' she went on pointedly, 'and I wish they'd realise it. I did apologise though, didn't I?'

'Yeah,' said Kilner, 'she did.'

'And so did they.'

Kilner grimaced. 'Took me ages to say it, mind.'

Jonesy laughed at her. ''Cause you're a stubborn bitch, that's why. God, it were a nightmare, though. Took wrong turn on motorway, I thought we were going to Scotland.'

Helen Garnett said, 'We had an atlas under seat, only none of us could find it. I kept saying to meself, Where's fuckin' Pennines then?'

The DJ came on, asking over the dark, packed pub if the crowd would 'Move all arses, glasses and handbags off the stage, please.' Tonight's act, Lee Star, bustled on to the little platform, a substantial vision sporting a tonnage of lipstick and lashes under a mountain of stacked and curly gold wig, expertly teetering on high heels, wearing stockings and a tight halter dress with a black-and-white pattern out of a Jackson Pollock painting. With her lips working overtime she mimed her way through a frantically expressive version of 'Lullaby Of Broadway', then launched into some deliriously breath-less patter. 'You, you haven't got a matching set, have you? Blonde hair, black pubes, I'll bet. Why? You know if you bang your thumb with a hammer it goes black? Well,' she said, rubbing her crotch, 'it's had that much fuckin' hammer . . . but look, I were stopped by a policeman on the way here. Where you going, he asks. Dolphin, I say. Are you a pouf then, he asks, I thought you were a woman. Well, I'll be blown. You will not, I say, I'm fuckin' late as it is. But will you put your hands together now, ladies and gentlemen, for our erotic dancer Donna . . .'

Donna and Lee worked through their routines, Lee coming back as Tina Turner in a black basque copiously decorated with plastic fruit, and then as Shirley Bassey. Among other things, Donna did a Janet Jackson job in a black fishnet bodystocking (and not much else) to Tom Jones's version of 'Kiss'. Lee's patter grew steadily more lewd and hilarious; he went back to the doctor to protest he wasn't satisfied with his new parts, so the doctor had a look, and told him he had a problem with his aviaries. 'Aviaries? Don't you mean ovaries?'

'Well I don't know, Lee. There's been a cockatoo up here.'

The crowd cheered him/her off, the music started again and the place, now heaving, danced its way to closing time. Helen Garnett, never mind her bad ankle, never mind that she'd broken her collar bone jumping fences on a BMX, danced on the stage; some revved-up young lad next to her, manically jigging in a Leeds away strip – Yeboah 21 – took off the shirt and posed for himself in the mirrors in a sweaty reverie. Helen gave him a shove and told him, 'Hey, pillock. Audience is that way.'

The DJ called closing time, and Lorraine looked at her watch. 'Looks like Dean's not let Kaz out then.'

Jackie smiled. 'She'll have a reet face on.'

Sarah Jones said of nights out with the Belles, 'I could go out with me mates from school, or from college. That'd be all right, I like 'em. But these . . . we've so much in common, haven't we?'

But what exactly was it, I asked, this thing they had in common? She shrugged; in her big brown eyes a polite hint lingered that the question was imbecilic. She said, 'Football, of course.'

16

An Absolute Shambles

They'd kept on winning, beaten Liverpool, beaten Croydon – but it had to hit the buffers eventually, and now it had done Paul and Sheila were almost glad. They'd come closer, in the circumstances, than they'd ever hoped for – but they'd been going into games racked with tension, watching the side scrape results on hard work and big hearts with their own hearts in their mouths, wondering who'd be hurt next, and once they lost Kaz, it became too much to ask. Paul said, 'As long as we had Kaz, we had hope. When Kaz went, hope went.'

So they talked about getting runners-up, about how Belles never finished third in their lives – but the pressure was off, the worst pressure they'd known, wondering every week if they'd have eleven they could put out, and for the trophies to be gone now was as much a relief as a sadness. On Sunday they'd looked at the team against Arsenal, only four left from last season's starters – and to make as much of a game of it as they had, there was pride enough in that. They didn't dwell on the loss; they looked instead to the positive, to the ones who'd come through, above all to Ann Lisseman. She'd been in doubt of her place when the season began, but for both of them now she was the club's player of the year; they'd told her her chance had come, and the way she'd taken it delighted them.

But then, so many had done well. 'It's indicative of the season,' said Paul, 'that we've had to take a young girl, Des, only just sixteen, tape up her ankle, she's not fit – in the warm-up she were limping, she couldn't sprint – but it didn't stop her marking, did it? It didn't stop her tackling, crunching in there, grit through the pain. She's another that's been magnificent, and she'll be the better for it next year.'

Next year was where their minds had turned to – especially as what remained of this year now stumbled into shambolic disarray. They had five games left, and only two of those had definite dates; it was mid-April, and any hope of finishing as they'd been meant to on 23 April was out of the window. The men's clubs by whose grace and favour they had pitches to play on would soon be done for the season, pulling up the posts, re-seeding the goalmouths; the FA couldn't make that any different, and the next few weeks would be the same messy scramble for venues they'd put up with in years past. But then, it was only women's football, wasn't it?

Women's football – an amateur sport that, for Paul and Sheila Edmunds, was above all else about enjoyment, about enjoying the game, and the people you played it with. So maybe, they hoped, with the title gone and the pressure off, the players could make the most of what was left, and never mind Arsenal. Because, Paul conceded, he wasn't too good a loser – but who'd want to play for that lot anyhow, when they'd won the league and they couldn't even smile about it after? He asked, 'Did you hear them singing? No. They don't know any songs, them. And I tell you, if they'd have lost as many injured as we have, and we were at full strength, would they have had a go like we did?' He smiled. 'I don't think so.'

They spent the rest of the Easter holiday with Laura, going swimming, going to the Disney Shop at Meadowhall, going to Twycross Zoo – and Paul looked forward to next year, never mind the football, because Sunday then could belong to his daughter instead of Belles. And he was glad he'd packed it in; he was becoming, he knew, too critical. However hard they worked, however well they played, he'd find himself looking at the young ones and thinking, they're not the old Belles, these. So it was time for someone fresh who didn't have that freight of bias, who'd take the new players at face value; it would do them all good to have that change.

A few days later, about midnight in the Palace on the North Bridge in Donny, the Belles were out dancing, and Tracy Kilner was slumped well gone in a dark corner. Kilner was one who'd had more flak from Paul for her attitude than anyone, and who'd made more surly faces at his back than anyone else in response – but seeing me talking with my notebook to some of the others she sat up, pointed at me and apropos of nothing she said, 'Write this in your book. I don't want Paul to leave. I love him to death. Best manager in the world. I'm going to cry when he leaves.'

'They know who you are, so they kick you. Well, Gill Wylie's never kicked me – I went up to her after, I said, Fancy getting in all that trouble without me there to look after you. And I don't mind, me, it's what you get for playing there – but I've never had owt like this.'

Kaz talked about how Belles had fetched tears to her eyes, the way they played against Arsenal, but there'd be more tears aplenty if she didn't make the World Cup. Ten days after she'd fallen, she went to hospital with Dean, and she was desperately nervous; the night before she'd chewed every nail to the flesh, and in her sleep she'd dreamed about it.

They were saying it was cartilage; when she'd first gone in they'd done X-rays and put a massive great strapping round her leg, layer upon layer padded thick with cotton wool. Gail laughed her head off when she saw it; Kaz was terrified what her mum would think. It was so fat, this thing, she couldn't get her trackie bottoms on. Gail had been waiting six hours by then; she stayed a little longer yet, making Kaz drive round and round the car park to be sure she was safe before she'd let her go home.

Kaz went back to the fracture clinic the next day and saw a consultant who'd seen Jackie and Skiller, a Mr Fagg. He said, 'So you're *the* Karen Walker,' and she were reet embarrassed – but he was very encouraging. He thought it might not even be a cartilage job, that she'd just generally jarred it; it was too swollen to be sure, but he gave her anti-inflammatories and said they'd have it sorted in good time. Since then, the swelling was all but gone; she still couldn't run, but she could get up and down stairs, and she was eagerly hopeful. She kept reassuring herself, saying how much better it was this morning, even compared to yesterday – but she was dreading what Fagg might say now.

So if it turned out it was bad enough that she'd miss the World Cup? She said, 'Just now, I'm more disappointed about missing Arsenal. I don't like to miss any game, me, I don't want to miss Southampton next Sunday – stood watching, I can't bear it. So it's not just World Cup, it's everything. Not training, it's awful; I've got all this energy and I don't know what to do with it. If I had a cruciate and I couldn't train for that long, God, I'd go off me head.'

We drove into Donny and waited at the infirmary for Mr Fagg. When he came into the bare little consulting room and the curtain was pulled he smiled and asked her, 'You fit to play yet?'

She said, 'You tell me,' rigid with tension.

He worked the knee, asked a string of questions, then told her there was nothing to suggest any serious problem. She was to ease herself back gently into training, to be guided by how it felt – and all the while she sat there just beaming, just glowing with relief and delight. He said, 'So, you'll be fit for the . . . Olympics, is it?'

He seemed a nice man, asking after Jackie and Skiller, and Kaz let the slip pass. She headed off to the pharmacy to get her prescription – and if her knee had allowed it, she'd have been bouncing off the ceilings. On the way out, the receptionist recognised her and said, 'So you'll not be scoring any goals for a few weeks then?'

Kaz looked at her, grinning enormously. She said, 'I don't know about that.'

Back home, Dean said quietly in the kitchen, 'Whatever she says, it's not about Arsenal or Southampton. She plays down World Cup, but if she missed it . . . football means an awful lot to Karen Walker. So there's a big smile on my face – and my only trouble is to stop her playing next weekend.'

In the next room, Kaz was laughing on the phone with Gail. 'What, there were nowt wrong with me and I were just attention-seeking? I'm going to kick your face in if you're not careful, you.'

Gail's call had come not five minutes after we'd got back through the door. But then, said Dean, the number of people who'd gone to see her in accident and emergency, the number who'd called – it was just the way Belles were.

That evening Mark Bright went training with them. When he called Paul to ask if he could come Paul thought, Christ, this'll be embarrassing, there'll only be five there. But he got a dozen (and, he said grimly, a dozen more crocked and watching) so he put Mark in goal, figuring that'd raise a laugh all round. Mark said later, with a wry smile, they were flying in at all angles; Kaz, meanwhile, pranced about behind goal telling them to go on, have a crack, this keeper won't stop owt. When he learned about her injury he arranged for the Wednesday physio to see her, and again the diagnosis was positive. While she was at Hillsborough, David Hirst told her to get herself signed on with them for Saturday, so she told him, 'Aye, you could use someone, eh?'

She was that cheered up you could have plugged her in and lit all Goldthorpe by her – and so too, training with England at Bisham Abbey, was Joanne. Copeland had them doing ball work, it was the kind of training she enjoyed; she wrote in her diary, 'I really concentrated and listened and did everything he said. Is this really me? But we had a meeting and it all sounds so exciting for the World Cup, I really want to go. It means more to me than anything.'

The last day, Thursday, they had a free morning, then a game in the afternoon, Copeland's first eleven against what Joanne called 'the splinter arse team', the lot off the bench. Why they couldn't play in the morning and get off home she didn't know – it was an arrangement that also irked Alan Burton in Yorkshire, who could have scheduled one of Belles' last fixtures that evening, if he'd had his England players back – but so long as she was playing, Joanne wasn't fussed. The way she felt, she'd have played in the middle of the night.

She was a splinter arse; the game ended 2–2, and she went off feeling she'd had a good one. She felt like Kaz did when she'd left Mr Fagg, jubilant – she was going to Sweden after all – and Kaz was happy about her being there too, by no means just for Joanne's sake.

A striker wants service – and, said Kaz, no one served you better than Joanne. Some of those Copeland picked, they were ball-greedy gits, she'd go a whole game barely getting a touch. But Joanne, 'She's that unselfish, she knows what she's there for, and her vision, her passing ability – you know if she's got it, you'll get it.' So to have her out now, she thought, would have passed all understanding.

But who understood Copeland anyway? He made Kaz feel like he didn't want her; when she was with England there were times she felt the worst player in the world, and that wasn't her at all. So even if the knee was all right, she fretted about missing the session, anxious about it threatening her place; it bothered her that she'd not been with them, not seen her mates Clare Taylor and Burkey from Liverpool, not had the chance to mess about with them. Besides, she said wistfully, that Holiday Inn, 'You get some reet snap there.'

When the Belles' bus left Donny for Hampshire at eight the next Sunday morning, Gill Coultard looked as happy as she'd been all season; there was a buzz and a bubble about them altogether, a real sense that what was left now was there to be enjoyed. Even Channy, with her hand in plaster, was smiling about it. She couldn't drive, couldn't brush her teeth, couldn't put her socks on or button her jeans; she said to Kaz, 'I only did it so I could sit next to you on bench.'

Gail asked her, 'Did you cry?'

'No. I were reet brave.'

The bus stopped to collect Nicky Davies at Woodall services; she hobbled down the aisle and Kaz asked her, 'How's your knee, Nicky?'

'Don't ask.'

Channy said, 'How's your knee, Nicky?'

She'd said she'd stop after Arsenal – but the Welsh management had assured her of her place in their squad for next season and with that concern allayed, and with so many others injured, she wasn't stopping after all. When I asked her if common sense didn't dictate that she rested it, she said, 'I ain't got none of that.'

Down the aisle in front of us, Kaz and Gill and Gail were mucking about, thwacking each other with cushions and water bottles and deflated balls. Gail warned Kaz that her and Gill, 'We're two size fours here, that makes eight. So watch it, you.'

Kaz told Gill, 'I've never seen you this giddy all season. Can't you go back to being boring?'

Evidently the England session had been successful. As the empty plastic bottles flew about the back of the coach, as they read the sports pages in the tabloids, they spoke about names and numbers on England shirts. Gill told Kaz, 'Walker nine, you.'

'More like Walker twenty-one,' she sighed, 'knowing him.'

Sheila told her, 'He'll only have you on bench once, the noise you make.'

Kaz said, with a sad little smile, 'I don't shout with them. I only shout with our lot.'

Debbie Biggins had enjoyed it, though. She'd had a hotel bed for two nights, that beat the back of the car – and, she said, 'I got me travel expenses. So I can afford to eat now.'

What followed was surreal in every sense. After a season of scrappy little grounds, of crumbling terraces and tatty tin-roofed stands in industrial estates and mining villages, in run-down 'burbs and out-of-the-way back streets, Southampton had got a pitch at the Sir John Moore Barracks of the Army Training Regiment outside Winchester. It was genteel, squeaky-clean, rurally idyllic; the sun blazed down on hazy fields and woodland, birds sang in the trees, the pitch was manicured, there were no benches or dug-outs, no tapes or barriers round the sidelines, just plush grassy banks, and to one side a smart new mess bar, with drinks at alarmingly cheap military prices. Des Shepherd, Belles' steward and programme seller when they played at home, who came with his wife Betty to every away game, a genial bod seventy years old, looked about him and muttered, 'Didn't have owt like this when I were in forces.'

Gail lay on the grass and sighed. 'Why is it always red hot where these live, and freezing cold where we do?' Walking past her, Kaz rolled up her trackie bottoms, wanting sun on her legs. Des said she looked like Stanley Matthews in his baggies, and Gail demurred. 'He were better looking, him.' Kaz kicked her and she yelped, 'Whoh. I were dreaming then, you. I were in sunny Spain.'

Paul watched them larking about, going through the motions in the warm-up, and everything about it worried him; it was like a picnic, not a premier league game, and he could see idleness creeping in all round. Even Sheila succumbed, sending someone to the bar for a spritzer. 'Don't get injured,' she told them, 'I'm supping wine. I'm not running on today.'

In the dressing-room Joanne stood against the wall, arms spread out as if for execution, making rat-a-tat noises. 'That's what you get if you lose,' she told them, 'shot at dawn.' In the bathroom there was a vaulting box; she said, 'You lose, you've got to get in that box and dig your way out. And if I go down injured, sound the bugle, eh?'

Outside, Kaz, Channy and Gail knocked a ball about amid the dandelions and the daisies; you couldn't keep Kaz still, she had to be at it, keeping the ball up on forehead and knee. Watching her Paul sighed, 'She's like a videofit of the perfect centre-forward. Quick, strong, brave, hard-working, scores goals. There's people you wouldn't cross road for, and there's others you'd go to the ends of the earth for. There's not enough of the second lot, and she's one of them.'

To make up for losing her he put Micky at sweeper, sending Gill back in the middle to go forward with Joanne and look for goals. He knew it'd make it harder, he knew if Gill was at the back she'd stop anything, they'd be more secure – but those were the roles they preferred, he wanted them to enjoy it, and Gill was all but leaping up the walls with pleasure at the change. Besides, Southampton were rubbish, doomed to relegation. Just so long, he told them, as you don't think all you've got to do is pull your shirts on and you'll win it, just so long as you work, we'll be right.

Southampton won 2–1; it was an absolute shambles. The referee was lamentable, but there was nothing new in that and it wasn't any excuse; Southampton just wanted it more, they kicked and pushed and pulled to get it, and Belles let them have it, let this lot of lard-butts and giraffes take three points. This fixture the season before, Belles had scored ten, they'd played like Brazil; this time, they didn't seem to bother barely playing at all.

As the frustration mounted it got naggy. Nicky Davies, clattered once too often on her bad knee, swung out at a woman ten feet taller than her, a ridiculous sight, this bustling little shorthouse pummelling fists into a midriff about level with her head; the pair of them got booked, and deserved it.

Worse, and more bizarre altogether, there was a ruck off the field. The day before, I'd been at Barnsley–Middlesbrough with Kaz and Dean, and before that there'd been bits and pieces going off all over, bottles flying, windows put in, runs and skirmishes round the bus station, moron drunks squaring up and swinging in scattered little packs, seething mad coppers lobbing louts into vans, 'Fucking shut up and get in there, you,' police dogs biting holes in people's trousers, other police on horses swinging truncheons on people's heads, 'You piece of shit,' thwack, take that – and that's men's football, right? You didn't ever think it went away, did you? But people scrapping at a women's game, that was truly weird.

It started with some local lad in a leather jacket slagging Belles in particular, and the North in general, all game. After an hour of this Bill Potter, one of the Belles' fans, rose to the bait and swore at this guy. So then some other local, a woman, went berserk, said something about people swearing in front of her baby, and attacked Betty Shepherd – attacked a woman sixty-eight years old. Northern scum, she called her – that were nice.

Seeing this from the far side of the pitch Des, seventy himself, wanted to protect his wife – so he ran right across the field through the game, and got mucked in himself. He could joke about it after – he said, 'At least I didn't get booked.' But at the time, it was bad enough watching the garbage on the pitch without having to look up and see people reeling about on the grass bank as well, fists and handbags flailing, that feckless, squirming, messy look a little set-to has about it as arms go round bodies, people trying to get after each other as others try to pull them away, the useless, insect-like milling of limbs in the air . . . it was deeply, deeply depressing.

Sheila said the woman who went after Betty was mental, that she'd tried to calm her down but she wouldn't be calmed, she kept saying, 'Scum, scum' – she said it were a good job her bucket were empty, or she'd have ended tipping it on this crazy person's head. And Belles and Southampton, they'd always had a good relationship; Southampton were left embarrassed, not knowing those who'd started it. One of them told Sheila, 'We never had fans like that before. We never had any fans before anyway.'

Sheila led Betty away, a normally placid old woman now shocked and shaken, her eyes swollen red with tears, and she was so much concerned to look after her that it was a while before the result sank in. The Belles had been beaten by Southampton? How in the name of God did that ever happen? It was, she said – as did Paul, and Gail, and everyone else – the worst Belles performance they'd ever seen.

Kaz said grimly, 'I'll show 'em how next week.'

17

New Belles

During the strike a decade back, when Skiller was sixteen, her first job was in a supermarket on Goldthorpe High Street. South Yorkshire, she said, felt like a place under occupation then, these thousands of police all come in from outside, and there was never any question which side you were on. She remembered when it went off down the High Street, police shoving miners ahead of them with their riot shields, and it started getting ugly – so they let men in shop, their brothers and their fathers, and they locked out police and stood shrugging. You're not having these, these are *ours* . . .

They'd take them their snap at dinner time on picket line; in Skiller's house, forty-odd quid she made at shop were near all that came in for a fair while. They'd get food parcels from abroad, dried peas in boxes, dented tins with foreign writing on; Skiller'd look at it and think, reet hamper, this, I'm not eating none of that. Her dad had a van, it were too tall to get in garage, so when tax ran out and he'd to get it off road, he knocked garage down. When it were over and they went back to work, first thing he did were tax van; they'd look back and think, he's lost his garage to keep his van. But after that, she remembered, he gave her so much, when she'd been sixteen and helped to keep them.

It had been, of course, the season the miners lost everything. Now, as spring came to Goldthorpe, and another season stumbled to an end while the sun emerged to cook up a veil of haze over the rape fields, they blew up one of the last pieces of the colliery, a tall bunker that used to be the first thing you'd see as you came to the town. Skiller's dad said the house shook when the charges went off, and now it lay on its side in a pile of rubble. When Skiller was a kid, they'd climb about on the bunker's conveyor belts; without it, she said, the skyline was empty.

In South Elmsall, up the top of the road beyond the warren of brick semis where Clare Utley lived with her family, Frickley Colliery was gone too. Where once hundreds of men went down into the earth, there was nowt left now – just a bare, dusty waste of flat concrete foundations strewn with dirt and broken brick, surrounded by a crescent of slagheaps. Earthmovers stood on the high tops of the heaps against the empty horizon, tidying up the village's history – but you can't clear the history out of people's lives. In the Utleys' front room among the family photographs they had three plates on the wall; one a memento for mum's fortieth birthday, another from Tenerife, and the third from the Yorkshire NUM, commemorating 'Frickley/South Elmsall Colliery, 1903–1993'. Clare's dad worked there eighteen years; he'd not worked for eighteen months since it closed.

When I said I might want to write about South Elmsall she said, 'It'll not be a very long chapter, will it.' It was a statement, not a question.

South Elmsall, said Jonesy, was 'a scrubber hole'.

At seven-thirty or eight on a Friday night the girls there go out to play, painted and bare-legged in miniskirts so mini they're more like belts than skirts. Jonesy said she used to wear that uniform, going out with people she knew from school; sometimes (not entirely a Belle yet) on a Saturday she still might go out like that, if they didn't have an early start on the bus for an away game next day. But things were changing; since before Christmas the new Belles had started going out on a Friday night, and Kaz or Micky or Gail would come, and Lorraine or Jackie, or all of them, and she'd be in a group then that meant so much more, knowing what they'd be doing come Sunday. With the Belles, though, she didn't go bare-legged in a black mini; they would, she said, tek mess summat rotten if she did. She'd be in jeans, Kickers, check shirt instead – and the number of times she'd turned up and she were wearing same as Kaz, it were embarrassing. But Kaz smiled fondly; she said of Jonesy, 'She's me little sister, her.'

Jonesy's dad was one of the lucky ones, still in work with BOC; they lived in a tidy little semi in South Kirkby, a short way down the road from where Des lived. Sat in the front room with *The Bill* on while Jonesy got ready to go out, her mum said football was the biggest thing in her girl's life, and she conceded that some people thought it strange; if a girl played up to sixteen, maybe, when she was still at school, nobody bothered about that. But to carry on after, when she might be out looking for men, some thought that wasn't right. Her mum herself, at first she'd not been bothered about the game, it was only her dad pushing their little girl on. But when she saw what it did for her, saw her writing in her diary that football was her life, she thought, Well, I better take an interest, hadn't I?

Sometimes she feared for her. She feared for her in her first year at college when the timetable kept her late in Wakefield, so if she wanted to go training she'd not come home, she'd have to take train straight through to Donny and not get back while gone nine, or even ten; she used to worry herself sick over that. Then she feared for her when she saw her play, our Sarah so petite, these grown women so powerful – 'cause you'd see them playing as kids, and you'd not think of them going higher. But she'd achieved it, hadn't she?

Her dad said, 'She's come on leaps and bounds since she went there. At school, every single report, it was always, "Sarah must learn to believe in herself." And through football she has.' He said, 'It's the best thing that ever happened to her, going to Belles.'

Clare Utley came out of Minsthorpe High in her white school shirt and her striped school tie, the road jamming round us with teenagers and cars. I looked about them and thought of the survey just out at that time, suggesting that a third of the country's fifteen and sixteen year olds had smoked dope already, and when I mentioned it she wasn't surprised, she saw it all about her. Jonesy'd said if she caught her little sister doing owt like that, she'd kick her head in; now Des said she'd known one lad at school, he'd been as good as her, he could have made it – and there he was wasting his life away.

But she was a serious girl, Des. When people said she could play for England one day she'd look at Kaz and think, OK – I have to run every day, get on weights, make that all the aim in me life? Fair enough, I could do that. In their sitting-room, she had trophies already gathering on a cabinet beside those won by her brother Craig. There was Junior Belles Players' Player of the Year '91–'92, Under-16 Player of the Year '92–'93, Reserves' Player of the Year '93–'94. The last two were the manager's pick, the first was the team's vote; in the first year, before she'd been suspended and broke her leg, Jonesy had been the manager's pick, and the two of them had grown up together through Belles. Des said of Jonesy, 'I can talk to her, she's more than a friend. I'd class her more as a sister.'

Des was five foot four, a well-built blonde with a strawberry-and-cream complexion; they'd called her Des for a couple of years now, after Des Walker, but in truth she was a more classical stopper than that, a stand-up-in-your-face Terry Butcher type. Aside from Walker, she said, she liked Neil Ruddock – that says it well enough. She'd played with her dad and Craig since she was five or six; from eight while eleven, she'd been on a lads' side in village. Then, when she was watching her uncle play for Carcroft, a Belle saw her kicking it about at half-time, asked her to come along, and she'd been there ever since.

Last summer in pre-season they had her play at the Reebok; she thought they were just giving her a run-out. But in September, an hour before kick-off against Millwall, Paul told her she were playing. The next sixty minutes she must have been on toilet twelve times, she were that shocked – and when it came, the game were faster than she could ever have believed. But in other ways, it was easier than reserves. Everybody wanted the ball, there was always a get-out and those around her, Flo, Ann, Micky, Gill, they'd talked to her, they'd eased her in.

No one at school thought it strange, what she did; in Des's generation, a girl playing football wasn't a freak any more. They all asked on a Monday how Belles had gone; when they picked teams, when they had sport at dinner time, she always got picked first. For her GCSE in PE she'd coached lads her age and she'd been nervous at first, wondering if they'd listen to her; after ten minutes, they were all doing what she said. But for all that, she didn't mean to stop at school. It were boring, she had no money, and it were no good Jonesy trying to tell her to stay on; she wanted out and, she said, she'd take owt to get out. She had her GCSEs coming up in a few weeks, she hoped for five or six passes, and she had her first job application in already, at a factory packing sewing machines for £100 a week. But all she wanted were football, and money so she could go out with the people she played with.

They'd not gone out, the reserves; the first team played harder off the pitch as well as on it, and they were a lot more organised about the way they did both. I asked if she felt different in herself, being with them, and she said, 'You do when Kaz is there. She lightens it all up. When I had to look after her . . . she don't sit down, wanders all over place, you lose her. She's off her head, her, wild. But it's like . . . they're not mates, they're more, they're family. You look at other teams – they're not sat together like we are.'

They called her their babby; when she curled her hair the first time they called her Madonna, and when she went swimming at Blackpool in her bra and shorts they called her Pamela, as in Anderson out of *Baywatch*. I asked if she felt older than sixteen and she said, 'I feel more responsible, maybe.' Then she smiled and said, 'I have to be older than sixteen, don't I? Otherwise I don't get in.'

Her mum knew what she got up to; her dad thought she went bowling. But she seemed old enough to me. She said, 'You're playing likes of Spacey, top level, it's reet good – but you don't think about it when you're playing. And it is harder against Arsenal than anyone else, Sammy Britton'll give you some elbow – but it's part of game, in't it? If you can't tek it, you shouldn't play.'

Jonesy worked fourteen hours a week at G.T. Smith, a super-market opposite Micky's bank on South Elmsall High Street; she did a couple of evenings after college and a full day Saturday, and she got forty quid for it. Near closing at eight on a Friday evening the place was deserted; scraps of paper and crumpled scratchcards blew about in the car-park. Inside, Jonesy stacked shelves with tea and coffee, her workmate sticking price tags with a hand gun on each box and jar; no laser-scan geewhizzery here. Jonesy said to her workmate, 'Say eh oop, Pete.'

'Eh oop, Pete.'

'She says eh oop to anyone, her.' She paused and shook her hair out, annoyed with it; she'd done it ready for going out before coming to the shop, but the curls had fallen raggy while she worked, and she'd have to do it again. She looked about her and said, 'Bet you'd like this job, eh?'

At her house I talked with her parents, while she went to tip her head upside down and get the diffuser at it again. Her dad talked about how he'd played, and run a pub team, and how she'd always come along since she were this high; he told how the first time she'd gone away on bus with her team track suit on, they'd stopped at Watford Gap and there were kids there saying, Ey, look, there's Donny Belles, and she were one of them. She'd come home and joked how she'd have to practise her autograph; he was so proud of her, you could have cooked toast on the glow.

Upstairs in her cramped little bedroom the walls, the wardrobe, the cupboard door, every spare inch was covered with pictures of Lee Sharpe. She said simply, 'I adore him.' Her mum would ask her, Why couldn't she bring someone like that home? And she'd think, 'Cause I don't often meet people who make thousands of pounds a week.

When we got in the car to fetch Des she asked gently, 'Did me mum and dad talk for England then?'

She was wearing light tan jeans; so, it turned out, when we got to the Coach and Horses in Donny town centre, was Kaz. Kaz smiled across her sweet Woody, 'Ee. Me little sister.'

It was Gail's thirty-second; she and Kaz sat like mother figures, quiet (relatively) against the back wall of the pub, the table around them spilling over with young Belles. Another girl I didn't know was sat next to Gail, staring across her in silence at Kaz; it turned out she was a fan, she'd seen Kaz and gone all soft, *you're Karen Walker, you*, and she'd been dumbly gawping ever since. It had happened in Blackpool too, someone asking for her autograph in the pub, and it made Kaz edgy, it were embarrassing, she wanted to curl up under table and die – especially when all the others started chanting, We're not worthy, We're not worthy, taking piss for next half hour. It were Friday – couldn't she just have a drink?

It was gone nine; the pub was packed, with a tiny little dance floor to one side of the bar thronged and jumping. At a table near ours a bunch of heavy metal types looked drugged silly, ashen-faced and nodding over their beer. One had unquestionably the worst haircut I've ever seen, a scrawny, limp, dangling mop of half-hearted and indescribably greasy curls two feet long. 'Rene Higuita', said Gail.

Kaz grinned. 'What's he doing in Donny then?'

'Let's get out of here, eh?'

It happened again as we were leaving, some bunch of lads, Rovers fans, recognising Kaz. 'Ee, you're star striker,' one of them blurted – but Kaz wasn't having it and she ducked by, trying to wear a polite smile and get away. She gestured behind her as she went, told him these others were Belles too – and, unwisely overkeen, this lad tried to start a conversation about the relative merits of Doncaster's male and female football teams, all the old stuff about how, in the end, men were better.

Belles swerved away after Kaz and the lad found himself with Helen Garnett in his face. She told him, 'I can piss faster than your lot can go down wing.'

Taken aback he said, 'Best season we've had in a while, come on.'

She raised her hands and cried, 'And John the Baptist has scored!' – then left him baffled and affronted in her wake. It wouldn't be sensible to get shirty with her, though – she's a southpaw.

I'd asked Kaz if they didn't get messed with sometimes, a bunch of women all out together, and she said of course they did. But anyone who did try it on, they didn't last long, not the way Belles could tek mess.

Asked the same question, Jonesy grinned and said, 'What,

you mean chatted up? Well, I do. Dunno about some of these others, mind.'

They went to the Palace on the North Bridge, a regular haunt because the music was better there, and you didn't get louts trying to pick you up or knock you over. (You might get knocked over by Kaz on her way to the bar, mind.) It was a smartly converted pub by the bus company's social club with a polished pine bar, the decor black and deep green, the walls hung with pictures of male models and monitors running videos; the management plainly meant it to stay smart, with little printed notices dotted about requesting you to use the ashtrays, not the carpet – not that any Belles smoked, excepting Flo back in Stoke with her Silk Cut.

Over the noise from the dance floor beyond the bar, Des said she missed Flo; she might be mental off pitch but she were serious for ninety minutes on it, and there weren't anyone quicker in all league. And Flo'd looked after her; if the player she were marking were giving her a 'mare, Flo'd swap for her, give her the easier one. But then, they all looked after you, didn't they?

The DJ was playing soul; on a black platform along one end of the stage, by a silver painting on the back wall of a muscled figure holding a flashing globe like a discus thrower, Kaz and Gail danced, oblivious in the music among the women in their short skirts, mosaic carousels of light flashing across the bodies.

Watching them before she went to dance herself, with other Belles all about her, patterns shifting within the group as they moved around, all talking to each other, Jonesy said of being among them, 'Everybody lets you have your say, everybody's ready to hear you. Even Kaz – everybody looks up to her, whatever she says people tek it in, and she could tek all glory to herself if she wanted. But she don't, she listens to you. At school, the main person were just that – but not here. And I used to do athletics, I used to run, I'm fast – but athletics or football, it's no contest. Football, you don't have one or two friends, do you? You have a whole team of them.'

She danced, went out, ate two double cheeseburgers, came back and danced some more; they danced until the Palace turned them out after two. I'd bailed out by then; the energy they had, I was entirely outpaced.

They told me later that seven or eight ended stopping at Jackie's house, talking through the small hours. Jackie said she wanted to walk her dog; Kaz lay on her back in the garden, looking at the stars, and told her she weren't walking no dog at three o'clock in morning. Jackie promised them a park, but Helen wasn't impressed when it turned out it was just a field, no swings, no slides, no roundabouts. 'Eh,' Kaz told her, 'a field's a park in Donny in't it?' She said, 'You tek what you get round here.'

Jonesy got up at seven and went to work at G.T. Smith – and after, she said, she'd not be going out in South Elmsall in any miniskirt. Like a good Belle she'd take it quiet on the Saturday night, ready to play Ilkeston away the next day.

While Jonesy worked, at eleven on the Saturday morning on the public pitches at the Straight Mile by the racecourse, twenty-five girls, twelve years old and up, got ready to train with Mick Meehan and Gary Wood, two cheerful souls unsung in the background of all the work Belles did. Bill Potter was there too, formerly a Liverpool scout for ten years, who'd fallen in love with Belles from the moment he first saw them four years ago, and who now put himself about bringing promising youngsters to the club. If people were injured he'd go to hospital, if the young ones like Des or Jonesy needed lifts he was there – but for the kids, what really made their Saturdays was Kaz.

She came streaking along the lane between the pitches and

the racetrack in her Escort, the car stacked to the brim with Friday night's survivors; one by one Jackie, Kilner, Helen, Des and Vicky Exley spilt out on to the grass, laughing and wincing in the sun. Jackie said, 'Poorly head, me.'

'Not me,' Kaz said firmly. 'I get plenty of practice, I do.' All in a rush she was stripping down, hastening to kick a ball, get amongst it – so was she playing tomorrow? 'Chuffin' right. I ain't watching no more, I can't handle it.'

The others watched her with the youngsters; slowly the bug spread among them, heavy heads or no. The back of Kaz's car was always littered with playing kit; jumble sale style they rummaged amongst it, until they'd assembled themselves some more or less ill-fitting, makeshift approximations of training outfits, and then they all went and joined in too. Bill Potter had to trot round the sideline to Des; she was still heavily limping, and he wanted to make sure she kept out of it. Desperate to do something, anything, she went in goal; throwing herself along the ground to stop a shot, she stood up unsteadily, and wailed. I thought, oh Christ, now what . . .

'Me jeans,' she cried, 'I've grass-stained me jeans. Me mum'll kill me.'

Among the impromptu volunteers, Jackie Sherrard was both the keenest, and the most nervous. Since her rebuilt knee had failed and been rebuilt again, for some weeks now, as the injuries rolled in, Paul had been joshing her, nudging her to get on and have a game. She was, he said, one of the best players, one of the purest footballers Belles ever had – and tomorrow, while the Belles were at Ilkeston, she was going to try a full ninety with the reserves against Huddersfield.

They worked with the kids on ball control, did shooting practice, then played two small-sided games, twelve to fourteen-year-olds in one, fourteen and older in the other.

Kaz hustled about among them, urging them on, praising them up. 'Who wants it then? Who's on our team?'

Helen went in too heavy in a tackle; from the goal Des called out, 'Steady, Helen, they're only kids.' Sixteen years old, she realised what she'd said, and smiled. 'Says me.'

'Boxing Helena,' Kaz grinned. 'Hulkomania.' Then Kilner got the ball and went surging up goalbound. 'Wide load,' Kaz screamed, 'wide load,' and there were that many laughing, it was all they could do to keep on playing.

Kaz said later she'd look at the young ones dancing, or she'd watch them playing, and she'd see them smiling, and for a minute then she'd get choked up. She'd think, They're Belles now, these.

18

England B

Training with the young ones that Saturday morning, Kaz wore a blue woolly hat with the three lions of England on it; it was embroidered in red, 'The home of football'. But when she looked at those words she snorted bitterly, 'Is it chuff.'

Copeland had dropped Joanne from the England squad. The letter went to her old place in Stoke, so she didn't see it; still on the sick, she was spending a lot of time in London, and she heard the news from a Croydon player instead. She was devastated; she was also mystified and angry. She'd thought he was giving her a chance – but what sort of chance was two days' training? She said, 'It's a bollocks, in't it? I go there, I do every session – unlike some others – and he drops me? What for? What have I done? And people say I don't deserve it – but it's not what you deserve with them lot, is it?'

The squad had six Croydon players in it, Debbie Bampton's team still winning more places than any other club. Of those six Kerry Davis, who'd transferred there from Liverpool, had roomed with Joanne at the training session – and she told her, with her spending time in London now, she should go training with Croydon. Bampton, she said, would put in a word for her then.

Joanne said fiercely, 'I wouldn't play for Croydon if they were the last team in the world.'

Paul thought it stank – but he had other problems racking up, and the biggest was Gill Coultard. After the débâcle in

Southampton, he needed to get the Belles back on the rails – but while they played at Ilkeston, Arsenal would be facing Liverpool in the FA Cup Final at Tranmere, and now Gill called to say Sky had asked her to be a commentator for that game. Paul said, 'I can't catch my fuckin' breath, me. She's captain of the club, we haven't got eleven who can walk – how can she even consider going there?'

In the event she didn't go to Tranmere, Bampton did – but, told by her manager that he needed her, she didn't go to Ilkeston either. She had, she said, a kidney infection – but as Sheila put it, 'When I were captain, I were there when I were dying.' And they had Kaz turning out on her rickety knee, they had Joanne turning out in the teeth of her disappointment; it was a good job, Sheila said, the young ones had those to look up to, because the captain wasn't much of an example.

It was a nightmare; with Claire Large down with flu, and Channy and Des still injured, Belles only had eleven. So Skiller got on the bus thinking she'd come to watch, there was no way her knee was right yet – and Paul told her she was playing. It crossed her mind she could go in goal – she wasn't a bad keeper, she'd joked after the knee went how Biggins better watch out for her place – but he said he wanted her up front with Kaz. She said she couldn't run; he told her, fine, 'Just walk about then. Joanne gives it to your feet, you lay it off for Kaz, and we'll be right.'

But he wasn't, in fact, even faintly confident. Ilkeston might have been only one spot above Wolves and Southampton in the relegation places, but on their day they were markedly stronger than either of those; they were strong enough that along with Arsenal, Liverpool, Wembley and the Belles, they'd recorded a win over the Croydon side now acerbically referred to by Paul as England B. And he thought, given the state his lot were in, Ilkeston might well be strong enough to get another win today – and then his last weeks with the Belles would be spiralling towards abject and unprecedented disintegration.

Ilkeston Town FC of the Beazer Homes League had a neat little ground, but the pitch was a sandpit. Joanne poked a toe in it and said, 'Are we playing in our flip-flops then?'

Behind us on Sky in the clubhouse, Liverpool went 1–0 over Arsenal, Karen Burke scoring with a strike so strong and true that if it had been *Match Of The Day*, they'd have been filing it for Goal of the Month. But Belles couldn't think about that.

Paul told them, 'First and foremost, we put out of our minds the fact that we'd like to be somewhere else today, or that maybe we deserve to be somewhere else. We're not, so forget it. And we also put out of our minds the fact that we've got absent friends – or not so friendly, maybe – 'cause we concentrate on the people that are here. In the face of adversity, when things are right down there, when things are looking bleak, people have to rally round – and I want to go back and say, Hey, we won anyway. *We didn't fuckin' need you.* That's what I want to say and that's swearing, and I don't care, 'cause I don't want to go back and hear her saying,' and here he put on a poorly, whining little voice, ' "Oh, you got beat, did you?" I want to go back and say, We had people playing on bad legs and bad knees and suchlike, and you couldn't even get off your arse and play for us. But we had people there who wanted to play for this club, people who knew what was the most important thing, and those people went and won us the game.

'Now, we've a bit of a patched-up team – certainly no selection problems today. Debbie one, Ann two, Jonesy three, Joanne B four, Joanne S five, Micky six, Vicky seven, Nicky eight . . .'

He smiled and shook his head as they laughed at him stumbling over the names, MickyVickyNicky . . .

'Kaz nine, Kilner ten, Skiller eleven. Debs in goal, Micky sweeps – and Joanne Sharp, you're central defence with Ann. I know you've never played there before but never mind, it's the easiest position on pitch, it even makes Ann look a good player.'

More laughter, and a great sympathetic chorus, Aaaah, don't be cruel.

'I'm only joking, Ann, you've had a reet season, you keep going.'

Beside him, Kaz stuck her booted foot in Sheila's bucket. Never mind the knee, her bad toe was red hot just from warming up. 'I've never been this injured in me life, me.'

'Scabby camel,' Sheila told her, 'that water was for people's faces.'

Paul said, 'We've let ourselves down last week, let's not have another one like that. And we've got the ability to do it, so let's do it together. All of us together.'

Ilkeston scored in the first minute; after that, they were nowhere. Stung, every Belle on the field responded with a raging brilliance, dredging up reserves of heart and imagination where they ought by rights to have had nothing left at all.

Their first goal, after thirteen minutes, was an absolute treat. Nicky, Kilner and Joanne Sharp were fannying about playing football in the right back slot, so Ann said, I'm not having that, got in there and turfed it upfield for Joanne. She brought it down, knowing where it was going as she controlled it, and laid it off quick and wide to Vicky Exley. Vicky streaked up the wing, crossed, Kaz arrived far post, no mistake, simple, pure, deadly.

Rocked, Ilkeston were climbing all over people, kicking and pushing and yelling, but it didn't help. Six more minutes, and Micky sent one over the top for Kaz to beat offside, one touch, keeper chipped, Belles ahead. A despairing Ilkeston voice roared, 'Hey, everybody's running away. Let's get stuck in, eh?'

They did, but Belles disdained it. With Joanne at the fulcrum, winning it when it was theirs, parading deft touches across the width of the park when it was hers, surging through clouds of dust and sand kicked up from the lumpen challenges, she was inspirational – and, inspired, Kilner laid in a lovely ball for Kaz to get her third on the half-hour. In the dug-out Gail smiled, richly satisfied. 'That's it, Kaz. We'll have three this half, three next.'

Sheila said, 'That's the difference, in't it? Just put her on pitch, and that's the difference.' They'd been beat twice without her – so back she came and scored three.

At half-time Jonesy limped wincing into the dressing-room, eased off her boot, and plastered Vaseline on a seeping pad of red-raw blisters; Sheila cleaned Joanne Sharp's bleeding knee. Kaz sat quietly smiling with Joanne Broadhurst in the corner, well content, and Joanne grinned at her, 'That ref, eh? They're knocking us all over the shop, and he tells me to pull my socks up. What a knob. Am I too scruffy for him?'

'Brilliant,' Paul told them, 'brilliant, I'm well pleased for you. 'Cause I tell you what, these are a much better team than them last week. But they've had it, haven't they? They're shouting and complaining at each other – when they were 1–0 up they were all, Oh, look at this, we're going to beat Belles here. Thought they'd done it. 1–1, 2–1, 3–1, they don't want to know now, do they? So let them argue. Us, we stay together, we help each other, we keep doing what we're doing.'

Smiling, laughing, they carried on where they'd left off. Skiller got the fourth with her head; she said afterwards, 'Well, I couldn't kick it, could I?' So she ambled about, lasting all the ninety 'cause she had to, taking the ball, holding it up, moving it on, while the eighteen- and nineteen-year-olds hared up and down all around her, all lifted and loving it because Kaz Walker was back.

And it had, said Paul, been difficult for the young ones. In an ideal season he'd have given them twenty minutes here, twenty there at the end of easy games they were winning – he'd not have made them do all this. And these last twenty now, they were the longest twenty in Jonesy's life, she was thinking, blisters, blisters, she could hardly walk – but they were winning, weren't they?

Kaz got the fifth from a free kick; Joanne put her through for the sixth. Joanne had gone down injured not long earlier, banged in the head, and she'd not been able to open one eye. Sheila told her to put her shades on, relax the muscle; Joanne told her bollocks to that, she weren't sitting on no football pitch wearing shades, she had her credibility to think about. Then she got up and carried on, like they all did, and the Belles beat Ilkeston 6–1.

When I got home, I called Gill. She was terrible, she said, couldn't barely get out of bed – so I asked if she'd heard the result. 'Yeah,' she sighed, '3–2.' I did a double-take before I realised she was talking about the score by which Arsenal had beaten Liverpool on Sky – but what her own team had done without her, it didn't sound like she wanted to know about that.

April became May; the Cup Final had been and gone, Belles had three games still to play, and the messy scramble to get to the end of the season continued. Rovers said they couldn't have Belle Vue any more – but Ilkeston were pushing to play the return game straight away the next Thursday, so the FA pressed Rovers to let Belles have their ground after all. Rovers agreed – then Ilkeston said they couldn't get a team up the motorway on a Thursday evening anyhow.

Alan Burton wondered why the FA couldn't have got on to Rovers earlier in the season, then some of this mightn't have arisen in the first place. But he didn't see any point getting shirty over it; he only hoped they'd come to understand that the women didn't have pitches of their own, and would learn to be more flexible in future about allowing them to fix their games and venues when they could. He said, 'They like to dictate when you will or won't play, there's no real compromise – but there's no way they can stop us clearing the backlog now, is there? Still, I'm sure a lot of it's just teething problems; at least I hope it is, I hope it's not an attitude problem too. Otherwise this'll go on for years to come.'

He went on casting round for pitches, pleading on the phone and in the post every day with welfare clubs in colliery villages like Thorne and Rossington for the posts to stay up a little longer. The confusion was compounded by an England trip to Sweden in mid-May; to get themselves used to it, they'd lined up two friendlies with a Swedish club side, and with the World Cup host's national team. As a consequence, it looked like Belles would have to wait to play their last two games – Ilkeston at home, Liverpool away – sandwiched into late May between that trip and the World Cup itself. For the England players involved it was far from ideal – but it was either that, or abandon the league.

Still, at least one date was settled – 7 May, when the Belles had Belle Vue for the last time to play host to England B. And Paul didn't know whether he had his captain or not – she'd not called, she'd not come training – but one thing he did know. For Joanne's sake, for Channy's sake, for all their sakes, he wanted Belles to beat Croydon so badly it ached.

He wasn't the only one, either. On the Wednesday, Channy came training; reluctantly, the doctor had taken the plaster off her hand. He'd have preferred to put another one on but he knew she'd play, so there wasn't any point – besides, she said, after two weeks it had got so the only thing she could think about all day was washing her hand. Inside the pot it stank, it itched, she hated it – and it was still swollen, she couldn't grip with it, she couldn't hold a pen or put her hair up – but strap it up, she said, and she'd be there.

Nor was she the only one back. After two years injured, to general delight, Jackie Sherrard had gone the full ninety with the reserves against Huddersfield – and, what's more, they'd won the game 4–3. Channy'd got home from watching the seniors beat Ilkeston, and she'd found Lisa near to crying afterwards; she'd smiled sweetly and said, 'Oh dear. Did our reserves beat you then?'

'What,' said Paul, bubbling, 'have I got selection problems then?'

Kaz was bubbling too. In the post that morning she'd got a pair of top range Adidas World Cup boots, had to be eighty or ninety quids' worth; it didn't say who'd sent them or why, but who cared, it was like Christmas. She was that chuffed, she wore them to do the washing-up.

They trained, laughing, panting, puffing under a chill pastel sky at the Straight Mile. The sun, lilac and gold, set through thin veins of cloud over wide stretches of brick semis across the dual carriageway; the racecourse ran away behind them, and the odd car crept past on the lane towards a patch of woodland beyond the pitches, people come to walk their dogs looking curiously through closed windows at these women working up a sweat in their shorts and bibs.

One of the ball-control exercises involved jogging backwards between a pair of markers, rolling your foot over the top of the ball to drag it with you as you went. Paul tried to demonstrate what he wanted them doing but it wasn't easy, and he stumbled and made a bog of it. He smiled and said, 'Knew I shouldn't have tried showing you that one. Still,

you'll be all right, you lot. Do it on the dance floor every
Friday night, don't you?'

The posts on the public pitches were all gone now, but the
Belles weren't finished yet.

At ten-thirty on a sunny Sunday morning, Paul went into the
garden with Laura to play wash-the-footballs. On either side
of them the neighbours were gardening and it struck him
how bizarre it must look, what he was doing with his daughter;
he thought, I bet they're thinking, Look at that prat there,
with his bucket and his bag of balls on a nice day like this.

When he got to Belle Vue, he found some prat of a greater
order altogether had nearly blown off the game. Rovers were
in turmoil, their Isle of Man-based 'football adviser' Ken
Richardson locked in long-standing disagreement with the
council over plans for a new stadium; at their last home game
of the season, the entire staff had been handed redundancy
notices not long before kick-off. These were subsequently
rescinded, as the manoeuvrings continued – but on the night
of 6 May some party, aggrieved at the wrangling, climbed
into the ground with a can or two of petrol and tried to set
fire to the main stand. Aggrieved, maybe, said Debbie
Biggins, but not very bright – they'd tried to start the fire on
concrete, when there was wood just a couple of rows of
seating away.

Chance and dim-wittedness having saved them a stadium
to play in, the Belles filed into the scratty little dressing-room
with its thin wood walls and its 'Keep Fighting' signs. Gill
was back, and she told Kaz she'd got a pair of them World
Cup boots in the post too; Joanne made a sad face and said,
'I didn't get none.' But she was, she said, resigned to not
going; she could only do her best, and hope against hope that
it might yet make a difference.

Kaz's knee, meanwhile, had clicked on Friday night (as

she sat down, she swore, to watch rugby league) and on Saturday morning she couldn't bend it. But she shrugged, 'Piss it, eh? I'll have a go.'

Jackie Sherrard sat beside her; Paul had picked her to play at sweeper. She said, smiling uncertainly, 'I'm that nervous.'

Paul told her, 'You get nervous in five-a-sides at training, you do.'

'Sherrard is back,' Joanne gently chanted, 'Sherrard is back. D'you know everyone's names then?'

'I know most of 'em.'

'No nutting me at corners,' Kaz told her, 'it's not the old days now.'

'Hey Channy,' Joanne smiled, and she held her hand up all fey and limp in front of her, 'no running about like that, eh? Or I'll laugh at you.'

'Right,' said Paul, 'we're playing our usual lot of England internationals here. Something to play for, in't there? So let's go out showing the attitude we did when we went down there, let's go out wanting to win. 'Cause they're a good side, regardless of what I might say; it's not their fault they get picked for England, they're good players, and you've got to be prepared to have a go at them, to go through pain and work and effort. And if you do, I'm sure we'll beat them – 'cause they've nothing to play for, these, but we have, we've pride to play for. And I don't know how you feel, but with three games left I know I feel that if we can't come first, then let's come second. Nothing less. I don't want it to die on us as if nothing's important now – I want to stay up there as best we can, and the people that can do it for me are these people sat in here. So let's have a togetherness, let's have that spirit we had last week, and let's beat them.'

What followed was a scrap, not a good game, but a tense and intensely exciting one. Belles scored early, Vicky Exley breaking through into the area off a lovely give-and-go with Micky, then pelting it home low on the deck. After that it was mostly Croydon, the Londoners lean, mean, fast, and well deserving to equalise on twenty-seven minutes. Paul was left yelling, 'We're stood about here as if we've never played before. Is it too warm for you?'

At least the Belles weren't as bad as the officials. The linesmen couldn't tell an offside from an apple cart, so much so that after Paul loosed off yet another salvo of sarcasm and frustration, the ref finally came and told him quietly in his ear to leave it out, it wouldn't get him anywhere. Trouble was, the referee was useless too; Croydon in general, and Kerry Davis in particular, were putting themselves about without compunction, Joanne getting the brunt of it, and he was letting chopped ankles and sly elbows all go by without a murmur.

They struggled to half-time and Paul gave them a roasting, shouting, pacing, demanding, furious. As they splashed water on burning red faces and necks, gulping down Gatorade, he wanted to know, were they going to stand about then? Were they going to let it all drift away after all? 'And don't use ref as an excuse either, 'cause we've played *crap* that half. So *get in there*,' he yelled, 'I haven't seen a decent tackle yet. The number of times they've run past us, for God's sake – and all the crowd are shouting same, don't you want to win? Let's work, Belles – you can hear them shouting it, *'cause it looks as if you don't want to work.* So you've got to go out second half and show these people, and show *me*, that you *do* want to work. You've got to fight and sprint and chase, you've got to go at them, pressure them – 'cause it looks like a practice match so far and they might want that, but I don't. I want you to show what we're capable of, and I want to win the game, 'cause I want to finish as high as we can. And they'll be sitting round saying, No wonder we've got six internationals, look how we're playing – *so get out there and show them what we're made of.*'

He strode up and down, repeating and repeating as he urged them back into the match that essence-of-football phrase, *get in there*, his fist flying through the air beside him as he said it, *whoomph* – 'cause these Croydon, he said, they get the ball, they want to look all nicey-nicey. But you look like you want to win it, they'll get out your road then . . .

Joanne said grimly in the corner, 'That Kerry Davis – does nowt but whine and nag all game, and she an't even been fouled yet. But her time'll come now.'

'Come on you scrubbers,' Kaz told them, 'let's whang some in, eh?'

In amongst all this, captain Coultard hadn't said much – but twelve minutes later she showed them how to do it, riding a tackle through her ankles as she got in the area, looking up, and chipping the keeper cool as ice to put Belles back ahead 2–1. And she was a strange person, maybe – but the way she could play, she was worth every one of those record eighty caps.

After she scored, the game went mayhem. Twice the Belles were denied penalties a blind man would have given – the first when Bampton and another Croydon defender crashed Kaz over in the area, leaving her seething in a heap, demanding of the referee, 'Hey, they've had a swing at me, them. Would you've give it if I were injured then?' Then the second, Kaz shot, and a defender blatantly pushed it away with both hands from in front of her – and everyone was yelling now, 'cause how in the world could that be let go?

I remember then, as the game rucked and scrapped across the field in the sunshine, how I disappeared in it, how I became an involuntary, twitching thing sat on the wall by the dug-out, muttering and snarling and sighing. I remember how, stung by another offside decision I couldn't believe, I sprang up on the dirt by the sideline screaming, 'Bollocks.

Bollocks.' Then I found I was looking at myself stood there shouting that, brain frothing in this near-empty, ratty, only-just-not-burnt-down little Third Division ground thinking, What are you doing? You're thirty-six, married, got two kids, and here you're losing all control over a dodgy linesman? Sheila said, 'It's all right, Pete. Football can do that to you.' But it was more than that, it was so much more.

I'd lost my heart to these people. I loved the way they played, and I loved the way they loved to play; I loved the way they made themselves something special out of football, and I loved the way that kept them going when there'd been so much against them, and I wanted them to win at that moment more than anything in the world because I loved them, period. I loved Nicky stumbling on game after game on her wrenched knee and her broken heart, I loved Kaz dancing red-eyed in the whirling lights at the Palace, I loved Channy smiling ironic at the counter of her shop in Elland Road, saying she better have a curry 'cause her stomach were bad; I loved Ann crying at Rotherham before she went home to catch bad guys, and little Jonesy with her blisters and her giant diffuser, and Micky on her feet all day in her uniform at the bank when her ankle was kicked purple. I loved Skiller, coming off on a stretcher at Croydon with the gashed scar livid on her swelling knee, and Channy's dad saying to her, Had she hurt that knee before then? And Skiller sighed and told him, 'No. I laddered me tights, didn't I?'

I loved them all, and none more than Joanne with her quick smile and her Waddle shirt, who used to dance laughing on the bar top at Mystique's in Stoke on a Friday night until her life fell to bits, and who was in everyone's twenty for Sweden except the England manager's. She'd covered so much ground all game, she'd won challenge after challenge, got up and given it – and for her now, as much as for anyone, I wanted Belles beating England B.

There were thirteen minutes to go when Croydon equalised; some messy scramble, I don't know what happened, and I didn't care. I only knew Belles should have been 4–1 up by then if the ref had known his job, and instead it was 2–2, and I was utterly, totally miserable, unable any more to bother taking notes, unable even to muster any more oafish desperate shouting. The game scratched and tussled toward the final whistle – and I shrugged. I thought, Story over.

In the ninetieth minute, Gill and Joanne worked a perfect one-two through the left side of the area. Gill gave it, she went, and as she went Joanne fed her on through, slipping it inside the full back to get her free on the byline. There wasn't time or space for her to get it on her right foot, and Paul saw that; he was thinking, Gill, left foot, could go anywhere this, she could even fresh air it, swing and miss altogether. But with her weaker foot she popped it up lovely, a little looper into the goalmouth; what Paul would later call, with contented admiration, a perfect nine-iron chip.

He looked for Kaz then – but it was Vicky Exley, nineteen years old, a new Belle, rising over the crowded box to head home the winner. 3–2 Belles, and a roaring happiness of blood in my ears, dancing on the sideline like a kid with my arms up high in the air. Then the whistle went and Debbie Bampton stalked off the pitch, not shaking hands with anyone. But it were a bit embarrassing, weren't it?

Sheila sat in the dressing-room with her head back against the wall, breathing hard as if she'd played all ninety herself. Jackie Sherrard stumbled in and Sheila asked her, 'Did you enjoy that then?'

'No.' She made a *whoooh* sound, a pained sigh of exhaustion, as if to say, It were never that hard two years ago.

Sheila grinned. 'These days all we do is biff it. We don't dribble no more, we biff it.'

Joanne came in jubilant, angry, edgy all at once. She couldn't sit down; she paced about downing pop, wildly grinning. Going out for the second half she'd told Kerry, watch your elbows, you, and Kerry'd said to her, right there by the ref, 'Fuck off, you wanker.' Joanne couldn't believe it, she were supposed to be her mate, that Kerry – and she couldn't believe all the ref had let go either.

She said sternly, talking fast, near hyperventilating, 'I were ready, me. I were ready to get sent off there. I called him a wanker, God, they're playing basketball, them. And Kerry's elbowed me in face . . .' She shook her head, and collapsed.

They were still too high to smile, even to know where they were, but Paul had the words for them, even though he was so wound up that the words he did give all came spilling in a rush. He said, or rather gabbled, 'I told you if it was between a club like Doncaster Belles and them, them with all these internationals – but they haven't got that bit of spirit about them, have they? We've got four people playing on one leg, people coming back after injury, but there were only one team going to win it and we've pinched it 'cause we've got character, 'cause you don't get to the top of the tree for fifteen years like we have and then just give it all away. And we're going back to the top, 'cause of these people sat in here. Right to the end, Vicky, that's what it's all about, eh? Gill, left foot cross, that's what it's all about. And it makes your Sunday that much better when you know you've beaten them. Well done everybody, that were *brilliant*.'

In just a couple of minutes, face taut and dense with emotion, mouth working richly expressive with pride as the words tumbled out, he brought them together, an exhausted, strung-out group of people gathered back in beneath the shelter of the secret language of their trade. And people always say, what does a football manager actually *do*?

I don't know – but the room erupted when he finished

then, all of them clapping, cheering, laughing, everybody talking all at once to everybody else, a great happy racket of Donny Belles noise.

When he heard a minute later that Bampton hadn't shaken any hands on her way off pitch, he said, smiling without any joy in his eyes, 'Is she so wrapped up picking England team she's forgot her manners then?'

19

Sad

The hardest thing was telling her nephew Liam that Aunty Gilly weren't captain of England any more. She said, 'I couldn't give him any reasons, 'cause I didn't have any.'

Gill Coultard was the youngest of eight; Liam's mother Glenys was the fourth child. Though Gill had left home at eighteen and didn't often see her many siblings now, these two sisters became close after their mother died three years back. Of her mother's passing she said, 'It still hurts to this day. Every time I play for England I think of me mum. I wish I could come home and say, Look, this is what I've won. Player of the Match. Or tell her how many caps I've got now. They say time's a great healer . . .'

The way she said it, plainly time wasn't doing his job – but there was a lot to be healed. Her father, a miner, had up and left when she was three; she didn't know him and she didn't much want to. She said, 'Me upbringing weren't one of the best. But that's a part of me that's been and gone.'

Without football, what would she have been? Still stuck there, she thought, stuck indoors somewhere, married, kids, fat – and the game had been her way out. She'd played for school teams 'til she wasn't allowed to play with boys any more; at that point, one of her teachers knew about Belles, and when she went there she was good enough that right from the start, thirteen years old, they took her training with England. She said, 'It were frightening, going against grown women. But you look at teenagers coming in now, and I wish

I'd had chances they've got. I'd have a hundred and twenty caps, not eighty.'

She remembered her debut against the Republic of Ireland in May 1981, when she was eighteen; England won 3–1. She remembered scoring the first women's international goal at Wembley, against Northern Ireland before a Charity Shield game. And she hoped, looking back, she could say she'd done well by the three lions for her eighty caps; she'd had a bad game in Belfast once when the place got to her, the atmosphere of the troubles, and the match against the Germans at Watford last December, the 4–1 trouncing, that had been bad – but she felt she'd earned her place in the record books, and you'll not find many who'd disagree. Playing through the years before anyone took notice, she'd been a permanent presence; only one other player came close.

Debbie Bampton had seventy-seven caps. Five years ago, she'd been captain; she fell injured and Barry Williams, who was manager then, gave the armband to Coultard. She'd kept it until the Italy trip in February.

Copeland told her before the trip that a decision about the captaincy was going to be made, but she didn't believe he'd do it. I asked why he did and she said, 'I'm still asking meself that three months on. I've asked him and asked him, and all he says is it was in me best interests. And he's the manager, that's what he's there for, I can't argue with it – but it's totally demoralised me, and that's rebounded on Belles. I'll put me hand up, I've let club down this year, I've not been a good captain, I've not set a good example. But I'm still demoralised now; I don't know now how I'm going to feel when we go to Sweden this week. That last training session at Maidenhead, I didn't enjoy it one bit. I were thinking, What am I doing here? Do I really want to be here? Do I want to go to World Cup? I do, more than anything in me life – but you have a setback like that and you wonder, don't you?'

She said, 'I were very disappointed in him as a person, when he left it as late as what he did, four hours before game. I had tears in me eyes, when we were lined up in tunnel – and if it weren't for Kaz Walker, looking at her then, I could quite easily have turned back. At that moment, I could quite easily have not gone to World Cup. And he says it were for me own good – but I still believe it did have something to do with that programme; other people were saying that. He says it didn't, but I do believe it did. So it hurts, and it always will.'

I asked what she thought of Copeland as a manager now. She paused a long while; she said, 'He's a very good coach.'

She was five foot nothing, eight stone five pounds, thirty-one years old; a stocky, rapid little barrel of a woman, immensely strong in her body, combative and wary in her manner. She'd left school with nothing, or nothing she could remember, and decamped from Thorne to Castleford; she'd been on the dole a year and a half, then landed in a factory making football boots and training shoes for Gola. From there, she got a job assembling gas valves at a plastics company in Leeds; the manager who took her on was Alan Burton.

He was a rugby league man really, but when she asked him a few years later if he'd take on being Belles' secretary he was happy to do it. He did say he'd only do it short-term – but, he said wryly, you take on these things, they have a habit of sticking with you. Besides, he, his wife Margaret and their daughters had become like a family to Gill, she was often round there; people like these, Gill said, or Des Shepherd cleaning out tunnel before a game, or Betty making tea, they were what made Belles special. It was a family club; it was nineteen years of her life.

It was sad, then, that this season which should have been the peak of her career was foundering in such discontent – but away from the game it had started badly, when the factory in Leeds gave her her redundancy notice, and from there it was one thing after another. At work they vacillated, said the job was still hers after all, but they could give no guarantees; she went to Pioneer instead, and started making CD players.

The factory was a tin barn off a slip road from the M62, just a few years old, with a spotless marble reception. Behind that, the corridors to the assembly area were featureless white tunnels of breezeblock. The workforce wore uniform pale-blue work suits and white cotton gloves; they were supposed to wear safety shoes too, which Gill didn't, saying they hurt her feet. It was, she said, 'Very regimented, very Japanese.'

Hanging from the tin ceiling over each production line, between a tangle of blue girders and silver ventilation pipes, an electronic board showed the line's overall target for the day, the running target, and their variance from it; each worker also had a target timetable pinned above her bench (they were overwhelmingly women) indicating that on today's shift forty-seven units were meant to go through between eight and nine, sixty-four between nine and ten-thirty, and so on through to four thirty-five. You worked, she said, 'Buzzer to buzzer', beneath the fans turning, by the packing cases waiting on their pallettes.

She did the same thing all day, one sequence among maybe fifteen people putting the product together down the line. The chassis came to her; with an electric screwdriver hung from a hook over her bench she screwed in the PCB board. Then she got the mains cable, wrapped and soldered the connections round the pins, tied it in and clipped the ends off the tie. Then pass it on, do the next, pass it on, do the next, and talk to her mate Tanya beside her on the line as she went. Tanya was a Man U supporter, she'd had a season ticket for years, and Lord knows what kind of hole that made in her wages – but she was having trouble at home, she was in a B&B, so she'd be round at Gill's tonight watching her team play on Sky.

The buzzer went, and the lines broke and scattered. Gill said, 'It's like Custer's last stand now. There's only one exit from the car park.'

People stood about outside getting nicotine in while the car park nudged and jostled to empty itself. I drove her the short way home into town, to a quiet, spartan, red-brick back-street of infinitely repeating two-up, two-downs, little houses where the front door opens directly into the living-room, and you go in by the back. She had a ginnel down the side of the house, and an alley down the back between her row and the next. Two lads in rugby league shirts kicked a rugby ball along the concrete in the alley. We went past them through her yard into a neat little kitchen extension, everything immaculately clean. The padded seats of the chairs round her dining-table still had the polythene wrap on them from the shop; there were no pictures on the walls. In the front room a porcelain dalmation sat by the trophies round the gas fireplace; there were only a few, the great bulk of them were in her bedroom, or packed away in the loft. The ones to the fore weren't won with Belles, but with the hockey team she played for on Saturdays, Rowntrees in York, winners in the last two seasons of the regional Costcutter League. She'd said to me once, 'I have me hockey Saturday, me football Sunday, and I'm happy.'

But that were when Belles won Double and Gillian Coultard were England captain, and she weren't happy now. She said, 'I want putting in a bag and shaking up, me.'

She said of how well Belles had done, when you looked at all the injuries, 'It proves it's not a one-man team, which everybody thinks it is outside of Doncaster. There is life after me, and there always will be.'

She'd been the prominent woman footballer of her generation, she'd been the centre of her team so long, it had been so much the essence and the making of her life, that she was finding it hard now, truly hard, to see herself coming towards the end and other players rising around her. I said she'd thrown that wobbly after the Southampton game at Stainforth, when she'd gone after Debbie Biggins, and she laughed. 'Real wobbly, that. It were frustrations, a lot of things. If I didn't walk out when I did I'd have said things . . . I'd have probably not gone back to club. Health-wise, England . . . I didn't let off steam when I lost captaincy. It just all boiled up.'

Did she regret that now? She said, 'No, I don't think I do. At the time, the way that game went . . . maybe I expect everyone to be like me, to be professional in everything you do, to be a perfectionist, to turn up and give ninety minutes' hard graft. I'm not bothered what they do off pitch after, so long as they give their all for Doncaster Belles. That's all I want.'

Why, then, had she said she was signing for Liverpool? It had been, she claimed, just a joke, it had been blown out of all proportion, they should have known her better – but the trouble was, I think, that they knew her very well, with her need to be the central figure. That perception of herself was plain in what she said of the aftermath of that week: 'We had a meeting on the Monday, that made it more worse, people getting upset, Betty saying you can't leave club, people pressing me, saying what were I doing? Everybody's waiting for you to jack it in, leave a sinking ship . . .'

When the ship sank, of course, against Arsenal and then Southampton away, Gill Coultard was playing. Kaz Walker wasn't – and when Kaz came back, while Gill sat with her kidney infection watching Arsenal–Liverpool, it was Kaz who refloated the ship with her five goals against Ilkeston.

Gill couldn't see it that way. She was gutted, she said, when Paul told her he needed her playing, not going on TV – and there was no recognition that there should, for her team's sake, have been no contest between those two options. She'd seen Sky opening doors for her, she could talk of it only as a missed opportunity (she didn't say this, but it was a missed fee as well, the size of which had been discussed with much relish by her team-mates) – and so, obliged to miss it, she fell ill. It was, she said, the stress of it all – and, I asked, the England thing was part of that? She said, 'It's been an underlying factor, oh aye, without a doubt. It's affected me health, it's stressed me out.'

It was Wednesday evening; as usual Gill (a perfectionist, professional in all she did) wasn't going to Belles' training. She said, 'I'm not wasting my time going seventy-five miles to be pratted about, people just tossing it off, thinking it's a joke. Kids today . . . they're not like we were fifteen years ago.'

They're not, are they? They're fifteen years younger and we're fifteen years older – and the frightening possibility opens up about kids today that they might even work out better. Moreover, there was more than a possibility, there was a near-certainty, that with the rise of the women's game, after all the years put in by people like Gill Coultard, these kids would get more recognition, and have more opportunity, than she'd ever had.

If she'd been a man, and had charted a comparable career in the professional game, she'd have been made for life; she'd have been a face universally known. But because she was a woman, the retirement she found herself contemplating was an abyss; all that achievement, and nothing beyond it but thirty more years screwing CD players' brains together for £200 a week. So it may be that she wasn't the best captain in the world, and it may be that Copeland, no matter how he handled it, had in fact made the right decision – but between that decision and the years rushing by her she was, as she admitted, going to her first and last World Cup well and truly messed up.

She said she'd told Paul that, in the circumstances, she'd hand the captaincy down. I went to training – from Gill's place to the Straight Mile was half an hour, M62, A1, no problem, not like coming from Burnley or Skipton – and when I got there, Paul had no memory of her telling him that. He said sadly, 'World of her own.'

He was laying out markers for the next exercise; behind him Belles were in a circle, all of them in rapid succession firing shots and lobbing high balls at Debbie Biggins in the centre of the ring. She heaved herself through the air, her with her bad attitude parrying and catching and falling on the hard ground, picking herself up, doing it again; when he called them to the next bit of work she collapsed on her back, gasping for air. She could just muster enough of a grin to say, 'Worst thing in world, that one is.'

Back in Castleford, Gill Coultard watched Sky.

20

Stumbling to the End

While Belles were training, Channy's dad had a heart attack. He was out with his mates and he started getting pains across his chest; his mates rang Channy's mum and Channy was back by then, so together they went to fetch him. Driving home, he was keeled over in agony on the back seat – and he gasped to Channy, 'How d'you go in training then?'

They got him into hospital; a week later he was home. The next day, Channy'd not been long at work when he called; he were reet ticked off. He'd called doctor, he grumbled, and they'd said he should stop indoors, he couldn't go to watch her play. Channy feared he would, mind – but then, as a number of her opponents had found, it takes a fair bit to knock over a Woodhead.

When Bampton stomped off at Belle Vue not shaking any hands, the young ones looked at her and thought, Is that the England captain then? Kaz was angry too. She said, when they met up with England, 'Does she expect me to talk to her after that?'

Nothing like team spirit . . . and they went to play Sweden, and Copeland didn't pick Kaz. He played some new for-mation, five across the middle, Karen Farley on her tod up front, and not a soul had a clue what they were doing. At half-time it was 0–0, so he came into the dressing-room and told them well done, Sweden hadn't scored, they were panicking, they didn't know where goals were going to come from – and Kaz thought, they looked like they had a chuffin' sight better idea where goals came from than England did. Sweden won 4–0, and England never had a shot all game.

Two days later they played a club side. This time he did pick Kaz, and England won 3–1; Kaz scored two of them, and hit the bar from forty yards trying to get herself a hat trick.

Joanne played the first half; the night before they flew, she'd been called up when Lou Waller fell sick. Her chances of going to the World Cup itself, though, didn't look too good. He'd played her wide, not her best position, and at half-time England were losing 1–0; second half she came off, he made other substitutions, and it was then they won the game. Still, she wasn't bothered any more; if she wasn't called, she said she'd not be devastated now, 'cause being with England just got worse and worse. It was, she said, 'Like being in prison, they barely let you out, you're stuck in your room for hours at a stretch – they don't cater for you as people at all.'

Besides, the football was bollocks. Him saying the Swedish didn't know where goals came from – her and Kaz, they were sat laughing, them. Swedes had hit post, hit bar, had one cleared off line – and he says well done, they haven't scored. It was so negative; she said, 'You're going to win World Cup that way, aren't you? Go there and not let any in.'

She wrote them a song, to the tune of 'I Will Survive':

> We've had enough
> Get someone new . . .

Paul listened to them laughing about the state of it, and shook his head. It sounded to him as if the limit of England's ambition was to avoid getting hammered; leave one up front, clog the midfield and come out the other end saying, well, we can hold our own in international women's football, 'cause we only got beat by two or three.

But maybe, in the end, that wasn't unreasonable. There were 35,000 registered women players in Sweden; the Swedish FA, like their German counterparts, had run women's football for twenty-five years, and their efficiently sponsored twelve-team First Division was watched by decent crowds, an accepted element in the sporting calendar. Players trained four nights a week; they were strong, they were fit, they were quality on the ball, and they'd had a full-time national manager since 1980. Karen Farley, who played in Sweden, told Kaz and the rest when she joined the England squad that they had no idea what was going to hit them – but they had a pretty good idea by now. Come the World Cup, they thought they could get through the first round past Canada and Nigeria – and after that, God help them.

Alan Burton got a pitch at RAF Finningley (the knock-on effect of whose imminent closure was thought to be another couple of thousand jobs gone) and you had to check yourself in past a guy at the gate with a machine-gun. A pair of guards with Alsatians wandered through rows of brick blocks housing living quarters and mess rooms; between the base and pitch stood tall fencing topped with wire.

Still, the dressing-room was neat and clean, the walls glowing yellow-orange with the evening sun refracted through a frosted-glass window. Kaz sat on the window-sill, Joanne stood beside her, and they told Paul stories from the Sweden trip, laughing themselves silly. 'Ee, that shot,' Kaz grinned, 'forty yards, that were. Get in, eh?'

'Forty yards, rubbish,' Paul said, 'don't talk to me about yards. I'm a carpet-fitter, me.'

'It were,' she told him, 'reet zoomer. From edge of circle. Well,' she said, 'all right then. Thirty-five.'

Channy smiled at her sweetly and asked, 'Were it a miskick, Kaz?'

'Your mate Sammy Britton,' Kaz told her, 'you know when World Cup's over, you chuck everyone in bath? So that physio, evil Edna, Sammy says we're all to get round her.' She grinned. 'And she says, "Then I'll punch her. Or if she's in vat, I'll bang her head on sink." Mental, her.'

The new girl, Joanne Sharp, sat quietly, watching Kaz command the room from the window-sill, and everyone laughing; she made a little smiling face at me then, as if to say, You get into something when you join these, don't you?

Ann Lisseman arrived, looking taut. She'd stopped work in Birmingham at five to four, got in car at four, taken two and a half hours to drive here; there were twenty minutes while kick-off.

Voting slips went round for players to choose their player of the year; Micky collected money for the awards dinner. Sheila, grinning broadly, had a go at Kaz for denting biggest trophy club had – taking it home one night after winning it, Kaz had volleyed it triumphant through taxi door into front garden.

Paul told her she were sub, if everyone turned up; he wanted to save her for Liverpool three days later. Joanne Broadhurst chortled and said, 'Just like England, eh?'

Kaz mock-wailed, 'I'm wanted nowhere, me. Nowhere.' But later she asked him sternly, 'I will get on, won't I?'

Against Ilkeston, in fact, he hoped he'd not need her. Ilkeston had secured their place for next season with a point from a 0–0 draw against Liverpool; Paul hoped they'd not be bothered now, and that Belles could get three points without too much trouble. It was his last home game, and Rob Kantecki's last game altogether; so he knew it'd be easy to think, end of season, nice sunny evening – but with three points here and three on Sunday they'd still come second, and he didn't want anything less.

Outside, I asked Channy how her dad was. 'Reet depressed,'

she said. 'He asked me to bring him. I told him, Could he promise not to jump up and down if we scored? He said he couldn't, so I made him stop at home.' And though she hid it, it was plain she was worried sick.

On the sideline a lad came to Sheila with a card and a box of chocolates, to say thanks for her coming to his school's Under-11 tournament. She told him, 'Ah bless. You didn't need to do that. It were good fun.' When he was gone she smiled. 'I got three or four handy little players, too.'

It was a gorgeous evening, the sky layered with soft drifts of cream and lilac cloud, the sun setting molten red. Long shadows stretched over grass tinted ember-orange; trees and bushes stood in pale white blossom along the railway line behind one goal. Ilkeston, on the other hand, were nothing like as pretty. 'I think they've come to defend,' Paul sighed, as they won a free kick, and left four players back marking Vicky Exley on her own. 'They could bore for bleedin' Europe, this team.'

The linesman asked him to clear people back from the sideline; he said, 'They don't take notice of me if I ask.'

Paul smiled. 'I don't either, when I'm playing.'

In the car park when I'd arrived, the ref had asked how the officials were going to come out in this book. Rubbish, I told him. He said, 'We always are, aren't we?' I told him I was a fan, and what did he expect? So now he was giving Belles everything – which wasn't exactly wrong, the way Ilkeston were barging and clattering and griping their way through a game played almost entirely in their half – but it did make a nice change, and the Ilkeston manager was moaning about it no end. Paul said 'I've never heard a team whine so much in all me life' – and he got that bored of it, he had to go watch from the other side of the pitch.

On the field, meanwhile, the game was largely a procession. Gill put one narrowly over bar first minute, Joanne put a free kick ditto from thirty yards, Vicky went outside post from twenty, Kilner shot at keeper, Vicky had another pop and hit side netting, Kilner tried again and hit post, Skiller fired a yard wide – it went on and on, and Paul grew more and more angry. Channy slung a corner a yard across goalmouth, and no one got after it; Paul shouted, 'Are we going to get in there?' He turned away muttering, 'Can't we hit bleedin' target?'

Gill was playing well; the rest were strolling, bar one other Belle. Joanne Sharp was heading it, booting it, running a thousand miles an hour (Kilner said later, 'She could catch pigeons, her') and on the sideline Kaz, Gail and Jackie were loving her for it. *Go on Joanne, well in Joanne, well played Joanne* . . . but there was nowt Belles liked better than a new Belle on board. One time, she was streaking with her player down the sideline, reet Billy Whizz, and the player stopped and Joanne didn't notice, she were that busy running she just kept on going towards corner flag. Laughter all round – but still no goals, and Ilkeston still bashing and pestering, and Kilner near losing her rag at it, coming close to taking a swing, and Gail calling, Steady, steady. The ref snarled at the player who'd provoked Kilner, 'Come here, come *here*, you. Don't you *ever* talk to me like that again.'

But there were still no goals. At half-time they lay in a circle on the pitch and Paul said to Channy, 'I want a better second half from you than that half there. You looked as though you never played football in your life, you're just jogging. So if you're not fit enough, I'll get you fit – you run like hell for twenty minutes then you say, I'm absolutely knackered, Paul, bring me off, and I'll bring you off. 'Cause I've got people here who want to play.'

Behind Channy Gail grinned, miming an exaggerated, elbow-whirling sprint on the spot. Sheila hugged her and said, 'You've no chance, you.'

Paul told them, 'Hard work. We'll beat them, 'cause they're

not as good as us – they're so slow at the back it's unbeliev-able, they've got that great big camel there – but you've got to work hard to do it.'

As we came off Gail was sprinting, making motor-car noises. Paul told her, 'Looking good, Gaily.'

'She's only fast,' Kaz grinned. 'She can't kick it.'

And the game went on the same, Ilkeston's giant six knocking Vicky over. Gail said, 'I'm retiring if I can't get round something like that when I'm back.'

Kaz sighed. 'They've got some reet players, these.'

'Ey,' Gail told her, 'it's still 0–0, in't it?'

Skiller went down; Paul said, 'Get ready, Wack.' Kaz's face lit up, a great big radiance; she started jumping up and down. Paul fretted, 'I think it's her knee.'

'Course it is,' Kaz said, 'we're all knees, us. Haven't got a decent knee in club.'

And she weren't used to being sub, she didn't know what to do; she wanted to run straight on, they had to hold her back by linesman while Skiller came off. She asked, 'What've I got to do here?'

'Score two,' Paul told her.

But it wasn't Kaz who scored, it was Ilkeston; Debbie Biggins dropped a corner and in the ruck someone bundled it home. So there was half an hour left and now Belles needed two. It only took five minutes to get the first – Kaz and Gill steaming into the area, panicking Ilkeston defenders going with Kaz, Gill taking it in on her own, a bursting surge through the line to charge down free on the keeper – so she rounded her and the keeper brought her down. The ref gave the penalty – but did he send the keeper off then for the professional foul? He didn't even have a word with her. Rubbish, like I told him – and you wonder, you really wonder where they get these people from.

Micky put the penalty home, 1–1 – and that was how it stayed. The rest of the game, Paul stood watching his last season fade out, Belles attacking and attacking and getting nowhere, Kaz not herself, Channy absent out wide, worrying about her dad, and a lot of other tired, hurt people stumbling towards the end of ten months – and it got to him, he got angrier and angrier. 'Nicky, get your head up, you're no good to us feeling bleedin' sorry for yourself. Channy, get involved – you an't kicked it for quarter of an hour.' Vicky shot over, and his head exploded. He screamed, '*Hit the target!*' then spun round spitting words out like they were burning his mouth. 'Centre-forward,' he growled, 'can't hit the bastard target.'

Gill got caught offside, Joanne not putting it through quick enough for her; he was virtually on tiptoe, gesturing, barking, telling them the same things again and again. And do they listen? Bloody footballers. And still Belles attacked, winning corners and wasting them, firing high, firing wide – but only Gill forced a save, one save all half. Gail sighed, 'Have they been up our end?'

They did get there once, on the break, and Channy cleared a shot off the line; it was the only decent touch she had all game and thank God she made it, 'cause to lose to this lot would have been ugly. But Paul's mood was ugly even drawing with them, and he came off snapping and snarling with Nicky Davies; somewhat unwisely she reminded him that these drew with Liverpool too and he spat out at her, 'So fuckin' what?' She walked behind him, muttering at his back how he should think what he was saying sometimes – and there were five minutes of evil temper all round.

Joanne said, 'They take the piss, these lot, don't they?'

Three days later, a Liverpool player told me how Ilkeston played eleven at the back against them too, and how one of them kicked her. So she was down on the ground and the

Ilkeston girl said she was sorry, but she had to do it 'cause they needed the point. And it's not happy-go-lucky any more, women's football; as Paul's time was ending, so too was the time for romance. The women were better every year now, their game was more competitive and winning mattered more – so there were more teams now who'd kick and bite for a result, if that was the way they thought they could get one. I remember John Jones saying to Paul once, 'It's easy to teach them to look after themselves, anyone can do that. But is that really the point?'

Paul told Belles he was bitterly disappointed and very angry. 'Still, looking on the bright side, think what it'd be like if you had to play for them lot every week – 'cause God almighty, that must be the most boring team in all the world. And if that's playing football, I don't want any part of it.'

But never mind them, or their tactics; it was Belles' performance that bothered him. He was sharply critical of the goal they'd let in, and of the dozen they'd missed – so much so that when they got home and he asked Sheila as he always did what she thought, she told him he'd been out of order. She knew how much he cared but there'd been no need, it was end of season, they'd not played that badly – so couldn't he just leave it go now?

Oh well, he thought wryly, at least we're finishing early this year. Season before, they'd still been playing in June.

At Finningley, Rob Kantecki walked away from his last game after four years as Belles' chairman. He was a sweet man, one of life's natural enthusiasts; when I'd first come to Belles a year back he'd seemed so artlessly, perpetually cheerful that I'd wondered about his motives, what he hoped to get out of Belles – but that was unfair. What he got out of Belles was the fun of being around them (they were, Sheila thought, like the sisters he'd never had) and without ever expecting anyone to go fawning or crawling to him, he'd put in thousands of pounds through those last four years to keep them going, money which more than a few doubted he could really afford.

So he had to concentrate on his business now – but once he'd got involved, for four years he'd stayed because he loved the way they were, and he wanted them all happy all the time. When anybody ever wasn't, he always took time to try and help; he was, in Paul's estimation, both daft as a brush, and entirely typical of the decent kind of people the club seemed to attract. And now he was walking away from a 1–1 draw with Ilkeston; he said, 'It's quite sad, this.'

But in the parking lot, when I said I was well depressed too, he forgot that he was low himself and tried to cheer me up. He said, 'As long as you've got your health and your wife loves you, you're OK. This,' and he waved behind him at the darkening air force base, 'this is just a diversion.'

Some diversion, all the time and money he'd put in – but the way I was feeling then, I thought, if he tells me it's only a game now, I'll kick dents in his bleedin' Merc.

He'd been struggling to give up smoking. Paul told him, 'Another game like that one, I'll be smoking myself.'

'I don't want Paul to go,' said Kilner, 'I'll be upset. I know he's hard to get on with sometimes, he's not me best mate or owt – but he's made Belles, an't he? He's got reet good attitude for game, he knows his football, and if you're doing owt wrong he tells you, he makes you want to prove a point. I know he's got me fitter than I would ever, ever be, and if he stayed next season I know he'd help me. We'll miss him, no doubt.'

Turned eighteen in March, Kilner lived with her family in a brick semi in Thurnscoe, by Goldthorpe; her father was a miner until a rock fell on his back four years ago, and her mother worked in a scotch egg factory. Kilner'd worked there herself for a while, but she'd walked out one evening when they'd not let her leave to play a game. She was on the dole a few months, then found a job as a bottlepacker on the Goldthorpe industrial estate – so next time you buy anything that comes in glass, spare a thought for Tracy Kilner.

Whisky, beer, milk, mayo, peanut butter, vinegar, Lipsyl, you name it – the company that makes the bottles packs them in cardboard layers on a pallette, shrinkwraps them, then sends them off to Kilner's tin barn. When they get there, fork-lifts whip the pallettes off the wagon, set them inside on the concrete floor, and Kilner and her workmates unwrap them. Layer by layer, they roll each bottle round in their hands to make sure there's no cracks or bumps or bobbles, then they stack them back on to new layers of cardboard, shrinkwrap them again and send them straight back. The day before, she and another girl had checked eleven pallettes of Rolling Rock bottles, 2400 bottles per pallette; a bottle every two seconds.

Rejects went in skips to one side of the workspace. The job were that boring, she said, sometimes you'd chuck away good bottles for the sake of a walk to the skip – or you'd drop one, for the sake of two minutes spent sweeping it up. She took home £93 a week for this – but, she said, it were all right; a job like that, it were what you made it. There were a lot of Man U fans in there, they talked football all day – and she'd not had to beg time off to play yet but the bosses were fair, she thought they'd probably let her have it. Though if they didn't, she said, she'd have walked out again anyway. 'If I had to lose me job for Belles,' she shrugged, 'I would.'

She'd seen them play a Cup Final on telly, and joined Under-16's; she'd gone with Des and Jonesy through that side and reserves, and now they'd landed up in seniors. When she started, she said, she'd been that shy she didn't speak for

a year. 'If one of them had said to me, Jump, I'd have said,
How high? But it's brought me out, football. If I didn't have
it I wouldn't go anywhere, I'd just be here. I'd be baby-sitting
every weekend, that'd be it.'

Or, she said, she'd be married. She'd had a boyfriend – but
football put paid to that. 'I were seeing me mates more than
I were seeing him, I were over there in Donny all time –
'cause going out with lasses, it's better, in't it? You have a
laugh, you're not bothered what you wear – you go out with
a boyfriend, you have to dress up, you have to act kind of
funny, you're not yourself. Is me hair reet? Is me dress reet?
With Belles,' she said, 'you relax, don't you?'

If she'd been shy at first, she was ambitious now; she
dreamed of playing for England one day, and some thought
if she got her head right, she had the strength and the skill to
be in with a shout. She was, she said, trying not to backchat
Paul no more; she was, said Sheila, one that took in what you
told her. She was five foot three, weighed ten stone, and she
had quick feet; if they'd gone in when she hit post against
Arsenal at Potter's Bar, or against Ilkeston last night, those
games might have ended very different.

'Story of me life,' she said, 'hitting post. But you're playing
grown women, you've a lot to learn. It's terrifying sometimes
– and there's games I get butterflies days before. Tomorrow
night, knowing it's Liverpool Sunday, I'll not sleep. And next
season'll be harder again, 'cause all teams are getting better,
there's players coming in from all over now. But that'll not
make me stop, will it?'

On the contrary – because football, for Kilner, was the
only way forward she had. She'd have liked to go to college to
do sports studies, she'd have loved to have been a PE teacher,
but at school she'd messed about; she'd got a few Es, Fs, Gs,
'Reet alphabet, me. Not like Jonesy – all As, her. So I'll be a
bottlepacker the rest of me life – but as long as it's fetching

money in I don't mind, 'cause I've got me football. Then there's World Cup on telly; you give it a few more years, I think we could be a big thing, I think there's more and more interest now. So you get up on a Sunday, and you feel you might get somewhere one day.'

21

All Wrong

I knew the squad for Sweden '95 before the players did. Mark Sudbury, the FA's press officer, produced a colour-printed information pack with contact numbers and a press release, mugshots and thumbnail biogs of the players, England's qualifying record and itinerary and the tournament schedule; it arrived the morning after the Ilkeston game. So I rang Kaz to see what she thought of Copeland's twenty, and she hadn't heard anything. I told her she was in, and Joanne wasn't. Kaz said, 'Don't you believe her when she says she's not devastated. She'll go mad, her.'

Joanne's omission had been on teletext the night before – thank God, at least, she didn't learn of it that way – so I asked Sudbury how the media knew before the players did. 'Well,' he said neutrally, 'I'm doing my job, aren't I?'

Here, then, were Copeland's twenty:

> *Goalkeepers*: Pauline Cope (Arsenal), Leslie Higgs (Wembley)
> *Defenders*: Clare Taylor, Becky Easton (Liverpool), Samantha Britton, Sian Williams (Arsenal), Donna Smith, Tina Mapes (Croydon), Louise Waller, Mary Phillip (Millwall)
> *Midfield*: Gillian Coultard (Belles), Karen Burke (Liverpool), Marieanne Spacey (Arsenal), Julie Fletcher (Millwall), Debbie Bampton, Hope Powell, Brenda Sempare (Croydon)

Forwards: Kerry Davis (Croydon), Karen Walker
(Belles), Karen Farley (Hammarby IF)

Throughout women's football, the reaction was bewilderment. Where was Broadhurst? Where was Arsenal's Kirsty
Pealling? That Croydon had more players selected than any
other club was, by now, no great surprise. That half the
defenders didn't play as defenders at their clubs, or that Julie
Fletcher wasn't a midfielder but a left-back was odd as well –
but more than all that, who was Mary Phillip?

She was eighteen; Millwall's manager, Jim Hicks, was
delighted for her. She was, he said, a quick, talented, athletic
young player – but on what basis she'd been picked he had no
idea. He knew Bampton would have seen her when Millwall
played Croydon; where else a recommendation might have
come from he couldn't imagine. As far as he knew, Copeland
himself hadn't watched his team all season; moreover, Phillip
had never been to a full England training session. Her only
experience with England came when, at the last session in
April, she and another Millwall player were called in to make
up numbers for the practice game on the last afternoon. But
if Copeland liked her in the practice game, why didn't he take
her on the pre-tournament trip to Sweden?

No one wanted to be hard on the player herself – it wasn't
her fault she'd been picked and it had to be hard enough
anyway, when she surely knew half the squad couldn't believe
she was in it – but everyone I spoke to was dumbfounded.
Never mind all the Croydon players; Vic Akers said, 'It's a
joke. I can't believe it. How can you take an eighteen-
year-old who's not been in the squad before ahead of
Broadhurst or Pealling? There's got to be something wonky
there, hasn't there? And I think the majority of people
concerned with women's football will really wonder on what
basis this team's being picked.'

But then, he said, 'I couldn't believe what they were doing in Sweden anyway, trying new players, new systems – two weeks from travelling and they're still experimenting? It's a bit belated, isn't it? It says to me they're in a state of turmoil; it says to me they're nowhere near ready for it.'

Amid that turmoil, the omission of Kirsty Pealling left him greatly upset for her. She'd figured in virtually all the qualifiers and training sessions over the previous year; she'd put in weeks and months of effort, despite the heavy demands of her course work at college, and she was widely thought to be a sound prospect at right-back for years to come – so he was bitterly disappointed. 'You'd think you'd keep faith, wouldn't you? And I'll have to pick her up; she'll be on the floor after this.'

As for Broadhurst, he said, 'She's got to be one of the best players around. Top twenty, no doubt. I've always been impressed with her, she's got experience too – I can't understand it at all.'

It was, said Jim Hicks, 'Amazing. What's Kirsty supposed to think about it? 'Cause if he wanted Mary, surely he had to look at her earlier? You can't even fathom the decision. As for Broadhurst,' he said, 'she'd be in my team, never mind my squad.'

At Wembley, John Jones thought the same. He said 'It's disgusting. What can I say to motivate my players when they see this squad? There are players that wouldn't get in my club side in there.'

He had a couple of young players who should have been contenders – but, he said, he was glad they weren't going. The way England was run, he didn't think it'd be a good experience. He said, 'It's very, very sad. We should be looking forward to the World Cup, being positive – and here we all are saying, What's going on?'

★

I assumed Kaz didn't know the squad because the postman in Goldthorpe maybe had a bad day; it was Friday, and players had been expecting letters any minute since they'd got back from Sweden on Tuesday, and the management went into conclave while the squad went home. Certainly, living in London now, and knowing the Croydon players, I thought Joanne would have heard by the Friday evening – but she hadn't, so I told her, and she asked me to read out the squad. When it came to Phillip's name she moaned as if she'd been struck. She said, 'Who? Oh fuck off, who's she? It's a joke, in't it?'

As I went on through the names she laughed at one of them, so I asked her why. She said, 'I'm just laughing at all of it.' But you could hear her falling to pieces on the other end of the line. She said, 'I've got eighteen caps or whatever, home and away, and he picks someone who's never even been with them before? You can't win, can you? And I bet Kirsty's pissed off. He took her to Sweden, he gave her ten minutes – I find it fucking incredible. They take you there and then they piss on you. And me, I thought I'd be all right. But I'm heart-broken now I know this; no one'll ever know what this feels like. I'm just empty, empty.'

She'd given them her London address and her phone number, but the phone never rang, and no explanation for her omission was offered. She didn't get the formal letter telling her she was on standby until the following Tuesday, four days after I knew she wasn't going.

The player many felt should have been captain of England – from her international room mate, Kaz Walker, to Vic Akers at Arsenal – lived in a pleasant terrace set above a cul-de-sac off a main road in Huddersfield. An attractive, strongly built woman, weighing ten and a half stone, standing five foot seven but looking taller, Liverpool's centre-half, Clare Taylor, was twenty-nine years old; she had shoulder-length black hair, a ready smile, a love of sport all round, and as well as her twenty-five caps, she'd also clocked up one experience that no one else in Copeland's twenty could lay claim to.

Playing cricket for England in 1993, she'd already won a World Cup; in her sitting-room were pictures of the winning squad, and of a moment of dancing jubilation on the field. She was an opening bowler; in the final against New Zealand at Lord's she took 2 for 27 off 11 overs, held a catch, and (she sounded a shade relieved here) 'Did not bat. Not required.'

The experience had involved two of the most extreme emotions of her life. They'd been beaten by the Kiwis in the qualifying round, and usually if Taylor lost something she wasn't one who'd die in a ditch over it – she wouldn't like it, but life went on. But that game, she said, 'For two days there, most of the squad couldn't believe we'd lost; I've never felt so low, I felt like somebody died. Then a week later we got them in the final and we steamrollered them, and the elation – bloody hell, *we're world champions* . . . I've got every single ball on video, I still replay it, it was brilliant. You had 4,500 people shouting, Mexican waves, pitch invasions, you're hugging anybody and everybody, people were that pleased – it was excellent.'

Realistically, however, she didn't believe she'd win another World Cup in Sweden. Of course they'd go there to win, and they might make the semi-finals if the draw was kind – but beat the Scandinavians, the Germans, the Americans? It might happen, anything can – but she couldn't see it.

Win or lose, it didn't take long in her company to see why people felt she'd make a good captain. Balanced, articulate, relaxed, she had a generous spirit and, without effort or rancour, was readily prepared to see any issue from different people's points of view. So if there were surprises in the squad, she said, you had to accept that the man would have his reasons for that.

None the less, I said, anybody who knew about women's football would surely have Broadhurst in their twenty?

'I'd tend to agree with you there. Personally, I'd have taken her. She's versatile, she's got the ability – it's a shock.' She said, 'It does seem a ridiculous decision.'

I asked if I could quote her on that; she thought about it and then said that I could, provided I put it in context.

The context was, firstly, that she thought Copeland was an excellent coach, that he knew his football inside out. Secondly, a lot of those who complained about him, or said that being with his England was boring, they should look at themselves – whatever it was like, it was up to them to make the most of it, and to try and see that the man only wanted to help make them better players. Besides, thirdly, he was the manager, he was the man who lived or died by his decisions – so whether you agreed with them or not, you had to respect them and get on with it. So, fourthly, if it was a horses-for-courses thing – if he had a game plan, and Joanne or anyone else didn't fit with it and other players did – then that was hard, but so was football.

In which context, however, the fact remained that she thought the omission of Broadhurst was ridiculous; there were some that were in, she said, who couldn't really touch her.

And then there were, I said, other issues, like all those Croydon players getting in . . .

She laughed. 'No comment on that one. No comment whatsoever.'

Born and bred in Huddersfield, Clare Taylor started playing football at eleven; a year or two later she saw a WFA ad in *Shoot*, wrote off, and was put in touch with Bronte in Bradford. She played there nearly fifteen years until, with other players leaving as the club fell out of the top division, she decided she needed something new; three seasons ago, she joined Liverpool.

It would have been easier to go to Donny, she knew a lot of people there – but precisely because Belles were so good, she wanted a bigger challenge. Knowsley, as Liverpool were then called, had a promising squad, and she wanted to be part of building something that could compete with Belles, rather than just slide into a team that was successful already.

Meanwhile, she was also playing cricket – and to pay her bills, she was driving a van for the Post Office. After university she'd been on the dole, she'd done casual work with them one Christmas, they'd called her back afterwards and she'd stayed – in part, because they'd been good about her sport. In her second year there, in 1988, she'd needed six weeks off for a cricket tour to Australia; all she'd wanted was to know there'd be a job when she got back, but they gave her the whole time off with pay.

Things had changed since, and in the new climate they weren't quite so generous; she did still get two weeks off with pay every year to play for England, but any time she needed beyond that she had either to use her holiday, or go unpaid. As a consequence, she'd not had a holiday since 1989, and even then she'd been playing netball for her mum's team in Barbados – but she wasn't complaining, not for a minute. You got the strong impression from Clare Taylor that when she played football and cricket for England, what kind of holiday did she need that could be better than that?

She loved football best, with cricket close behind – but she was the kind of person, she said, if tomorrow you told her she couldn't do those things, she'd not waste time turning in on herself and mourning, she'd find something else. And she loved her spacious, airy house, she loved her home town, she loved her neighbours – the terrace that Saturday morning,

the day before Belles went to Liverpool, was like a soap
opera, people popping in and out from one door to the next
– so the house, and the job that paid for it, remained of
necessity her number one priority.

A lot of the problems with England, she felt, stemmed
from the management's failure to understand that. She said,
'I remember when we first met Mr Hughes, the Director of
Coaching, he came down to Bisham. He's saying they've
taken over, they want us to do well, and I've said to him,
that's well and good – but what you've got to understand is,
I work shifts. I might work twelve hours for a bit of extra dosh
and it's difficult combining the two. You're coming from a
professional background where you can say, we meet on
Wednesday, you'll be there – and the men, all they do is play
football, so they can do it. But us, it's not so easy. And his
reply to me was, If you want to play for England, young lady,
you'll find the time. As if to say, these are the rules, and if you
can't keep to them we'll find someone else. Which to me is all
wrong – because if you're a good player, why should you be
penalised if you can't find time off? And they keep saying
we've got to act more professionally – well, if they paid me
£150 a week to train, I'd do it. But they don't, do they?'

But the problems, of course, were more specific than that.
She said she respected Copeland as a coach; if he was talking
football she could listen all day (being the person she was,
she could talk back as well). Trouble was, however, 'On the
man-management side, getting the best from your players –
sometimes I feel he's not up to scratch on that. But his
attitude is the FA attitude, it's football football football. So in
a way Bampton's a good captain for that – well, I'm not
saying she's a good captain, but that's why she's got the job,
because she thinks football all day. And there's times for that,
but there's also times you need to relax. I'm not saying you
want to go out and get absolutely blathered – but I can learn

more from and about a player over a glass of beer, just chatting, than you ever will in some classroom. "Right – why didn't we do this? Why didn't we do that?" Some people clam up then, don't they?

'So you look at the cricket. When we won that World Cup we didn't have the best team technically, we didn't have the best players – but we had spirit, we had a laugh, and everyone helped each other and fought for each other, on the pitch and off it. Whereas in the football, that's not there with us at the minute. You take a young player like Fletcher, it's no good bawling her out on the pitch, what the eff d'you think you're playing at? – 'cause knowing Julie, that'll have no good effect. But to me, sometimes Bampton loses sight of that, and the management do too. You can bawl at me, OK, I don't mind – but some can't take it. And you've got to know your players, you've got to know individuals.

'So he tells me not to get involved with other people's problems, to think about my own game – but I'm afraid I can't do that, that's not me. Firstly, I don't like seeing people upset – and secondly, it's a job they should be doing themselves, but they don't. They need to tell people why they're dropped, or what they've done wrong, so they can go away and work on it. It's the worst thing, when they leave people in the dark. Classic case, after that 4–0 drubbing in Sweden – OK, we did play bad – but he tried a new system, different people in different places, there's going to be teething problems, so it's not as bleak as everyone's thinking.

'But we got on the coach, and I'd scored an own goal and I was trying to claim another, "Two-nil to the Taylor", just trying to lighten it up – well, if looks could kill. But what can you do? You've lost, so get it out in the open. Only that night, we'd have usually had a team meeting, given out Man of the Match, it was Fletcher's first cap, you'd give her the cap – forget it. Nothing. It was, Right, tea's at so-and-so, back to your rooms, like you were naughty kids – you'll have your tea and go to bed. To me, that was worse than sitting us down and giving us a bollocking – all these people creeping back to their rooms wondering what they did wrong. But he's not spoken to anyone for hours after – and that's all wrong, isn't it?'

Clare Taylor, like so many, had high hopes when the FA took over – but eighteen months on, the England camp was marred with mistrust and exasperation, while the National Division was a shambles. They'd been supposed, like the men, to have it all done and dusted in time for the Cup Final showcase – yet here they were three weeks later still playing, and the situation for Liverpool was even worse than it was for Belles. Tomorrow, 21 May, at least Belles finished then – but Liverpool still had games left after that against Croydon and Arsenal too.

They'd tried to get Arsenal to come up midweek; it was arranged, then Vic Akers cried off. That didn't sit too well; Liverpool had been obliged to play Leasowe when all their England players were in Sweden, under threat of a fine if they didn't, so how come Arsenal could back out? Since they had done, however, it now looked as if Liverpool might have to play those two games in two days the next weekend, just two days before the England players got together for the World Cup. And it was no way what the women deserved, the league lurching to this meaningless, disorderly conclusion; it was, to borrow Taylor's often-used phrase, all wrong.

It made it hard, she said, to get geed up any more. Liverpool's season finished when they lost the Cup Final; these last games now, them and Belles, they came second or they came third – so what? They hadn't come first, and it didn't matter any more. True, she'd not been on a team that had beaten Belles yet, and she did want to win – but she didn't think too many would be that bothered. Besides, she had other things on her mind.

Next Monday she'd be thirty and her neighbour, Eileen, two doors down, had turned fifty today. They'd had the bar at Huddersfield Sports Centre booked for months for a joint party this Saturday night – and there was no chance now she was going to act all good and temperate at her thirtieth birthday party, just 'cause the season had dragged on and she had to play the next day. She had, instead, invited Kaz; she told her they could get hangovers together, then mark each other the next day wearing shades.

The party started about eight; the Sports Centre bar was a long, dark room with a little stage at one end by a dance floor for The Travelling Billberets. Maybe two hundred came, among them Gail and Channy as well as Kaz, and a number of the Liverpool players. Kaz was bubbling, drinking sweet Woody by the pint; she told the Liverpool lot not to stand on her toe, not on the dance floor nor on the football field neither, 'cause in a fortnight they were flying to Sweden. She said, 'It's an adventure, in't it? I've been reading itinerary – I've never done owt like this in me life, us sleeping on overnight trains, all that. I've never slept on a train before, me. And I doubt I ever will, either.' She talked about the BBC having the rights, too, how they'd get shown on *Match Of The Day*. She asked, how many millions would watch that then?

'So,' Gail told her, 'you'll be even more famous then.'

'I'm going to slap you, me.'

Channy announced she'd booked her holiday for July; she was going to Turkey. Kaz rounded on her, wailing; she and Dean had booked for Turkey then too. They grinned at each other in mutual mock-horror; Channy gasped, 'Where you going, you? I'll die if I hear your gob. I'm cancelling.'

'Channy,' Gail told her, 'Turkey's quite big, you know.'

'Not big enough to avoid Kaz.'

Kaz wandered off, heading helium balloons tied to the chairs as she passed; Channy found one of the young Liverpool players and introduced us. 'Pete, this is Nicky. Nicky, this is Pete. She'll be marking me tomorrow.'

Gail looked at her askance and told her, 'No, Channy. You'll be marking her.'

'No,' Channy insisted, 'she'll be marking me.'

'Channy. You're a defender. She's an attacker. Or are you going to have a rush of blood again?'

'Nicky, this is Gail, she's me personal coach. And I wish just once in a while she'd get behind me.'

'Every week I'm behind you. Fuckin' chasin' you to get back.'

Nicky asked me, 'You're writing a book?'

Gail told her, 'There's a chapter on Channy.'

'Why?'

'It's a long one.'

'Why?'

Channy said, 'I'm not talking to you again. And Gail, get behind me – She's marking me, all right?'

'No, Channy. You're a defender.'

'I'm an *attacking* defender . . . '

Clare Taylor knew who she was marking tomorrow; she told Kaz to get her cider in. Eileen, her neighbour and co-host, came round to introduce herself to everyone; she said to Channy, 'You're Clare's friend, right?'

Channy put on her innocent face and told her, 'I came for a game of squash, actually.'

To one side, Kaz and a group of Liverpool players were roaring with laughter over an old Channy classic – the time she'd rung Kaz, said she had tickets for Leeds–Man U on a Sunday and she couldn't use them 'cause she was playing football, so did Kaz want them instead? So Kaz says, Er, Channy – I play for same team as you . . .

They danced to the Billberets playing party staples, Lou Reed, Van Morrison, Eric Clapton; it wasn't Belles' music, but then Kaz'd dance to people banging bin lids together. Her toe was hurting, though, so she went for a consultancy at the back of the room with Liverpool's Becky Easton. Easton was studying podiatry; she took Kaz's foot across her lap and examined the toe, stroking it, working the joint. The diagnosis, she smiled, was obvious; Kaz shouldn't play tomorrow . . .

It was difficult to give a reasonable diagnosis, mind, when the patient was holding her shoe over your head threatening to whack you if you hurt her. And it was gone midnight, so I left them to it and went outside to call a cab.

Opposite the payphone in the Sports Centre lobby there was a board listing the Huddersfield Sporting Hall Of Honour; there were fifty-four names on it, athletes, fencers, golfers, cyclists, swimmers, shooters, showjumpers, gymnasts, crown green bowlers, footballers, lots of cricketers – and two of the names were Clare Taylor, listed separately for cricket and for football. So I suppose, whatever else was all wrong, at least someone had noticed one of these women somewhere.

22

Decent Honest People

He knew it was time to pack in when they had all those spare Sundays in the winter and he found himself thinking, we haven't got a game – good. He could see Laura, he could visit his mother in Askern, he could have a Sunday dinner; he knew a manager shouldn't think like that, he should get the team together to train on the free day, or he should watch the reserves – and on a Saturday morning he should have gone to see the young ones a few times, shown his face, let them know he was interested. But on a Saturday morning he was swimming with Laura and you couldn't have both, could you?

The conflict was frustrating. The men, they had all week to train – and the women were that good now, they had that much ability and that much potential, he'd have loved the time to work with them like that. But as long as there were no crowds there wouldn't be any income; and as long as there was no income there wouldn't be any time.

Besides, he didn't want it going professional, not if it meant it started mattering so much that people cheated, cut corners, poached players, played long ball, packed their defence – and that was all beginning now. At Belles, they paid expenses to players who had to travel, a little help towards their petrol money – and he could see it coming when those expenses would begin to be incentives, the way it was in the men's amateur game. One club would offer twenty a week, another thirty, a third that much more – it was, he thought, probably happening already – and he didn't want any part of it. The game would get better, the players' work would have reward, but the soul would be dimmed – and there would not, he thought, be another team like his Belles had been.

So if you asked him how much time being manager had taken out of his life, he'd say this season it hadn't taken as much as it should have – but when you knew a thing was ending, ending in more ways than one, then sometimes it was hard to give it all that you might. At least his phone bill would drop a bit – but it wasn't that, or the time the job took, that he was getting away from. It was all the stuff in his head; he'd be teaching, watching Sky Sport, writing essays, lying in bed, and all hours of the day and night he'd be wondering who was fit, and who was best to play where, and whether they'd get three points come Sunday.

For all that, in moments of weakness he'd still want to stay on. He was a teacher, after all, he liked to see good pupils learn; he saw Joanne Sharp and he thought, I'd like to get her next autumn, tell her she's done really well, and how good she could be – she looked, he thought, more like Flo every game, this skinny, fierce blonde tearing about that fast, all hard bone and clenched teeth. Or there was Vicky, Kilner, Jonesy, Des; there was Channy's mate Izzy that used to be at Bronte, who'd come to watch them tonking Ilkeston 6–1 – she was a handy player, and on the sideline he'd said to her she should come to Belles next year. Then he'd thought, why am I telling her that when I won't be here? But he knew, when the ref blew the final whistle at Liverpool, he'd still be thinking of all those things – what he'd like to do in pre-season, what he'd like to do with this player or that one. He knew, most Sundays, he'd see Sheila go out the door and he'd think, I wish I were going. Then other times, he knew, he'd thank God he wasn't.

Sheila said it wouldn't be many Sundays before he was asking everything that had happened before she'd barely got back through door. She, of course, would still be going; she'd go for ever. Joanne said, 'What would Belles be without Sheila?'

Joanne: it grieved him, her not going to Sweden, he felt every cut in her heart. Never mind what Copeland thought of her; if he'd been Belles' manager next season, he'd have moved heaven and earth to make sure she stayed. It wasn't just her ability, or her knowledge and experience, though that would have been a huge enough hole to try and fill; it was her influence on the atmosphere too. He said, 'She's fun, isn't she? She's good company, she makes you laugh – and she has this very important quality of not taking herself too seriously. I know one or two others,' he said, 'who could use a bit of that.'

Why Copeland wasn't taking her escaped him entirely – but since the man didn't talk to him he could only presume he wasn't just looking for a certain kind of player, he was looking for a certain kind of person. Which, when you looked at England's men, with a former captain among them who'd done time for drunk driving and two others in the courts, frankly struck him as nonsense.

He said, 'You should look at two things only. Can they play? And are they committed? Not, Do they swear when out socially, or do they wear the wrong trousers – 'cause if he's condemning her for having the wrong attitude, I tell you, she's not got the wrong attitude to football, has she?'

He'd miss her, and he'd miss Kaz and Gail; more than anything, he'd miss those people you were just happy to be around. He said, 'This club, there's been so many good people like that. In ten years, I've met so many decent honest people because of Doncaster Belles.'

Liverpool, like Belles, were left scrambling for a pitch, any pitch – and two of the best men's teams in the country would not, I think, have put up for too long with the venue they'd had to settle for today. But then, it was only women's football . . .

The dressing-room was a dank, chilly, ill-lit pit. It had a bare concrete floor, filthy smeared walls, a badly lagged boiler in one corner, ratty coathangers dangling awry from bent clothes hooks, and a monster spider in a hole in the wall. So Gail went to try and pick it up and the others all ran screaming away from her. Kaz and Jackie cowered in the far corner, trembling; Kaz said, 'Looks a bit chunky, that does, I couldn't touch owt like that. 'Ere, what you doing with it, Gaily? Where's it gone? Oh,' she grinned, 'it's on Channy's head. No, that's her hair. But how we supposed to pay attention to Paul with that thing running about?'

They sat round the benches with their hoods up, in case the spider took a leap down the back of someone's neck. But Paul wasn't there anyway; Sheila said, 'He's still out there somewhere looking for pitch.'

The pitch was down a rough track past a jumble of crumbling sheds and a clutch of abandoned tennis courts, all brown, dug earth and torn, rusting wire. The surface was hopelessly bumpy, tussocks of grass patched through with streaks of bare dirt; the centre spot was a barren crater. It had a perceptible slope, too, angling down diagonally from one corner to the far one. 'Garrincha stadium,' sighed Paul, recalling the great Brazilian winger who'd had one leg shorter than the other. 'But', he smiled, 'I don't suppose these'll know who Garrincha was, will they?'

'Ey Channy,' said Gail, 'you going to run like you were dancing last night?' She mimed a juddering, jelly-kneed, imbecile quiver.

Laughing, we looked about; the pitch, it appeared, had another significant defect. There weren't any goals . . . Kaz pointed to the area. 'What do I do when I get in there then?'

No goals, but plenty of litter – crisp and fag packets, pop

cans, cracked plastic beer glasses, chunks of wood and skeins of cotton wool, a toddler's flowery leggings, a severed doll's leg. Kaz and Gail played cricket with a rotten orange and a nail-encrusted plank; Kaz lobbed the orange at Gail's head. Gail said, 'Does someone sensible want a go?'

And it wasn't Liverpool's fault, this place – stumbling to the end, you take what you can get – but you wouldn't walk a dog on this, never mind play football.

In the dressing-room, Paul smiled; the game may not have meant much, but fifteen players had still made it. He had four subs, the biggest squad of the season – he asked, did they have enough shirts? And because he wanted it to end happy, he apologised for being so angrily disappointed over the draw with Ilkeston – then he asked them for a win to see his time finish on a good note, and sent them out to warm up. With an interruption when some bloke butted in to get nets for the goals from a great padlocked iron chest on the floor by the boiler, there wasn't time to say more – and there wasn't much more to say anyway.

Nor could anything he said have changed what happened; Liverpool came out of the blocks on fire, went 2–0 up in ten minutes, 3–0 inside twenty. Jan Murray was unrecognisable from the player who'd done so little at Stainforth; she tore Nicky Davies to bits, thwacked in the crosses all game and got a goal for herself, while Debbie Biggins waved at things like she was seeing off relatives at the airport. Watching Murray, Paul sighed, 'It's such a shame she's not going to Sweden. She'd go down the line, she'd pop in the cross, Kaz'd score on the end of it – she'd solve his left-side problem in one go. But he's put her off, hasn't he? Disaster, that.'

He stood apart from the subs, talking to himself as the season melted away. He felt they were letting him down – Channy was hiding, Micky was strolling, Gill was being shown up something awful by Karen Burke – but there was no point yelling at them now, he didn't want it ending bad-tempered. Besides, they hadn't given up – Vicky hit the post, Joanne missed a sitter – but Clare Taylor was finally achieving her ambition, to play on a team that beat Belles. She'd say later, 'Best birthday present I ever had, that.'

At half-time, Paul tried to raise them – but it was half-hearted, sat about on this wretched pitch on a grey dull day playing a game no one cared about, and they were only half listening. They sat in groups, a few here, a few there, a few alone, the season over; he fell silent among them.

Channy was putting Vaseline on her sock; Sheila told her, 'Your socks don't get blisters, Channy. Your feet do.'

'Trust me, Sheil. It's nice and gooey. I like to hear it squelch.'

She squelched on for the second half, Belles played better, it ended 4–1, and the season played out to the sound of some crazy old drunk in a sailing cap shouting gibberish about Everton on the unpeopled touchline.

Paul said, 'Outside, they'll say we've achieved nothing, 'cause there isn't any silverware. But within our club, we know what we've done; there's a lot who've come on this season. And if the mountain was too high to climb, well – we still passed base camp, didn't we?'

The Doncaster Belles finished third; the bus took them back along the M62, and Paul Edmunds went home to write an essay for the Open University on 'Curriculum & Learning: Learning Theories in The Classroom'.

On a bright, crisp, cloud-flecked Sunday evening, the Belles' cars peeled away from the Waterdale car-park, and as I watched them drive off into their other lives I felt my gut hollowing out, a physical pain, an aching emptiness directly akin to the ending of a broken romance. It wasn't that they'd lost, that didn't matter – after Arsenal took the league at

Stainforth, proving a point over Croydon had mattered, but nothing much else. It was, instead, the realisation dawning that my time with them was over; that there were no more Sundays to be had laughing with these people and loving to watch them play, no more messing about on bus rides to grubby little grounds with peeling changing rooms and empty terraces, no more feeling privileged that they'd let me in, no more people taking the piss about what a crap dancer I was on a Friday night. Writing this book was like having fifteen extra sisters for a year, and to see them scatter away broke my heart fifteen times.

I drove across the North Bridge and went a mile past the mess of tin barns, Curry's and carpets and B&Q; turning west for Barnsley I couldn't bear it any longer, and in the Aldi car park I swung round and went back. In McDonald's I found Des and Vicky and Jonesy supping pop, waiting for their lifts home with Bill Potter – and together we agreed, the summer stretching away looked blank and tedious.

But not entirely – because Kaz (who else?) was organising five-a-sides for Wednesday nights at the Dome where Joanne Sharp worked, to keep them all together. And then, it didn't look blank to Jonesy anyway. She had her sights set on university and, she said, that had to matter more than football. She said, 'It's not be all and end all, is it?'

In unison the other two gasped, 'It *is*.' Vicky said, 'Life's crap, in't it, without football.' But she was unemployed; I'd asked her once what her life would be like without football and she'd said simply, 'I wouldn't have a life.'

'I want to party,' said Jonesy, 'and I want a degree and a decent job. I don't want to work in no factory. I want to get most out of life, me.'

Vicky laughed, 'I can't believe how square you sound.' Then she sighed, 'She's right though. But we're all different. She wants a career – and I want to play for England.'

They asked if I'd be back next season – but people had been asking me that for weeks now. I said I hoped I would, and felt guilty and treacherous – because writing's a mercenary game. You get your matter, you pick it up and turn it round, you write it down, you walk away. My wife would tell me, when they asked if I'd be back, they didn't know me – when the book was done, she said, I'd be gone like dust, my head filling with something new.

But when I'd turned round at Aldi, and at that moment in McDonald's, I didn't want to believe that, and I didn't want to leave them – not Belles in general, nor these three now: Des who wanted money in her pocket for her Friday nights, shy Jonesy with her firm ambition, Vicky with that different ambition of her own. Only teenagers still, the last months had helped steer them towards being three more of Paul's decent honest people – and I didn't want to leave them because I wanted to see how they'd turn out, and I never wanted less in my life to walk away from a subject than I did right then. So I said I'd be back next season.

Still, they said, don't fuss – this one's not over yet, is it? There's still awards night, in't there?

When Belles had gone to Millwall in November, Jim Hicks had looked at their team sheet – no Borman, no Broadhurst – and he'd thought, we've got a chance here. Then after the game he told me, 'They work so hard for each other, they're such a unit. And,' he smiled, 'people say they don't have a youth policy. So who were all those kids who just beat us 4–1?'

On the morning of the Belles' end-of-season party, Mick Meehan took a group of young Belles to an Under-12 tournament in Worksop; there were eighteen teams playing six-a-side games, ten minutes a game, and in their group the Belles won four, drew three, and lost once to a side called Bright Sparks from Halifax, who went on to win the tournament. Kaz went – imagine that, God in your minibus – and when it was over they all jumped on her in a heap and tipped a bucket of water on her head.

That evening, at Le Bistro in Donny town centre, those kids all got certificates acknowledging their participation in the season, as did the Under-14's. Belles had taken over the upstairs bar and dance floor, there must have been two hundred there, and amid the buzz of chatter in the yellow light parents watched their daughters go smiling and excited to the table where the trophies were, thronging round Mick in a happy cluster. Rob Kantecki said, beaming, 'Four years ago there was nothing like this. And every year all I've ever heard is how Belles have had it, they've nothing to fall back on – but look at this now.'

Kaz and Dean watched at the back, Dean in a pale orange check shirt; he looked at Kilner, Exley, Biggins all in a row and said, 'Check shirts are in tonight then.'

Kaz said, '£2.99 and a free lucky bag, that were.'

'I bought an ice-cream,' Dean smiled. 'The shirt came with.'

Later, before their parents took them home, the babbies had a dance and Kaz danced among them; the Pied Piper, making their day.

Gary Wood gave awards to the Under-16s, Lorraine Hunt to the reserves – then Paul stood up, clasped his hands before him, and said he hoped they could all hear him. 'As people know, I've not got much of a voice, I don't shout very much. Now my last season (ironic cheers), it's been difficult, hasn't it? Twelve months ago I'm thinking, we've won the Double, let's celebrate – but twelve months on I'm thinking the same, 'cause I'm proud of what we've achieved. And it's been a tradition in the club to give a trophy to everyone who's turned out and helped us achieve it – so with all the injuries we've had, just bear with me now while I hand out ninety-five trophies.'

One by one they came up, the room full of clapping and smiles. 'Kaz Walker, a promising young player, we've high hopes of her in future. Ann Lisseman, who's had a *very* good season for us. Jonesy, we're all impressed by the blouse. Channy, just beamed down from Planet Channy, wearing those trousers for a bet. Debbie Biggins – don't drop it, Debs. My favourite player at training – Tracy Kilner.' He went through them all, until there were four left on the table, and no one to collect them – but a few had fled to Ibiza to collapse in the sun already. He smiled – 'sums up our season, that' – and he was stood there holding Joanne Broadhurst's little trophy when the cry went up from the back that she'd arrived. As she bundled through the crowd he said, 'Never misses a night out, Joanne. Be last one out, too,' and on the dance floor they embraced.

When everyone had their mementoes, finally he gave out his own award for the Sportswoman of the Year, for the player he though had best exemplified Belles – giving her best, taking responsibility, loving her football – Ann Lisseman. Plainly, as she stepped up, she couldn't believe he'd picked her, her glasses flashing as she shook her head, the Brummy policewoman who'd wondered in the autumn if she'd ever get off bench. But I remembered against Arsenal at Rotherham, the way at half-time she'd spoken quietly, urgently in Nicky Davies's ear as they waited to go back out, encouraging, her hand on Nicky's shoulder – and the way Nicky had been twice the player second half. Amid the applause you could see everyone agreeing with his choice, faces shining over white table-cloths, halves of lager trembling as everyone clapped, sparkles of light from glass and jewellery – but then, they all knew there was another award coming yet.

There were the supporters' awards first, and the Anne Marshall trophy commemorating a player who'd died in a road accident, given to someone every year who put in special work for the club – Mick Meehan got that – then Sheila said, 'We give the best last. The Players' Player always means the most, to be picked by your team-mates is special – but when I looked at the votes, it obviously wasn't a hard choice this year. Last September I've said to this person, This is your chance, you take it, and he can't possibly drop you – well, she's not been dropped all season. Ann Lisseman.'

She couldn't believe it; when you looked at the players Belles had, she'd never thought for one minute that anyone could vote for her. She'd voted for Kaz herself, her second choice was Des – and now here she was walking across the little dance floor to Sheila for a second time, stunned, barely able to speak. She said thank you – it didn't seem enough, but nothing else would come out. Then she went back and set the two trophies together on the table in front of her and stared at them. She was a hoarder anyway, one that kept every programme – but these, she thought, if she lived to be a hundred she'd still be dusting and polishing them. She'd look back and think, Was that really me?

They all stood to applaud when Gill gave Paul his engraved glass tankard; he turned it round in his hands to read the inscription, then set it carefully back in the box. 'C'mon,' he smiled, 'let's get drunk.'

At the bar Channy smiled too, claimed she'd voted for herself twice and she didn't win owt. Her trousers had a complicated black-and-white-check pattern, like something went wrong with your test card, and definitely raised questions about her suitability to play for England. She said, 'I'm shy and reserved, me.' But her dad was with her (promising not to get too excited) and Channy was beaming.

Jonesy's blouse was pink, with short sleeves, she'd got it at Meadowhall specially. She told Paul, delighted, 'I says to Des, I bet you any money he says something about it.'

'She'll do well, her,' said Sheila. 'And if she gets to university, she can always come back and play after.'

Paul asked Joanne, 'What you going to say in dressing-room next season then?'

'Stay on your feet, enjoy yourselves, watch the line. Be in your memory for ever, that.'

They looked back together, turning over nine months of moments; if anything would stick in his mind, Paul said, it was Kaz in the 3–3 at Wembley. 'Best individual performance I've ever seen in women's football.'

The kids went round with their certificates, getting everybody to sign them. One of them handed Paul a red pen with hers and he told her, 'I'm used to red pens. I'm a teacher, me.'

Joanne smiled at the girl giving her one to sign; she asked her, 'Why d'you want me?' She laughed and said sadly, 'I'm a has-been, I am.'

The parents took the juniors home and the older people said their goodbyes, until the big room was left for the Belles to dance into the small hours. I remember Ann stumbling by, bumping into a table, and Sheila grinning, 'She's won two trophies, thinks she can knock everything over. Where's referee then?'

In the empty, mirrored room, on the dance floor littered with scraps of party debris, in the half-dark pierced with lights flashing red, blue, green, purple, they dragged Paul in amongst them; they swayed in a circle, arms locked round each other's shoulders, and Joanne danced with Paul in the centre. The song said,

> If I can't have you
> I don't want nobody baby

Which, after a year with the Belles, are the best last words I can think of.

23

Sweden '95

The opening game of the second FIFA Women's World Cup was played on 5 June in Helsingborg between Brazil and the host nation, Sweden. It was watched by the Swedish Deputy Prime Minister, by FIFA President Joao Havelange, by a fervently partisan full house of 14,500, by 150 journalists from around the world, and by sixty photographers in luminous bibs.

One of these stood out, a stout skinhead in red shorts and orange trainers. Julian Lillington, a Leyton Orient fan, discovered women's football in 1989 and had followed it ever since. A shy, wry fellow, he said mildly, 'After watching Orient for twenty years, the women – it's a godsend, innit?' To get into the World Cup he'd applied for a photographer's pass under the aegis of the fanzine, *The Leyton Orientear*, and when it came through he thought, Blimey – better buy a camera. He got a second-hand Minolta and now, as the teams ran out, he was wondering what to point it at.

Any of the Brazilians would have done. Never mind what it said on the team sheet, on their shirts they called themselves Meg, Suzy, Sissi, Fanta, and in the case of the number nine, Michael Jackson – because, when she first turned up for training, she had shades and dancing feet. At the back they had a clogger called Elane who'd kick anything – waiters, bus conductors, passing dogs, no one was safe, in another game she even managed to get herself booked *after* the final whistle – and with a spirited combination of reckless tackling and inimitable deftness, Brazil beat the fancied Swedish team 1–0.

In the stand, twenty Englishwomen cheered. In their shared hotel they'd been getting on with the Brazilians like a house on fire and they were delighted for them – but attending the game had been a thrill all round. There'd been a funfair, a bank, touts – a pair of canny British lads working the pavement, selling £6 tickets for a tenner – and there'd been the atmosphere, fans everywhere, fans with faces painted yellow and blue, draped in flags, parping hooters, wearing inflatable Viking helmets, a real actual football crowd watching women.

Then there'd been the opening ceremony, dune buggies zipping about the pitch carrying the flags of the twelve contestants, hundreds of dancing young girls doing the obligatory Nuremberg-meets-MTV routine with which all sporting events now commence, mixed with folkloric fol-de-rol and a raft of solemn speeches. So, sure, when they'd got together to fly out, the FA had handed each player a grand's worth of Umbro kit, track suits, training tops, sweatshirts, T-shirts, shorts, boots, it was Christmas revisited, that was something – but now they'd seen the opening game, the reality of the World Cup hit home.

They went back to the hotel thinking, Tomorrow that's us out there.

Canada had spent the last few months wandering the time zones, losing eight matches in nine. They'd managed a draw against Japan B, but that was all, and they had, they said, no great expectations; they were skilful players, but there wasn't much substance about them. England should have murdered them, and they did score three – two penalties and a cracking header from Gill – then they let in two howlers at the end and scrambled gasping to the whistle. Still, they had three points, they'd won their first game, they were jubliant – and it was probably the best moment of the trip.

The extraordinary organisation of the tournament required the women not only to play three games in five days – a schedule no men would have tolerated – but to travel between venues on overnight trains between those games as well. (The Germans, of course, ignored the regulations, chartered a plane for DM40,000, and flew.) So the euphoric England team went from the stadium to the hotel to the railway station, left Helsingborg at one in the morning, got into Karlstad in central Sweden seven sleepless hours later, went bleary-eyed to the Stadshotellet, and found when they got there that their rooms weren't ready. Exasperated, Copeland cancelled training and, as soon as he could, sent everyone to bed.

The next morning, monsoon rains fell for five solid hours. The River Klaralven was near bank-full, there'd been floods upriver and across the border in Norway; in training, Copeland tried to do some defensive work, but it was more like swimming than playing football. Still, defending was all they did that evening anyway; England played Norway and the traffic was fourteen lanes one way. Norway won 2–0, and if it hadn't been for Arsenal's Pauline Cope in goal it could have been seriously embarrassing.

Cope, a butler with a catering firm in the City, was, said Copeland, 'The best keeper in the world'; she was also a character. Before the game, a FIFA official came to the dressing-room to tell them today's bureaucratic latest (the tournament was mired in pettyfogging officialdom) and he was a loomingly tall blond Luxemburger with feet as big as flippers. Cope looked up at this vision and gasped, 'Ooh, hello big boy.' Collapse of stern official. Copeland, who wasn't a wholly humourless man, loved that – but he liked the performance in the game rather less, and the daily torrent of amended rules not at all. Before one game, the back-up staff had to spend four hours unpicking the Umbro logo off the

England shorts, because it was fractionally bigger than the regulation twelve square centimetres. A good job, then, that the gift from the Norwegian delegation had been sewing kits. As for the dope-test sample bottle that turned out to have a hole in it . . .

Another FIFA rule (whose details changed almost daily) concerned the introduction of time-outs, one per side per half. FIFA said coaches wanted them but really, of course, it was about finding a way for television to show more ads during a game, so that FIFA (still hungry to sell football to Americans) can get even richer. Copeland, to his credit, didn't use his time-outs; they broke the flow of the game and he wanted none of it.

He wanted none of the Stadshotellet either. It was a great hotel, a baroque orange turn-of-the-century palace outside, a bizarre warren within – but, months before the tournament, it had warned FIFA with scrupulous honesty that, during Sweden '95, it would be hosting Karlstad's graduation balls, and that this might not mean restful nights for footballers.

FIFA stuck them in there anyway – Japan, Brazil, Germany, Norway, Nigeria, England, teams coming and going in a cavalcade of track suits. Japan were like an artillery brigade, hordes of chain-smoking bagmen humping huge boxes of oriental kitchenware; Nigeria were more regal, the head of their delegation being the copiously robed Princess Bola Jegede. They also had the youngest average age of any squad there, just twenty years old – and you didn't catch any of them complaining about night trains or graduation balls. If the Swedish wanted to go crazy in the summer, if they wanted to drive about all day on tree-garlanded pick-up trucks, then stay up drinking and dancing all the bright-skied night in ball gowns and sailor suits, that was fine. Have you seen the rush hour in Lagos? And these Nigerians, they were students, they were shopworkers, a few were paid to play at clubs called the Pelican Stars, the Ufuoma Babes, the Dynamite Queens: paid £20 a month . . .

The English weren't interested. Deflated by Norway, kept awake by revving bikes and pounding discos into the small hours two nights running before the Nigeria game, they wandered about glazed of eye, hoarse of voice. Clare Taylor said, 'They kept singing, "What shall we do with a drunken sailor". I made loads of suggestions, I can tell you.'

But she was more angry with some of her own lot than with any Swedish party goers. She said, 'You get the feeling there's a few here who think, I've got my Umbro kit – so we lost, so what? And when you look round the pitch and you see people who aren't trying, they're not bothered – that hurts more than losing.'

Maybe some weren't trying, and maybe some were just knackered. The English game has many promising young players coming through, but though the WFA ran an Under-21 squad, the FA hadn't continued that – and, in stark contrast to the Nigerians, Copeland had instead brought a squad with the oldest average age in the tournament. Players like Bampton and Coultard, with all their caps, had played through all the years when nobody paid any notice; now they were getting their last strut on the big stage, they were too old for it, and people were running right round them. As the German manager would say later, with a comfortable shrug, 'You have no midfield.'

Whether Joanne would have made any difference, who knows? Copeland didn't rate her (like Graham Taylor, he didn't rate Chris Waddle either) and he said she wasn't fit. Was she any less fit than Gill Coultard, who hadn't trained with her club since he took the captaincy off her? Was she any less fit than Croydon's Donna Smith, who'd been injured all May, and was still injured now? But Smith had transferred to

Croydon from Hemsley's side in Brighton and she went to Sweden – where she never played – and Joanne didn't.

Hemsley said, as she would, that she and Ted knew what they were doing, and that they'd brought the best twenty. The fact that Akers, Edmunds, Jones and Hicks all disagreed – people who, unlike her or Ted, watched the best teams playing every Sunday – was of no account. They were, she said, entitled to their opinion, but she and Ted were doing a good job. They were doing such a good job, she said, that now the FA were running women's football, the Germans and the Swedes were coming to us to see how we were running it.

Well – I suppose they might be coming to have a good laugh. Compare the set-ups otherwise, I don't think there's a whole lot we could teach them. Karen Farley, a quality player, an in-your-face, hustle-bustle striker and a delightful, vivacious character with it, had gone from Millwall to Sweden four years ago. Now fluent in Swedish – no mean achievement in itself – she played for a club in Stockholm and, she said, 'The opportunities girls get here, the possibilities – you can get proper coaching twice a week when you're twelve. There's so much backing and sponsorship, we've got all the facilities, we never have to worry about a pitch. And people know you in the street, it's in the sports pages every day – it's so different. But it's just the way this society is, isn't it? The way it's always treated women, never mind women's football – it's just better, isn't it? I wouldn't go back.'

England had to beat Nigeria. And maybe some weren't bothered, some were knackered – but others were growing restless and vexed. Copeland had them spending hour after hour in their rooms, they were hardly ever let out – they were meant to be resting, you could see his point – but they were beginning to climb up the walls. How many episodes of *High*

Chapparal did they have to watch? How much old *Dallas* can a woman take? And what, asked Kaz, is this *Melrose Place*?

Tired and out of sorts, against the manifestly inferior Nigerians England gamely strove to snatch defeat from the jaws of victory; they let in two dreadful goals, and it was a good job they scored three at the other end. Farley got two and the third, Kaz Walker's header from Farley's cross, was as good a goal as any you'll see anywhere – but you had to feel sympathy for Copeland. No coach born can stop his players giving the ball to the other side's strikers, can he? Clare Taylor was dispossessed on the edge of the area for one, a basic blunder; Leslie Higgs, deputising for Cope in goal, kicked it straight to one Rita Nwadike for the second. On the other hand, Higgs was probably a sack of nerves; she had, according to John Jones, returned from the pre-tournament trip to Sweden so utterly dispirited by the state of the England camp that she hadn't wanted to go back for the World Cup at all.

Back at the Stadshotellet, any sympathy for Copeland evaporated. Now they'd made the quarter-finals he said he'd let them relax, but his idea of relaxation was a bit of walking round in the street, followed by Hemsley chasing them down like a schoolmistress and shepherding them back to their rooms. Once in those rooms, they weren't allowed to receive phone calls after ten o'clock at night . . . smiling, Clare Taylor said she didn't mind that. When I asked later if she'd had any feedback from home she said, 'Well, I've had me mum ringing saying if I play in the quarters I'll be very lucky, 'cause I was garbage against Nigeria. So the sort of feedback I'm getting,' she laughed, 'I'm better off not being allowed any phone calls at all.'

Meanwhile, I suggested to Copeland's physio that now they'd got through, and had three days before the quarter-final, maybe letting them unwind with a beer somewhere mightn't be a bad idea. The management, after all – as the players well knew – didn't mind a beer or two themselves. For that suggestion, however, I got my head bitten off – totally unprofessional, that. But they don't get paid for it, do they? And do the men not have a drink? Mind you, this was the physio who thought me and Andrew Longmore of *The Times*, the only two writers the English press could be bothered to send, constituted 'media pressure'.

The players went upstairs to indulge in an orgy of track suit swapping with the Brazilians; the media pressure retired to a deeply Anglophile institution called the Bishop's Arms. In there we found Gail Borman, Pauline Cope's brother, Jim Hicks with Tina Lindsay, one of his players at Millwall, Marieanne Spacey's dad and her boyfriend, the splendidly named Gary Rumble, along with Lillington of the *Orientear*, now dubbed Lord Lichfield. Like England fans anywhere, they were having a ball – playing football at the campsite, dropping alarming sums of money on beer – and like England fans anywhere, they were glumly malcontent about their team.

But it wasn't just who was picked, or how they played; it was the fact that these people were amateurs, that they'd come all this way to support them, their sister, their girlfriend, their daughter, their team-mates – and they felt Copeland acted like he didn't want them around. Spacey's father, a finance officer for an educational charity, said, 'It wouldn't be a bad idea to make people feel welcome. Then the players could feel they were playing for something, that there are people here who care. And you get the best out of people if you let them relax, don't you? Any organisation, you get the best out of people if they're happy – and I don't know if that's the case here.'

We moved two hundred kilometres to an exceedingly dull provincial town called Vasteras, a company town for the engineering firm ABB. The hotel was a businessman's box on an industrial estate; lovely.

England got some rest, played Germany in the quarter-final, and again had Pauline Cope to thank for preventing hideous embarrassment. Weary and spiritless, we didn't have a shot all game, the Germans attacked for ninety minutes, and it ended 3–0. We played like we knew we were beaten before it started; marred with mistrust down the faultline of the Croydon issue, hamstrung with disrespect for the manager and his sidekicks, England had no fire, no desire, no nothing. Kaz came off shaking her head and said sadly, 'Frustrating, in't it?'

I asked Copeland if he'd let them have a beer now it was over and he said he'd buy them one. But when I bought a few of them a drink myself that evening, he sent Bampton over to tell them to go to their rooms. 'What's he going to do,' Kaz sighed, 'send me home?'

In Norway, 50,000 women play football; when they reached the final, well over a third of the population watched them win it. In that country, as in Sweden and Germany, players train three or four nights a week, with clubs and national sides alike attracting generous sponsorship. In Japan, the women's league is professional, drawing players from Canada, Scandinavia and Australia with salaries and benefits worth up to $100,000 a year. Between commercial endorsements and wages paid by the United States Soccer Federation, American players earn similar money, and some of them rather more; the American squad, champions in 1991, semi-finalists in Sweden, were in training camp in Florida for six months before this tournament. Some of the Englishwomen, by contrast, had trouble getting time off work to go to Sweden at all – and when they got there, the FA gave them £15 a day.

Asked why the women's game is successful in Scandinavia, Norwegian manager Even Pellerud shrugged and said simply, 'Because the Nordic countries very early respected women. We are much more even between the sexes.'

German manager Gero Bisanz, whose side lost the final 2–0 to the Norwegians, made a similar point. The German FA have run their women's game for twenty-five years, the national side are sponsored by Mercedes, and Bisanz had been managing them since 1982; in his day job he was, significantly, their FA's technical director, their number one coach. He said, 'In Germany it's not women's football, men's football. It's just football.'

So what do we do about it? After the German defeat, BBC commentator Clive Tilsley shrugged and said, 'Well, we've only been going for two years, haven't we?' – and that is, perhaps, what the FA might want you to think, as if 1993 were Year Zero and nothing that went before was of any account. But there have, of course, been people working in our women's game for years – among them, John Jones.

He said, 'We really need someone who's qualified as a manager of women – and that can't be an internal FA appointment, because they don't know anything about it. And there's very few who've had the experience – so the next manager *has* to come from within the women's game, and the opinion of people within the women's game *has* to be listened to.'

Anybody listening?

Doncaster Belles '94–'95

Staff

Robert Kantecki	Chairman
Alan Burton	Secretary
Paul Edmunds	Team Manager
Sheila Edmunds	First Aid
Lorraine Hunt	Reserve Team Manager
Gary Wood	U16's & U14's Manager
Mick Meehan	U12's Manager
Bill Potter	Youth Development
Des Shepherd	Chief Steward
Betty Shepherd	Tea

Senior players

Debbie Biggins	goalkeeper, part-time waitress
Michelle 'Micky' Jackson	sweeper, treasurer, assistant bank manager
Mandy 'Flo' Lowe	centre-half, pottery worker
Ann Lisseman	right-back/centre-half, policewoman
Chantel Woodhead	left-back, Leeds United mail order
Gillian 'Sprout' Coultard	captain, midfielder, factory worker
Joanne 'Fash' Broadhurst	midfielder, forklift truck driver
Nicky Davies	midfielder, football community worker
Karen 'Skiller' Skillcorn	midfielder, shop manager
Gail Borman	forward, office worker
Tina Brannan	forward, sweet seller
Karen 'Kaz' Walker	forward, civil servant
Jackie Sherrard	gazza knee, office worker

Up from the reserves
Clare 'Des' Utley   centre-half, schoolgirl
Sarah Jones   left-back, student
Joanne Sharp   midfielder, leisure manager
Tracy Kilner   midfielder, factory worker
Claire Large   midfielder, farm labourer

Transferred from Sheffield Wednesday
Vicky Exley   forward, unemployed